P9-BAU-459

WHITE
NIGHTS,
RED
MORNING

Books by Judith Pella

Blind Faith

Lone Star Legacy

Frontier Lady
Stoner's Crossing
Warrior's Song

The Russians

*The Crown and the Crucible**
*A House Divided**
*Travail and Triumph**
Heirs of the Motherland
Dawning of Deliverance
White Nights, Red Morning

The Stonewycke Trilogy*

The Heather Hills of Stonewycke
Flight from Stonewycke
Lady of Stonewycke

The Stonewycke Legacy*

Stranger at Stonewycke
Shadows over Stonewycke
Treasure of Stonewycke

The Highland Collection*

Jamie MacLeod: Highland Lass
Robbie Taggart: Highland Sailor

The Journals of Corrie Belle Hollister

*My Father's World**
*Daughter of Grace**
On the Trail of the Truth†
A Place in the Sun†
Sea to Shining Sea†
Into the Long Dark Night†
Land of the Brave and the Free†

*with Michael Phillips †by Michael Phillips

9606

BETHANY HOUSE PUBLISHERS
MINNEAPOLIS, MINNESOTA 55438

Cover by Dan Thornberg,
Bethany House Publishers staff artist.

Published by Bethany House Publishers
A Ministry of Bethany Fellowship, Inc.
11300 Hampshire Avenue South
Minneapolis, Minnesota 55438

Printed in the United States of America.

Library of Congress Cataloging-in-Publication Data

Pella, Judith.
White nights, red morning / Judith Pella.
p. cm. — (The Russians ; #6)
1. Russia—History—Nicholas II, 1894–1917—Fiction. I. Title.
II. Series: Russians (Minneapolis, Minn.) ; 6.
PS3566.E415W45 1996
813'.54—dc20 96–25282
ISBN 1–55661–360–1 CIP

To

Jeannie Holmberg

who is all a big sister
should be.

JUDITH PELLA is the author of five major fiction series for the Christian market, co-written with Michael Phillips. An avid reader and researcher in historical, adventure, and geographical venues, she has exceptional skill as a writer. She and her family make their home in northern California.

A Word From the Author

History is not like fiction—it is real. The things that happened in the past cannot be changed, altered, or ignored, though we may wish to do all those things at times. Interpretations, of course, may vary, but the basic facts do not change. As a writer of historical fiction I'm acutely aware of this with every word I write. And because of this I am committed to interpret history as honestly and with as unbiased a view as I possibly can.

Unfortunately, history is not always a pretty thing—neither are the characters who people it. And that is probably doubly true about the history of Russia. In a country where millions have been slaughtered in war or various political purges, it is inconceivable that an account of these things could be rosy. I'm certain this has already been noted by readers of previous books in THE RUSSIANS series. But this particularly is the case in *White Nights, Red Morning*. I could have taken the easy route and avoided the many sensitive elements involved in the era in which this book is set. It would have been safer to focus on World War I and to treat Rasputin lightly. But I believe the events surrounding Rasputin are extremely relevant to an understanding of a crucial time in Russian history. Thus I have forged ahead, often negotiating precarious waters, but always with a sense of responsibility both to history and to my readers. This commitment has constrained me not to whitewash or skip over the facts, though some may be distasteful or even shocking.

My intent is *not* sensationalism, nor even realism for realism's sake. In fact, *White Nights, Red Morning* relates only a portion of Rasputin's corrupt reign—and the least shocking at that! The line between truth and vulgarity in this case is a very thin one. I ask you, the reader, to proceed not so much with an open mind as with a mind constantly aware of the old adage, "He that ignores history is doomed to repeat it." My hope and prayer is that you will see beyond the sordid facts of Rasputin's life to the courage and strength of the other people in the multifaceted story of THE RUSSIANS.

CONTENTS

I

Troubled Times

1905–1906

1

A gust of wind scattered the leaves beneath a spindly elm struggling to maintain life in front of the busy market on Vassily Island. Somehow through many winters it had managed to survive in the middle of a bustling city but each year always seemed as if it might be its last. Its barren branches were almost bare now, and the single leaf that blew against Anna Fedorcenko's stocking was nearly the last of the season. Wistfully Anna glanced down at the dry, yellow leaf, then she shook it away. She continued to watch as it tumbled for a few more moments down the sidewalk until it was finally trampled by an unobservant passerby.

Then she turned her wandering attention back to the task at hand. The noisy jostling crowd in the market in no way mirrored the aimless tumble of the leaf. But for all the activity of the people trying to press against the bakery door, the line, such as it was, had hardly moved a handful of inches since she had taken her place there an hour ago. She had known of course when she left the apartment, while the cold morning dew was still thick on the doorstep, that she'd be spending a good part of her day at market. She'd already spent three hours purchasing a half pound of cheese. Since the railway strike, panic had spread through the city. Food was already scarce, and with the prospect of the strike, it was feared that soon nothing at all would be found on the shop shelves. As much as Anna hated crowds, her family had to have bread. Raisa Sorokin, with whom Anna shared the apartment, had offered to go. But in spite of the mobs, Anna desired the chance to get out of the flat, away from the presence of memories.

Anna hated to think how she or Raisa would manage the market trek when winter set in. She prayed daily the troubles in the city would heal by then. But since the terrible events of last January, since Bloody Sunday, matters only seemed to be worsening in St. Petersburg.

Anna had hoped the end of the war with Japan would bring relief. In March, practically the entire Russian navy had been destroyed by the Japanese in Tsuhmia Straits. It was a horrible tragedy, but it had speeded up an armistice. By then, however, many in the military were so incensed by the disastrous and futile war that they were ripe for the rhetoric of the revolutionaries. In August, the tsar had enacted a new law establishing a parliamentary body called a Duma—if it were ever convened. According to Anna's brother Paul, who was quite involved in political matters, the powers of this Duma would be rather limited. But people had been clamoring for representation for years. At least it was a step forward.

However, instead of the law bringing peace to Russia, it seemed to ignite the fires of revolt even more. When the Duma did not readily convene, the whole country erupted into chaos. This spontaneous revolt took everyone by surprise, even the revolutionaries. The outbreak was initiated not by political dissidents, but rather by the masses.

General strikes broke out not only in factories but everywhere. Even among doctors and bank clerks and the corps de ballet of the Maryinsky Theater. St. Petersburg had been all but crippled; food and fuel for heat grew scarce. The city's water supply, substandard as it was, had nearly ceased, and had only been saved by locking in the workers. But electricity was gone, and at night the city looked as if it had reverted to the medieval times of Ivan the Terrible. A searchlight perched on top of the Admiralty Building and operated by naval generators gave some illumination to Nevsky Prospekt. Yet it still was unsafe to venture out into the city streets at night. Hope for things to improve before winter set in was becoming more and more remote.

The city was also plagued by the constant upheaval of street demonstrations, rallies, and the ever-present threat of violence. Many times Anna had considered returning to Katyk. But she didn't want to be that far from her sons, who were in school. Besides, things had changed in Katyk too, and Anna's ties there were growing more distant. Two months ago Mama Sophia had died. When Anna had returned with Paul and her daughter Mariana for the funeral, she had suddenly realized that she no longer belonged in the home of her birth. Her sister Vera was still there, of course, but they had never been close, and the years apart only emphasized that fact. The Burenin izba and small plot of land went by common assent to Vera's eldest son, who now had his own little family.

Life had become unbearable in the city, but it was still home for Anna. The people she cared most about were there. Even if she sometimes felt as if her life had ended with Sergei's death, her sons and adopted daughter had established themselves, and it seemed unfair to uproot them just for her own satisfaction. And oddly, Anna had no serious desire to leave St. Petersburg. The memories here were painful at times, but they were her only link to her dear Sergei. She wasn't ready to cut herself off from them, and never would be.

Thus, one way or another, Anna managed to cope. She gave thanks to God when she felt good, when moments of happiness penetrated the gloom. And the other times . . . well, she was just learning how to accept them.

"Mama!"

Anna turned toward the familiar voice that somehow rose above the noisy sounds of the crowded market.

"Yuri! Whatever are you doing here?"

Elbowing his way through the crowd, Anna's eldest son strode toward her. He seemed to have sprouted several inches in the last six months. Cutting a path through the mass of shoppers, he could have been a man, not a fifteen-year-old boy. But as he drew close, the smoothness of his beardless cheeks revealed his youthfulness. Still, he was already nearly as tall as his father had been, with a lean, strong figure. His resemblance to Sergei and the Fedorcenkos was still marked, even though, unlike Sergei, Yuri's hair and eyes were dark brown. His high forehead and well-sculpted jaw bore all the pride of the family whose nobility predated even the Romanovs.

"You shouldn't have to be spending your day in these lines," said Yuri.

"It must be done," Anna replied. "But you still haven't answered my question. What are you doing here? Why aren't you in school?" One thing Sergei had desired more than anything was that his sons get a proper education. Anna was determined to see that through, no matter the hardships it brought.

"School has been canceled, Mama."

"What?"

"No electricity, no food to feed the students, no transportation for those who live too far to walk." Yuri shook his head. He was obviously not pleased. His education was as important to him as it had been to his father. "Even some of the teachers have joined the strike. Some students, too. I've heard most of the schools in the city are closing."

"What next?" sighed Anna.

"I hate to tell you."

"What do you mean, Yuri?"

"It's Andrei."

Anna closed her eyes and sighed. Andrei was probably deliriously happy about the cessation of school. The only reason he attended at all these days was because of Sergei. But now schools were closed, and revolutionary activity had escalated in the city. Anna felt her stomach tighten in apprehension.

"I thought I should find you, Mama," Yuri went on. "Maybe you can stop him."

"Stop him?"

"He wants to join the demonstrations. He would have gone directly downtown, but I talked him into coming home first. I told him—" Yuri faltered and glanced down. But he wasn't the type of person not to see a task through to the end, even if it was unpleasant. "I told him it would be a terrible thing if something . . . happened to him and he hadn't seen you first."

Yuri bit his lip. The memories of his father's sudden death were still raw and tender. Anna wanted to weep; she wanted to embrace her son, hold him as if he were a child. But it would not have been fitting in that public place, so she merely patted his arm.

"I tried to get Andrei to stop by Uncle Paul's on the way home from school," Yuri continued, steadied by the diversion of his talk. "I thought Uncle Paul might be able to talk some sense into him. He wasn't home, but Aunt Mathilde said she would let him know we wanted to see him."

Anna glanced at the line in front of her. It had crept forward only slightly since Yuri's arrival. So little food was coming into the city; people were apt to drop any task at even the slightest hint of the arrival of a shipment of bread.

"We must have bread," Anna said.

"I know, Mama." Yuri obviously perceived her conflict. "I'll wait for the bread."

Mother and son exchanged looks that went far deeper than the words they spoke. Shared grief and loss had brought them close, but they had always had a level of mutual understanding that had never developed between Anna and Andrei. Was it because Yuri was so much like his father? Or simply that his sensitive nature had lent itself more naturally to closeness?

Anna had always had a more difficult time with her younger son. His manner, his sense of adventure, his passion were alien to Anna. He was more like his aunt Katrina in that way. But instead of opposite personalities enriching each other as they had between Anna and Katrina, the differences between Anna and Andrei only created a chasm between them. Sergei had been much better with Andrei. That had been Sergei's gift, after all. He had been a man who could bridge chasms—between servant girl and prince, Cossack and gentleman, or illiterate peasant and intellectual.

But Sergei was gone.

Anna nodded toward Yuri, then turned away from the market. She had to depend on herself now. She had to learn to meet the crises of life alone. Well, she wasn't truly alone. God was still with her.

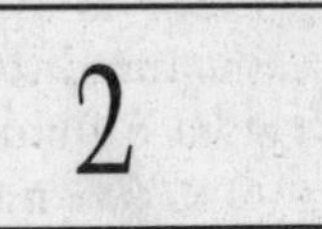

2

Paul was sitting in the parlor. Andrei was nowhere to be seen. When Anna entered the flat, Paul jumped up from where he had been sitting and strode toward her.

"Anna, you've come home just in time!" Paul said.

"It's not the coincidence it appears to be. Yuri found me at the market and told me about Andrei's crazy intentions."

"I just finished talking to him—"

"And has he left?"

"I tried to talk him out of it," Paul said defensively.

"I'm sorry, Paul, that was unfair of me."

"Don't worry about it. You have every right to wonder. Trusting me to discourage a revolutionary is like entrusting a hen house to a fox. But he hasn't gone yet. He is in his room changing out of his school uniform into clothes he deems more appropriate for radical demonstrations—whatever that might be!"

"Would it help for me to talk to him?" The sincerity of Anna's query was real, for, despite their differences, she knew her brother, Paul, to be a wise man.

"I doubt that you will be able to just let him go."

"I can't very well lock him in his room, can I?"

"It wouldn't help. I should know."

"What should I say to him, Paul?"

"Many years ago a very wise young woman told her impulsive brother that he should give himself time to grow up, to get his education and learn about life before he jumped into its many frays. Had circumstances not conspired against me, I would have listened to that advice."

"If only I could be as naive as the girl you spoke of . . ." Anna closed her eyes as if she might be able to conjure up an image of that girl who now seemed only to exist in their imaginations. "She's gone, Paul. In her place is a woman who has seen perhaps too much of life."

"Go and talk to your son, Anna. You will do fine."

Andrei was gathering together a few items on the table he and Yuri used as a desk. Andrei let Anna into the room then continued with what he had been doing. Anna watched as he put his sketch pad and a packet of charcoal into a satchel. Lately, he hardly went anywhere without these things. As with his grandfather Viktor, Andrei's grief had unearthed an artistic talent within him that helped him emotionally as no human had been able.

Anna recalled his first drawing. He had hesitantly showed it to his mother, a look of wonder on his face.

"Andrei, this is very good. I didn't know you could do this sort of thing."

"I didn't either. It . . . just came. It was almost like someone else did it."

"It looks so much like him."

"Do you think so, Mama? That's why I did it, you know. I was so afraid I'd forget what he looked like."

Now Anna glanced at the wall where the drawing hung. She felt a sudden tightness in her chest as she gazed into her Sergei's tender eyes. Andrei had not only made a likeness of his father, but he seemed also to have captured Sergei's very soul. She could almost hear Sergei's gentle, vibrant voice say, *I will never leave my beloved family, as long as I live in your hearts*.

Anna somehow received strength from the simple charcoal drawing. She took a breath, stepped into the room, and closed the door behind her.

"Andrei, where are you going?"

"Mama, please don't try to stop me."

"Could I?"

"Papa wouldn't try. He let me go to Father Gapon's march."

Anna bit her lip. Andrei had no sense of diplomacy. He usually said the first thing that sprang to mind, thinking about his words only later, if at all.

"And that is the only argument you can give me?" said Anna. "It hardly makes me any more eager to send you into . . . heaven only knows what."

"You don't need to be afraid for me—"

"What makes you think you're so invincible?" Anna spoke more sharply than she intended, but all she could think of in that moment was her Sergei leaving one morning full of life and hope, and returning a lifeless form in the arms of a peasant. Didn't Andrei understand that she feared the same thing happening every time her sons left her sight? Sometimes she awoke shaking from nightmares in which the bodies of Andrei and Yuri were being carried to her in the strong arms of a stranger.

"Mama, I won't die."

"Because you will it? Because God wills it? How can you be so sure?"

"Will you try to protect me for the rest of my life, then?" he snapped. Then he added more contritely, "Mama, it's not a good thing to live in fear. Don't make me live that way. Please!"

"Andrei . . ." Anna sighed.

He was only thirteen years old. A child, though he often tried to act like a man—a brash and cocky one sometimes. But his wide-set pale gray eyes and blond hair, as unruly and curly as Anna's, and his broad, open face gave him the look of childish innocence. The appearance of a cherub, not a hardened revolutionary. He had definitely inherited his grandfather Yevno's look of honest simplicity along with his solid, muscular build. But Andrei was in no way as uncomplicated as old Yevno had been. The simple innocence was but an exterior shell around the burning passions and convictions that lay within.

Until Bloody Sunday, Anna had always been amused by Andrei's affectation of the radical persona. The family had chuckled when he spouted jargon he'd obviously heard from the students his father tutored or from things he'd read. But that one horrible day—that day when the tsar's troops had fired on peaceful demonstrators, killing and wounding hundreds—had wiped away forever all sense of amusement.

Perhaps Andrei *had* become a man that day. After all, he had watched as his father was shot down, and he himself had been seriously wounded. Just as an entire nation had lost its innocence that day, so had Anna's youngest son. The Russian people had lost their Little Father; Andrei had lost his father. And as the people's devotion toward their beloved tsar and undying faith had crumbled, so had the faith of a little boy.

"Son, I know your beliefs mean a lot to you," Anna said. "It's an admirable thing to be a . . . person—" She couldn't bring herself to use the word *man*. "A person of conviction. I only wish that you would let yourself grow up a bit more. Finish your schooling, at least. You know that's what your father would want." That last statement was perhaps unfair, but she was running out of arguments.

He was silent for a long time, but the slight movement of his mouth and eyes indicated he was in deep thought. He plopped down on his bed and rested his chin in his hands.

"I'll probably never be old enough," he said. "Not in your eyes."

"You are my baby, Andrei, but I promise if you give a little now, I will try to give a little later."

"Okay," Andrei grunted reluctantly.

"Thank you," Anna said, then withdrew and left him to his thoughts.

When the door clicked shut behind his mother, Andrei got his sketch pad and a piece of charcoal and resumed his seat on the bed. He turned over a fresh sheet in his pad and began drawing from memory a scene he had observed on the way home from school. A beggar had been standing on a corner with tin cup in hand. A gentleman in a fine cashmere suit and natty bowler hat, carrying a mahogany walking stick with a gold handle, passed the beggar, pointedly ignoring him. Another man, a poor working man in coarse clothes and tattered cloth cap, paused and dropped a coin into the fellow's tin cup.

Andrei's keen artistic eye had taken in the most minute details of the scene—the sharp line of the gentleman's nose and the likeness of a serpent on the golden head of his stick; the jagged scar on the working man's cheek and the homemade mittens on his hands. But Andrei had especially noted the surprise on the beggar's face, the brief flicker of hesitation as he perhaps debated returning the hard-earned kopeck to the fellow.

The sketch that grew on the blank sheet did not have the representational detail that Andrei's grandfather Viktor used when he drew. It was more Impressionistic in style, the lines at times vague. Yet when Andrei completed the drawing, the haughtiness of the gentleman, the humility of the worker, the wonder of the beggar, were in no way compromised by the style. Even the serpent on the walking stick bore an unmistakable arrogance.

Andrei studied the work in progress. Perhaps he was too young to join those who clamored for freedom, but no one could stop him from embracing their plight in his heart. And suddenly an idea struck him—a way to obey his mother but at the same time strike a blow for freedom.

After fleshing out the sketch, Andrei paused, thought for a minute, then wrote a phrase at the bottom of the picture.

"Give your all to fight the oppression of the boyars!"

He drew a border around the entire drawing as he had once seen on a handbill posted on a wall. He started to sign the drawing with his own name but on a sudden impulse he wrote instead, *Malenkiy Soldat*, "Little Soldier."

Andrei smiled. He liked the idea of a pseudonym; all the revolutionaries had them. His *nom de guerre*.

A knock at his door made him look up. For the first time, he became aware of the passage of time. It had to have been at least two hours since he had spoken to his mother.

"Come in," he said.

It was Yuri. Andrei would never have thought to knock on the door to his own room so as not to interrupt his brother's solitude. But, then, that was Yuri.

"Look who I've got with me!" Yuri announced.

Andrei saw a diminutive figure peeking over Yuri's shoulder.

"Talia!" Andrei grinned. "What are you doing here in the middle of the week?"

"I could ask the same of you," Talia replied. She followed Yuri into the room and shut the door.

"But they hardly ever release you from that prison of a ballet school."

"The ballet is on strike, so they couldn't very well keep the students without instructors or mentors." Talia paused and wrinkled her nose with disapproval. "I just hope it doesn't go on for too long. I'm already getting a late start at the school, and missing time can't be good for my career."

"Oh, you and Yuri!" Andrei exclaimed with a hint of disgust. "Such slaves to your educations. I say we couldn't be luckier."

Yuri raised his eyebrows. "That's because you don't give a fig about your future."

"I only care about the future of my country," retorted Andrei.

"All right, you two," Talia interceded, "I may not have a very long holiday, and I don't want to spend it being a referee."

She plopped down on the bed next to Andrei, and Yuri, not really angry, followed.

Andrei didn't care what they thought of him for hating school. Any holiday was to be greatly appreciated, especially if it could be spent with his best friend, Talia. The daughter of Raisa, their housemate, Talia was twelve, a year younger than Andrei. She had always been petite, with fine, expressive features. Demure, quiet, at times even self-effacing, she was as loyal a friend as anyone could desire. She and Andrei and Yuri might have been thrown together by chance when their parents decided to live together, but the friendship that had grown between them was a real and vital one. For the last five years they had been practically inseparable. And, though their various boarding schools now forced them apart much of the time, the ties between them were still strong.

A year ago the three had participated in the childish rite of becoming blood brothers and sister. The little wounds on their fingers where they had drawn and mixed their blood were healed now and nearly invisible. But because the rite itself had only been an expression of the devotion that had already been present, the reality would never fade away.

Still, Andrei always felt more confident about Talia's friendship when they were together. Yuri would always be his brother, but there were no blood ties, childish rites aside, to guarantee Talia's fidelity. She had been in the ballet school only a few months, but that new world might one day steal her away completely.

"What have you got there?" Talia tried to get a look at the sketch, but Andrei's arm obscured part of it.

Andrei, never shy about his drawing, lifted his arm.

"Are you going to tack that up on the Winter Palace?" Yuri asked with some amusement.

"I doubt I'll ever get out of here long enough to do that," Andrei said, ignoring his brother's condescension. "Mama makes it awfully hard."

"Well, there'll be other demonstrations." Yuri made an obvious effort to be more understanding. "I can't see the Romanov dynasty falling anytime soon."

"I guess it's pretty terrible to hope it waits for me."

"Like Yuri says," added Talia, "there will be time for you. And even if there is a revolution tomorrow, the new leaders will have to look toward young people like yourself to work for the new government."

"Yeah, but I'll still miss all the excitement."

"Maybe not . . ." Talia tapped her lip thoughtfully.

"Who's this?" asked Yuri, pointing to the signature on the drawing. "Little Soldier?"

"My new pseudonym," said Andrei. "What do you think, Talia?"

"I like it. I can hear the people saying, 'Who is this Little Soldier, with such a powerful revolutionary message?' "

"You won't be much of a soldier," Yuri interjected, "if Mama won't let you go to the battle."

"I was thinking," said Talia. "Maybe you couldn't get all the way to the Winter Palace without being found out. But I'll bet we could slip out to St. Andrew's market."

"There's no demonstration there," said Andrei.

"But that would be a very public place to post your drawing—"

Andrei laughed. "Maybe that ballet school is doing you some good after all!"

"And what if we're caught?" asked Yuri. Obviously he had no intention of letting them go alone.

"We are just children," Andrei answered cunningly. "We would just be sent home to get spanked by our mothers. Let's go!"

Talia jumped up eagerly. Yuri followed with more hesitancy. But they all trooped out together on their holy mission.

As it should be, Andrei thought. *Together.*

3

Andrei's poster, tacked to the wall of the busy market on Vassily Island, was seen by many. It had been both admired and reviled. And, indeed, there was some curiosity about the identity of the mysterious creator. But the first rain that came washed out most of the charcoal and obscured the fine art work. It was never expected to have a major impact on events in Russia, anyway.

Tsar Nicholas was already well on the way toward taking action against the upheavals wracking the nation. Sergius Witte, the political genius who had been battling the emperor for years in his attempt to convince him to adopt a constitutional government, had finally prevailed. Or, perhaps more accurately, the *people* had finally prevailed. Without the crippling strikes, the tsar might have continued to nurse his illusions that the Romanov autocracy was still as viable as it had been two hundred years ago or even fifty years ago.

For good or ill, all Nicholas the Second's illusions were starting to die. One of the most sacred vows he had taken upon ascending to the throne was to maintain the absolute autocracy he had inherited from his father. And one of the dreams of his life was to pass the Crown, inviolate, on to his son and heir.

Yet events were conspiring against him, forcing him into a position in which there seemed no possible compromise. He was primarily responsible for his own plight, of course, because he had embroiled Russia in an impossible war. But Nicholas now found himself in a position in which his only choice was between two appalling evils. On one hand, he could step in with military force, crush the rebellion, and strong-arm the nation back to work. The cost in blood would be high, far worse than the tragedy on Bloody Sunday.

The only other choice was to give the people their civil rights, along with a constitution.

The manifesto now lay before him. It was surprisingly brief considering the vast implications it contained. In it the tsar declared he would:

> *Grant the people the unshakable foundations of civil liberty on the basis of true inviolability of person, freedom of conscience, speech, assembly, and association.*
>
> *Immediately institute a State Duma, without suspending the scheduled elections. And insofar as it is feasible in the brief time remaining before the convening of the Duma, admit to participation those classes of the population that are now wholly deprived of the rights of suffrage, leaving the further development of the principle of universal suffrage to the new legislative order.*
>
> *And finally, establish as an inviolable rule that no law can come into force without the consent of the State Duma, and that the representatives of the people must be guaranteed the opportunity of effective participation in the supervision of the legality of the actions performed by our appointed officials.*

Nicholas read the paper once more. Could he really initiate such a thing? It was the same as a man cutting off his own legs. He had pointedly omitted the use of the word *constitution*, a term he wondered if he would ever come to grips with.

While his wife urged him to stand firm, a majority of his advisors were pressing for him to adopt the manifesto. The more moderate ones suggested that government be made into a military dictatorship with the tsar's cousin Nicholas Nicholavich as the dictator. Witte, though he said he might support this idea, declared that he could never have an active part in it. Of course, Witte wanted the constitutional monarchy in which he hoped to be Prime Minister.

The sudden sounds of a disturbance in the anteroom diverted Nicholas's thoughts. He looked up just as his door burst open. He was shocked to see his cousin, completely ignoring court protocol, rush into his office.

"Nicholas Nicholavich!" the tsar exclaimed.

"Nicky, I've heard what you are considering. You can't do it!" The strapping, six-foot-tall military man shut the door behind him and strode toward the tsar. He might have looked rather menacing if the tsar hadn't grown up with the man and played with him as a child.

"I myself am not sure what I am going to do," said the tsar calmly. "What specifically are you talking about, Nicholasha?"

"That ridiculous idea of forming a dictatorship with me as the head."

Suddenly, the Grand Duke Nicholas drew his revolver. The tsar gasped, then the grand duke jerked up the gun and pointed it at his own head.

"I swear, Nicky, if you do such a thing, I will shoot myself," declared the grand duke.

"Calm down, Nicholasha, please."

"Tell me you will adopt Witte's proposals—then I'll calm down."

"I'm debating my decision at this very moment."

"Then you *are* considering this military dictatorship?"

"No, especially if it means I shall have to scrape your innards off my carpet."

"What about Witte's plan?" Appeased, the grand duke slipped his gun back into its holster.

"I . . . don't know."

"Nicky, it's the only way. Surely you must realize that. You must adopt it—for the good of Russia."

How much his cousin's outburst influenced his final decision, the tsar couldn't say. But he did have to make a choice, and it did help that people he respected were encouraging the path he at last conceded to.

So, late in the month of October of that fateful year 1905, Nicholas the Second, Emperor of Russia, ended the absolute rule of a dynasty that had survived nearly three hundred years.

After signing the decree, Nicholas returned to his study. Half an hour later, his secretary, Prince Orlov, found him sitting at his desk, weeping.

Orlov, obviously flustered at finding his sovereign in this state, turned to leave.

"Don't go, Orlov," Nicholas pleaded. "I can't bear to be alone right now. I feel like a murderer because I have destroyed the Crown. What will I give my son now? I fear it is all finished . . ."

Cyril Vlasenko tried to sit up in bed.

"I want to see the stable!" he demanded petulantly.

"The stable is gone, Father."

"Humph!" Cyril snorted. "So much for the tsar's manifesto."

The manifesto, in fact, had not brought about the immediate results Nicholas might have hoped for. Disturbances continued throughout the country until Witte had to call out troops to quell them. Some lives were lost, but at least it wasn't the bloodbath the tsar had feared.

But the demonstration in Vlasenko's own territory of Katyk had turned especially ugly. Five peasants and two Cossacks had been killed; thousands of rubles in property were destroyed, including Cyril's own stable. And all because Cyril had one of his servants flogged for refusing to work.

"It's too far, Father," Cyril's son Karl continued to protest. "Besides, there's nothing left to see."

"I don't care! I'll walk there today or, by the Saints, I won't walk at all."

"You need to walk, Father. It's the only way you will rebuild your strength. But the stable is too far."

"What do you know?"

"I am a doctor, you know."

"You're a quack."

"Please, Father."

"Anyway, *you* said I'd never walk again."

"Well, perhaps I was hasty in my prognosis—"

"Hasty, ha! You couldn't make a proper diagnosis to save your life."

"I resent that, Father," returned Karl, but in too weak a tone to impress his father.

Cyril knew that his son would never get over the fact that it was no doctor at all who had been instrumental in Cyril's miraculous escape from certain death.

Cyril fell back against his pillows, ignoring his son's protest. Nine months ago he had been critically injured by a terrorist's bomb. He had spent weeks in a semicoma, then months bedridden. His three-hundred-pound frame had shrunk to two hundred. Before the bombing, the tsar had assured him that he would be promoted to the coveted position of the Minister of the Interior, vacated when Minister Svyatopolk-Mirsky had been fired after the debacle of Bloody Sunday. At last all Cyril had ever hoped for was within his grasp.

Then that cursed bomb. He was all but certain it had been planted by that crazy malcontent Basil Anickin. In all likelihood Anickin had also been responsible for the death of Cyril's assistant, Cerkover. But Anickin had been killed shortly afterward, and Cyril had been robbed of seeing him punished for his crime. Told that he would never walk again, Cyril then fell to brooding about his failures. He became totally apathetic, hardly caring if he lived or died. Everything he had worked for had also been demolished by that bomb. His family had feared he might do himself harm, and, in fact, Cyril had thought often about taking his miserable life.

After two months of this, Cyril's wife, in desperation, had called upon the *starets*. Cyril had always disdained these holy types, so-called men of God. Cyril was not a spiritual man. When Father Grigori had come to the Vlasenko country estate, where Cyril had retired as a virtual recluse after the bombing, Cyril had at first refused to see him.

Grigori Efimovich Rasputin was a dirty peasant who smelled as bad as Cyril's stables, with greasy hair and matted beard. What Poznia and the aristocratic ladies saw in him was a mystery. They acted as if the man's wretchedness was a sure sign of his spirituality—having scorned outward adornments and such so as not to distract him from God. But to scorn even a bath! Cyril couldn't understand that.

But even Cyril had to admit there was something compelling about the *starets*. When Cyril had shouted at the man to go away, Rasputin had come into his bedroom anyway. Since the accident, Cyril had seen no one but his family, his doctor, and the servants. So, he rose out of his lethargy enough to protest this intrusion. Cyril yelled, but Rasputin had stood over the bed in silence, staring down at Cyril with those intense, penetrating eyes of his.

Cyril tried to escape that gaze, tried to turn his head away, but he couldn't. Despite the fact that Father Grigori hadn't laid a hand on him, Cyril was held as firmly as if in a vise.

"Go away," Cyril finally said, but weakly, without force.

"Is that what you truly want?"

"Yes."

"And then will you take the revolver you keep in that drawer by your bed and put a hole in your head?"

How did he know about the revolver? Even Poznia was unaware of it.

"It's none of your business," said Cyril.

"Look at me Cyril Karlovich."

What could the man mean? Cyril couldn't *stop* looking at him.

"What do you want, Father?" asked Cyril, swallowing hard, still trying to extract himself from the *starets'* hold. How he hated to be under any man's control!

"Why don't you fight them the way you are fighting me?"

"Who?"

"The demons of defeat and despair that own you."

"I . . . I . . ."

"You don't like to be owned, do you?"

Cyril's mouth was dry; all he could manage was a negative shake of his head.

"Then throw them off. Fight them! Get up and walk!"

For a brief, fleeting moment Cyril felt as if he could do just that. He squirmed in bed, strained against his afflictions. But before anything happened, he fell back exhausted.

"I can't," he moaned. "I'm an invalid."

"Bah! You are a coward!"

"No."

"A coward and a weakling, I tell you! Half a man. Worthless!"

The words incensed Cyril. No one would have ever had the nerve to call him such things before. But what truly galled Cyril was the fact that he had often hurled those same words at his son.

Were they now also true about him? No!

"Shut up, you stinking peasant," Cyril screamed at the *starets*. "Get out of my house!"

Rasputin said not another word but turned on his heel and left the room.

If it had been Rasputin's intention to make Vlasenko draw upon the baser elements of his character to find the strength he required to triumph over his disabilities, it had been successful. Cyril drew upon his hate, his anger, his vindictiveness, his ambition. He would not be reduced to the pathetic level of his son. He refused to be helpless. He had once before risen from the dust of obscurity—he would do so again!

He'd prove the whole lot of them wrong! All those who thought he was washed up, all those who *hoped* he was finished. He'd show them all!

He immediately set out upon a regime of exercises while still bedridden. When Karl brought him a wheelchair, Cyril flew into a rage. He would never use one of those wretched contraptions—never! Within a few months of Rasputin's first visit, he had actually gotten out of bed and taken a few short steps. With the aid of another of Karl's contraptions—a wooden cagelike thing, a sort of two-handed cane that stood waist-high and which Cyril could grip in front of him with both hands as he walked—he steadily began to build up his endurance.

One day, shortly after Cyril's first attempt at walking, Rasputin had returned to visit. This time Cyril welcomed him. He didn't know what part the *starets* had actually played in his recovery. Since Cyril believed he was master of his own destiny, he was convinced his recovery was due to his own tenaciousness. Yet, he couldn't deny that Rasputin had somehow caused the will to live to be rekindled in him. He saw no reason not to give the *starets* his due. Besides, a man like Rasputin might one day be a useful ally. Cyril had heard that the empress was quite taken with the holy man.

And Cyril was going to need all the help he could get to regain his lost influence. Perhaps even the help of God.

But before Cyril could hope to take on the government, he first had to get his own house back in order. The peasants would not have gotten out of hand so quickly if he had been his old self. Even now, if they could glimpse him on his feet, a force still to be reckoned with, they might come to their senses. For, even if the troops had dispersed the riots of the last week, there was still no guarantee that there would not be a repeat of the violence that had, among other things, been the cause of the razing of Cyril's stable and the subsequent loss of several fine horses.

"Well? What's it going to be?" Cyril's thoughts returned to the problem at hand.

"Such a long distance for your first time out . . ." Karl hesitated.

"I'd rather die *doing* something than rot in this bed."

Karl hurriedly crossed himself. He had definitely inherited all his mother's superstitious tendencies.

"Don't speak like that, Father."

"Stop it—please!" said Cyril, his tone filled with sarcasm. "You'd simply love to have your inheritance speeded up."

"Not that you've left me anything to inherit," Karl snapped.

Cyril grinned. He loved it when his son showed even a hint of backbone. And Karl's statement was unfortunately too near the truth. Since Cyril's injury, the always-precarious Vlasenko holdings had begun a serious decline.

"All right, let's quit this senseless discussion," ordered Cyril. "Get me that walking contraption. I'm going to the stables. I want to see what those worthless peasants have done. Then I want to see the magistrate because I'm going to have every one of those scoundrels arrested."

"That'll mean half the countryside. At least a hundred stormed the estate last night."

"Then, so be it."

Cyril inched himself into a sitting position on the edge of the bed as Karl brought the walker to him, then put slippers on his feet. As Cyril's feet touched the floor and he put his weight on them, pain shot up through his legs. He winced slightly but for the most part concentrated on ignoring it. There was going to be pain. The doctor had hinted that Cyril might have to live with pain for the rest of his life, even if he did learn to walk on his own. But Cyril knew better. People thought he was irascible, selfish, and callous, but he was also strong willed. He had given in to depression for a short while after his incapacitation—he was only human—but that had merely been a brief lapse in the tenacity that was his true self.

It took twice as long as it normally would have to reach the stables, and at the end of the trek Cyril was panting and perspiring. He might have dropped fifty pounds, but he was still a middle-aged, sedentary man who had just suffered a near-fatal injury.

Smoke rose from the charred remains of the stables. The bricks of the blacksmith's forge were all that was left—of the building at least. The burned carcasses of four horses lay among the rubble. The stench of charred flesh permeated the air, and there was no wind to disperse it—a fact that had saved other nearby buildings from being destroyed also.

"Curse them!" breathed Cyril. "That nincompoop of a tsar gave away the country with that despicable manifesto of his, and what good has it done? He should have made those ungrateful people face ten thousand Cossack rifles. He's so afraid of a little blood, but that's all these dirty peasants understand. And I swear, if they ever try to harm my land again, that's what I'm going to do." He turned savagely on his son. "I want you to see to it that our supply of weapons are restocked. I want ten loaded rifles at the ready at all times."

"And who do you think will use them?"

"I have a few faithful servants left. I'll put one in your mother's hands if I have to." He pointedly didn't mention his son's ability to help. He knew Karl wouldn't have the guts. And Karl didn't correct the omission. "I'm ready to go back now," Cyril said as he maneuvered an awkward turn. "It must be lunchtime. I'm starved."

Ironically, many of the revolutionaries thought no better of the tsar's manifesto than the reactionary Vlasenko. Trotsky, ever the ebullient orator, said, "The tsar has given the people a constitution, but retains the autocracy. Everything is given—and *nothing* is given. The people still must contend with the police hooligan Trepov and that cunning shark, Witte. All they have now is a whip wrapped up in a fancy constitution."

Paul Burenin found his own reactions more mixed. A year ago he had severed his official ties with Lenin's Bolsheviks. He had never been able to buy into the Party doctrine with the single-minded passion that Lenin required. Paul had never wavered, however, on the importance of the complete removal of the monarchy from Russia. So, while he saw the new constitution as a positive thing, he believed it was merely a stepping-stone toward a republic—preferably a democratic one.

That is, if the constitution worked. Paul had little hope it would.

The initial euphoria had already begun to dissipate as various factions perceived the reality—that the manifesto gave far too much to please the conservatives, and far too little for the satisfaction of the revolutionaries.

When were the monarchists going to realize the futility of such placating actions?

Paul lifted the page he had just finished writing and reread it. The article reiterated the "too little, too late" theme and called for the workers to continue the struggle. The worst danger of the manifesto was that it would succeed in pacifying the proletariat.

Tapping his pen against his chin, he tried to think of a rousing conclusion, but the ringing of the telephone disturbed his thoughts. He picked up the receiver thinking, not for the first time, that this modern instrument was as cruel a master as the tsar.

"Hello," he said in a tone revealing his frustration.

On the other end of the line, a voice spoke with urgency. "Paul, you must come to the office immediately."

"What's wrong?"

"I can give no details over the phone, but we are expecting an important visitor. I don't think you will want to miss him."

"I'll be right there."

Paul hung up the phone. Forgetting his article, he jumped up, grabbed his coat, and started for the door. Then he stopped, returned to his desk, and jotted down a hasty note to his wife, who was out visiting friends.

Paul headed for the office of the newspaper *Novaya Zhizn*. He had begun writing for the radical paper a couple of months ago. It was published by Mariya Andreyevna, the beautiful actress wife of Maxim Gorky. There were Bolsheviks on staff, but there were a number of non-Bolsheviks as well, so Paul felt comfortable in his association with the paper.

He took the tram from his flat on Vassily Island to downtown Petersburg. From the tram stop he had to walk only three blocks to the apartment of the editor, which served as a covert office for the underground paper. When Paul entered, the rooms were crowded and buzzing with activity. The fellow who had telephoned him, Chirikov, met him at the door.

"I'm glad you got here so quickly," said Chirikov, a small man with an excitable, somewhat nervous bearing. "Lenin will be here any minute."

Paul had heard Lenin was in Russia. The Bolshevik leader had only arrived a day or so ago, but Paul wasn't surprised one of his first stops was the newspaper office. Lenin well knew the value of the printed word. But the thought of Lenin's direct involvement in the paper was not appealing to Paul, who knew intimately how the man operated and how controlling he could be.

Chirikov, also a non-Bolshevik, voiced Paul's immediate fear. He spoke in a low tone so only Paul could hear. "I've already heard rumors that Lenin plans to take over the newspaper. Where do you think that's going to leave us?"

"I think we better start looking for another job," said Paul gloomily. "Lenin won't tolerate any non-Party staff."

"That's what I was afraid of—"

Chirikov stopped abruptly as the door opened and Lenin himself swept into the room. He was accompanied by three or four others, including Mariya Andreyevna.

"As you'll see, we operate on a shoestring," she was saying.

"And why should you be any different from every other party organization?" Lenin asked.

Paul noted that Lenin had changed little in the months since they had last seen each other. He still looked more like an ordinary shopkeeper than a revolutionary leader. Only the intensity of his small, narrow eyes was remarkable about him. His deeply receding hairline made him look older than his thirty-five years.

"If I had but one jewel on the tsar's crown," Mariya said, "what I couldn't do!"

"Someday we will have all his jewels," said Lenin.

"But then we'll be in control and won't need them."

"We'll always need them."

"Nevertheless, despite our lack of funds we have a fine staff." Mariya gestured toward the others in the room who had ceased their talk and activity and had riveted their attention upon Lenin.

Lenin gave the group a quick appraisal, pausing as his eyes encountered Paul. His incisive gaze, though not openly hostile, lacked the warmth of two friends meeting after a long separation. Not long after Bloody Sunday, Paul had written to Lenin telling him he was withdrawing from the Party. Lenin had never responded to the letter, but Paul had heard Lenin had been hurt by Paul's decision.

"Pavlikov," Lenin said formally.

"Ilyich," said Paul, using Lenin's more intimate name. They had been close at one time, and although their politics had taken different paths, Paul still respected, and even admired, Lenin. He didn't want to see ill feelings between them, yet he knew Lenin's nature was such that he could never accept as an associate, much less a friend, someone who was not a Bolshevik.

"You look well," said Lenin stiffly, but with an obvious attempt at cordiality. "Your decision to return to Russia was good for you."

"Yes, it was. And I am glad to see you back where you belong also."

"Even if it means I will shake things up around here?"

"I would expect nothing less from you."

"Well, it is time to get to work," Lenin said, then with a parting nod at Paul, turned back to Mariya. "Let's have a look at your next issue."

"Come this way. Our lead articles are ready to go."

Paul watched them a moment. What would Lenin say when he saw that one of Paul's articles was on the front page?

"This will become a Party organ in no time," came a voice at Paul's shoulder.

Paul turned and saw the big figure of Stephan Kaminsky. He had changed considerably from the peasant lad who had left Katyk years ago to seek a university education, but instead found a place among Russia's revolutionaries. The yellow-haired boy Paul had met in St. Petersburg years ago had a tougher, more experienced visage now. His crooked nose and intense brown eyes, which had once been in balance with the softness of his chin and hair, now dominated all, giving him a rather intimidating appearance.

"I've no doubt about that," said Paul dryly. Despite the fact that Stephan was from his own village, Paul had never warmed to the fellow. In fact, while they had worked together with Lenin in exile, Paul and Stephan had often clashed. Kaminsky had become a passionate Bolshevik, and, if it were possible, was probably more intolerant than Lenin.

"You may as well start packing," said Kaminsky.

"That, too, I assumed."

"Those who never joined the Party are better off than those who turned their back—"

"Please, Kaminsky, I don't wish to hear you preach. I have work to do."

"Like gathering your things?"

"Exactly." Paul turned abruptly and strode away.

Stephan Kaminsky had come far, at least in his own mind, since those forgettable days in sleepy old Katyk. He had always wanted out of that mean and hopeless peasant village, away from the stifling weight of his poverty-stricken family. When a sympathetic *barin* had seen promise in Stephan and decided to support his way through the university in Petersburg, Stephan had jumped at the chance. The fact that he had been all but engaged to Mariana was hardly an obstacle. He figured she would follow him wherever he went. He hadn't counted on her fortunes changing so radically.

He had a high enough opinion of himself to think the beautiful girl was unquestionably his. He thought it would make no difference if he ignored her and put his own activities before her. He also saw nothing wrong with flirtations with other women, even though he still wanted Mariana and cared for her. Mostly, though, what he desired in Mariana was a beautiful conquest and even a beautiful wife at his side. She couldn't expect that a man of the world, such as he was becoming, would not have other romantic trysts. That was simply life.

When he lost Mariana to that American reporter, he hadn't been happy. It was all right if Stephan misused her, but the idea of *her* misusing *him* grated against his ego. But Stephan was a handsome, desirable man, and he soon learned that he could have his pick of beautiful women. Besides, the women in his circle were not as archaic in their morals as Mariana. Stephan could thus have his freedom, to boot.

Still, Stephan harbored no great affection toward the Burenin clan, especially after Paul had become another thorn in his flesh. He hated the fact that, although he and Paul came from the exact same background, Paul had far more natural intellectual gifts. Stephan had to work at understanding all the fine nuances of politics. Although he was a devoted Marxist, he had a hard time grasping the fine precepts of Marx and Engles. Paul, on the other hand, not only understood Marx, he had done a translation of *Das Capital* into Russian that was used widely among Revolutionary circles.

But these things were only irksome to Stephan in a small way. He had no major reason to envy either Paul or his niece, Mariana. He had succeeded in his own right. He had risen to a prominent place in Lenin's inner circle. Lenin wanted loyalty more than intellectual acuity. And Stephan was loyal, if nothing else. And because of it, he had been made Lenin's personal bodyguard. As much as he had at one time desired intellectual pursuits, he now realized that his beefy, muscular frame was no small asset, perhaps even more so than his mind.

If the Bolsheviks succeeded in overthrowing the monarchy and Lenin rose to power, Stephan knew he would reap the spoils of that victory. And a side benefit would definitely be putting the arrogant Paul Burenin and the faithless Mariana Remizov in their place.

6

The year 1905 ended as it had begun—in violence. The national unrest that had continued even after the tsar's manifesto erupted at the end of December into a violent outbreak in Moscow. Another general strike was called for, but when a group of several thousand demonstrators was surrounded by the police and many arrests made, the people responded by throwing up barricades and breaking out weapons. Street fighting broke out all over the city.

The tsar, this time encouraged by Witte, met the rebellion with a decisive show of strength. He dispatched the ruthless Semyonovsky Guards to Moscow. The outbreak was crushed with a thousand casualties. Then the guards went on to do the same in other parts of the country.

The final closure of the disturbances of 1905 came when the newspapers announced the murder of Father Gapon, the man whose peaceful demonstration on Bloody Sunday had touched off the revolution. Gapon had fled Russia after Bloody Sunday and spent several months in Europe, where he met once with Lenin. The Bolshevik leader was moved by Gapon's sincerity and zeal but recognized a great deal of naiveté in the man. It was probably that very quality that got him embroiled in several covert plots, finally to be recruited as a police agent. A little over a year after the ill-fated march on the Winter Palace, Gapon was executed by a small group of Social Revolutionaries who believed him to be a traitor to the cause.

Thus, as the winter snows melted, Russia returned to at least a semblance of order. St. Petersburg went back to work, food and goods reappeared in the markets, as did electricity and most of the other modern conveniences.

It seemed to Anna that it was time for life to move on, to enter a new phase. It was time for the mourning clothes to be laid aside and for the future to be attended to.

No one need know that Anna's heart still ached at the loss of her husband. Even Sergei—especially Sergei!—would have insisted that Anna and his family find joy and happiness in life once more. He would not even have wanted to be mourned for as long as a year. No doubt he would tell Anna to find herself another husband, too. But Anna was far from ready to take that step, if she ever would be.

Nevertheless, their adopted daughter, Mariana, had waited long enough to take that step toward matrimony. She and Daniel Trent had waited almost too patiently to be married. Mariana assured her mama that after Sergei's death she had no heart for a wedding celebration. A few months after Bloody Sunday, however, Mariana and Daniel had traveled to America to meet his family and friends. Then Mariana first truly understood the wealth of the Trent family. Of course, American wealth was rather dull and colorless compared to Russian wealth, but no one could doubt its presence, despite the lack of superficial display. When Daniel and Mariana set a date for a wedding in April, Daniel's brother said he would see to it that any of the Trent family who wished to attend would be provided traveling expenses to Russia for the wedding. Imagine! Committing to such an expense with no hesitation at all.

And, it was a good thing the Trents would be present, for there would be few other guests. Only family and a few close friends would attend the simple ceremony in the Remizov St. Petersburg home. It would be a Protestant ceremony, and for that reason Mariana had decided not to include others beyond those close to her and Daniel. It would simply have been too awkward. Even Mariana's grandmother, Countess Eugenia, had refused to attend the non-Orthodox wedding.

Despite the size of the wedding, Daniel encouraged Mariana to spare no expense.

"I only plan on getting married once," he said. "So, let's make the most of it."

He had already planned a wedding trip that would take them all over Europe. He insisted Mariana go to a fashionable French designer in St. Petersburg who was famous as the dowager empress's personal designer. Unlike her daughter-in-law, Alexandra, the Empress Marie had always been a social person, loving parties and the gowns and jewels that went with them.

What the Frenchman turned out was a gown simple but elegantly exquisite.

"Like you, my love," Daniel had said when Mariana attempted to describe the dress using those very words.

"I only hope I have a daughter to pass it on to," Mariana said. "Then I won't feel so bad about the expense."

"I don't want you to feel bad about anything, Mariana. If any of this makes you truly feel awkward, then we can dispense with it all—except the marriage, of course!"

"I enjoy all the beautiful things, Daniel. Oh, I couldn't live this way all the time, but I don't mind it for an occasion like our wedding. And I think all the preparations are good for Mama. She has been having fun spending the money you've given her, ordering flowers, food, new clothes for her, Raisa, Talia, and the boys. I think everyone needs a festive occasion."

"Yes, it's been a hard year. Even your father's wedding wasn't enough to make up for what we've all been through."

Mariana's real father, Dmitri, had married Princess Yalena Barsukov on New Year's Day. Though Count Dmitri Remizov was far beneath Yalena's social and financial station, and twenty years her senior, almost everyone considered it a good match. Yalena, having lost the love of her life a year before meeting Dmitri, had been on the verge of joining a convent. Her parents welcomed anything and anyone who would distract their daughter from that path. Count Remizov might have had a reputation as a playboy, but since his engagement to Yalena, he had been a model of fidelity and devotion. Maybe age and maturity had left a good mark on Dmitri. And the Barsukov fortune, which was enormous, could easily withstand even the extravagant tastes of the count, especially for Yalena's happiness. Besides, Yalena seemed to truly care for Dmitri. Perhaps she had finally put her broken heart well into the past.

Their wedding in Moscow had been the social event of the year. Scores of grand dukes and grand duchesses were in attendance, the recent violence in Moscow notwithstanding. The dowager empress had also attended, representing her son, who had been unable to attend because of the unstable political situation in the Capital. There were hundreds of guests, and food and champagne flowed without end. Yalena's gown cost twenty thousand rubles. Mariana's gown as maid of honor cost half that, but still more than her own wedding dress. Mariana thought the opulent affair suited Dmitri more than Yalena, whose quiet, simple nature would probably have felt more comfortable with a wedding like Mariana's.

Mariana was glad she had decided to have a small wedding. She hadn't really enjoyed her father's at all. It was all so impersonal, not to mention stressful in the planning and execution. She had only been the maid of honor but she had been nervous days before. And she had needed days of coaching, also, to learn proper protocol.

Mariana's wedding was tomorrow, and she felt as relaxed as a napping kitten.

The bride kissed her new husband, and a great cheer rose from the small group of guests. There was definitely something to be said about the simplicity of a Protestant ceremony.

"I feel as proud as if she were my own," Misha whispered in Anna's ear.

Anna remembered how close that had come to being true. When Anna had decided to abide by Princess Katrina's last wish and adopt her newborn daughter, Mariana, Anna had not been married. Sergei had been imprisoned in Siberia, and there seemed no hope of her ever seeing him again. Misha had offered to marry Anna in order to provide a proper family for the infant Mariana and to diffuse the gossip. But before a wedding took place, Sergei had miraculously appeared, having escaped from Siberia. Anna and Sergei married and became Mariana's adoptive parents.

Anna glanced at Misha. The big Cossack would have made a good father. For all his rugged visage, he was a gentlehearted man. Anna often wondered why he never married. When the subject came up occasionally, he'd say the military was no life for a wife. He was a captain of the Imperial Cossack Guard. He looked ten years younger than his forty-nine years, and could probably hold his own with his strongest, youngest recruit.

When Anna had first met Misha, he had been involved with a noblewoman, the daughter of a lady-in-waiting to Marie Fedrovna, who was now the dowager empress. Anna never knew what became of the noblewoman or Misha's relationship to her. All she knew was that it had dissolved long before the death of Katrina and Misha's proposal of marriage to Anna. He'd had a few female acquaintances since then, but none had developed into anything serious.

Actually, now that Anna thought about it, she knew very little of Misha's life apart from his long-standing and devoted friendship with her and Sergei. Somehow, when the three of them had been together, the talk had always centered upon Anna and Sergei's life and family. Was that because they had been self-involved and insensitive to Misha? Or had Misha adroitly channeled conversation away from himself? If the latter had been the case, he had been very successful.

Suddenly curious, Anna said, "Misha, I was wondering—"

"Mama!" Mariana called, not realizing she was interrupting. "The photographer wants to take some pictures."

Anna excused herself from Misha's side and went with her daughter over to where a camera was set up. She took one backward glance at Misha; he was watching her, rather intently, she thought. He quickly smiled. Was that embarrassment she detected on his stoic face?

Andrei was more interested in the table of food, and especially the cake, than in having his picture taken. While he waited with the rest of the family to be called by the photographer, he kept one eye on the refreshment table. Luckily almost everyone in the group would be included in the pictures, so he wasn't likely to miss out on any of the food. Nevertheless, he was getting hungry and impatient, and it didn't help that Yuri was engaging the photographer in conversation, asking the poor man countless questions. At that rate, it would take forever to get through the picture-taking.

Then, to his added dismay, Talia sauntered up to Yuri and the photographer. She quietly listened to Yuri's questions about the workings of the camera and to the photographer's answers. Andrei noted that, although she once in a while glanced back and forth between the two speakers, for the most part her gaze was focused on Yuri.

What a cow-eyed expression she was wearing! What was wrong with her?

Andrei never had been the most intuitive of boys, but it suddenly dawned on him that the look Talia was giving Yuri was very similar to the looks he'd seen Mariana and Daniel often exchange in the last year.

Could Talia be in love with Yuri? How could that be? She was practically like a sister.

Andrei gave Talia a closer appraisal. It had been months since he had last seen her, not counting the few days before the wedding. The last time had been in October when they had sneaked down to St. Andrew's market and tacked his poster up on the church wall. When she had been home for the Christmas holidays, he had been in Moscow for his uncle Dmitri's wedding. Almost six months had passed since last fall.

And, though Andrei had seen Talia yesterday, he hadn't noticed until now that she had changed. Maybe it was the fact that she was all dressed up. The shimmering blue satin gown she wore as a bridesmaid made her look very grown up, even though her slim, willowy figure was still childlike in many respects. Andrei was beginning to notice the blossoming of other thirteen-year-old girls of his acquaintance, but Talia had not yet shown any of that. Still, there *was* something older, more mature, about her. Her dark brown hair, falling in soft waves to the middle of her back, was no different than it had always been. Her dark eyes, almost too large for the rest of her dainty facial features, and fringed with long, thick lashes, were, as always, those of a fanciful child. Andrei thought he'd like to sketch her because her eyes would be a fascinating study. Yet they were hardly mature.

Perhaps then the changes were more in the graceful way she moved, with assurance and confidence. That must be a result of her ballet training. He could almost visualize her gliding around a stage, the lovely swan, or the beautiful, tragic Giselle. For a moment Andrei forgot all about the beckoning food and his impatience. And momentarily his young eyes glimpsed life as an artist, not a cocky adolescent. He felt the kind of sensitivity he'd always mocked in others. And for an instant he could understand and appreciate beauty without being embarrassed by it or by the sensitivity itself.

He also felt a strange tightening of his throat, and he suddenly wished Talia would look at him as she was now gazing at his brother. He licked his dry lips.

"Hungry, my boy?" A voice intruded into his thoughts.

It was his grandfather.

"No . . ." Andrei's voice squeaked nervously. "I mean . . . yes, I think so." He began to regain his composure. "Will these pictures take forever?"

"They'll want you in a minute," said Viktor.

"Do I have to?" Andrei easily slipped back into the guise of the petulant teenager.

"Years from now you'll be glad you did."

Andrei shrugged.

Viktor went on. "How are things going at school for you these days, Andrushka?"

"I think I'm passing everything."

Viktor smiled. "That's something, isn't it?"

"I'm satisfied."

"It doesn't bother you that your brother makes perfect marks and will probably graduate at the top of his class?"

Andrei glanced once more toward Yuri and Talia. The photographer was busy taking pictures, and Yuri and Talia were by themselves now, talking. No, there were other things besides school grades that Andrei thought would bother him far more.

Andrei said to his grandfather, "He has to get good grades for what he wants to do; I don't."

"And what do you want to do?"

"I guess I'm not sure. But I do know it's not going to be anything that'll require math or science or even grammar. Maybe I'll be an artist."

"Really?"

Andrei was just as surprised at that impulsive notion as his grandfather. But now that he thought of it, it sounded like the perfect path for him. It wouldn't require an education, and, as with the posters he was making and tacking up around the city, it could be a perfect way for him to express his political passions.

But he shrugged again. "I don't know. Do I have to know what I want like Yuri?"

"No," said Viktor. "Oh, there was a time when I would have believed so. I was very hard on your father when he was your age. I felt he had to fit into certain molds and do so at the expected time. I wanted to stamp out his natural instincts. Now I would encourage you to seek that which makes you happy. However, Andrei, goals in life are not entirely bad. I wouldn't like to see your indecision and uncertainty cause you to take the path of least resistance, or worse, to carry you away wherever the winds will blow. There is a saying about being master of your own destiny. You mustn't let others control your future."

"No one's going to push me around, Grandfather, you can be sure."

"I hope not," said Viktor. "I think the photographer wants us now."

They went to where the family was being posed around the bride and groom. Viktor was whisked away to a prominent position next to Daniel. Much to Andrei's relief, he was directed to a place on the fringes. Yuri was placed beside him.

Then the photographer said, "And this pretty young lady . . ." He smiled at Talia. "You are a member of the family?"

When Talia hesitated, Yuri quickly said, "Of course she is—our sister. Come on, Talia, get between Andrei and me."

"Perfect." The photographer grinned. "A rose between thorns."

Andrei smirked at the lame attempt at humor, then moved to accommodate Talia. The photographer went to his camera, which was on a tripod, looked through the lens, then returned to the place where the young people stood.

"You must move in closer so I don't cut off any arms or legs," he said, giving Andrei a little push toward Talia.

As Talia's frame pressed against Andrei's chest, he felt a strange sensation tingle through him. Heat crept up his neck and his heart started pounding.

Talia glanced up at him apologetically, almost as if she sensed his discomfiture. "Am I crowding you too much, Andrei?"

"It's okay. I just wish they'd get this over with." He nervously ran a finger between his neck and stiff collar. He suddenly needed some air.

"Young man," the photographer chided Andrei, "this is a joyous occasion, not a funeral. Try to appear as if you are glad to be here."

Andrei hated every minute of it, except for the nearness of Talia, but that made him more confused than happy. Nevertheless, he composed his face in what he thought, and hoped, was appropriate for the occasion. But, when he wasn't looking at the camera, he found his gaze strayed toward Talia. Unfortunately, she was always looking at Yuri.

7

Anna felt melancholy. Perhaps it was, as Raisa had suggested, just a letdown after the excitement of Mariana's wedding. True, Anna had let herself become completely absorbed in planning the big day. She had probably gotten a bit carried away, but Daniel had insisted that she do whatever she and Mariana wanted. For nearly two months the wedding had been her life. Her escape. She hadn't had time to dwell on how much she missed Sergei. Some days she'd go one or two hours without thinking of him at all.

Now the wedding was over, and Anna felt as empty as she had when Sergei had first died.

She wandered into the parlor of the flat she and Raisa shared, alone now that the children were all away at boarding schools. Raisa was sitting at her sewing machine, busy altering a gown for a countess to wear on Easter Sunday. The machine stopped when Raisa glanced up and saw Anna.

"I didn't mean to interrupt you," said Anna.

"I don't mind."

"You're busy."

Raisa finished the seam she was working on, took the garment from the machine, then said, "There, now I have only handwork. Stay, Anna, I can sew while we talk."

"I don't know if I really wanted to talk. I was just . . ." Anna sighed and sat on the couch. "Raisa, I think I'll go crazy with boredom. If only I still had the children to teach. It seems I lost everything at once. I know of little other work to do. I've thought about hiring myself out as a servant again."

"Most of the houses would require you to be a live-in." Raisa's tone betrayed an edge of dismay at that thought.

"That's why I haven't pursued it. It's not that we need the money, thanks to Daniel. But . . ."

"I know, Anna." Raisa reached her plump arm out and took Anna's hand. "I could teach you how to sew. I always have more work than I can handle."

"I suppose . . ."

"But you'd rather be a teacher yourself."

"I loved teaching our children. But no one would hire an old peasant woman as a tutor."

Raisa let go of Anna's hand, turned to a pile of sewing projects, withdrew a gown, and held it out to Anna. "This is all I have to offer right now," she said. "This dress and several others need hemming. They are all marked and need only to be sewn, and you do a fine hemstitch, Anna."

Anna took the dress. "I'll be happy to help." She didn't have the heart to tell her friend that she found sewing tedious. At least it was something to do. Maybe she *should* learn to sew. She had always admired the beautiful embroidery work that Raisa did so well. It seemed a bit more challenging than simple dressmaking. Perhaps she'd have Raisa teach her that.

Two days later, Misha came by for a visit. Had Raisa spoken to him about Anna's melancholy? He seemed especially solicitous. But she welcomed him gladly and was happy to hear it was his day off, so he could stay for as long as he wished.

"So, do you miss Mariana terribly?" Misha asked as he and Anna sat at the kitchen table with cups of tea, freshly drawn from the samovar, before them.

"Of course. But she has been gone before and I know I'll see her again." Anna sighed.

"Anna—"

"Misha—"

They spoke simultaneously, chuckled together, then Misha said, "Go on, ladies first."

"I was just going to say how I've appreciated your company this past year. You've always been such a dear and faithful friend. That's all. Now, what were you going to say?"

Misha hesitated. "I'm glad to have been there for you, Anna. You've helped me as much as you say I've helped you. Anna, maybe it's time . . ." He paused.

"Yes. . . ?" prompted Anna.

"Oh, nothing important." Misha looked away, then focused on his tea.

"Misha, is something bothering you? You know you can always talk to me."

"I know that, Anna." He picked up his cup and took a long sip of tea. "I did have something I wanted to mention to you." Anna sensed this wasn't his initial concern, but she nodded for him to continue. "Raisa spoke to me the other day about how all your idle time is affecting you."

"Poor Raisa. She has to put up with so much."

"You know that's not what bothers her. She would lay down her life for you if it would help—as would I. Anyway, I have a little problem at the barracks, and it's just possible you might be able to help."

"Me? Help out the Imperial Cossack Guards?" Anna chuckled. "Pray tell how—I'm very curious."

Misha smiled. "I don't need your help with the entire unit, just with one guard in particular—actually a former guard, one of my officers who was killed in Moscow last winter. Shortly after his death, his wife committed suicide in despair. Their two young children were orphaned. Well, they did have a grandparent with whom they went to live, but now the grandparent has also died."

"Oh, those poor children!"

"Yes, it is a sad case."

"What can I do to help?" Anna asked eagerly.

"There is another relative, an aunt who lives in England. I'm trying to locate her, but she apparently departed Russia after some family dispute and has cut herself off."

"Do you think she'll take the children?"

"In her suicide note, the mother mentioned the aunt—her sister. The dispute had not been between them, but they lost contact anyway. The two were quite close, and the mother wanted her children to go to the aunt if she could be found. In fact, she had specifically not wanted them to go to the grandparent with whom they ended up going, because he had been the cause of the family dispute. Her last wish was ignored at first, but now it seems we are finally forced to regard it."

"I still don't know what you want of me, Misha."

"The children, a boy age three, and a girl age six, will have to go to an orphan home—"

"Say no more, Misha!" interjected Anna with rising excitement. "Unless Raisa protests—and I know she won't—you must bring them here to live until you find their aunt."

"I was hoping you'd agree—"

"Agree!" Anna laughed. "If you hadn't asked me, I would have begged for them."

"It's so good to hear you laugh, Anna . . ." His voice trailed away as if he wanted to say more but decided against it. An intensity remained in Misha's eyes.

"You won't worry about becoming attached to them, then having to give them up?" asked Misha. "It wouldn't be too hard on you?"

"I'm sure it will be hard, but not more than I can endure. Certainly the rewards would far outweigh any difficulties. Misha, I have so much love to give—so much more than is needed these days by anyone close to me."

"Not everyone, Anna." Misha stopped abruptly, and his gaze dropped.

"Misha . . ."

"Every time I see you, I try to hold my tongue."

"I don't understand, Misha."

"Come, Anna, I think you do." His tone held a hint of rebuke. "But you have made it hard on me."

"That wasn't my intention. I was only afraid."

"I know." Misha's voice was gentle again. "Were you afraid for me, or for yourself, or for Sergei's memory?"

"A little bit of everything, I suppose." Anna paused in wonder at the sudden turn the conversation had taken. One minute they were talking about her taking in some orphans and the next—

"Anna," Misha went on quickly, as if he feared he would lose his nerve again, "I love you—"

"Misha . . ."

"God forgive me, Anna, but I always have. I cared for Sergei as my dearest friend, as a brother. But I envied him his wife—she who would have been mine but for a twist of fate."

"Please don't—"

"It's out now, Anna. I may as well say it all. I tried to be honorable all these years, but perhaps the most honorable thing I should have done was to leave you two alone altogether. Instead, I used Sergei to be close to you. It only made it worse when I grew to love him as well. Yet, that didn't change my feelings for you."

"I never realized." Anna felt her face flush with the shock.

"I would have killed myself before I hurt either of you."

"My poor, dear Misha."

"Anna, I'd rather you hate me than pity me."

"Why should I hate you, Misha? As you said, you were always honorable."

"Cursed honor!"

"That's part of why you are dear to me."

"Anna, I love you! Not as a brother or a friend. I love you with a passion I have had to restrain for many—too many!—years. Do you understand that?"

Anna nodded mutely.

"And I have waited another year, Anna," Misha went on, "during which I've fought an endlessly conflicting battle between grief for my dear, lost friend, and hope that I might yet have a chance to win his wife." He shook his head dismally. "Oh, God! I am a worthless, wretched creature. He should send me directly to hell for my sins."

"God understands, Misha."

"And you, Anna? You understand also. But why?"

"Because I know your heart." Anna reached across the table and laid her slim, pale hands over his. "And I love you, dear Misha."

"But not in the same way, right?" His tone was so hopeless Anna wanted to weep.

"My heart and my life are still too full of Sergei," said Anna. "I don't go to bed at night or wake in the morning without missing him, yearning for him, wanting him."

"I'd pray for death myself, Anna, if I knew you'd do the same honor for me."

"Maybe someday . . ."

"But don't you see, Anna? If it can't be now, it just can't be. I'm no longer a young man. I can't go on for another day as I have been."

"But you've already given it years."

"I had no choice. You weren't free. Now . . . it would be torture. A ghost is a much more fearsome presence than a living man."

"When my grief for Sergei subsides, you would be the only man I would consider—"

"Anna, you are not a selfish woman. But to ask me to continue to wait under such circumstances is just that."

"Yes, of course."

"I asked you to marry me once, Anna. But, if I did so now and you refused, I don't think I could ever ask again. I suppose that's why I've been so reluctant this past year. I've been waiting for the right time. It never came. Sergei was still between us. Maybe he always will be."

"I don't know. I can't predict the future." Anna looked up into Misha's fine, tender eyes. "I won't ask you to wait, either. But then what? Will I lose my dearest friend?"

"If I were a stronger man, I could have let things go on as they have been forever. I'm sorry, Anna."

"I'm the one who should be sorry. I *am* sorry."

From somewhere in his heart, Misha managed a smile. "Well, at least I didn't ask the fatal question. I didn't force your final rejection."

"We can still be friends, then?"

"I will always be your friend, Anna."

The next day, the two orphaned children came to stay with Anna. They were there two months—two of the fullest months since Sergei's death. Anna poured all of her unused love out on the children. She almost didn't notice that Misha wasn't visiting as much as had been his habit since Sergei's death.

When the children's aunt was located, Misha did come to fetch the children.

"It's been a long time, Misha."

"I know. I've been so busy."

"Why don't you come to dinner tonight. The flat will seem so quiet after the children leave."

"I . . . all right. I'll see you then."

Anna did miss the children, and when Misha came that evening she welcomed him gladly. She, Misha, and Raisa enjoyed a nice meal, almost like old times, until Misha delivered his news.

"I've been transferred to Moscow."

"How can they do that?" Raisa asked.

"*They* didn't do it." Misha glanced at Anna. "I requested it."

Anna didn't have to ask why. She knew he hadn't done it immediately after their talk two months ago because of his commitment to finding the children's aunt. With that commitment fulfilled, he was free to do what they both had known was inevitable. He had said he couldn't go on for another day as it had been. And only duty had kept him here this long. Now he was making the break. His love for Anna could not permit him to be near her any longer without hope of it being requited. And her love for him could not let her stand in his way. She couldn't be that selfish.

As he left, Anna could not resist the impulse to embrace him.

But she wished she had resisted. He embraced her with passion; all she had to give in return was affection.

"Maybe someday," was all Anna could say.

"Maybe . . ." Misha said as he left the flat for the last time.

In the years that followed, they did not see each other again. But Anna thought about him almost every time a new houseguest came to stay in her home. Misha had opened Anna's eyes to a way in which her life could have meaning again. And she had no doubt that Misha had spread the word to certain needy people that Anna and Raisa's home was one in which hospitality could be found. After that, there was a steady flow of orphans, students in need of housing, homeless widows and their children—anyone in need of a home full of love.

As Anna's own children grew and became more and more independent of their mother, she found many outlets for her abounding love. She became happy again. And through this outlet the pain of grief was gradually healed.

But, except for occasional, hasty letters, she heard nothing from Misha. He seemed to be gone from her life forever. He would never give her the chance to reject—or accept—him again. She couldn't blame him. But what she regretted most was that she had lost her dearest friend.

Still, she prayed that one day she might see him again. She didn't know what such a meeting would bring. She didn't know what she *wanted* it to bring.

II

Coming of Age

Summer 1912—Fall 1913

8

The little boy was five years old. He fidgeted as he lay on the examination table, despite the fact that his every movement seemed to cause pain. Yuri Fedorcenko gently lifted the boy's bare leg on which was a large, swollen bruise.

"I'm going to bend your knee," said Yuri. "Tell me the moment it starts to hurt, Vasily, all right?"

"It hurts *now*," whimpered Vasily.

Resisting the urge to immediately drop the leg so as not to cause the child further suffering, Yuri let it down slowly, gently. He eyed the older man standing across the table from him.

"So, Prince Fedorcenko, what do you make of the boy's injury?" asked the man, a tall, husky fellow with small eyes and thinning hair. He looked as if he'd be as comfortable plowing a field as tending a medical clinic for the underprivileged.

"The limited range of motion suggests the possibility of bleeding in the joint. Yet the child says he merely bumped his knee against a table. I see no indication of broken bones besides the marked swelling, which is just not of the type that accompanies fractures."

"Have you ordered X rays?"

"Of course, Dr. Botkin," said Yuri, his tone betraying his insult at the implication that he might have overlooked such a routine procedure.

Botkin smiled. "Oh yes, I forgot I am addressing the great physician-to-be, *Doctor* Fedorcenko."

"I'm sorry, Dr. Botkin, I didn't mean—"

"Never mind, young man. Self-confidence is a quality that shouldn't be lacking in a doctor. However, it ought to be mingled with perhaps a touch of humility."

"Yes, sir." Yuri infused his voice with every ounce of humility he could muster. After all, Botkin was not only the head of the clinic, he was also physician to the Court of Nicholas the Second. He was a man in a position of great power and influence in the medical profession, but more than that he was a fine doctor, worthy of respect if only for that.

"Would you care to offer a preliminary diagnosis?" asked Botkin.

"Without the X rays and the other tests I've ordered, I'd be taking a stab in the dark."

"Not to disparage the wonders of modern medicine, Prince Fedorcenko, but it can be risky to rely entirely upon them. A test does not *see* or *feel* the actual flesh and blood. It is important that you hone your innate perceptions. Don't ever let them be made dull by gadgets and machines." Botkin turned to the patient. "Vasily, we will leave you for a few minutes. I'll send in your mother and a nurse with something to ease your pain."

"Thank you, Dr. Botkin," said the boy, gazing at the older doctor with awe and trust.

"Now, Fedorcenko, step outside with me so we can discuss this further."

They stepped into the corridor where the mother was waiting. Botkin sent her into the examination room, then told a passing orderly to fetch a nurse. Finally, he returned his attention to Yuri. "There. Now we can talk. Tell me, then, what you think of the boy."

"Well, Dr. Botkin, I must admit that my 'innate perceptions' are quite baffled. There is internal hemorrhaging inconsistent with the severity of the wound. There appear to be no broken bones. If I were to take that stab in the dark, I would almost say this was a case of . . ." He let his words trail off, reluctant to make a fool of himself before this important man.

"Go on, Fedorcenko."

"You must understand, I am simply extrapolating."

"You'd be surprised how much of medicine is extrapolation. Now, do continue."

"In my hematology course, I recall learning of a disease called hemophilia—the bleeding disease. It's very rare, and thus we didn't spend a great deal of time studying it. But some of the symptoms are similar to Vasily's."

"What do you know of that disease?"

"It is a failure of the blood-clotting mechanism, incurable, and there is little but symptomatic treatment known for it. A hundred and ten years ago an American, John Otto, discovered that hemophilia is a genetically transmitted disease, carried by females but manifested in males only."

"This is the first case you've observed?"

"If, indeed, this is hemophilia, then it is my first case. Have you ever seen it before, Doctor?"

Botkin paused a long moment before answering. "Yes . . . I have seen it."

"I've heard it called the 'royal disease,'" said Yuri.

"So, you think it impossible for a peasant boy like Vasily to be afflicted with it?"

"No . . . but I think it would probably go far better for a crown prince to have such a disease."

"Why is that?"

"Royalty can afford to live pampered lives, and pampering is perhaps the best treatment for the illness. Vasily lives on the streets. If he does survive to manhood, he will have to engage in physically taxing manual labor. Look what a mere bump against a table did. Imagine the poor boy in one of our textile factories. Thus, hemophilia is far better suited to one who lives a life of ease."

"In some respects you are correct. Yet, you haven't taken into consideration the intense emotional duress of the disease, not only on the patient, but on the family as well. Even royalty are not free of that. And, if a mere inconsequential bump can induce severe symptoms, then even the most sedentary person could be affected."

"May I ask you a question, Doctor?" When Botkin nodded, Yuri went on. "If Vasily does indeed have this hemophilia, what is his prognosis?"

"Let me clear up one point first. Vasily is indeed a bleeder. He has been in the clinic on two or three previous occasions. I should be surprised if the child celebrates his tenth birthday."

Yuri shook his head, frowning. He had only a year left of medical school and had engaged in some practical experience, but he was still rather a novice where death was concerned. The only terminal patient he'd ever worked with had been an old man, and when he died, death had come very naturally. A dying child was totally different. Yuri sensed this would be the true test of his mettle, his ability to be a doctor. On most levels, he did not doubt himself. After all, he was at the top of his class at the St. Petersburg University School of Medicine. And he certainly exuded confidence in his medical prowess—so much that he had a reputation for a tendency toward arrogance among his peers and even his professors. If only they knew that on a level unseen by them, and often not even recognized by Yuri himself, he was a mass of doubts and fears. That was his basic nature, which he expended much energy trying to cover.

But now he was conversing with the great Dr. Eugene Botkin; he mustn't let his thoughts get away from him.

"Does the boy know, Dr. Botkin?"

Botkin shook his head. "How do you tell a mere baby that death lurks for him around any given corner? How do you make him understand that any day might be his last?"

"Even *you*, Doctor?" Yuri said the words before he realized he had spoken his shock aloud.

"Do you suppose, Prince Fedorcenko, that a physician becomes hard and heartless as he becomes experienced? It has always been my sincere prayer that such is not the case. I hope it never becomes easy for me to inform a patient he is going to die. I hope my heart always aches at the sight of a child, or even a man, in pain. You are one of the best students at the university, Fedorcenko, but you have learned nothing if you cannot grasp this highest lesson of all. Never allow knowledge and know-how to usurp your basic humanity."

"But, Doctor, how can you come face-to-face with pain and suffering every day without some shell of protection?"

"Trust God, young man. It is the only way."

At that moment, a nurse carrying a small tray of medication approached.

"Ah, good, sister," said Botkin. "After you've given the boy his injection, find a bed for him. I'd like to keep him overnight for observation."

"Yes, Doctor." Then the nurse took a paper from her pocket. "This came a few moments ago. It's from the tsar."

"But the tsar is out of town."

"It's a telegram."

With a mumbled word of thanks, Botkin took the telegram, opening it quickly. His high color paled.

"Dr. Botkin," said Yuri, "is something wrong?"

Botkin made a noticeable attempt to shake away his initial reaction to the message. "No . . . nothing at all, really." He stuffed the paper into his pocket, then turned to the nurse. "Sister," he said with more sharpness than Yuri had ever heard from the man, "why aren't you giving that child his medicine? He's been waiting too long already."

"I'm sorry, Doctor." The nurse hardly finished speaking before she opened the door and hurried into the room.

"I have to go, now," said Botkin to Yuri, his tone distracted. "See to it that Vasily is made comfortable. Dr. Tevele is familiar with the case and will take over in my absence."

"Yes, Doctor."

Botkin started to go, then paused and said, "Fedorcenko, I was about to invite you to my home for dinner. I'd like to talk further with you. Unfortunately, I must go away for a while. But when I return, I hope you will accept my invitation."

"I would be honored, sir."

With a sense of awe, Yuri watched the doctor leave. It was no small thing to be invited to Botkin's home. The man was known to take certain promising students under his wing, acting as a sort of mentor to them. If Yuri should be so honored, it would mean a tremendous boost to his medical career. Too bad the invitation had to be postponed. What if Botkin forgot about it in the ensuing time? He was, after all, a very busy man with many duties on his shoulders—not the least of which was the well-being of the tsar of all the Russias.

9

In the fall of 1912, the commemoration of the hundredth anniversary of the defeat of Napoleon took place. After an exhausting string of ceremonies lauding the battle of Borodino in which the Russian army at last stopped the march of Napoleon's armies, the tsar and his family traveled to Poland for a holiday.

Dr. Botkin had already planned to join the family in Spala, but those plans had been preempted by the tsar's telegram requesting that he come earlier than planned to the royal family's first destination of Bialowieza. The tsarevich had taken a spill from a rowboat and injured his upper thigh. The doctor immediately confined the boy to bed. In a week the swelling had diminished, and Botkin gave Alexis permission for limited activity.

Botkin thought of the child in the clinic and Prince Fedorcenko's rather naive perception of the rare illness afflicting the child. Botkin had been Court physician for five years now and had observed the little tsarevich at close hand, and never once did Botkin think the heir was better off than any other victim of hemophilia. It was possible that Alexis, now eight years old, would also never see his tenth birthday.

After Alexis appeared to recover from the fall in Bialowieza, the royal family traveled to Spala, also in Poland, to their hunting lodge. It was an idyllic place, rather rustic to be sure, but peaceful in its isolation. The thick forests surrounding it were rich with fall colors and the game was plenteous. It should have been a wonderful respite for the family. The tsar could hunt to his heart's content, the tsaritsa was spared hateful public appearances and Court intrigues, and the children could enjoy the healthful out-of-doors.

But their tranquility was shattered when the tsarevich suffered a relapse. During a particularly jostling carriage ride with his mother, Alexis began to experience terrible pain. By the time he returned home he was almost unconscious. Botkin found the old thigh wound had turned black and ugly again. Specialists were called in from St. Petersburg, but to no avail. The internal bleeding could not be stopped. The tissues, swelled by blood, caused intense pain, and before a week was over, the boy was feverish. The doctors, hovering almost constantly around the critically ill heir, were helpless.

Finally, Botkin had to tell the tsar that the public should be notified about the tsarevich's condition. It was the first time any official word had been made regarding the heir's illness. Of course rumors had always circulated around the Court and circles close to the throne. But even now the exact nature of the tsarevich's affliction was not released. Newspapers speculated everything from a hunting accident to a terrorist's bomb. The only thing they were now certain of was that the heir to the throne could die at any minute.

Sometimes Botkin had the feeling people forgot that a *child* was suffering and probably dying. He was thought of only by virtue of his position. The tsarevich. The heir. And the effect his death would have upon the throne of Russia.

They might think differently if they could hear the poor boy's screams of pain echoing up and down the corridors of the lodge. Or if they could see the wasted, empty countenances of his equally suffering parents. Botkin had actually seen the tsar break down in tears upon seeing his son, then flee from the boy's room. Alexandra was holding up better, though how much longer she could last under the dreadful strain, Botkin did not want to guess.

What was even worse—and somewhat bizarre—was the fact that the social life of the royal couple continued. Local aristocrats were entertained. The tsar went hunting. Even Alexandra received guests. Nicholas and Alexandra had become experts at maintaining the superficial guise of officialdom. Even those who visited the lodge never truly knew the tragic extent of the Imperial family's distress.

It wasn't true that only a mother could truly feel the pain of a sick child. Alix knew Nicky was suffering as much as she. Yet there was one kind of anguish he would never know—that of the burden of responsibility. The fact that she had taken Aleshka out in the carriage was only a small part of it. There had been other bleeding incidents in which Nicky or even the girls had blamed themselves. But none of them had to face the awful fact that Aleshka had, in the first place, gotten this horrible disease from her. Not a day, hardly even a moment, passed when that reality didn't haunt her.

And now every time the boy screamed from his internal torture, it pierced Alix like a sword of retribution.

"Mama, help me!"

Alix reached over and wiped a cool cloth over his forehead as if that was what he wanted.

"I'm here, my baby." *Not that it does any good,* she thought bitterly.

She was past wishing she could exchange places with her son. She once thought fleetingly of ending the boy's suffering once and for all. Or, even better, ending her own life so she wouldn't have to watch his pain any longer. But she was too much of a fatalist to seriously consider such measures. They were in God's hands. His will be done.

When the doctors came in that evening—there was one doctor or another examining the boy nearly every hour—their grave expressions did not alter.

After eleven days, Alix wondered how much longer this could go on. Even Alexis sensed his end must be near.

"Mama, when I die, I'd like to be buried in the pretty woods."

"Oh, Aleshka, don't say such things!" Alix quickly crossed herself. "You will be with us a long . . . long time."

"I only wish it wouldn't hurt you and Papa so much."

"My child!" But Alix could say no more. Though she tried to hide her emotion from her son, it now spilled out like the tears that dripped from her eyes.

That night the priest administered unction, and the tsar's secretary sent a bulletin to the Capital, which they all believed would be the last before announcing the death of the heir.

When the service was over, Alix chased everyone from the sickroom except her dear friend Anna Vyrubova. Anna had come to reside at the Court several years earlier when her marriage had failed and Alexandra had taken pity on her. The two had become almost inseparable. Anna was a round-faced, plump woman who was as pious as the tsaritsa herself. Some said Anna was too mystical for her own good and probably for that reason had few friends at Court. She and Alix were, for that very reason and others, kindred spirits.

"Your Highness," Anna Vyrubova said humbly as she sat by the tsaritsa, holding her hand, "don't you think it is time we notified *Our Friend*?"

"I should have done so long before this," said Alix. "But—" The empress couldn't say exactly why she had waited. There had been some trouble recently concerning Father Grigori. Many at Court and in the government didn't understand the great *starets*, Rasputin. They tried to make accusations against him, calling him false and ambitious. Alix knew differently. Since that first meeting seven years ago, Father Grigori had been devoted to the royal family, never asking anything in return, always giving freely of himself. On two or three other occasions, Alix was certain his prayers had healed her son. But perhaps that had been part of the cause of her reluctance in calling him now. Things had been going so well lately with the tsarevich that Alix had believed he had been healed completely. This relapse had shaken her faith.

"Your Highness, we know Father Grigori isn't perfect," said Anna, almost as if she could read the tsaritsa's thoughts.

"I thought he might be upset with me for allowing him to return to Siberia."

"The backbiters and intriguers forced him to retreat from the Capital, not you."

"I could have stood up for him. Instead, I refused to see him after the newspaper published those letters."

Recently some of the tsaritsa's private letters to Rasputin had fallen into the unscrupulous hands of the press. Of course the people, who were always anxious to find fault with her, had misinterpreted her dramatic turn of a word. She had written quite innocently: "My soul is only rested and at ease when you, my teacher, are near me. I kiss your hands and lay my head upon your blessed shoulders. I feel so joyful in those moments. Then all I want to do is sleep, sleep forever on your shoulder, in your embrace . . ."

They had no right to ridicule and demean the cries of her heart. She was empress of Russia. Her husband was absolute monarch with the power to—well, since that horrid constitution, his powers were rather cloudy—but nevertheless, he and his royal family were deserving of respect, if nothing else.

"Could *Our Friend* blame you?" Anna was saying. "You were shocked and hurt that your private and personal life was made a public spectacle. It had been careless of *Our Friend* to lose track of the letters."

"I should have been angrier at the people who had the nerve to think—oh, I want to forget the entire horrid incident."

"And no doubt the *starets* wishes to do the same. Besides, I think he believed it was God's will that he leave the Capital, for a time at least."

"And now?"

"Do you think he will turn his back on you?"

"No, he wouldn't." Alix paused and looked at her son. He had begun to moan again. His sweet, fine-featured face was so pale. "Anna, would you go to the village and send *Our Friend* a telegram?"

"As you wish, Your Highness." Anna rose quickly, went to a small desk in the room, and withdrew paper and pen from a drawer.

Alix took the writing things and jotted down a brief note: "Father Grigori, my son is dying; you are my only hope. I know if you pray for him, God will hear your prayers."

The note seemed so brief, yet what more needed to be said? In those few words, days of anguish, fear, and desperation were expressed with all the eloquence of a literary masterpiece. As an added touch, Alix drew at the bottom of the message a swastika, her favorite lucky charm.

Rasputin's reply came the next morning before the sun had risen. He said simply: "The little one will not die. God has seen your grief and heard your prayers. Have faith and try to keep the doctors away from the child as much as possible."

For the first time in nearly two weeks, Alix felt peace. Had the *starets* actually been able to transfer his power to calm and heal over the lines of the telegraph?

She was certain of it when, the next day, Alexis's hemorrhaging stopped. She didn't care what anyone said now, she would see to it that Father Grigori returned to the Capital. He was her only hope. And perhaps he would still be God's instrument for healing her son completely.

10

Cyril Vlasenko hobbled up the steps of Count Ignatiev's home, ebony cane gripped firmly in his right hand. His wife was at his side and two footmen hovered protectively behind him. He was certain he could manage without the footmen, but, even though the bombing had occurred seven years ago, he still felt vulnerable when alone. Thus, when he went outside, he always had an escort of some kind.

This evening, however, his thoughts were far from danger and fear. His life was looking decidedly better than it had in years. He had just been appointed Assistant Minister of Agriculture. Perhaps it wasn't much to brag about for a man who had been on the verge of becoming Minister of the Interior. But it was a move in the right direction.

It had only been four years since Cyril had returned to government service, and he practically had to begin at the bottom again. It helped that he now had an important ally at Court. Without the influence of Rasputin, Cyril would still be wallowing in provincial government. It had been fantastic insight on his part to stay close to Rasputin, who, even a few years ago, was gaining stature at Court. Cyril knew he had made the right move when he saw that even Count Witte was friendly to the *starets*. Witte had also retreated from government in 1905, though the cause was more his own doing. He now was ambitious to return to power and, like Cyril, saw Rasputin as a tool to that end.

Witte, however, would not be at Ignatiev's home tonight. This was entirely a gathering of right-wing adherents who were, among other things, devoted to reversing the disastrous constitutional reforms of 1905. They were closely related to the Union of Russian People, and some, like Cyril, were even members of the more militant Black Hundreds. Tonight, however, was to be a purely social gathering. Rasputin himself would be in attendance. And Cyril would have to thank the *starets* for his recent appointment.

In the last several months since the tsarevich's near fatal illness, Rasputin had risen enormously in power. It was said the tsar counted on Rasputin to look into the eyes of prospective Imperial appointees in order to discern the particular man's worthiness for office. Cyril had no doubt that he himself had been so scrutinized. For once he was in the right place at the right time—this evening's invitation proved it even further. He was certain the *starets* had wrangled it for him, and because of it he could now hobnob once again with some of the highest ministers, church officials, and aristocrats in the country.

Cyril and his wife, Poznia, were received cordially by the Ignatievs and the other influential guests. None had forgotten that once Cyril had wielded some power himself—and that as a former director of the Third Section, he knew more about their affairs than they did themselves.

Rasputin arrived later and was received with great affection, especially by the women. Poznia all but fawned over the man, but Cyril didn't mind. His wife spent a great deal of time with the *starets*, and when she wasn't meeting with him, she was sending him flowers and sweets—almost like a courting lover. All the other women did the same. Cyril had no idea what went on between Rasputin and the women when the men were not present, nor did he want to know. Many believed the worst. Cyril, however, agreed with the tsaritsa when she defended the *starets*, saying, "True saints are never accepted in their own country. And, as far as those low rumors go about him kissing women . . . well, one only has to look in the Bible to find that kissing is an accepted mode of greeting."

And Cyril would continue to agree with the empress as long as it benefitted him. And he would turn a blind eye toward his wife's involvement. It kept her happy, and it hadn't hurt Cyril.

When Rasputin arrived, he became the instant center of attention, a fact that he seemed to revel in. No one seemed bothered by the *starets'* rather crude behavior. He grabbed food from the table with his bare hands—quite dirty hands, too. He talked with his mouth full of that food and seemed to have no use at all for a napkin, using the sleeve of his dusty old cassock instead. He laughed louder than anyone and drank more. He appeared more the lusty peasant than a man of God.

The talk that evening turned to the upcoming tercentenary celebration of the Romanov dynasty.

"Here's to three hundred more years!" said Ignatiev, raising his champagne in a toast.

All drank heartily. They knew their own political health depended mightily on the longevity of the Romanovs.

"Sometimes I think it will be a miracle if we make it three years, much less three *hundred,*" exclaimed one of the men. "Every day revolutionaries and liberals rob more and more of the prestige of the throne."

"I, for one, believe in miracles," said Rasputin. "Come now, let's drink to miracles!" He tipped his glass to his lips and drained it.

"What do you think of the Duma, Father Grigori?"

"They are a bunch of dogs collected to keep other dogs quiet!" The *starets* laughed loudly at his wit and was joined by everyone.

"Father Grigori," Cyril asked, anxious to be part of the interchange, "will the tsar dissolve this Duma as he did the others?"

"It's only a matter of time," said another guest.

"He will, if he's smart," another chimed in.

Rasputin said, "Do you wish a prophecy, my dear Count Vlasenko?"

"Prophecy or keen insight, Father Grigori," said Cyril diplomatically. "You could offer either."

"That ragtag bunch of ruffians and revolutionaries some broadly refer to as an official government body will *self*-destruct one day, even if the tsar does nothing." Rasputin smiled. He must dearly hope that time would be sooner rather than later, for much of the debate in the Duma of late had involved censorship of Rasputin himself.

"You can be sure, Grigori Efimovich," said Ignatiev, "that no one with an ounce of sense places any stock in the gibberish spoken in the Duma."

"I know," said Rasputin, "but the tongue is a dangerous beast. A very small member, yet more difficult to tame than a wild lion. It is the flaming gateway to iniquity, defiling all in its path, sparked by the very fires of hell. Yet, oh, how man is ruled by this ravenous animal! How can both blessing and curse flow from the same organ? But it does, stirring envy and strife in the hearts of men. Only by true, godly wisdom can we rise above the ravages of that instrument of evil. And is not the fear of the Lord the beginning of wisdom. . . ?"

It was in moments such as this that Cyril almost regretted his association with the *starets*. Once Rasputin got going on his sermonizing, he could go on seemingly forever. Half of what he said made no sense, especially to a man like Cyril who knew little of spiritual things. And, as much as his relationship to Rasputin was getting him more and more attuned to his neglected spiritual nature, Cyril still hated sermons. But no one dared interrupt as Rasputin rambled on for the next fifteen minutes.

Later in the evening, Cyril was certain his perseverance had been worth it. He managed to get Rasputin alone for a moment.

"I want to thank you, Father Grigori, for my recent good fortune," said Cyril.

"And what might that be?"

"You must be aware of my appointment to the agriculture ministry."

"That is only the beginning, Cyril Karlovich."

Cyril beamed and afterward celebrated so heartily on champagne and sweets that, upon leaving Ignatiev's, he needed the support of his footmen more than ever.

11

Paul Burenin was certain stranger things had happened, but definitely not to him. He still found it hard to believe that a former terrorist and exile could suddenly find himself thrust into a position in the government he was all but sworn to destroy. It had happened quite by accident, almost as a lark. His friend Alexander Kerensky had suggested the preposterous idea last year.

"I've been approached by a branch of the Social Revolutionary Party," Alexander told him. "They've asked me to stand for election to the Fourth Duma. They are expanding the Party to include a broader populist faction."

"Are you going to do it?"

"Yes, I am. I've always sympathized with the Populists. And I think you should try for one of the positions yourself."

"Me?" Paul laughed, thinking he was joining in on a joke.

But Kerensky was serious. "This is our opportunity to have a real impact on the government."

"I think, Sasha, I would feel a bit hypocritical employed by a government I have worked so long to destroy."

"It's the monarchy we are dedicated to destroy. The Duma represents a step toward that final goal of a representational democracy. Even the Social Democrats, a few Bolsheviks among them, are represented."

"I know. But all that aside, Sasha, I am a nobody. Who would elect me? You, at least, have made a name for yourself as a barrister."

"I see people every day who have read your articles, Pavushka. You don't give yourself enough credit. There is, however, one requirement for running, and that is land ownership."

"That shouldn't be a problem. The Burenin family plot, though managed completely by my nephew, is in my name as the eldest male in the family."

Before he knew it, Paul was swept into the Duma elections and, by a true miracle, was elected to represent the Akulin District. He couldn't say that being a member of the oft-abused, oft-ineffectual body was the fulfillment of all his dreams. He viewed it more as a way station on the political road of his life. Despite his lifetime involvement in revolutionary activities, he had never pictured himself as a politician. His main talent had been in stirring support through the written word. He had at one time enjoyed debate, but the tedious, nit-picking debating of the Bolsheviks had soured him on that aspect of politics.

The Duma, however, was reviving this almost atrophied talent of his. The debate in the Duma did get extremely lengthy at times, but there was such a broad base of opinion that it never got boring. He still often wondered if the Duma was truly a potent force in Russian politics. The tsar had shown by dissolving the first two Dumas that the power of autocracy was not fully broken. The Third Duma had run its natural course, but more often than not at complete loggerheads with the monarch. Still, at the very least, the Duma gave Paul a legitimate outlet for his political views.

The major issue in the Duma of late was the "Rasputin Question." Hardly a session went by when there wasn't some debate of the man's outrageous behavior. The animosity between the "Holy Devil" or "Mad Monk," as some referred to Rasputin, and the Duma was bound to come to a head, and it did so at the tercentenary celebrations.

The celebrations in February of 1913 were to be opened by an inaugural liturgy at the Kazan Cathedral. The president of the Duma, Rodzianko, was to deliver the one and only speech to be allowed at the ceremony. Yet in spite of that honor, the members of the Duma had been given the worst viewing positions of any officials. When the oversight was noted just prior to the service, Rodzianko took the matter up with the master of ceremonies in a rather heated discussion.

Rodzianko might be at a far different political pole from Paul, but Paul had to admire the man his unflinching championship of his cause.

"You will remember," Rodzianko pointed out firmly, "that it was an assembly of the *people*, such as the Duma represents, not of officials, that elected Michael Romanov as tsar three hundred years ago!"

As a result, the Duma members were given the place that had been reserved for the Senate. Rodzianko had the spot cordoned off and guarded by members of the Duma sergeant at arms. But when the Duma representatives began to trickle in, they found someone else was attempting to infringe upon their place. And of all people, it was Grigori Rasputin. Paul had a feeling it wasn't a coincidence that the Mad Monk had chosen this very spot to take his place.

Rodzianko, who had last year been instrumental in forcing Rasputin to leave the Capital, now accosted the *starets* with mighty indignation.

"What, may I ask, are you doing here?" demanded Rodzianko.

"What business is it of yours?" retorted Rasputin with an insolent smirk.

"You better speak with a little more respect to me—I *am* the president of the Duma."

Rasputin moderated his tone. "Well, then, what do you want?"

"Clear out of here!" ordered Rodzianko. "You don't belong in a place of worship."

"I'm here at the request of persons more highly placed than you." Rasputin showed his invitation.

"I don't care! You swindler, who can believe a word you say? Now, get out, or I'll have the sergeant at arms drag you out."

Rasputin grasped his hands together, as if in prayer, and directed his gaze upward. "Oh, Lord," he groaned heavily, "forgive this man his sin."

Rasputin then departed. But the enmity between him and the Duma, and Rodzianko in particular, had not been improved by the incident. Paul understood that Rasputin was becoming a real thorn in Russia's governmental flesh and a cause of the Crown to lose face, but he also believed much more could be done for the country if the Duma could focus on more practical issues like land reform, modernizing education, and international affairs.

Was there no aspect of political involvement that was free of frustration? Paul was beginning to wonder. Yet, he had devoted too much of his life to it to give up now. Lately, he was feeling more certain than ever that Russia was coming to a crossroads. It was obvious to even the dullest person that the Crown was becoming sicker and sicker. Paul saw the rise of Rasputin not so much as a cause of that sickness, but a symptom of it. And he secretly believed that if the *starets* was just given a free hand, the much-anticipated demise of the Russian monarchy would come sooner rather than later.

Nicholas viewed Rasputin not so much as a holy man than as the consummate Russian peasant. Grigori's crude simplicity could be rather refreshing after a few hours with the highborn and haughty, but the man's crudeness was unsettling at times.

Watching him now as they shared tea with him in Alexandra's boudoir with the children gathered around, Nicholas had to choke back criticism of Grigori's deplorable manners. He hated for his impressionable children to observe such behavior. Yet the children enjoyed the monk's company. He was kind to them and always had amusing stories to tell.

Rasputin now launched into one of his stories. "That brings to mind a couple of cows in my village." He paused, grabbed a loaf of bread from the tea table with his hands, tore off a chunk, took a big bite, then proceeded to relate his story with his mouth full of bread. "It came time to mate the beasts, but neither had a liking for the bull—"

"Father Grigori," Nicholas cut in hurriedly, "do you think that an appropriate topic . . . for children, I mean?"

Rasputin glanced at each of the children, then laughed heartily, spraying a good deal of the half-chewed bread into the air. "I am a foolish peasant. Forgive me, Papa. You can take the peasant out of the village, but you can't take the village out of—hmm . . ." He scratched his dirty beard. "That didn't come out right, did it? But you know what I mean, eh?"

"We know, Father Grigori," said Alexandra with an affectionate smile, "that God can use even a peasant to do great things. Perhaps he can *especially* use a peasant because of your uncluttered soul."

"You are too good to me, Mama!" Grigori stuffed another bite of bread into his mouth, washing it down with a big gulp of wine, which he preferred over tea.

"Tell us another story," said the tsarevich. He was especially close to the *starets*—and no wonder. He had come to believe, like his mother, that Grigori was directly responsible for his recovery from that terrible injury in Spala.

"Another time," said Nicholas, trying to be the firm father. "It is bedtime for you and your sisters now."

"Can't we have just one story?" implored Alexis. The girls gave vigorous verbal support to their brother.

"I will take them to bed, Papa," said Grigori. "I will tuck them in and tell them a story—a nice story . . . from the Bible perhaps." He winked at the tsar.

"Well, all right," said Nicholas.

Excited, the children jumped up—that is, the girls jumped and helped their brother, who now had to walk with a brace on the leg he had injured in Spala. They would have dashed off immediately with the *starets*, except for Nicholas's gentle reminder that they mustn't forget their manners.

All five children then paused and gave their parents respectful good-night kisses before they skipped out with Grigori, each child vying to hold the *starets'* hand.

"He is a good man," said Alexandra when she and Nicholas were alone. Had she perceived her husband's doubts?

"A bit eccentric, though, I should say."

"But you must admit he gives us all such a sense of peace and security. The children feel it, and I know you do also, Nicky."

"Yes, I can't deny it. I wish, however, I could explain it."

"Why? It is the most natural thing in the world to find peace in the presence of a true servant of God."

Nicholas nodded, rubbing his beard thoughtfully.

In a few moments, Grigori returned.

"What delightful children! Baby will grow up to be a fine monarch," the *starets* said as he sat in one of the mauve chintz chairs.

Alexandra rose from her own seat, came to the *starets*, and knelt before him. "And you shall be his wise counselor, dear Friend," she said dreamily. She took his hand and kissed it. "What a grand kingdom we shall have when Alexis the Great ascends the throne of Russia."

Nicholas did not mention the fact that for all this to happen he himself would have to be quite dead. He shared the same dreams of passing his crown on to his son, and of Alexis perhaps reigning over the Golden Age of Russia.

Alexandra lay her head in Grigori's lap, and the *starets* gently caressed her hair. If this made the tsar at all uncomfortable, he only had to remind himself that Grigori was a lifeline to them all, but especially to Alix. She suffered most from Baby's illness. She alone had to bear the awful pain that it had come from her. Nicholas would never refuse her the comfort and strength she drew from

Grigori. Though others might misinterpret it, he knew in his heart that their relationship was as pure as the breath of God. And, in many ways, Nicholas was grateful to Grigori because of that relationship. Nicholas did not have the kind of strength his wife needed. Nicholas and Alix needed each other, yes. They loved each other passionately, of course. But Nicholas was as helpless and as impotent as anyone to save the one thing that was more important than life to Alix. Only Rasputin appeared to have the power to sustain the life of their son and perhaps, as a consequence, the life of Alix, too.

No, he would never deny her that lifeline. Never.

12

Andrei did not much like family gatherings. He liked national celebrations even less. How unfortunate for him then when several such events all coincided in the same year. February of 1913 had brought the glorious tercentenary celebration of the Romanov dynasty. "Glorious" of course was how the Imperial government termed it. Andrei called it "three hundred years in chains" and had published in an underground newspaper a political cartoon with just such a theme. It had been reproduced on handbills and plastered all over town. Andrei was quite proud of the fact that for days everyone was talking about the "Little Soldier," the pseudonym he had kept all these years.

At twenty-one, Andrei was still a political zealot. The desire for the overthrow of the Romanov dynasty continued to run strong in him. Yet lately, though he hated to admit it, his art often robbed him of some of his political zeal. He was glad he had found a way to combine the two with his newspaper work, yet, at times, it was a precarious mix. Too often the revolutionary zealots with whom he associated tried to demand a more total dedication from him. And haunted by his father's death, he felt guilty about being more passionate about his art than his politics.

But if he was occasionally torn between his political friends and his art, he was even more conflicted with his family. Unfortunately, they understood neither his politics nor his art, and thus Andrei was reluctant to frequent family gatherings. Three years ago he had moved away from home into a flat with a half dozen others with similar interests as his. It had simply become too hard to live at home, especially after he had quit secondary school a year before he was to graduate. His mother tried to be accepting, but he always could sense her disappointment even if she never *said* as much. Yuri had been more verbal.

"Papa would turn over in his grave. You know how important our education was to him."

"I think our *happiness* was far more important to Papa," Andrei had retorted.

Down deep Andrei knew he had let his father down. But he could not have stood another moment in that bourgeois school, listening to government propaganda disguised as lessons. He had been miserable, and his grades showed that fact clearly, if nothing else did. If he hadn't quit, he would probably have flunked out, anyway.

Besides, he didn't need an education for what he planned to do with his life. He had already sold two paintings, and a gallery wanted to do a showing of his art if he could deliver at least two dozen works of the same quality as those that had sold. He was certain he could make a living with his art—in fact, other artists he knew, who had been at it seriously far longer than he, had not even come close to his present success. He also earned a modest income doing artwork for three radical newspapers.

How many other people could say they were doing what they loved, making a difference in the world, and earning a living, to boot? Well, it was probably not exactly a *living*. He had been forced to work at some rather menial odd jobs to fill in the financial gaps, and still there were days when he didn't eat. But he would rather starve than sell out his dreams and convictions.

If only his family could understand. Yuri was fulfilling his dreams and convictions, too. The only difference was that Yuri's were more socially acceptable than his.

Yuri, the scholar. Top of his class.

Yuri, the fine doctor.

Yuri, the protégé of the Court physician.

Yuri. Yuri. Yuri.

Andrei. . . ? Well, you know Andrei.

Nevertheless, there had been no way Andrei could escape this particular family event without breaking his mother's heart.

So now, in the summer of 1913, he was sitting next to his mother, surrounded by his family, attending his brother's graduation from medical school. Once more he must suffer under the weight of Yuri's laurels.

Still, he simply could not turn completely away from his family. Many of his friends had done that very thing. In some cases, if they hadn't renounced their families, the families had renounced them. But that had never been the case with Andrei. Sometimes his mother harped at him, and Yuri had a tendency toward arrogance and lecturing, but they had never withheld their love. And he could not deny his love for them. Even Yuri.

Andrei glanced toward the front of the auditorium where the medical students were seated. Yuri was up on the stage with the special honorees. His robe was covered with the evidence of his accomplishments—sashes and tassels and braid that said, *Here is a man who has achieved great things*.

And Yuri deserved all the accolades he received. Yuri had worked hard, sacrificed much. Their brother-in-law, Daniel, might have paid for Yuri's education, but no one but Yuri had devoted unceasing labor to making it come out as it had. Andrei had witnessed many times when his brother had stayed up all night doing schoolwork or rewriting whole papers that he believed were inadequate.

All Andrei wished for was that his own accomplishments would be thought of as highly as Yuri's, not swept under the rug in shame and embarrassment. Even his success in the art world was not understood. His political work aside, his painting should have warranted some praise. But Andrei had strayed from the kind of art that was found socially accepted. He had stopped doing representational art, or even Impressionistic art, three years ago. He was seeking his own identity, and though he hadn't yet fully discovered his place as an artist, the paintings he had sold were of a neoprimitive style. Lately, however, he had been experimenting with suprematism and cubism.

He had recently shown one of his paintings to his mother and brother. It was an abstract of a peasant woman baking bread. It had received much praise from his peers, and even Kazimir Malevich, one of the leaders in the new Russian art movement, had seen the work and admired it. Andrei's mother had given it a perplexed look, then, speaking as if she were trying hard to say something nice, commented, "It's very colorful, Andrei."

Yuri had been more critical. "Where is the bread? And why is her hand—I *think* that's her hand—bent in that way? It's anatomically impossible."

Only Talia had really understood. "I like her, Andrei. I mean, not only do I like the painting, I like *her*. I see her strength and her stoicism, yet she handles the bread with a kind of tenderness, as if she knows it is the means of her family's survival."

Andrei glanced at Talia, who was sitting next to him. She alone made family encounters bearable. She was simply not around as often as he would have liked. Her ballet training had been all-encompassing over the last seven years. He saw far less of her than he wanted, and he doubted that would change even when she graduated in two weeks. They would both be involved in the art world and perhaps their circles would intersect, but they would still have to expend a great deal of effort if they were to maintain their friendship. Nevertheless, she would always be his best friend—even if she would never be more.

Talia must have felt his gaze. She looked up at him and smiled. "I'm so glad you came, Andrei," she whispered, leaning close. "It's not so bad, is it?"

"Only because you're here."

"That means, then, that you will be at my premier performance?"

"I wouldn't miss it."

"I'm already getting nervous over it."

"You'll be wonderful—"

"Wait!" Talia said suddenly, "Yuri is about to speak."

Andrei restrained an ironic smile. Again Yuri came between them. But Andrei had long ago accepted the fact that Talia was hopelessly in love with his brother. Of course Yuri didn't have a clue about this, and when Talia had confided it one day to Andrei, she had sworn him to secrecy. Why Talia was so reluctant to make her feelings known to Yuri, Andrei couldn't guess. But he had no problem complying with her request. The moment she told Yuri, he would have to hurt her by telling her he didn't have the same feelings for her. It was best for all that they keep these romantic notions in check. They were friends, above all else, and romance had a way of ruining friendship. That was certainly at least part of the reason why he never revealed *his* love for Talia to her. He didn't want to lose her friendship. He also didn't want to face her sure rejection.

What a triangle! he thought. Twisted and hopeless. Sometimes Andrei wondered if they would ever find real happiness. He doubted they could do so apart. Yet it also seemed impossible to be happy *together*, except as friends.

13

Yuri glanced at the clock above the mantel. Eight o'clock. He didn't want to be impatient to leave his own party, but he had told some friends he would meet them at nine. Yuri hadn't thought his mother's party would last so long. Everyone was having such a good time that no one seemed to want to leave—no one except Yuri. But he had to stay at least until Daniel and Mariana arrived. They had attended the ceremony at the university, but immediately afterward Daniel had been called away on business. He said it would take only a few minutes, but it had already been an hour.

"Yuri, you gave a wonderful speech today." Yuri's grandfather, Viktor, came up and put an arm proudly around Yuri's shoulders.

"Thank you, Grandfather. I'm glad you could come."

"Do you think I would miss this proud day?"

At that moment Andrei passed close to Viktor, who quickly reached out and snagged Andrei's arm. He then placed his other arm around Andrei. "Ah, my boys! I haven't seen the two of you together in months. You are the finest young men I know. I'm as proud today as a grandfather can be. And I know your father would be proud of you both also."

After a few moments, Viktor's wife approached. "Do you mind if I steal you away, Viktor? There is a gentleman who would like to meet you."

"Will you excuse me, boys? But I will have more to say later, since your mother has asked me to deliver a little speech."

When Viktor was gone, Yuri and Andrei remained where they were, quietly and even a bit awkwardly.

Finally Yuri said, "Thanks for coming, Andrei. I know how you feel about these things."

"Are you kidding? I wouldn't miss the most important day of my brother's life."

"I appreciate the sentiment, but . . . if this turns out to be the most important day of my life, what do I have to look forward to?"

"There you go, intellectualizing everything! Yuri, you're going to have a fine life, accomplishing great things. I've no doubt about it. *You* will never disappoint our mother."

"And I suppose you think you will?"

"I already have."

"Bosh."

"It doesn't bother me very much. I realize she can't have two perfect sons—that would take its toll on her humility."

"Come on, Andrei—"

At that moment the front door burst open and in swept Daniel, Mariana, and their two children. Scattered conversations around the room ceased and attention turned toward the new arrivals.

"Forgive us for being late," said Daniel. "I had to send a telegram to the States giving approval to some business matters. The international wires were jammed up. It seems Bulgaria has invaded Serbia."

"Again?" Andrei looked up. "They just signed a peace treaty less than a month ago."

"Those countries are always at each other's throats," Dmitri said.

"Let's just hope they don't involve Russia." Viktor shook his head.

"I hope they don't involve anyone," said Daniel. "There is such a tangled mess of alliances and pacts in Europe now that the whole continent could well be drawn into the fray."

"No more politics," Mariana insisted. "This is Yuri's party; let's not spoil it with depressing news." She turned to her cousin and adopted brother, embraced him, and kissed his cheek. "I am so proud of you, Yuri. Or, should I say, *Doctor* Fedorcenko?"

"I do like the sound of that." Yuri grinned.

Daniel threw an arm around Yuri. "You've earned it!"

"I couldn't have done it without you, Daniel."

"Nonsense! You are a brilliant man. You would have achieved

success even if you'd had to beg on the streets for money."

"Well, thank you, anyway." Yuri started to shake Daniel's hand, then, suddenly full of emotion, gave Daniel a full and hearty Russian embrace.

An hour later, when he made his excuses and departed the party, Yuri felt torn. Most of the guests had left already, but the people he cared most about were still there—his mother, his grandparents, Raisa, Talia, and Daniel and Mariana. Andrei had left almost immediately after Daniel's arrival.

It would have been different if Yuri, like his brother, didn't enjoy his family's company. But he did. His circle of friends were important to him, too, and, unfortunately, the two elements didn't mix very well. It was understandable that his mother didn't fit in; she was from an entirely different generation. But the others also seemed to shy away from the social set Yuri associated with. Andrei did more than shy away—he was openly hostile.

"How can you demean yourself by rubbing shoulders with all that aristocratic riffraff?" Andrei often said.

Andrei still used the surname Christinin, the name their father had taken while he was a fugitive. As far as the family title went, its use, to Andrei, was akin to a curse word.

Reaching the street outside his mother's apartment, Yuri walked for some distance until a cab drove by. He told the driver his destination, then climbed in. It was a ten-minute ride to the fashionable St. Petersburg club called The Bear. He sat back and continued to muse about his brother.

Sometimes Yuri missed his brother's company. Their times together as children—he, Andrei, and Talia—were among his fondest memories. But over the years they had drifted further and further apart. It was as much his fault as Andrei's.

Then again, maybe it was no one's fault. They were just two different people—they always had been. But sometimes it seemed as if Andrei was trying to be different, trying to do everything he could to distance himself from Yuri. The better Yuri's grades in school, the more "fails" Andrei got; the more Yuri associated with his aristocratic friends, the more zealous Andrei's revolutionary fervor became. Now that Yuri thought about it, Andrei had dropped out of school the same year Yuri had entered the university.

Was Andrei trying to prove something in his behavior?

Yuri wanted nothing more than to make his family proud, to return the Fedorcenko name to its former glory. He believed he owed it to his father and his grandfather, a duty that had become even more important, considering the fact that Andrei seemed to be doing all he could to shame the Fedorcenko name. He would not even claim it as his true name. Maybe that was just as well. Sooner or later Andrei was bound to run afoul of the authorities, and in that event it was better only the Christinin name suffered.

Yuri's cab pulled up in front of the nightclub. He paid the driver and entered the building. Everyone who was of any importance at all in St. Petersburg at one time or another crossed the threshold of this place. Glancing around, Yuri saw the sons and daughters of Imperial ministers, grand dukes and duchesses, generals and admirals. Yuri made a pointed attempt to conceal his awe. Actually, he seldom came here because his budget hardly allowed for the extravagance of such a place. More than that, if the truth were known, Yuri had not yet achieved the highest level of Russian aristocracy. His friends and associates were of the type that mingled on the fringes of the true upper crust. Some were wealthy but lacking in titles; others, like him, had the titles but not the accompanying amenities and influence.

Yuri longed to move up the social ladder. In his youth, especially since his father's death, he had constantly pumped his grandfather for information about the Fedorcenko family. He had learned about the fabulous St. Petersburg estate lost to that conniver Cyril Vlasenko. Viktor told him about the hundreds of servants, one of which had been Yuri's own mother—a fact Yuri tried to forget; about the rooms full of priceless artwork and antiques; about the parties at which hundreds, including tsars, had been entertained. Viktor had to be pressed sometimes, but he even told about how he and his ancestors walked the corridors of the Winter Palace as men who influenced tsars and national affairs.

Andrei forever prattled on about how the aristocracy would be torn down with the monarchy, along with the capitalist bourgeois. He said all wealth would be distributed equally among the people, and a man's worth would be determined by his character, not by some title in front of his name. Yuri believed his brother was naive. Such a utopia was impossible. There would always be rich and poor. Even republics like America had class divisions. Look at the Trents. And they were not even in the highest class because their money wasn't old enough.

Yuri believed that if he had the initiative to better himself, then why should he not do so? Wasn't that what freedom was truly about?

"There he is!" shouted a voice above the din of the nightclub. "The man of the hour."

Yuri turned and saw Count Vladimir Baklanov standing across the crowded room waving. Vladimir, a fourth-year law student at the university, was a friend Yuri had met several years ago at a party. They had liked each other immediately, and it was only later they learned that their grandfathers had once been close friends. Vladimir was a year younger than Yuri, several inches shorter, husky of build and extremely good-natured. His round, florid face sported an enormous handlebar moustache and a constant grin. He was full of laughter and mischief.

"Come on, Vlad, you'll embarrass me," Yuri said as he slid easily into a chair.

Also at the table was another of Yuri's close friends, Count Boris Kozin, youngest son of the wealthy banker. He was as close as any of Yuri's friends to the inner circle of St. Petersburg society, but for the most part his family's dealings with the highest nobility were centered around business more than pleasure. Occasionally Boris was invited to the best parties, but not often. An economics graduate, Boris fervently hoped to marry *up* and have the income of a large estate to control. As the youngest of three brothers, he had little hope of getting much from his own family. Thus far, his patrician good looks had attracted many fine girls, but none to suit his high hopes.

Boris lifted a bottle of champagne from a sterling silver urn filled with ice. He deftly popped the cork and, as a cascade of foam bubbled from the bottle, filled three glasses, passing them around to his companions.

"We were ready to have the champagne without you," said Boris.

"You know how these family things go," Yuri said. "It's easier to escape from the Fortress. But I'm here now, so let's drink this champagne before it goes flat."

"First, a toast," said Vladimir. He lifted his glass. "To our resident genius! The most decorated graduate of the Petersburg University Medical School, Prince Doctor Yuri Sergeiovich Fedorcenko."

"Are you sure it's 'Prince Doctor'?" said Boris. "I think it should be 'Doctor Prince'—"

"Never mind. Drink up!"

The three drained their glasses quickly, and Boris refilled them. In no time the bottle was empty and another ordered.

"Speech, Yuri!"

"I've had it with speeches," Yuri said. "But I do want to thank you for—well, for everything."

"Why thank us?" chuckled Vladimir. "Don't you know you're getting the bill?"

"I don't care," said Yuri. "It's worth it to share this momentous occasion with my two best friends in the world."

"Then, perhaps you don't want the gift we have for you. . . ?"

"Vlad, you didn't have to—"

"See, he doesn't want it!" taunted Boris.

"I certainly wouldn't want to hurt your feelings," said Yuri.

"Give it to him, Boris." Vladimir drained another glass of champagne. "I can't stand the suspense."

Boris rubbed his chin as if he were considering what to do, then slowly he slipped his hand into his inside coat pocket and withdrew an envelope. Handing it to Yuri, he said, "*Bonnes Fortunes!*"

Yuri took the envelope with a perplexed brow. Why would his friend wish him luck with the ladies? Surely they hadn't . . .

He was relieved when he saw upon opening the envelope that it was an invitation to a party.

You are cordially invited to
celebrate the engagement of

Prince Felix Feliksovich Youssoupov

to

Princess Irina Alexandrovna

at the Moika Palace
on June twenty-fifth, 1913 . . .

"I don't get it," Yuri said, trying to prevent his jaw from slackening in awe. It was probably just the champagne, but his head was starting to spin.

"You've always wanted to rub shoulders with the crème de la crème, have you not?" said Vladimir.

"Yes . . ."

"Well, there you go."

"I'm to crash the party of the year?"

"It's hardly crashing," said Boris with mock affront. "That's a bona fide invitation sent to my father and his family."

"I didn't know even you mingled with such personages," said Yuri skeptically.

"I tell you, this is completely on the up-and-up! My father served with the elder Felix in the Chevaliers-Gardes. Granted, they were never close friends, but a month ago Youssoupov and my father cut a business deal at the bank. The invitation was Youssoupov's way of showing his gratitude."

"But—"

"Yuri, you know what they say about gift horses and looking too closely."

"You really expect me to attend? I . . . I couldn't. Why, the tsar himself might be there!"

The Youssoupovs were doubtless the richest family in Russia. Some estimates had them even richer than the tsar. Felix Youssoupov, since the death of his elder brother, would be the heir to all that wealth. But that was hardly the half of it. Irina Alexandrovna, his fiancée, was the tsar's niece, her mother being the tsar's sister. The idea of Yuri walking into a gathering such as this was as stupendous as when his mother had nearly collided with Tsar Alexander II at the Winter Palace. Yuri liked to allow himself to think that because he was a Fedorcenko he was a man of certain standing. But underneath the air of importance he sometimes attempted to assume, he was aware of his background as the son of a peasant maid who had been raised in a St. Petersburg tenement.

Yes, he had longed for the society of such as the Youssoupovs. His grandfather had once been on an equal footing with them and their ilk. But what if the working-class peasant boy got the better of Yuri, and he made a complete fool of himself? Perhaps, after all, the imagining and the longing were better than the fulfillment.

Yuri said to his friends, "This was very kind of you, but—"

"We won't hear any excuses, Yuri," said Boris.

"Do you plan on giving up your place to attend, Boris? I would never ask you to make such a sacrifice."

"Would I be so magnanimous?" Boris smiled slyly. "Look at the envelope. Who is it addressed to?"

Yuri turned the envelope over. "To the family of Alexsie Vladimirovich Kozin. So am I your country cousin?"

Boris nodded. "Visiting from . . . hmm . . . Kiev, and of course, they wouldn't expect us to leave you at home."

"I don't know . . ."

"You'll be there, Yuri. A legion of demons couldn't keep you away."

14

On Saturday the twenty-fifth, Yuri prepared himself to attend the Youssoupov party. He had only one formal suit with white tie and tails. It was a bit out of fashion and snug around the shoulders and waist, where he'd filled out slightly over the years. But it didn't look bad, and he had worn it only two other times, so it still was new-looking. Vladimir loaned him a new top hat which was a little too big, but if Yuri wore it back on his head it worked well enough. In fact, the effect gave him a somewhat rakish appearance. Boris added a walking stick and gloves.

"I truly look like your country cousin, Boris," said Yuri as he examined himself in the mirror. They were in Boris's bedroom, where they had gathered to dress for the party.

Vladimir gave Yuri a critical appraisal. "Tilt the hat to the right." Yuri obeyed. "Not so much," said Vladimir. "There, that's perfect."

"I suppose I'll pass, if I can only remember not to eat anything."

"Yes, please!" Boris chuckled. "I couldn't bear the embarrassment of you splitting your seams."

"I'll try not to embarrass you." Yuri grew pensive. "Can I really pull this off?"

"I only wish I could see you there," said Vladimir. He had to remain behind—it would have been pushing too far indeed for Boris to bring *two* country cousins. "Just remember, Yuri, you are *Prince* Fedorcenko; your grandfather did walk with tsars. This is where you belong."

"I wish I felt as certain of that as you, Vlad."

"Come on," said Boris. "I've got a carriage waiting. Let's go."

The Youssoupov palace was situated on the Moika Canal not far from the Maryinsky Theater near to the center of St. Petersburg. It had been a gift to the family from Catherine the Great. It was one of four Youssoupov palaces in Petersburg—there were another three in the Moscow area, several in the Crimea, and thirty other estates scattered throughout the rest of Russia. While in Petersburg, the family resided in the Moika Palace, which was a vast labyrinth of rooms—galleries, ballrooms, parlors, reception areas, dining rooms, and even a theater. Of an eighteenth-century Empire style, it was as much a museum as a home, filled with priceless works of art, including an original Rembrandt.

A butler opened the door for them, and there was a short, tense moment as the man studied the invitation. Both Yuri and Boris let out barely audible sighs of relief when the butler let them pass and a footman appeared to escort them to the ballroom.

As Yuri entered the foyer, resplendent with gilt and finery, he thought about the Fedorcenko St. Petersburg Palace. He had never been inside, but he had walked by it two or three times. From what he had heard it once had been every bit as fine as the Youssoupov palace, though perhaps not quite as large. He felt a sudden longing for the "olden days" of which he'd heard so much. He used to fantasize about convincing Daniel to buy the palace back from that scoundrel Vlasenko. But what then?

Did Yuri really wish to live like the Youssoupovs, even if he could? He disdained much of Andrei's politics, yet he did see the unfairness of the enormous gap between the rich and poor in Russia. There was very little in between. Of over a hundred and twenty-five million citizens, less than five percent could even aspire to a secondary education. The noble class who controlled the majority of the wealth and power in the country comprised only a fraction of a percent of the total.

Yet it was said that Felix Youssoupov gave freely of his time and fortune to help the needy. Even he must realize that in this new era, when revolution and anarchy lurked around every corner, the opulent lifestyles of the rich must be placed into better balance with the surrounding poverty. That's what Yuri hoped to do with his medical career—give of himself to those in need. But that didn't mean he and his future progeny had to be reduced to the same level of poverty. There must be a way to make all this work in proper balance. Perhaps he'd have a chance to talk to Youssoupov himself about these things.

But in the meantime, he and Boris were drawing near to the ballroom where Yuri could already hear music and voices and laughter.

The footman announced, "Count Boris Kozin and Prince Yuri Fedorcenko."

The man's voice was not so loud that it caused any disruption of the activities of the three hundred guests. Yuri diverted his gaze from the glittering ballroom with several crystal chandeliers and yellow marble columns to focus on a small reception line at the door. Two older couples, the parents of Felix and Irina, shook hands with the new arrivals. Yuri's hand trembled as he realized he was shaking the hand of the Grand Duke Alexander and the Grand Duchess Zenia, the tsar's sister! All thoughts of the downtrodden Russian poor fled from Yuri's mind.

Princess Irina, the bride-to-be, apologized that her fiancé had been called away briefly. "I welcome you in his stead," she said. "I will see to it that he greets you later."

Though Yuri did want to meet Prince Felix, he felt it would probably be best if he got through the evening as anonymously as possible.

He and Boris then moved in among the guests, some of whom were dancing to a traditional waltz, while others were milling in small groups talking and sipping champagne. Neither young man saw a familiar soul. Thus, they stood in an awkward clique of two, trying to engage in easygoing conversation so they appeared as if they were having a good time. The last thing either wanted was to do anything that would draw attention to them.

"Look over there," Boris said, cocking his head toward where a small knot of three young women were standing. "They appear unattached. Shall we forge ahead?"

As Boris started in the direction of the girls, Yuri clutched his arm. "Boris, how about something to drink first? I'm parched."

"Don't be such a coward, Yuri. This is our big chance to meet women of substance—" Boris stopped suddenly. "Don't look now, but I think they've discovered us, too."

"Oh, wonderful," said Yuri without enthusiasm.

Making a great effort to appear casual, Boris glanced in the direction of the girls and smiled. To Yuri he said, "The pretty blond one smiled at me. Are you coming or not?"

"All right." Yuri felt like a man resigned to his execution. As they approached the girls, he kept silently reminding himself that he was a *prince*, and not a bad-looking one, at that. And he was a doctor with a promising future. Even if he had no money, he had a lot to offer a young Russian debutante.

Boris, who was far more the suave charmer than Yuri, immediately struck up a conversation with the blonde.

"Forgive me for being so forward, but when I saw you I simply couldn't take my eyes off you. You look so familiar to me. Have we met before? But surely I would not have forgotten meeting such a beautiful woman."

"I really don't think so," she said in perfect French. "I am Mademoiselle Blanche Fortier. I've only been here a short while from Paris."

"Ah, French . . . how delightful."

Yuri watched in awe his friend's masterful approach. He, himself, could only smile awkwardly at one of the other girls. She smiled back, but he couldn't think of anything glib or charming to say. As he searched his mind for some other line besides "Have I met you before?" two other men approached and moved in.

Soon Yuri was left standing alone, silently cursing himself for his cloddishness. With a disgusted grunt, he strode toward the refreshment table. Even if he did risk bursting his suit, it was better to do *something* other than merely standing around like a boorish lump. But as he looked at the food, and an elegant spread it was, he realized he was far too nervous to have much of an appetite. He took a glass of champagne instead.

As he turned away from the table, he collided into a woman. A tidal wave of liquid leapt from his glass, but Yuri only noticed the young woman's silky amber-colored hair, cut and styled daringly short, and a flash of her brilliant blue eyes. It took his breath away almost as much as the mishap itself had. Luckily the flying champagne seemed to land only on his clothes, not hers. Nevertheless he was still flustered and apologetic.

"I'm so sorry! Are you all right? I haven't ruined your dress, have I? I shall never forgive—"

"No harm done," she replied, giving herself a careless appraisal. Her stylish gown of lavender tulle and satin trimmed with pearls appeared undamaged. She eyed the damp spot on his suit. "But I'm afraid you are going to be stained."

"Oh, it'll dry and won't show a bit then." He paused. She was a beautiful young woman. . . . If only he could think of something clever to say. But his mind went blank.

"If you'll excuse me, then," she said, "I'll continue on my mission."

"Can I assist you?" he said hurriedly. "To . . . uh . . . make up for my clumsiness." Hardly clever, but it was something, at least.

"There's no need . . ."

"I'd like to, really."

"Well—"

Yuri grabbed a plate. "What would you like?"

"I only wanted some champagne," she replied.

Yuri glanced at the plate, feeling even more foolish. He started to replace it but in the process bumped a dish of canapes that was perched on a pedestal. The dish tottered precariously, but Yuri caught it before disaster occurred.

The young woman made a poor attempt to restrain a giggle. Yuri felt the blood rush up his neck and cheeks.

"I think I'd best get you away from this table," said the girl. "Even the Youssoupovs can afford only so much breakage."

Much to Yuri's surprise, the girl took his arm and led him a few paces away. "I'd suggest we dance," she continued, "but I fear you might have the same grace on the dance floor that you do at a refreshment table."

"Not . . . not quite the same."

"Then, shall we?"

Almost before he realized what was happening, his arm was about her waist and they were gliding away to a waltz. Seconds after they had begun to dance, the music stopped.

The girl laughed. "My goodness! I do believe we are jinxed."

"I hope not," Yuri said.

She looked him up and down in a rather frank appraisal even for a modern society girl. "Yes . . ." she said meaningfully.

"Maybe we ought to try to get off on a better foot."

"Quite literally!"

They laughed, and Yuri relaxed a little. The more time he spent with this lovely girl, the more he did indeed want to improve his disastrous initial impression.

"I'm Yuri Fedorcenko," he said, offering his hand. He thought about adding *prince*, but he had already gotten off to such a bad start with her he didn't want to appear pretentious. The use of *doctor* was so new it didn't even occur to him.

She took his hand with slim, graceful fingers. "And I am Katya Zhenechka."

"The vodka Zhenechkas?"

"Yes. Isn't it terrible? Some say my father is the cause of all the woes of Russia."

"I'm sure the people would find a way to get vodka whether your father produced it or not."

"And what do you do, Mr. Fedorcenko? You wouldn't be related to—"

A new voice suddenly intruded into Yuri and Katya's conversation. "I've found him at last! Our party crasher."

Yuri's insides gave a jarring leap as he spun around and found himself face-to-face with the party's guest of honor, Felix Youssoupov.

15

Prince Youssoupov wore a grin that contrasted sharply with his startling words. He was a handsome man, slim, with sensitive, deep-set eyes, a long, finely chiseled nose, and expressive, thin lips. Twenty-five, according to the society newspaper columns.

Yuri stood there, stunned and thoroughly confused when Youssoupov came up to him and slapped him on the shoulder in anything but a hostile manner.

"At the time of your arrival, it didn't dawn on my parents who you were," Youssoupov continued, "until you were quite lost in the crowd. But I had to appease my curiosity—"

"Excuse me," Katya said suddenly. "I really think I shall take my leave, if you don't mind."

Yuri watched helplessly as she turned to go. "Please, Katya, I—" But he couldn't think of what to say in his defense. He *was* a party crasher. He let her walk away.

Youssoupov then realized he had stirred up something unpleasant. "Goodness! Did she think I really meant that about you?"

"Didn't you?"

Youssoupov laughed. "Why, it almost sounds like you believe it also."

"Well, I wasn't exactly invited here."

"You would have been, had we known. You are one of *the* Fedorcenkos? But, of course, you must be. How many Prince Fedorcenkos are there? Still, you dropped out of society for so long, I thought the name was lost forever. Whatever happened? I heard about old Prince Viktor, of course. But for the rest of the family to disappear also—"

"It's rather an involved story."

"Perhaps someday you can tell it to me in detail. In the meantime, you won't have to crash another Youssoupov party again."

"That's very generous of you, Prince Youssoupov. But I must tell you honestly that the Fedorcenko family has fallen somewhat from its former status."

"Do you think I care about status? At one time our grandfathers were friends. That is what's important. But I am curious about what brings you back here now."

"I just graduated from medical school."

"Ah, so you are a doctor."

"Just barely."

"Well, I have a soft spot in my heart for physicians. You know, I was a sickly child and had doctors attending me always. Thank God I have overcome all that. Thank those doctors, also."

"If you ever have need of medical assistance again, I will gladly be at your service."

"Thanks so much. Now, what shall I do about Countess Zhenechka?"

"I don't understand, Prince—"

"Felix, please. Well, did I break up a budding romance?"

"We'd only just met."

"Then I've spoiled your first impression."

"I had already done that, I'm afraid."

"Come now. A good-looking, intelligent man like yourself should have no problem with impressing a beautiful woman. I'll go see if I can repair the damage I did."

"You need not trouble yourself, Felix, really."

"Never mind. You just wait here."

Youssoupov hurried away, and after ten minutes, Yuri decided he'd not see his host again, nor would he see Katya. He found a chair near a wall, sat and tried not to look as miserable as he felt. Boris came up once and tried to interest him in dancing with some other girls, but Yuri had lost his enthusiasm. After five more minutes, he was ready to find Boris to tell him he was leaving. Then he saw Katya approach across the crowded dance floor.

He was again keenly aware of her shimmering hair, the light from a chandelier highlighting its amber hue. But he now realized that the distinctive hair color was merely a frame surrounding the true work of art—blue eyes, a slightly upturned nose, pale lips with but a hint of lip rouge. But those lips seemed to say more with a smile or a pout than a Tolstoy novel.

She was smiling now, and Yuri felt every ounce of courage and strength of will ebb from him. He acknowledged her approach by standing, but he felt, irrationally, that he should kneel before her instead. He could be her slave if she wished.

"I'm sorry I left so abruptly," she said.

"I don't blame you. It was rather awkward."

"I felt if there was a scene, you wouldn't have wanted anyone around."

"I appreciate that." There followed an uncomfortable pause. Finally Yuri said, "Would you care to sit?"

"I'd rather have some fresh air. The gardens here are quite worth a visit, anyway."

Yuri was glad to leave the ballroom, which had grown stifling. But more than that, the prospect of being alone with Katya was almost dizzying.

They left the ballroom, passing through several grandly arched arcades all lined with statues and fine works of art. A final archway that resembled a Grecian temple opened out onto the garden. Now, in June, a soft breeze brought the scent of lilacs and roses. The white night glowed above the couple as they strolled down the path between fragrant shrubs and flowers. Yuri thought that if Katya looked beguiling under the bright chandeliers, she was breathtaking outdoors on a summer evening.

They were quiet for a few moments as they walked. Only the distant sound of music could be heard.

Katya's voice, slightly husky with an intensity that made even her most trivial words seem important, floated over the silence. "Felix told me all about you."

"Well, you came back, so it must not have been too shocking to you."

She smiled rather mysteriously, then said, "Just intriguing. You came back to be a doctor, he said. But from where? Did you leave Russia?"

He wasn't exactly ashamed of his family's convoluted history. He could hardly hide all of it anyway, since some was already a matter of public record. But why complicate his still-precarious relationship with this girl by airing all the sordid facts? It was best to keep things simple.

"I've been abroad," he said.

"Was your family exiled?"

"In a matter of speaking."

"You speak excellent Russian for not having been exposed to it."

"Well . . . uh . . . my parents didn't want me to lose my Russian heritage. They hoped one day I would return."

"They are alive?"

"My mother is." Yuri seized the momentary pause to change the topic of conversation. "I'm glad you suggested walking outside. I've had my nose between the pages of books for so long, I've almost forgotten what pleasure there is to be found in a place like this."

"Medical school must have been difficult. I'm thankful my father is a die-hard conservative who believes education is for men only."

"You've no interest in learning, then."

"That's different, isn't it? I'm learning things every day. I don't need to go to school for that."

"You sound like my brother. I have to admit, I loved school, and now that I'm through, I feel a bit of a letdown. But I do have internship ahead of me, and I think I've chosen a profession in which learning and challenge never stops."

"Then, you'll be happy." She said it as if she were speaking of some alien emotion, something as removed from her realm as the suffering and poverty that existed less than a versta from this grand St. Petersburg palace.

"And you, Katya. . . ?" The sound of her name felt good on his lips.

She laughed as if mocking him. Or was she mocking herself? "I have everything." She shivered. "It's chilly."

"Do you want to go in?"

"No."

He was acutely conscious of her moving closer to him.

His voice nervously rose an octave as he said, "Why did you come back, Katya? Did Youssoupov make you?"

She laughed again. He was coming to love the sound of her laughter. And the sight of it, too, for when she laughed her eyes sparkled like starlight. He realized her laughter wasn't always merry or even happy; sometimes there was ire and mockery in it. But it was never cruel. It was filled with honesty and even a kind of purity.

But perhaps he was getting carried away, hopelessly enthralled with Countess Katya Zhenechka.

"You wouldn't believe that I was lured back entirely by your magnetic charm?"

"We both know that can't be true."

"Maybe I believe in fate."

"Perhaps we were fated to be jinxed?"

"Oh, my, this is getting complicated." She stopped walking, turned and tilted her head back so she could direct her gaze at him. "The truth is, I was bored, Yuri Sergeiovich. Bored with the very kind of suave gentleman you were trying so hard, and so unsuccessfully, to be. If you hadn't nearly knocked over that compote, I would have left immediately. Felix's arrival only confirmed my interest. If he hadn't spoken to me, I would have found you anyway."

"I'm glad I could amuse you." He tried to sound affronted, but it was difficult to pull off since his heart was racing because of her nearness. At least she had come back.

"I didn't mean to insult you. I really meant it as a compliment. So many society men are completely bankrupt of character. Be thankful you've been away from it."

He hardly heard her. All he could think of was how much he wanted to kiss her.

"Let's have a better look around this garden," he said. He had to do something before he made more of a fool of himself than ever.

They walked for a while, then sat on a bench. They talked for an hour. But when they rose to return to the party, Yuri wondered what they had talked about. He hardly knew any more about her than when they began—and he wanted to know everything!

Inside, they finally danced together, and Yuri was thankful that two years ago he had asked Talia to teach him to dance so he could attend society functions without embarrassment. The effort was more than rewarded now as he held Katya close, the sweet perfume of her hair intoxicating him.

The first time another gentleman cut in, Yuri gave her up reluctantly. But she returned to him at the first opportunity. There were other such interruptions, but each time they found their way back to each other. But eventually the evening had to end altogether.

"May I call on you?" Yuri asked as he helped her with her wrap.

"Well, I . . ."

Yuri felt himself fall from his euphoric cloud. Had he imagined everything this evening?

"I understand," he said, trying to cushion his fall.

"No . . . Yuri, I would like to see you again. But I'm leaving tomorrow for the Black Sea. I'll be gone for some time."

"Oh . . ."

She lay her hand on his arm in a gesture, incredibly intimate for all its simplicity. "Do call on me when I return."

Later, when he told his friends about the meeting, their reactions surprised him.

"You've never heard of Countess Zhenechka?" said Kozin. "But, I forgot, you had yourself practically entombed in that university."

"I don't understand," said Yuri.

"Listen, Yuri," said Vladimir, "Countess Zhenechka has . . . well, a bit of a reputation, if you know what I mean. Of course, we here in Petersburg only know the half of it since she spends a great deal of her time in Moscow, but I have heard that she is—"

"Don't say it, Vlad!" Yuri interjected harshly. "I don't want to hear it."

"I won't say she is a *fallen* woman, Yuri, but she is extremely modern. She goes out with men unchaperoned. I've heard she even drives a motorcar."

"I never thought you were such a prude, Vlad. Those things are hardly immoral."

"Leave him be," said Kozin. "She's beautiful and rich. Who cares about her reputation?"

"You have no idea what you are talking about," retorted Yuri. "It's because of people like you, spreading wild rumors, that decent women like Katya are ruined. You should be ashamed of yourselves."

He left his friends in a huff, forgetting to offer them a final thanks for their part in his attending the Youssoupov party. He had met an angel tonight, and he'd never believe any slanderous remarks about her.

16

"You are doing what?"

"I'm going to the Crimea tomorrow."

Andrei shook his head with disgust. "What about Talia's performance? You can't miss it."

"She'll understand."

"I've never seen you so anxious to see Grandfather before," sneered Andrei.

"Andrei, I've met a girl—a wonderful, beautiful girl. I have less than two weeks left of my holiday before I have to start working at the hospital. If I don't go now, it could be months before I will see her again."

"And when did you meet this girl?"

"Yesterday at the Youssoupov party."

"Youssoupov? No doubt she is some aristocratic—"

"Don't start, Andrei! Because no matter how hard you try to hide it, you are an aristocrat also."

"All right. Let's not get into that. But will you devastate Talia for a girl you've only known one day? You are more self-centered and crass than even I thought."

"This girl is different. She is the girl I plan to marry."

"Love at first sight, eh?"

Yuri ignored the mockery in his brother's tone. "I'm going to go talk to Talia now."

"You'll never get in; you know how they are at that ballet school."

"That's why I'd like you to come along."

"Me!"

"I need some moral support." That was hard to admit considering Andrei's response thus far, but Yuri knew it would go easier with Talia if Andrei was there. Besides, the element of intimidation afforded by Andrei's size and bearing could impress upon the school officials and perhaps get them in easier.

In the end Andrei agreed to go, as Yuri knew he would. Despite their many differences, they were still brothers . . . and friends.

The ballet school was a few blocks off Nevsky Prospekt, down a quiet street that bore all the characteristics of a place that didn't want to be bothered with the strife and demands of the real world. The first obstacle presented to these two outsiders was the closed and locked outer door of the school. But they didn't have to stand there long, wondering how they would get past this barrier. As a young student exited, Andrei rushed up the steps and grabbed the door before it could close automatically and lock them out again. Slipping quietly inside, they found themselves in a small outer room with a few chairs, which the brothers knew to be a visitor's waiting room. They had waited there twice before to meet Talia. But then, unlike now, they had been expected.

Yuri hitched back his shoulders and tried to look the aristocratic doctor that he was. He spoiled the effect, however, when he glanced at his brother for confidence. Andrei shook his head and smirked, then took the lead himself and strode into the next room where they met their most formidable barrier yet. She was a petite, gray-haired lady whom Andrei had once nicknamed the Gray Cossack. As the school receptionist, she took her job as seriously as an Imperial Guard.

"How did you get in here?" she asked in an ominous high-pitched voice.

Andrei said with authority, "My employer"—he indicated Yuri with a nod—"*Prince* Yuri Sergeiovich Fedorcenko, wishes an interview with one of your students."

Yuri smiled to himself. He knew that what Andrei was doing went against his political grain, and it made Yuri that much more grateful to his brother. Yuri tried harder to keep up his part by striking a haughty pose. He hoped the woman didn't recognize them, but he didn't see that it would matter if she did.

"Has he made previous arrangements?" asked the woman. She shuffled through some papers. "I don't see his name on my list."

"An emergency has arisen."

"A death in the family?" Her tone made it clear that anything less would be unacceptable.

Andrei snorted derisively. "Do you think he would trouble the school for something trivial?"

The Gray Cossack tilted her head back and studied the two

young men. "You've been here before."

"Of course we have."

"Who do you wish to see?"

"Miss Sorokin, Prince Fedorcenko's adopted sister."

"You say this is a family emergency—"

"Never mind this!" Yuri interceded sharply. "I do not have to stand for this cross-examination as if I were some subversive. I'll just go see the grand duke. Come along, Andrei."

"Which grand duke might that be?" asked the woman, the threat diminishing from her voice.

"What grand duke contributes most to this school?" Yuri couldn't have answered that question himself, but he felt fairly certain *some* grand duke must support the school. He prayed the woman pressed no further.

"I don't think there will be a need for you to bother *him*," she said. "You wanted to see Miss Sorokin, correct?"

Yuri and Andrei nodded.

"Please have a seat in the waiting room." The Gray Cossack lifted her telephone receiver.

As the brothers settled themselves to wait, Andrei said, "Yuri, under no circumstances must you tell Talia why you are going to the Crimea."

"And why not?"

"She wouldn't understand."

"Talia? She'd be the first to cheer me on. You know what a romantic she is."

"For an intelligent man, you are incredibly dense."

"What do you mean by that?"

"Nothing. I just think—"

But just then a side door opened and Talia entered the room. She looked pale and her large eyes were even larger than normal, filled with fear. They stood as she entered and she rushed toward them.

"It's Mama, isn't it? She's dead."

Suddenly Yuri realized his and Andrei's scheme had not been very well thought out. They had never considered what Talia would be told.

"Your mother is fine," said Yuri reassuringly.

"Not your mother . . ." Talia gasped.

"Everyone is fine. No one is sick or dead."

"But—"

"We're sorry, Talia. We were just trying to get past the Gray Cossack. We didn't think—"

"*I* didn't think," said Andrei. "It was my scheme. Forgive me, Talia."

A sob broke through Talia's fine, soft lips and tears came in a rush. Yuri placed his arms around her and patted her head, trying to comfort her.

"There, there, Talia dear," he cooed. "Come and sit down."

"I hate to think what you would have done if one of us *had* been dead," said Andrei, in an obvious attempt to lighten the situation. Talia only cried more.

"In those few minutes," she said through her sobs, "my whole world ended. My mama and Aunt Anna, and you two—" She sobbed again. "You're all I have."

"You have your career," said Yuri, trying desperately to lift her dismay.

"Don't you know I'd give it all up, throw it all away, for you? It's just something to do, it's not my heart and soul."

No one could respond to that. They just sat quietly for several minutes as Talia collected her emotions. Yuri reproached himself again and again for what he was about to do and wondered if he could go through with it. But he kept trying to convince himself that she would understand. Nevertheless, he began to formulate a plausible lie to tell her. But still he could not find the nerve to tell her his plans.

Finally Talia took a deep, calming breath and said, "Now, why are you two here? Surely this isn't merely a social visit."

"Are you going to tell her, Yuri?"

Yuri's head jerked around. Was there a touch of smugness in Andrei's voice?

He swallowed. In his mind he conjured up an image of Katya; it wasn't difficult to do since she had been at the forefront of his thoughts since last night. Her iridescent blue eyes, her hair the color of gold reflecting a vivid sunrise, her throaty, pure laughter . . .

Talia would understand.

"Talia, something has come up and I won't be able to attend your performance."

"Oh, Yuri, no!" She looked as if she might start crying again.

"I promised my grandfather I would visit him this summer," he went on quickly. "He stayed only a short time for my graduation because of that promise. Now, it appears this week and part of the next will be the only time I'll have off from my hospital work for months. Your performance comes right in the middle of that time, so it will be impossible for me to do both. I wouldn't even think of doing this to you, but Grandfather is getting old—who can say how much longer he will be with us."

Yuri felt like a scoundrel, but it was done now. He'd make it up to Talia somehow.

"I see, Yuri," she said. Did she really?

"I feel terrible about this."

"You mustn't disappoint your grandfather. He *is* an old man."

"Oh, Talia! You are the best person . . . the best friend! And I'll never miss another of your performances—"

"Don't make another promise you'll have trouble keeping, Yuri." Her voice was almost too controlled.

Yuri tried not to think about how much he might have hurt her. Someday she would fall in love, and then she'd truly understand.

17

Ensconced in tulle of pale pink that billowed around her like the first tentative clouds of morning, Talia was poised like a statue on the stage. The light that picked her out from the other dancers was dim at first, only gradually brightening as her performance progressed.

Andrei sat in the third row from the front with his mother and Aunt Raisa. Not an enthusiast of ballet, he had waited patiently for Act III of the ballet *Coppélia*. He had tried to enjoy the preceding acts by viewing it with an artistic eye, seeing shape and color and even texture more than sound and movement. This was not his first ballet, but the fact that this was of particular importance to his best friend Talia made him far more attentive than at other times. He made a real effort to not only make himself sit still for such a long time, but also to appreciate it. He knew that as long as Talia was a dancer, he'd be attending many more ballets.

So, as the light settled on his friend, he prepared himself to concentrate. Before he realized it, he was so caught up in the enfolding scene that he was leaning forward in his seat, eyes fixed, heart pounding.

She was "Dawn."

Andrei immediately felt from her a certain melancholy of a day as yet unrealized. Her head was bowed, her shoulders slumped slightly, her hands clasped in front of her—her whole bearing was one of sadness, not hope. Was Dawn weary of having to begin another day of unrealized dreams? Or was the dreariness of night simply too encompassing to shake off easily?

Andrei was close enough to see her face, eyes closed with a drawn look of suffering. He sensed the struggle of the character she was playing and felt his own tension rise. He had never truly realized until now what passion had been locked inside sweet, shy Talia. Or was her melancholy real because she was thinking of the empty seat in row three where Yuri should have been sitting?

Then the still figure of Dawn began to move. Her toes, on *pointe*, shuffled slightly, and her bent shoulders trembled. Andrei held his breath. Her head began to lift and her arms to reach out, physically pushing away the darkness of night. As she moved toward the audience an incredible transformation occurred. The day was victorious over night; the Dawn grew and the frail beauty of the dancer became as powerful as the hope of a new day. Her large eyes opened, glimmering; the expression she wore brightened, and Andrei felt certain the increasing light was emanating from her rather than from some mechanical source.

The sun had risen. And for Andrei, he glimpsed a new facet of Talia that only deepened his love for her.

Following the show, there was a lengthy time of congratulations and praise. The matushkas hugged Talia, and Raisa lost no opportunity to brag about her daughter to passersby in the theater. Everyone said she had stolen the show. Then Raisa and Anna took their leave, the crowd dispersed, and the performers disappeared into their dressing rooms to change.

"Would you wait, Andrei?" Talia asked. "Remember, we talked about going out to celebrate after the performance."

"That was when Yuri was to be here."

"I still want to celebrate. I want to be with you."

He smiled. "Where do you want to go?"

"Most of the performers are going to The Club to await reviews."

The Club was a cafe about a block from the Maryinsky where the show people often socialized. After Talia changed from her costume into an evening dress of pearl gray satin and lace, she and Andrei walked to The Club. The night was sultry. It had rained earlier in the day, and the streets shimmered under the evening gloaming. A passing automobile drove through a puddle, splashing water onto the sidewalk. Talia and Andrei sidestepped and barely missed being soaked.

"That was a *pas de deux* worthy of Pavlova and Nijinsky," Andrei quipped.

"Perhaps you missed your calling, Andrei."

"Imagine me in tights, flitting around a stage—"

Talia burst out in laughter.

"It's not *that* funny," Andrei said, pretending to be insulted. But on visualizing the ridiculous scene, he, too, erupted into laughter.

They fell on each other in their uncontrollable mirth, and it seemed to grow rather than subside. It took a full three minutes before they had regained their composure enough to start walking again. All the tensions and disappointments and exhilarations of the day were absorbed into the merriment and, at least for a time, healed by it.

"Thank you, Andruska!" Talia was trying hard to recapture the proper reserve of a ballerina.

"For what?"

"I needed so much to have a good laugh."

"Well, you know you can always count on me for that."

"I can always count on you—period!" She put her arm around him and squeezed him affectionately. She had no idea what that gesture did to Andrei.

As a man who thrived on impulse, he quickly returned the gesture and neither let go until they reached their destination.

When they arrived at The Club, everyone cheered Talia's entrance, and she blushed and smiled demurely at the attention. She changed a bit in the crowd, seeming to close in on herself. There would be no way that she'd laugh as freely in this group as she had when she and Andrei were alone on the street. She had been different on the stage, too, more like the laughing girl on the street, more animated and alive. Talia was as at home on the stage as she was with her family, Andrei mused. As the enfolding Dawn, it was the only other time, besides with him and Yuri, that Andrei knew Talia to be completely uninhibited and free. In the cafe, he could feel her draw closer to him as if for protection.

After exchanging greetings and words of encouragement, Andrei and Talia found a vacant table for two, near enough to the others so as not to be obviously isolated, but apart enough so that Talia began to relax a bit. They ordered two piroghi and tea. Occasionally they were drawn into the banter of the larger group, but for the most part they talked quietly together.

"Did you see Mama?" said Talia. "I thought she was going to explode."

"She had every reason to be proud."

"She hardly knows a thing about ballet."

"One doesn't have to know anything about the art to appreciate the beauty and power of your performance. Talia, while that light was on you, every person in that audience was under your spell. It was inspiring. In fact, it's given me an idea for a painting. I can hardly wait to get home to start it."

"I'm glad to hear that." She paused, collecting her thoughts. "Andrei, when I'm up on that stage, I . . . it's so hard to describe, but something happens to me."

"I saw it, Talia. All your timidity crumbles, and that passion I know is in you emerges. It was like rebirth, truly the dawn of a new day, the beginning of spring!"

"I wish you were one of the critics writing the reviews."

"You have no need to worry. They will shower you with praise."

"There were times when I knew I was off my mark and when my extension was poor. I fumbled one pirouette—"

"Even you must know, Talia, that the bottom line is not mechanics, but the emotion a performer evokes from the audience. And you did that without a doubt!"

"I didn't know you had such an understanding of ballet."

"Art is art, and ballet is as much an art as painting. You are trying to achieve the same thing on a stage that I want to do on canvas."

"I wonder what Yuri would have said about my performance," Talia said suddenly.

Andrei felt as if his balloon had been pricked. The excitement he had been feeling all evening vanished.

"I mean as a scientist," Talia added quickly.

"He would have thought you were beautiful," replied Andrei, trying to resume his earlier mood. "He would have praised the fine musculature of your legs and the glow of health on your face."

Talia giggled. "He's not *that* artistically stifled."

Andrei shrugged. "Well, he was stifled enough to miss the best performance of the year."

The arrival of their food and beverages interrupted them. Andrei was glad. He didn't want to spend the evening talking about Yuri. But, much to his dismay, that seemed exactly what Talia wanted to discuss. After they tasted their food, Talia lifted her eyes, fixing Andrei with a haunting gaze.

"Andrushka, tell me why Yuri really didn't come tonight."

"He had to see our grandf—"

"The *real* reason, Andrei. Don't try to protect me."

"What makes you think there is a real reason?"

"Yuri is a terrible liar."

"Drat him!" Andrei took an angry gulp of his tea.

"Tell me," she prompted again with that quiet insistence that was hard to refuse.

"Let it go, Talia. Why do you have to know, anyway? It's not important."

"Tell me, Andrei."

"No! I won't."

"Who are you trying to protect, him or me?"

"Not him, that's for sure. He can go to blazes, for all I care!"

"Don't talk that way about your brother."

"After what he did to you, how can you defend him? He's a self-centered boor, putting some floozy society girl before his dearest friend—" He stopped, suddenly realizing his slip. He cursed his troublesome tongue.

"I . . . I thought it was something like that." She bit her lip, her eyes filled with moisture. But she didn't cry. "He must really care for this girl."

"Bah! He met her less than a week ago. He thinks he's in love but he doesn't know the meaning—"

"You were right, Andrei," she broke in abruptly. "I wish I hadn't found out. But I guess it had to happen sometime, didn't it? I was lucky his studies had kept him too busy for women in the past."

"You should tell him how you feel." Andrei felt somewhat safe now in making this suggestion—safe at least that Yuri wouldn't return the sentiment.

"What good would it do now? All it would mean is sure rejection. And I know Yuri. He would feel so bad about it that in the end it would still ruin our friendship."

Andrei shook his head. "You should tell him anyway."

"Give me one good reason why."

"Because you are his friend, Talia, and friends are honest with each other." Andrei regretted the words the moment he spoke them, but he hadn't realized until they were spoken how hypocritical they were.

"You're right again," she said.

He couldn't meet her eyes. "So, you're going to tell him?"

"I still can't, Andrei, in spite of the fact that you are right. I hate having the huge, horrible lie between us. But I couldn't bear him looking at me with pity, telling me how he loves me as a sister only. Why did I have to fall in love with him? It's spoiled everything!" A tear finally escaped the corner of her eye. She brushed it away.

Then something occurred to Andrei. Perhaps this would be the perfect time to reveal his secret to her. It might make her feel better to know how he felt. It might make her forget Yuri. He opened his mouth to speak—he wasn't going to further weigh the issue with more thought.

But he never got a chance to speak. The cafe door burst open and a young fellow rushed in.

"The first reviews are here!"

The whole place erupted into excited clamoring. Andrei never found another opportunity that evening to take up again the dangling thread of their conversation. Perhaps it was for the best. Talia wasn't the type to flit quickly from one love to another. It would take a long time for her to get over Yuri, if she ever did. It was possible she'd hang on to her futile hopes until he was standing at the altar with another woman.

Still, Andrei felt the lie between him and Talia as acutely as if it were a wall of burning fire.

18

For a while Andrei attempted to overcome his frustration through his work. Talia's performance had inspired an idea, and it took him several days to make a preliminary sketch of the exact scene he wanted. Talia would be the focal point, surrounded by prisms of light. Availing himself of the cubist style, he intended to capture the ballet more as the mind might perceive it than the eye—from many angles at once.

He would have liked to make a couple minor adjustments to his final sketch, but he was running short on paper and his trash was now full of crumpled sheets. He had heard that privation and hardship were good for the artistic soul. In that case he ought to be a Rembrandt by now. But on principle, he refused any help. His brother-in-law Daniel had even offered himself as a patron.

"Many artists have them," Daniel had argued.

"If I ever acquire a patron," Andrei told him, "I want to know it is because of my talent, not the blood that flows in my veins."

But there were times, such as this, when Daniel's offers were tempting. Andrei was at the point of having to choose between supplies or food. He had six months to get together a respectable representation of his work for the gallery showing. He could not take an outside job right now and expect to meet that goal. He was even going to have to curtail his submissions to the newspapers.

But how could he?

Glancing through his supply of oils, he realized he was expecting the impossible. He barely had enough paints to finish one project, much less two dozen.

Sighing, he went to the crate where he kept copies of his old newspaper sketches. Maybe a newspaper would reprint something from the past, and he could thus generate some income without the intensive labor. Perhaps if he just changed a bit here and there, put a new slogan with something, giving it a slightly new slant . . .

He riffled through the sheets. They were in terrible order, many were creased and wrinkled, and there were other miscellaneous handbills, pamphlets, even trash mixed in. At last he came to one section near the bottom that was in better order. He remembered when Talia had come to visit him sometime ago and had tried to organize things. She had labeled three or four large folders and filed the drawings in them by subject. Unfortunately, he hadn't kept it up.

As he picked up one of Talia's folders, it slipped from his hand and the contents scattered over the floor. Then the apartment door opened and one of his roommates walked in.

"Oleg? What time is it?" Andrei asked.

"Three o'clock, same time I always get home."

"Oh no! I didn't realize it was so late." Andrei hurriedly gathered up the sketches and tossed them carelessly into the box. "I should have left half an hour ago."

"Where are you off to?"

"An S.D. meeting."

"Well, I'm too tired to go. Give them my regards."

Andrei jumped up, then paused and took a couple of sketches at random from the box. He wouldn't have been so anxious to drop his work and attend the meeting except that there would doubtless be some representatives from one or two of the underground newspapers there. He might be able to sell something to them and get a bit of quick cash. He grabbed his sketchbook and pen, too. There was a lengthy tram ride to reach the meeting.

By the time Andrei traveled from his flat, downtown to the meeting place a few blocks from the university on Vassily Island, he had redone one of the political cartoons. He had also come up with an entirely new one based on an altercation he had observed between the tram driver and a gendarme, which he had titled, "Who are the real criminals?" He might only make five rubles per sketch because the papers ran on bare-bones budgets, but if he humbled himself and ate a few meals at his mother's, it would be enough to buy a few supplies.

Much to Andrei's surprise, the flat was crowded. The membership of the Social Democrats had diminished in the last few years because of the break between the Mensheviks and Bolsheviks. Lenin had become far more demanding and exacting in his membership requirements. Andrei doubted he would qualify as a Bolshevik by Lenin's stringent standards, but, after many long discussions with his uncle Paul, he had decided to continue supporting the Party, even though he had not become a member yet. Paul had not tried to influence his nephew one way or another, though he himself had long ago withdrawn from the Party completely. Andrei respected his uncle, but he was still drawn to the Party because of its aggressiveness.

Andrei was no intellectual. He did not prize scholarship and debate for their own sakes, as was the case with many revolutionaries. He understood politics and political theory well enough. But he simply didn't have the patience for the hours and hours of discussion, nit-picking, and hairsplitting that went on at political meetings. It was torture to attend Party meetings, and he did so only to support the things he believed in and the mission of revolution. He enjoyed demonstrations, strikes, and handing out pamphlets far more. It wasn't so much the thrill of possible danger that enticed him to these particular activities—it was merely the fact that he was *doing* something.

All the chairs in the apartment were taken, as was most of the floor space. Andrei leaned against a wall. The group was buzzing with conversation; the meeting had begun half an hour ago but there was now a short lull between speakers. Andrei spoke to a couple of acquaintances nearby, one of whom was an editor of a radical paper. They talked about the previous speaker, and Andrei managed to show the editor his drawings, which received a favorable reception.

The next speaker was announced as an emissary from Lenin—Stephan Kaminsky. Of course, Andrei knew the name, though he hadn't seen Stephan since he was a boy in Katyk. Kaminsky proved to be a dull speaker, completely lacking any polish or charisma. But what he lacked in these areas he quite made up for in sheer length. For an hour he droned out the Party line, precept upon tiny precept. Andrei would have fallen asleep if he hadn't been standing up; but he did hear a snore or two from others in the group.

After the meeting Andrei decided to rekindle the old ties. He and Kaminsky were, after all, from the same village, which made them almost brothers. He strode up and introduced himself.

"Andrei Sergeiovich Christinin," he said. "From Katyk."

"Ah, yes." Stephan nodded. "You were the youngest, weren't you?"

"I still am."

"And a rambunctious, headstrong lad, if I recall."

"I still am," Andrei repeated, this time with a grin. "The rebel of the family."

"Not the only rebel. Isn't Paul Yevnovich your uncle?"

"Yes."

"And you are a Party member?"

"Not yet."

"I'm surprised Pavlokov hasn't soured you against the Party."

"He still admires Lenin immensely, despite the differences that caused him to break with the Party."

"Is betrayal the way your family shows its admiration?" Kaminsky's previously pleasant tone turned caustic. Andrei gaped at the sudden turnabout.

"I would hardly call doctrinal differences *betrayal,*" Andrei replied.

"The only way to achieve the goal of revolution is through wholehearted commitment to the cause. A double-minded man weakens the cause—thus, betrayal."

"I still think that's a bit strong."

"And now he has given over completely to the Establishment as a member of their Duma."

"There are Bolsheviks in the Duma."

Kaminsky chose to ignore Andrei's logic. "One day the Duma will crumble along with everything else, when a new order arises in Russia. Betrayers will not be tolerated."

"My uncle has devoted his whole life to the cause. He spent years in exile, ruining his health in the process. He continues to live constantly under the threat of arrest each time he speaks out for the cause in the Duma, which he does frequently. He has never betrayed a soul, least of all Lenin. In fact, because Lenin couldn't give just a little, he lost one of the most faithful men he could have had."

"If you think so highly of your uncle, why do you support the Party he . . . spurned?"

"Because I believe in Lenin."

"What about Bolshevism?"

"Lenin is Bolshevism, isn't he?"

Kaminsky cocked a bushy eyebrow. He appeared momentarily taken aback by this logic. A full minute passed before he spoke.

"So, what have you done for the Party?" Kaminsky spoke as if relieved that he'd thought of a way to handily change the subject.

Without hesitation, Andrei opened up his sketchbook. "Perhaps you'll recognize my style."

"*Malenkiy Soldat* . . . I've seen his work. You are he?"

"I am."

Kaminsky turned several pages of the sketchbook, giving each drawing a seemingly critical appraisal. If he were an art critic, Andrei would have been worried by the stern expression on Kaminsky's roughhewn, rather intimidating visage. He hadn't even considered, when he had shown his sketchbook, that Stephan might represent some new opportunities.

Finally, Stephan said, "We have a new Party organ, *Pravda*. We could use material like this."

"Really?" Andrei was genuinely surprised. Thus far he had only worked on small publications. *Pravda*, like its predecessor *Isrka*, was a major Party voice, Lenin's personal vehicle.

"Could you come up with a sketch a week? Something along this line—" Stephan poked a finger at the drawing Andrei had done on the tram. "But meatier, if you know what I mean."

"That was only a rough draft."

"Good. How about it? The pay isn't much, but the exposure is double, or more, of the papers you've worked on in the past."

"It sounds tempting, but . . ."

"You hesitate about working almost directly with Lenin himself?"

Andrei felt foolish for his hesitation. Kaminsky was right. This was a fantastic opportunity. It could well bring him into Lenin's inner circle. He could at last have an integral part in the coming revolution. It's what he had wanted all his life. The gallery showing represented a dream from only the last couple of years. Could it possibly mean more to him than his political ideals? Yet giving up that dream, regardless of its newness, was not an easy thing to do.

He said to Kaminsky, "I didn't think you'd have someone work on an organ like *Pravda* who wasn't a Party member."

"That is a situation that would have to be remedied. You'd have no problem with that, would you?"

"No, of course not." Andrei couldn't admit to someone as obviously narrow-minded as Kaminsky that the sacrifices involved might be too demanding for him.

But perhaps Kaminsky was more intuitive than he appeared. "You have a great talent to give the Party and the cause," he said. "Don't waste it away, as I see many artists do, in self-involvement.

Too many are more willing to squander their talents on making pretty pictures for the bourgeois to hang in their fancy houses."

"I don't believe that's out of any sympathy to the bourgeois," Andrei countered. "Rather it's an artist's need for acceptance and recognition of his work."

"All aspects of self-fulfillment must be subject to the needs of the Party."

"Perhaps the Party would be larger if it showed more sympathy—"

"Bah! Lenin would rather have a few who are totally committed than a horde of ineffectual half-hearts."

"Some men have families to support."

"Do you speak for yourself, Christinin?"

"No . . ."

"Are you willing to give your all for the Party? It's only through total commitment that liberty can be achieved."

Andrei felt the heat rush up his neck—not of anger, but of humiliation and a sense of self-reproach. He had been vacillating, holding back for a long time, because he hadn't been able to give up the work that had grown so near to his heart.

Desperate to exonerate himself, he said, "My father died for the cause! Don't tell me about sacrifice."

"I don't know what cause your father died for, but it wasn't Bolshevism. Regardless of that, how long do you think you can ride on your father's heroism? Isn't it time you made your own mark for the cause?"

Andrei was silent for such a long moment that finally Stephan impatiently thrust the sketchbook back at him and turned his attention elsewhere. But that moment of silent debate was all Andrei devoted to his dilemma.

"Kaminsky," he said. Stephan turned around. "I can do those drawings. Where do you want them delivered?"

A gleam of triumph filled Kaminsky's eyes. "I, of course, can't guarantee they will be accepted. But they will go to a man named Stalin—"

A fellow standing nearby interjected, "I don't think so, Stephan. Stalin's been arrested again."

"Now there is a faithful Party man, that Stalin," declared Stephan with a pointed look toward Andrei. "He spends more time in Imperial prisons than out. He'll go far in the Party."

Andrei left as soon as he got the information about how to deliver his contributions to *Pravda*—a rather intricate process designed to elude police detection. His mind was in a turmoil over all that had transpired. He wasn't certain if he was angrier at Kaminsky for his reproachfulness or at himself for being the cause of his own humiliation. He should have known Kaminsky was the kind of die-hard Party man who would never accept anything less than total commitment.

But was Kaminsky expecting too much?

Andrei wondered about that as he began to walk home. There had been a time in his life when the destruction of the monarchy had been the most important thing to him. After his father died, he thought that consuming passion would burn inside him forever. But what had the years done to it all? It was still there; he believed in the cause. But he had to admit he had for the most part only gravitated toward the Social Democrats because he had several friends involved in the Party. Not being an intellectual, he mainly saw the surface of things, and from that view, Marxism seemed to suit Andrei's idealism. The precepts of even distribution of wealth and "Dictatorship of the Proletariat" were appealing.

Uncle Paul often pointed out that this dominance of the working class was at the expense of the peasantry, which Marxism absurdly disregarded. How could the peasants be so coldly brushed aside when they comprised eighty percent of the population? Marxism promoted a classless society. What was wrong with that? Paul's answer was that such a society risked the dehumanization of the individual.

Andrei didn't want to be bothered with all the theoretical debates. All he wanted was freedom for Russia, and Lenin seemed to offer the best hope of realizing that dream. True, Uncle Paul had felt the same way once, but eventually he had to come to terms with the basic differences between his instinctual regard for the *people* and the Bolshevik line.

Andrei wondered if he would reach a similar turning point. But his dilemma didn't seem as straightforward as his uncle's. His choice wasn't between two sets of doctrines but rather, it seemed, between the cause he believed in and the work he loved. Even if he chose to follow some other doctrine besides Bolshevism, Andrei knew Stephan was right in demanding commitment. But Andrei also knew he would never be as fulfilled by politics as he was by his art. Only when he worked at his art did he feel truly alive and free.

How could he give it up for his beliefs? Why should he have to?

All at once Andrei realized his footsteps were heading toward his mother's flat. Talia had mentioned she would be there today. As he approached, much to his delight, he saw her sitting on the front steps reading a book and enjoying the late afternoon sunshine. This was the first time today that Andrei was even aware of the bright, warm sun.

He sat down next to her and immediately poured out all the experiences and debates of the day. They had never needed small talk between them.

"I can imagine," she said when he finished, "that you are quite worn out with all this."

"If I hadn't run into Kaminsky, I could have gone on forever contentedly on the fringes."

"Forever?"

"I don't know—no, probably not. He only forced an issue that was bound to surface sooner or later. But, Talia, why do I have to be torn like this? It's just like my uncle. Why? I see people like Kaminsky who are fervent in their beliefs—whether they're Marxists or Narodniki, or of some other party—and I wonder why I can't get fervent over a party doctrine. But it's more than that, Talia. It's like the things I was zealous about as a boy have faded a little. Other things have become more important, I guess. I still want freedom for Russia. I despise the ruling class and the monarchy and will rejoice when they crumble. But that's not enough these days. There's so much conflict and backbiting between parties and debate over the most minor of details that one is almost forced to take a side. Why can't I?"

"Andrushka, I see that what you're expressing is complex. You won't be offended if I give you a simplistic answer?"

"That's what I want more than anything. I want things to be simple!"

"This just came to me as you were talking," she answered. "I was thinking of your father. He achieved the very thing you seek, Andrushka. But he never joined any political parties. I don't think he was even a member of Father Gapon's Worker's Assembly. He certainly never told me why he didn't join them, but knowing your father I think I can guess why. You see, Andrei, your father didn't die for liberation or for the overthrow of the tsar—he died because of love and compassion. He supported the workers because he loved them and cared about them. And I'll wager if your father were here now, he'd tell us he also loved the Marxists and S.D.s and S.R.s—and even the monarchists!"

Andrei felt his throat tighten with emotion as he heard Talia speak about his father. "That was my father," he said. He blinked back tears.

"Don't you see, Andrushka! One of the very foundations of compassion is tolerance."

"Something of which the likes of Lenin and Kaminsky know little," Andrei added.

"But *you* were raised with it. You breathed it like sweet air from your father. Is it any wonder you can't throw yourself wholeheartedly into those narrow-minded parties? And, from what I know of your grandfather Yevno, it's probably the same for your uncle Paul. Compassion, tolerance, and love are too much a part of you. Does Marx teach about these things?"

"I don't think so," said Andrei. "To tell the truth I tried reading *Das Kapital*, but it was too boring and I quit after ten pages. Talia, are you saying Lenin isn't a compassionate man because he believes in these things? His fervent single-mindedness is what I admired most about him."

"I can't answer that."

"And here's something else. My father wasn't a vacillating, wishy-washy sort. He was a man of strong convictions. Yet, tolerance suggests a kind of double-mindedness, doesn't it?"

"Not the kind your father had."

"What kind was that?"

"If I knew the answer to that, I'd write a book about it and probably become rich and famous for solving the world's problems. He never gave you a lesson on it. He lived it. And you lived *with* it during the most influential part of your life."

"I wish he were still here," Andrei said quietly. A tear escaped from the corner of his eye.

Talia reached up and tenderly wiped it away.

It embarrassed him that she was seeing him cry, yet he didn't try to hide it. He offered her his emotion, his grief . . . even as he wanted to offer his love.

19

Yuri had a hard time keeping his mind on his work. His thoughts kept wandering back to that glorious week on the Black Sea. In the drab surroundings of the hospital, he had to remind himself frequently that the time in the Crimea with Katya had been real. Nearly a month had passed since he had returned to St. Petersburg, but he still remembered every detail as if it had only just happened. The fact that he'd heard Katya had returned to the Capital only heightened the sweet memories in his anticipation of seeing her once again.

His trip to the Crimea had been a risk, presuming to show up in the middle of her holiday. At first, it had seemed as if he had ruined his chances with her forever. When he went to her estate that first day, he had done so without telephoning ahead. His grandfather had no phone, and it would have meant a trip to their nearest neighbors, half a mile away, to do so. He debated about whether or not to take the chance, finally deciding that she'd be less likely to turn him away in person than over the phone. When she first laid eyes on him, he thought she *would* turn him away.

"I know it was rude of me not to call first," he said in a rather pitiful attempt to apologize.

"This is just such a surprise." Her voice had been strained.

"I'm not usually given to such impulsive acts, but . . ." He let his words trail away unfinished. He couldn't come right out with the truth, that he was madly in love with her and couldn't stay away.

"You came here just to see me?"

"My grandfather lives here, you know. But, yes, I came because of you." There was an awkward pause, then, gathering all his boldness, he continued, "May I . . . come in?" He had been standing in the foyer where a maid had left him to seek her mistress. Yuri had the feeling uninvited visitors were not common at the Zhenechka Crimean estate.

Katya glanced nervously over her shoulder. "It's such a lovely day, why don't we walk in the garden?"

Yuri beamed delightedly. She was throwing him a crumb, but it was all he needed.

She seemed to relax a bit as they walked in the beautiful garden that stretched over an acre south of the house. The roses were in bloom and the sweet scent filled the air. This time of year also saw a riot of many other varieties of shrubs and flowers in full bloom. Mentioning that her grandmother, who apparently was the mistress of the estate, had a penchant for horticulture, Katya pointed out several rare plants. There was even a greenhouse with fabulous orchids that bloomed nearly the year round. Yuri listened attentively, not only because he found her conversation interesting, but because her voice drew him like a magnet, endearing her more to him with every word. He knew in his heart that the rumors about her were untrue.

He left that afternoon with an invitation to return. When he did so the next day, she must have been watching for him, because she met his carriage outside as he came to a stop in front of the house. After that, he saw her every day. Once or twice he went to her estate, though he never again went inside. She always met him in the yard. Usually, however, she met him at his grandfather's, in her carriage. There was never a chaperon present except for the driver, who kept a discreet distance.

They picnicked by the sea under the warm summer breezes, or they visited the picturesque Tatar villages where the women still dressed in full-flowing Turkish trousers with tight-fitting, ornately embroidered jackets. The men sported astrakhan hats and baggy trousers with brightly colored shirts. Yuri and Katya laughed gaily as they shopped in the markets, trying to bargain with the canny Muslim residents.

Once she did, indeed, drive him on a short excursion in her grandmother's motorcar. And she spent the afternoon teaching him to drive the contraption also. How they had laughed as they jerked and bounced over the rutted roads of the countryside.

And by the seaside, Yuri tried not to show his shock at Katya's daring swimming costume with a skirt that rose well above the knee of her shockingly bare legs. He had to admit that she *was* a modern woman, but that still did not reflect upon her basic character.

"This is the twentieth century," Katya said, responding to his wide eyes. Her own eyes glinted mischievously.

"I can be a progressive man," he said, trying not to be defensive.

"Then wipe that leering grin off your face. This outfit is the height of seaside fashion, and before long all truly liberated women will be wearing similar ones."

"I only hope it won't cause the sun to taint your lovely skin."

"Do you worry about everything, Yuri Sergeiovich?" She then bent down and scooped up a handful of water and tossed it playfully at him, drenching his own swimming suit.

Before he could react, she raced off into the gently rolling waves. They played like children, Katya bringing out in Yuri a sense of release and freedom he had thought was long departed from him.

And so their time together went, Yuri feeling more alive, more vital than he'd ever felt in his life. But in addition to the fun and laughter, they also talked—that is, Yuri talked and Katya listened. He told her everything about his family, the smallest detail, the most shocking secrets. But she wasn't shocked. She said she was greatly impressed, and had she known Sergei Viktorovich, she would have admired him. And she wanted to meet Yuri's mother—who, she said, sounded like a *real* princess.

But Katya said very little about herself. She lived part of the year in St. Petersburg with her grandmother and part in Moscow with her father. The summers she usually spent in the Crimea. Her parents were divorced—a bit of information she revealed reluctantly, saying, "You'll probably find out anyway." It seemed her mother had, several years ago, left her father for a Cossack. They now lived in a Cossack village on the Don, and Katya's mother wore peasant clothes, ran barefoot through the fields, and was still producing Cossack babies for her husband.

"She was very young when she married my father," Katya explained. "She was only seventeen when I was born. My father was twenty years older than she."

"You defend her, then?"

"She is my mother, though I haven't seen her in years."

"It must be very hard on you."

She shrugged as if it was a minor thing. "We all have our lives to live."

"Yes, but—"

She cut him off abruptly. "I'm starved. Where is that picnic lunch?" She jumped up from where they had been sitting in the sand and fetched the basket. Their conversation never again drifted to the topic of her family.

But Yuri felt no need to press her. Although he wanted to know everything about her, every tiny detail about what made her the person she was, he was content enough just to be near her. The last thing he wanted was to do something that might push her away, and he instinctively sensed that to dig deeper into her personal life would do just that.

On his last day, however, he impulsively nearly did that very thing. But he couldn't restrain himself. He was too full of feeling for her not to express it.

As they walked again on the beach under the warm sun—they had never met in the evenings, only by day—he mustered the boldness to open his heart entirely to her.

"I love you, Katya!" he proclaimed, his joy swelling inside him.

"Yuri, please . . ."

"Don't think me frivolous. I know it is sudden, but I've given it a lot of thought."

"I'm only your first love, Yuri. You'll get over this."

"Don't you feel the same, Katya?"

"I . . . I don't know how I feel. This *is* sudden."

"I understand. I'm willing to give you time. But I can say with more certainty than I have felt about anything ever before that this is no passing fancy. You have touched something within me, Katya, that I know without a doubt no other woman will ever be able to touch again. At first it was just your beauty, I'll admit. But it has nothing to do with that now."

"You hardly know me, Yuri."

"I know what I need to know."

"There are things—"

"They wouldn't matter."

"How do you know?"

"I know!" He then slipped his arm around her and drew her near. When she didn't pull back, he bent his lips toward hers and knew the sweetest ecstasy of his life. Her lips responded to his, melted into his, and for a brief moment, a moment that could sustain him for life, she was his.

Then she drew back.

"I must go," she said, breathless and flushed.

"Have dinner with us tonight, Katya. My grandparents enjoy your company."

"I can't."

"Not even on my last night here?"

"I've already spent the whole day with you."

"What have you to go back to? Why, I would almost think you are hiding a husband back on your estate."

She laughed, a pointed attempt to diffuse the intensity of the moment. "And I suppose that wouldn't bother you, either," she mocked lightly.

"I can be as progressive and outrageous as you."

"Ha! Down deep, Yuri, you are as old-fashioned and stilted as a peasant."

He only smiled and kissed her again. "Then, if we are to say good-bye, let it be now and here, where I've known my greatest happiness."

He left her to be driven home by the coachman while he walked the two miles to his grandfather's estate.

20

Those weeks after returning to St. Petersburg, Yuri had been miserable. He felt as if a sudden famine had come upon his soul after a time of fabulous plenty. But he was tied to the hospital where interns were too low in the pecking order to expect much time off. His next holiday would not be until Christmas, if he was lucky.

When his friend Vladimir had mentioned that he'd seen Katya the previous day in town, Yuri had been surprised. But she had probably only just arrived and had not had a chance to call him yet. Or perhaps she had tried. She would have trouble reaching him because he was so busy at the hospital. So the first thing Yuri did when he stopped for lunch was to call her from a hospital telephone.

"Hello, my love!" he said eagerly when she answered. "Imagine my ecstasy when I learned you were back in town."

"Yuri . . . hello."

"I can't wait to see you."

"Well, I . . ."

"I know I should give you time to unpack and get settled, but you won't torture me too long, will you?"

"I have plans for the next two evenings."

"What?" Then he noticed the distance in her tone, which he had at first attributed to the quality of the phone connection.

"I have been gone so long and there are people who wish to see me. You must know how that is."

"I know. I'm one of those people."

"Of course . . . and I want to see you."

"Can I come tonight?"

"As I said, I have a previous engagement."

"I don't understand." Was this the same person he had been with in the Crimea? Yuri felt his insides knot up with fear. "How could you have so many engagements already made if you only just returned?"

"Did I say I had just returned?"

"No. That is, I thought—"

"Yuri, I'm just spending the evening with some friends. Why don't you join us?"

He hesitated. He had often had a vague sense that Katya was giving him crumbs, but this was the first time he truly felt like a dog begging for scraps from the master's table. He wanted to tell her no, that he had better things to do with his time than spend it with an unfeeling, insensitive woman. But even as his ire was stirred, he found himself answering, "Yes, I'll do that. What time?"

"Nine o'clock."

So late in the evening, it couldn't be a dinner invitation. Would her other friends be coming for dinner? No matter. At precisely nine o'clock that evening he took a horse-driven taxi to the Zhenechka estate, one of the grand estates on the island known as Petersburg Side. The Grand Duchess Zenia, the tsar's sister, lived near the Zhenechkas. As the cab approached the estate, he thought about the old Fedorcenko palace—far larger and more fabulous than Katya's home, or even the grand duchess's, for that matter. He wondered, not for the first time that day, how Katya would have treated him had he grown up in that palace on the hill, heir to all the wealth and power that had once been at the command of the Fedorcenko name.

But he now felt far closer to his peasant roots in Katyk as he knocked on Katya's door.

A servant received him at the door and led him up a flight of winding, wide stairs and down a long corridor to a drawing room. On the way, he passed substantial indications of the Zhenechka fortune. In the drawing room, there were already half a dozen people including Katya. Yuri nearly forgot his hurt feelings as he set hungry eyes upon her. After the four-week separation, she was even more beautiful than he remembered. And he wasn't even shocked at her daring evening dress, which fell from her waist in satin folds and ended two revealing inches above her ankles. The coral satin of the dress set her hair to dazzling so that it looked like tongues of flame.

Katya greeted Yuri with a smile that, though warm and even friendly, held none of the passion he had felt from her on their last day in the Crimea. Again, he wondered if he had misread the entire week, especially that final day.

He was introduced to the others present, none of whom he knew. They were all about his or Katya's ages; one couple was engaged to be married, the others, two men and another young woman, were all single. They all had titles before their names and looked the part of young Russian aristocrats. Yuri noticed immediately that he was "odd man out." But surely Katya would not have invited him if one of the other single men present was her specific escort. And, in truth, the other two men didn't seem attached to any particular woman, even though the fellow named Count Pytor Prokunin did seem a bit more solicitous toward Katya than to the other girl. Yuri despised the man immediately.

The group visited together, drank wine, and ate canapes for an hour. Yuri tried to overcome his misery and keep up his end of the social banter. The group interacted as old, familiar friends, but the conversation was far from deep or stimulating. The women talked about clothes and gossip, the men talked about automobiles and hunting and gossip. Yuri knew very little about any of these topics, and when he tried to talk politics or philosophy his attempt fizzled out quickly.

After an hour or so of this, one of the men suggested that they go out for the rest of the evening. Someone suggested going to see the gypsies—an idea that was eagerly adopted by the rest of the group. Katya ordered her grandmother's motorcar around, and though it was crowded, the entire group squeezed in. Yuri was forced to sit up front with the driver.

It was too early to see the gypsies, who often didn't perform until after midnight, so the group stopped at a couple of fashionable nightclubs first. Well after midnight, they piled once more into the motorcar and ordered the driver to take them to the Novaya Derevnya district, commonly called The Islands because of its many interlacing canals on the Neva. There they sought out the Villa Rhode, one of the most popular gypsy clubs.

Although visiting the gypsies was all the rage among the avant-garde of Russian aristocracy, Yuri had never been to any of their clubs. He had, of course, heard many stories of the fiercely independent gypsies who practically formed a class, even a race, of their own. Set apart by their dark skin, ebony hair, bright clothes laden with gold and silver jewelry, they were most famous for the grace and beauty of their women and the unbridled passion of their music.

Parties were received by appointment, and though Katya's guests had decided impromptu, one of the men had called ahead and reserved a place for them. They were led into a large, brightly lit room. In contrast to other clubs that were traditionally dim, the gypsies liked their lighting as bright as their clothing. There were already about thirty other guests in the room, which was furnished with long divans, armchairs, and low tables on which to set refreshments. The performance had not yet begun, but there was a charged atmosphere in the room. Gypsies, in their red and green and indigo costumes sparkling with baubles, circulated among the guests serving refreshments.

Count Prokunin found six seats together, then, when he realized they were one short, smiled sheepishly at Yuri.

"Yuri, be a good fellow and see if you can fetch yourself another chair."

Yuri pulled over another chair and managed, while Prokunin was distracted ordering drinks, to snag a seat next to Katya.

"Well, what do you think, Yuri?" she asked. "I know this is your first time."

"Quite gay. But I'll reserve judgment until I've heard them perform." Feeling encouraged by her responsiveness, he added, "I feel as if we haven't had a chance to talk all evening."

"This is an evening for fun, not talk."

"So, that's it then, why you seem so distant?"

"Now, Yuri, no more of this seriousness or I won't let you sit by me."

"I'm so sorry, Your Highness," he said sarcastically. "Your wish is my command."

She giggled. "It's good to see you are not always so earnest."

"Katya—"

"Look, over there! It's Father Grigori."

"Father Grigori?"

"You know, Rasputin." Katya leaned across Yuri to speak to Olga, the other single girl in the group. "Olga, do you see who is here?"

Yuri hardly heard Olga's answer. As Katya pressed close to him, a heart-pounding surge coursed through him. He forced himself to focus on the conversation.

Olga squealed when she looked where Katya directed her. "Katya, we must invite him over here."

"I don't know, he's with his own group."

"It would be rude for us not to speak with him."

Yuri asked, "What is a priest doing in a place like this?"

He had heard about the escapades of the infamous Grigori Rasputin, of course, but he had attributed the rumors to vile gossip. Stories had circulated about drunkenness, even sexual orgies. They certainly couldn't be true. Wasn't he a man of God and a confidant of the emperor and empress? Still at the moment Rasputin didn't look like much of a priest. He was dressed in a richly embroidered bright blue silk peasant shirt and black baggy trousers tucked into high boots that were shiny and new.

Olga answered Yuri with a deprecating shrug. "Father Grigori isn't to be judged on the same level as mere mortals like us. He is above all that. If he does something, it can't be wrong."

"You sound like he's not a flesh-and-blood human being."

"Don't you know?" put in the third single man, Alex. "He's practically a saint." His tone was laced with sarcasm.

"Oh, what do you know, Alex, you cynic," Olga said.

As the two engaged in this dispute, Yuri turned to Katya. "What do you think of him?"

"I've known him in the past, although I haven't seen him in a long time," she replied, the first hint of sincerity in her tone. "He helped me a great deal . . . a while ago."

"Helped you?"

"Yuri, you are a man of science. You wouldn't understand."

"I have faith also," Yuri defended himself. "I was raised in a deeply devout home."

"Maybe you should meet him, then."

Katya started to rise from her seat, apparently to approach the *starets*, but at that same moment the musicians started up their music and the performance began. For the next hour Yuri was so mesmerized that he forgot his former misery. It was as if the singers cast a spell over him. He could hardly take his eyes off them. They not only sang, they *enchanted*. At one point a middle-aged gypsy woman took center stage and sang in a deeply moving contralto. True, Yuri had had more wine that evening than he was used to, but the woman made him feel positively euphoric—and not from wine.

The only time Yuri was distracted from the performance was when at one point, while several gypsies were singing and dancing together, they danced to where Rasputin was seated. Laughing merrily, they began to rifle his pockets, pulling out trinkets which, by the congenial look of all involved, had been put in the pockets precisely for that purpose.

Rasputin laughed loudly. "Gypsy pickpockets are robbing me!"

He then grabbed one of the gypsy women and danced around his table with her. He moved with the hearty gusto of a drunken peasant, uninhibited and full of mirth.

When the performers took a small break, Katya rose from her seat and resumed the mission that had been interrupted before. She went to Rasputin, who, upon seeing her, jumped up from his chair and gave her a vigorous embrace. In another moment, they were coming Yuri's way.

"This is my friend, Father Grigori," Katya said, indicating Yuri. "Prince Yuri Sergeiovich Fedorcenko. He is a doctor."

Yuri stood, and Rasputin stepped so close to him that Yuri could smell the man's fetid breath, reeking of wine. "A doctor?"

"An intern, really," Yuri said.

As if he hadn't heard, Rasputin continued, "Oh, Physician, heal thyself!" Then he laughed. "It's not so easy, is it?"

"But I'm not ill."

"Is the physician sent to the healthy? No, it is to the sick that he comes." Rasputin spoke in disjointed sentences. Yuri had a hard time following him. "Naked and ye clothed me, sick and ye visited me, in prison and ye came unto me," Rasputin went on. Yuri wondered if either he or the *starets* had missed something.

"I . . . I don't understand," said Yuri.

"Oh yes, you are a man of great intelligence, yet you have no understanding. I'm not surprised. It is not to the healthy that I have come." Rasputin focused his eyes on Yuri. "Where are you from?"

"St. Petersburg."

"You're not married, are you?"

"No."

"Have you a woman?"

"I . . . no." Yuri felt weak all over. Between the man's unsettling gaze and the interrogation, his head was spinning.

"You are sicker than you think, Yuri Sergeiovich. No medicines can touch the pain that haunts you."

"Well . . . I . . . I . . ."

"Come and see me tomorrow evening. We will talk. I have medicine you have never heard of." Rasputin turned to the others. "It is so good to see all my dear friends. We must spend an evening together soon." He directed his hypnotic eyes toward Katya. "You especially, Katichka. It has been too long." Then he turned and rejoined his other friends.

Yuri was silent the rest of the evening. He would have left right then, even if it had meant a long walk home. But the minute Rasputin departed, the gypsies began to sing again—almost as if they were all conspiring to keep Yuri where he was. He tried hard not to think of Rasputin, but with no success. Had the man read into his very soul? That, too, was rumored to be one of the *starets'* talents. It was almost as if Rasputin had seen things in Yuri that even the young prince was unaware of—or, at least, afraid to admit.

His mind fixed on Rasputin's invitation. He would not go, of course. An innate fear gripped Yuri, but he could not tell if it was a fear of Rasputin . . . or of himself.

21

The next afternoon Yuri received a telephone call at the hospital. It was Katya.

"I spoke to Father Grigori," she said. "He wants to make sure you haven't forgotten about his invitation."

"No, but I'm surprised he remembered—he seemed quite drunk last night." Yuri made an effort to sound glib.

"I suppose he can take more wine than most men." Katya was definitely defensive. "Are you planning to go?"

"I have to work late at the hospital. I won't get off until ten tonight."

"That's all right; Father Grigori thought you might have to come late."

"Second sight, is it?"

"Yuri, sarcasm doesn't become you."

"You liked it last night."

"I think I was a bit tipsy myself."

"Perhaps that explains a lot of things."

"What about tonight, Yuri?"

"I don't know."

"He wants me to bring you."

"You?"

"Yes . . ."

"Well . . ."

"I really want you to talk to him, Yuri."

"Should that matter to me?"

"Please, Yuri. I know I don't deserve your kindness, but I truly believe it would be a good thing for you to see him."

"It's you I want to see, Katya."

There was a long pause. Finally she said with—he was almost certain—regret in her tone, "I can't promise anything."

"Shall I come to your place?"

"That would be too much out of the way. Why don't you meet me downtown at Nicholas Station? It's close to where Rasputin lives."

After Yuri hung up the telephone, he had a difficult time keeping his mind on his work. Was he doomed to forever lap up Katya's small, careless concessions? Would he never be able to say no to her? What kind of man was he? He'd always imagined himself to have more character than that. Had love made a complete fool of him?

And then there was Rasputin. He was the last person Yuri wanted to see. But—again—Katya wanted him to go, so he would go. What did Katya see in the man? It was quite obvious she did see *something* in him. Her hard shell seemed to soften when she spoke of the *starets*. She had said he had "helped" her. How? Yuri tried not to think of all the rumors, especially those about the man's cavorting with women. But even last night Yuri saw that women seemed more attracted to him than any other men. In the group Rasputin was with at the Villa Rhode, there had been half a dozen women and only two men. But certainly that was not an indictment against the man. St. Petersburg gossips could be vicious.

Yet Rasputin had gazed at Katya with more intimacy than even Yuri dared, and he had called her Katichka with great familiarity.

Stop it! Yuri silently reprimanded himself. He feared he was going to work himself into a frenzy of jealousy, an emotion that had always disgusted him in others. With more determination than ever then, he threw himself back into his work. But when, shortly before dinner, he ran into Dr. Botkin, he could not keep himself from broaching the subject of Rasputin.

In the last year, and especially since his internship had begun, Yuri had developed a friendship with Botkin. Actually, it was more a mentor-student relationship, but, nevertheless, they had become close. Yuri visited his home often in Tsarskoe Selo, and, though they talked mostly about medicine, Yuri felt he could confide in the man.

"Dr. Botkin, do you have a moment?"

"Of course, Yuri Sergeiovich."

They found a little alcove with two or three chairs and sat down. Yuri launched immediately into his concerns.

"Last night, I had a most interesting experience," said Yuri. "I was out for the evening with some friends, and I met Grigori Rasputin."

"I should say, then, it must have been interesting!" Botkin gave a knowing smile.

"You must see a great deal of him at Tsarskoe Selo."

"I doubt he frequents the palace as much as the rumors have it."

"What of other rumors about him?"

"May I ask if there is a reason for your sudden interest in Rasputin beyond the meeting last night?"

"He has asked me to visit him tonight. I find myself rather reluctant. If it wasn't for—" He stopped suddenly. He hadn't wanted to bring Katya into the conversation.

"For what?"

Yuri reddened. "Well, I suppose there is a young woman I'd like to impress."

"I see." Botkin did not smile or in any way appear amused.

"Can you tell me something about him, Doctor?"

"You know, Yuri, I am most reticent to discuss my dealings with the royal family. They count on my discretion."

"And would speaking of Rasputin so compromise that?"

"The tsar and tsaritsa think very highly of the man."

"Is it true they believe he is responsible for the health of the tsarevich? Never mind. I don't expect you to answer that. But what do you think about the man himself?"

"I do not pretend to understand the ways of God. I believe in medicine, yet there is a spiritual realm of which I am all but ignorant. Who can say what power lies in that realm?"

"But surely you don't give credence to a man like Rasputin?"

"What I think is of little consequence in the spiritual realm. I'm sorry I can't be more direct with you, Yuri."

"I understand, Doctor."

"I will tell you one thing. Whether Rasputin's power is real or imagined or faked, he is not a man to be taken lightly, to be dismissed as merely the 'Mad Monk,' as some are wont to call him. If you must see him, Yuri, I suggest you do so with caution, remembering that you are a man of science. True, there is a spiritual side of you, a sensitive, emotional side, yet I see no reason why you shouldn't measure the spiritual with the scientific, at times. Balance, my boy—always remember balance."

"Thank you, Doctor. I appreciate your kindness in talking to me."

"Let me know how your visit with the *starets* goes."

Immediately after Yuri's dinner break, the fairly easygoing pace of his day exploded.

At first Yuri didn't recognize the frantic woman who rushed into the hospital with a child clutched in her arms.

"My baby! My baby! He's dying!"

"Madam, please calm down and tell me what happened." Yuri placed a consoling arm on the woman's shoulders. Then he saw the face of the child in her arms.

Little Vasily!

"What happened?" Yuri said with more urgency as he quickly directed the woman and child into an examination room, calling a nurse as he did so.

"He was running to dinner—oh, he's such a rambunctious boy! He tripped on a piece of torn carpet. Doctor, I was so proud of that carpet. It was old and threadbare, but we were the only family in the building . . ."

Yuri let the woman ramble on for a moment; she probably wasn't aware of half of what she was saying. In the meantime he had her lay Vasily on the examination table. The black and blue mark on the boy's head glared out at him.

"Vasily, can you hear me?" Yuri said.

The child's eyes fluttered. He was barely conscious, but he managed to say, "It . . . hurts . . ."

"I'm going to shine a light in your eyes, Vasily, so I can see what's going on inside your head." Yuri had the nurse bring in an electric light, then he pried open each of the boy's eyelids and flashed the light into them. The pupils hardly responded.

Yuri looked at the nurse. "See if Dr. Botkin is still in the hospital."

"I know for a fact that he left, Dr. Fedorcenko."

"Dr. Tevele, then?"

"I'll look for him."

After the nurse left, Vasily's mother asked beseechingly, "Doctor, how is my baby? He . . . seems so still."

"Vasily!" Yuri called. "Vasily!"

The child was breathing shallowly now and did not respond to his name. Yuri was completely helpless, and he knew no other doctor could help the boy, either. Nevertheless, he desperately wished another physician would come. He didn't want to stand here alone and watch the child die.

"Just an hour ago he was playing and laughing . . ." wept the mother.

Words of comfort stuck in Yuri's throat—lame, stupid, worthless words. He had no comfort for this distraught mother. Her child was dying. There was nothing he could do. He suddenly thought of Rasputin and how he was reputed to have been responsible for the tsarevich's recovery last year from his near-fatal illness. It was completely irrational, but Yuri had a sudden urge to run to the telephone and call the *starets*. It was said that Rasputin had healed Alexis all the way from Siberia.

Oh, God, help this child. I can do nothing. But Yuri's prayer sounded as ineffective as his medical power. Maybe a man like Rasputin did have some special connection to God, something a sinner like Yuri sorely lacked.

Yuri noticed the mother's lips were moving. She, too, was praying. She crossed herself. Yuri did the same, but mostly out of respect for the woman's faith. He felt suddenly drained of all faith. But he was drained also of scientific prowess, too. No balance. He was walking on a tightrope with a lead weight in one hand.

Desperately needing something to do, he examined the boy's pupil reaction again. It was worse than a few minutes ago. Where was the nurse?

"We need a priest," said Vasily's mother.

"Yes. But I don't want to leave the child," said Yuri.

The woman stood motionless. "He's my baby, you know. I have three grown children. Vasily came late in life. We doted on him so. We . . . loved—*love*—him so. They say I gave him this disease. Will God ever forgive me for killing my baby?"

"Don't talk that way," said Yuri. "You are not to blame." He wanted to tell her he was more at fault than she for being so helpless. This was the twentieth century. Modern medicine had advanced tremendously in just the last fifty years. Yet at that moment, Yuri felt as archaic as a medieval bloodletter.

Then the child stirred and his lips moved soundlessly, distinctly forming the one word, "Mama."

"Doctor!" said the mother hopefully.

Yuri took Vasily's hand. It was cold. But the fingers twitched slightly against his grasp. Yuri glanced at the boy. Maybe there would still be a miracle.

Then the child's hand went slack. Yuri could not bring himself to look again at the face. The child was dead.

22

Yuri was so distraught that he probably should not have met Katya that night. But by the time he left the hospital after dealing with the bereaved mother and all the other awful details a physician must attend to in the wake of death, he was too drained to think rationally. He walked to Nicholas Station, almost forgetting why he was going there. When he saw Katya, for a moment he thought it was mere chance. Then he remembered the telephone conversation, and his miseries were compounded.

"What's wrong, Yuri?" she asked when they met in front of the train station. Her concern seemed so real. Yet he could only think that she was a faithless woman, using him for some purposes he didn't understand.

"I'm fine." But his voice was empty of all except despair.

"It's obvious you're *not* fine. Please, what is the matter?"

Something snapped in Yuri, and he felt in that moment that Katya was the cause of all his troubles.

"Why should I tell you?" he snarled. "I once tried to open my heart to you—and you ground it into the dirt."

"You just don't understand, Yuri. There are things—"

"I don't want to hear it! There's no excuse for the way you've treated me. And I won't take it anymore. I'm through groveling at your feet. You're not worth it!"

"If only I could explain."

"I don't believe there is any explanation. You are just a frivolous, empty—"

"It's not true!" Her eyes were glistening with moisture. She looked more than ever like a vulnerable child. His anger began to melt. He wanted to embrace her. Her gaze was steady, filled with that honesty she could wear so expertly. How could he actually believe his awful accusations?

"Then, tell me what is true?" he beseeched.

She looked at him a moment longer, then her gaze fell. "I . . . I can't. It's better this way, Yuri."

"What way?"

"That we don't see each other again."

He stared mutely at her, as if her words came totally unexpectedly, as if he hadn't only a moment before suggested that very thing himself.

Katya took a slip of paper from her pocketbook and handed it to Yuri. "Father Grigori's place is just three blocks from here; you should have no trouble finding it."

He took the paper; he didn't know why.

"How can you do this, Katya? So cool, so calm. Did our time in the Crimea truly mean nothing to you?"

"Walk away, Yuri, while you can. It's for the best." She turned and strode to her motorcar, which was parked by the curb.

He watched silently as the driver opened the door for her and she stepped in. He kept on watching as the engine started and the wheels began to roll away from the curb. Then, all at once, he seemed to stir to life.

"Katya!" he called.

But the car turned a corner and disappeared from sight.

Katya wept all the way home—quiet tears that seeped from her eyes in spite of her attempt to hold them back by chewing on her lip. She couldn't make a scene that the chauffeur might see and report back to her grandmother. But she tasted blood on her lip and still the tears flowed.

Why did Yuri Sergeiovich keep coming back for more? Why couldn't he see that she was a terrible person, not worthy of him at all? It was his fault that she had to be so cruel. Other men did not press her so, demand so much of her. Why him?

Yet, was the problem with Yuri, or was it only with herself? It had always been fairly easy to brush off other men, at least the few she had allowed into her life. They never minded being kept at arm's length—enjoyed, played with, then left alone or dropped altogether. Probably the others had only been out for a good time, just like she was. The last thing she wanted was to fall in love. That's what had nearly destroyed her life before.

For the past two years she had done a marvelous job of avoiding meaningful relationships with men. It hadn't been difficult. She had a rather low opinion of men anyway, and most in her social circle easily affirmed that opinion. They wanted one thing from a woman, and all their behavior focused on ways to get that thing. The best way to deal with these men was to fight fire with fire. If they were play*boys*, she made for herself the reputation as a play*girl*.

Almost every evening was filled with parties, visits to nightclubs, the theater—any event where the Russian nobility mixed and mingled. She let the rumors spread about her free and easy lifestyle, supported by her daring fashions, her frequent flirtations, her excursions to places where genteel ladies would never be found. She let the rumors fly that her relations with men went beyond mere flirting. And because of this, she was not the most sought-after marriage candidate. Men were proposing to her all the time, of course—though love was not their motive for doing so. But the parents of these men usually steered their sons away from the wild Countess Katya Zhenechka. They wanted their precious boys to marry ladies of quality and breeding, not a trollop who had obviously inherited her mother's unstable and unsavory character.

Her behavior and the rumors surrounding her had incurred the constant wrath of her father, but it was a small price to pay for the benefit of remaining single and free.

But from the beginning Yuri had shaken her carefully constructed world. He was new to society, and he didn't know all the rumors about her. She wondered if he was still ignorant of them. Or did he simply have the uncanny ability of seeing past all that into her soul, her real self, which she had always worked so hard to hide? He loved her—really *loved* her. It boggled her mind. No one had ever loved her like that before. Should it be any surprise that she had been drawn to him? He made her let down a little part of her solid emotional wall. He had begun to reach a deep need in her that she had always tried so hard to deny. And, in moments of weakness, she found herself succumbing to him. She would then pull back as soon as her good sense returned. But in the process, she hurt him—more than once, too. She hurt him again and again because she just didn't have the strength of character to cut him off completely.

But she must.

It was the only way. Yuri was an honorable man, and he'd probably accept her past. He was like the biblical Joseph, accepting the seemingly tainted Mary because it was the right thing to do. Unfortunately, Katya was no Virgin Mary. And it would hurt Yuri in more ways than one to get involved with her. He was a rising star in the medical profession and in the circles of Russian nobility. It was important to him to be successful in these areas. And an association with someone like Katya could only harm his ambitions. Her past could not be kept a secret much longer. Only her father's force of will had kept Katya's secret hidden. Yet, there were vague whisperings—mostly in Moscow, but they would trickle up to the Capital sooner or later.

Katya tried to slip into her house unnoticed, but her grandmother was coming down the stairs at the same moment Katya entered.

"There you are," said the older woman. Countess Elizabeth Zhenechka was tall and regal, described by many as a "handsome woman." Not beautiful, but with such *presence*. She was a reserved, somewhat distant woman, much like Katya's father. Yet her grandmother had a tender heart, a caring heart. Some said Katya's father had no heart at all.

"Hello, Grandmother."

"It is not seemly for you to be out so late—and unescorted, too, I suppose."

"I had an appointment."

Countess Zhenechka closed her eyes and sighed. "Why can't you pay more attention to propriety, child?" It was more of an entreaty than a reprimand. The woman came to the bottom of the steps and put an arm around her. "I'm only concerned for your future, Katya, dear. You must be careful of your associations if you hope to make a decent marriage. Heaven knows it's going to be hard enough as it is."

"I don't care about marriage, Grandmother."

"Whatever became of that young man who visited you in the Crimea? Prince Fedorcenko, wasn't it? I know the family has fallen considerably from its former status but . . . well, we must be practical, and it may be the best match we can hope for. He is a doctor, and that is respectable, if nothing else."

"Please, Grandmother, I don't want to talk about this."

"Oh, Katya . . ." The woman gave Katya an affectionate pat on the shoulder.

She didn't need to say more. Katya knew she had not only ruined her own life, but that of her family as well. They would all have to live with her mistake. It wouldn't go away. But that didn't mean she had to drag Yuri into it, too. She cared for him too much to do that to him.

23

Rasputin lived in flat number twenty at 64 Gorokhavaya Street. For a counselor and intimate of the emperor and empress of Russia, it was not among the best St. Petersburg locations. But perhaps the *starets* had a need to maintain some ties, however flimsy, with his common roots.

Yuri climbed up three flights of stairs to the third floor and found number twenty. He still wasn't certain why he had come. The only reason he had even considered the visit in the first place was because of Katya. Now she was gone, perhaps forever. Yet Yuri needed something to fill the terrible, empty void that had so suddenly replaced his burning love. He wasn't in the mood for his friends who would want to have fun, perhaps in a nightclub. He certainly couldn't face his mother—she would see right through him and encourage him to talk about his troubles.

The more he thought about it, a visit with Rasputin was just what he needed. The curious man with his odd idiosyncrasies would be a perfect distraction. Yuri rapped briskly on the door.

The *starets* received him cordially. He was dressed in the same clothes he had worn the previous night at the Villa Rhode, but the strong odor emanating from him could hardly be due merely to unwashed clothes. But Yuri didn't hold this against the man. Like many, he had a vague notion that holy men had higher things on their minds than personal hygiene, and thus a lapse in that area was acceptable in them.

"Come in. I'm glad you decided to come," said Rasputin. "Where is Katya?"

"She . . . some emergency came up and she couldn't make it. She sends her regrets."

"That is too bad. She is such a delightful girl. But at least you have come. Would you like tea—? Ah, but you look as if you could use something stronger."

"I've had a difficult day."

"Come . . . we will talk. What better use of a man of God, eh? Someone for the distressed to unburden themselves to."

He led Yuri from the large anteroom to a dining room. Rasputin's flat was furnished simply but solidly, more middle-class in appearance than aristocratic. In contrast to the simplicity, however, was the profusion of icons throughout the place. It was very much what Yuri might have expected from the man. The dining room was furnished with massive oak. On a sideboard, a samovar was heating; and the table was laid with crockery and dishes of various cakes and other delicacies, along with a large bowl of flowers. It seemed the priest had gone to some trouble for his guest.

Rasputin opened a door in the sideboard and withdrew a bottle and two crystal wine glasses.

"While we wait for the tea water to heat, eh?" Rasputin filled the glasses from the bottle. Handing a glass to Yuri, he said, "This is good Russian Madeira, not that puny stuff they pass off elsewhere."

After finding a seat on one of the high-backed chairs, Yuri gulped the wine. It was indeed strong. He tried to think of something to say, but he had never been talented at small talk and found in his present mood he was less adept than ever. He was spared for the moment when the telephone rang and Rasputin excused himself. The phone rang almost constantly during the visit. There were also several other visitors who came and went, some of whom Rasputin received in another room. From the sounds of their voices, Yuri deduced they were all women. Catching a glimpse of a couple of them through an open door, Yuri saw they appeared to be respectable society ladies, despite the fact that ten o'clock at night was hardly the hour when such ladies usually paid calls.

Nevertheless, except to answer the door and telephone, Rasputin spent his time with Yuri, leaving the other visitors alone in other rooms to entertain themselves. This made Yuri distinctly uncomfortable.

"I don't wish to keep you from your other visitors," he said.

"Don't give it a thought. They will keep, won't they?" The *starets* smiled and Yuri noticed his yellow teeth. His beard, too, was matted and sprinkled with what appeared to be crumbs of food.

"Grigori Efimovich," said Yuri, "I don't understand why you wanted me to come. Surely it wasn't entirely for a social visit."

"I've never had much fondness for doctors, you can understand, can't you? What with the general skepticism of the medical profession toward the miraculous. But I realize mine is not a very Christian attitude. Isn't the very foundation of Christianity brotherly love? Did not God call His people to love and mercy? 'He that loveth not knoweth not God. For God is love.' And isn't it so that if God loved us, should we not love one another? For only then shall we see God. If we love our brothers, then truly God dwells in us."

Rasputin went on for another ten minutes in this vein, sermonizing on the merits of love. Yuri had a hard time following it all because the *starets* would easily get off track onto some other subject such as giving or sacrifice. Yuri soon learned that Rasputin loved to preach and often launched into a sermon whether it had anything to do with the topic at hand or not.

Finally Rasputin said, "With you, I could redeem myself, Yuri Sergeiovich. Your heart was troubled, and no human hand could touch the pain I saw in you."

"What pain?"

"I feel it now stronger than before. Share your pain with me, Yuri Sergeiovich. I can help you."

"I wouldn't even know where to start."

"What about Countess Zhenechka? Does she spurn your love?"

"How could you know that?"

"They say I can read into people's hearts. It is a gift of God."

"Then you ought to know what a fool I am. You ought to know how I've sold my heart to a faithless woman."

"Is that truly what you think of little Katya?"

"What else can I think?"

"Do you really know her, Yuri Sergeiovich?"

"Do you, Grigori Efimovich?"

"Of course I do, but it has been many months since I last saw her. Ours was a brief, but meaningful encounter. It is possible she has changed in that time, but I doubt it's been such a dramatic change. She is young and innocent and perhaps confused about life."

"I knew there was something I couldn't see, that I couldn't love her if she was really as shallow and insensitive as she tries to appear. Tell me about her."

"Those who come to me expect confidentiality."

"As a doctor, I understand that. But if she won't tell me, and you won't tell me, how will I ever find out?"

"Have you asked her?"

"She never talks about herself."

"And so you gave up on her?"

"What else can I do?"

"Have some faith, young man. Don't you know that a little bit of faith can move a mountain? Have you heard what power there is in a tiny mustard seed? Faith is the substance of things hoped for, the—"

The telephone rang, sparing Yuri another sermon. Rasputin left to answer the call. When he returned he appeared agitated.

"Duty calls," he said. "Mama and Papa have need of me."

"Your parents?"

"The parents of all Russia, our beloved sovereigns. Despite what others say, Mama and Papa need the anointed one of God. They will not listen to the lies of the devil. Even though the Duma itself speaks slander, our rulers know they are the words of the Evil One trying to get rid of the Lord's anointed."

Yuri rose, duly impressed. "Then, I won't keep you. Thank you for seeing me."

"Remember the things I've said. And come back to visit me—come with Katichka."

As Yuri left, he wondered if that would ever be possible. He doubted she would see him again. Yet Rasputin had said to have faith. Maybe Yuri had given up on Katya too easily. Maybe he should give her another chance. Perhaps he should have asked Rasputin to speak to her on his behalf. Maybe he would call the *starets* tomorrow and request it. And, surprisingly, Yuri felt lighter at heart than he had all day. With the *starets'* words bolstering him, he felt he could truly have hope again.

Katya stood on the sidewalk outside Father Grigori's building. Last night she had wanted to see Father Grigori almost as much as she had wanted to see Yuri. She was disappointed when her argument with Yuri had forced her to excuse herself from that meeting. She was so confused, and she needed to talk to the *starets*. She needed his prayers. It had been some time since she had last seen Rasputin—almost a year. She hoped he didn't hold that against her, nor the fact that it appeared as if she only sought him out during times of trouble. But he was a man of God; of course he wouldn't hold anything against her.

He had been such a help to her a year and a half ago when she had gone through that terrible time. He had embraced her spiritually and emotionally, never once disdaining her for her mistake as others, even churchmen, had. Through him she had fully understood God's mercy toward sinners. Only because of Father Grigori had she not committed the worst sin of all.

How close she had come, though! She had even bought the poison. It had seemed the only way. Her shame had been too great to face, and she believed she would never have the strength to face her father. Ending her life seemed the only possible answer. But Father Grigori had gone all the way to Moscow with her to be there for the confrontation with Count Zhenechka and had held her hand the entire time. She didn't care what anyone said, the man was indeed a saint. And she wondered now why she had been so lazy in maintaining the relationship. But this was her first time back to Petersburg since then. And her life had changed so dramatically that it had all but eclipsed her previous encounter with the priest. Maybe he could help her understand her conflicting feelings about Yuri.

When she knocked on Father Grigori's door, uninvited, he greeted her with a grin, greatly allaying her worry that he might be upset with her. "Ah, my little Katichka! I missed you so yesterday."

"Forgive me, Father Grigori—"

"I can forgive with ease, my dear, because I have known great forgiveness. Don't you remember when Our Lord said of the woman who had anointed his feet with her tears, 'Her sins which are many are forgiven for she loveth much. But to whom little is forgiven, the same hath little love.' I love you, my Katichka, dear." He threw his arms around her. "Now, come, let us be together."

His arm still around her, he drew her into his home. They went to the parlor where two other women were already seated. Katya knew them and they exchanged cordial greetings. But she soon sensed a coolness from them as Grigori lavished her with most of his attentions. He sat very close to her and kept his arm around her. She didn't remember him being this affectionate before. It was almost as if no time at all had elapsed since they last spoke.

"Lydia," he said to one of the other women, "go get us some tea."

Lydia rose obediently, though his request bore no "please" or "thank you." When she returned with a tray of tea things, she contrived, after setting the tray on a table, to sit on the divan on the other side of Rasputin. But he continued to all but ignore the other ladies.

"Tell me about the young man, Katichka, sweet?" he asked.

"He . . . is an acquaintance."

"Is that all?"

"I . . . I don't know. He's a nice man."

"Tell me, dear, what troubles you. Have you forgotten how Father Grigori can help?"

"I know it's been such a long time . . ."

"But I don't hold that against you. Open your heart to me as you did before. Remember what good it did."

A sudden knot rose in Katya's throat and, quite unexpectedly, a sob broke through her lips. "Oh, Father Grigori . . ." Tears seeped from her eyes. "I thought my life was better, but it's still a mess." She hated to break down like this in front of the other women. She had to be careful of her secret. Yet she needed so to talk to Grigori.

He took her chin in his hand, and she hardly noticed the dirt embedded in his fingernails. Without words he somehow made her gaze up into his eyes, and she felt that gaze from those pale, yet brilliant, blue eyes draw her and nearly take her breath away. His eyes seemed to caress her and penetrate to her very soul. It occurred to Katya how, before, she had been able to lose herself in his eyes, forget all her pain and confusion. She remembered how good it had been to feel the tension fall from her body like loosened chains.

"Oh, Father . . ." she murmured, desperate for peace to wash over her again.

He jerked his eyes from her for a moment as he spoke to the other ladies. "Leave us."

Katya hardly noticed the women exit, for he immediately turned back to her, and she eagerly latched on to his gaze once more. "I so want peace," she said.

"And you shall have peace, my dear. The peace that passes all understanding." He pressed closer to her. "Come, let your papa bear your pain. Hold me." He put both his arms around her, stroking her hair and kissing her hair and forehead. "There, there," he cooed.

And Katya felt like a little girl able to rest in her papa's arms, as she had never been able to do with her own papa. Maybe she never would have ruined her life if she'd had a papa like Father Grigori.

If she'd been held and kissed, shown even the tiniest bit of affection.

"Open up to me, dear Katichka. Let me help you find your way to God." His eyes once more sought hers. "My peace I give unto you," he cooed softly, "not as the world giveth give I unto you.' "

A heaviness crept over Katya's spirit. Father Grigori wanted to help her find inner peace. It had helped before. But something nagged at her and she couldn't quite grasp at it, something disquieting. What was it? She felt a greater intensity from the priest than before. Perhaps she was more troubled than she thought.

Father Grigori's stroking hand pressed harder on her hair and shoulders. She could feel the heat from his hand. "Do you know how beautiful you are, little one? I have so hoped you would come back to me. I knew there was more for me to give you."

Part of her wanted to draw back from his intensity and the foul odor of his nearness. Yet another part of her reasoned that he was a man of God, he must know what was best for her.

"Oh, God . . ." she breathed.

"Yes, little one, I am His prophet."

She let her shoulders relax, and the priest moved ever closer. The ringing telephone made her start. Rasputin cursed under his breath.

"One of the ladies will get it," he whispered.

"They left, didn't they?"

The telephone rang persistently.

He shuddered and shook himself. "It may be Mama and Papa." But in spite of the possibility that it might be the Imperial couple, he rose with great reluctance.

His voice was brusque on the phone, and she knew that it couldn't have been the tsar he was talking to.

"You want to come now?" he said, then paused for the caller's response. "I'm busy now." Pause. "All right. Come in half an hour." He replaced the phone not at all gently, then returned to the parlor. "That was a friend of yours, Katya dear."

"Really?"

"Yes, that doctor. He wants to see me. I think he wants advice about you."

"Is that what he said?"

"Not exactly, but I can tell these things."

"He is coming here?"

"In a little while." Rasputin sat back on the divan.

"I should go."

"We still have time." He placed his hot hands on her shoulders. "Besides, wouldn't you like to see him?"

"No, I don't think I should."

"As you wish. But, Katichka, we have time. You still need my help."

"I know, Father Grigori, but—" She rose abruptly. "I really should leave."

He rose also and took her hands in his. "Don't stay away so long again, Katya, dear. Papa will miss you."

"I won't, Father Grigori."

Katya hurried away from the priest's flat. And when she got outside, the air somehow seemed so fresh and clean and sweet. She took a deep breath and felt as if it had been a long time since she had really breathed.

24

Talia's next big performance came when the Maryinsky Ballet opened the fall season with *Giselle.* True to his promise, Yuri was there. Two weeks had passed since his visit with Rasputin. He had telephoned the *starets* the following day to request his assistance with Katya, but Rasputin had little to offer but vague and somewhat trite solutions. The man had been drunk, to boot, and had been far more interested in bragging about his association with the Imperial family. Within a few days Katya had left for Moscow, and it seemed Yuri was going to have to allow time to have its way with their relationship. He did not intend to chase after her again.

The ballet proved an excellent distraction, especially when on that particular evening there was a bit of a scandal. All the facts did not come out until the party after the performance, but, by then, everyone was talking about how the dowager empress had left in the middle of the ballet in apparent outrage. It seemed the dancer

Nijinsky had appeared on stage in a costume far too skimpy for the Empress Marie's Victorian tastes. Rumor had it Nijinsky would be expelled from the ballet.

"He's one of the greatest dancers in ballet—perhaps the greatest dancer of all time," said Talia. "They can't keep him away long."

"Such things wouldn't happen in a government established for the people," said Andrei. "Men and women would have free artistic expression."

Yuri wasn't in the mood for his brother's political rhetoric. Since he hadn't seen the two all summer, he changed the subject by asking what they had been doing while apart. What followed was a continual flow of chatter between them as they filled each other in on the intervening months. It was almost like old times. Yuri spoke mostly about his hospital work, never mentioning the Crimea or Katya. He did tell about his meeting with Rasputin.

"I've never met anyone quite like him," Yuri told his friends.

"Is it true he counsels the tsar and tsaritsa?" asked Talia.

"They telephoned him once while I was there and requested him to come to the palace."

"Leave it to our esteemed tsar," Andrei muttered, "to seek counsel from a debauched priest."

"You're speaking out of ignorance," Yuri said.

"All of St. Petersburg read the stories in the newspaper last year, which all but said Rasputin and the tsaritsa were having an affair—"

"Rubbish," Yuri snapped. "Only left-wing malcontents would believe such lies."

"And why, then, upon their publication was the so-called *starets* summarily dismissed from the Capital?"

"But he is back, isn't he?"

"Only proving the tsar is so weak-kneed he can't even say no to his wife. But what really surprises me, Yuri, is that you, after one meeting, are defending Rasputin. Has he got you under his spell, too?"

"Never mind!" Yuri sulked. He wasn't entirely certain what he thought about Rasputin, and he hated being forced into a position in which he had to defend the man.

"Good heavens! He has!"

"Shut up, Andrei! You don't know what you're talking about—as usual."

"He's just concerned about you, Yuri," put in Talia. "I've heard stories myself about how Rasputin can hypnotize his subjects."

"I'm sorry I even brought up the subject." Yuri shook his head. "Just forget about it."

"How can I forget it when I see my own brother seduced by such evil?" Andrei pressed, his voice laced with conviction. "Don't you see, Rasputin represents all that is most despicable about Russia—the backward barbarism steeped in superstition. And, of course, the tsar supports this creature because he knows these attitudes are the surest way to deaden the force of the class struggle. He as well as the landowners and the bourgeois have used the concept of God only to exploit their own interests. Lenin has rightly called God the opiate of the people—"

"Oh, Andrei!" Talia interrupted. "Don't say such things. What would your mother say?"

"Yes, Andrei," Yuri challenged, "do you deny God, then?"

"I deny anything that would oppress and deceive the very people it purports to help. I deny the tsarist presentation of God. Perhaps Mama worships a different God."

"There is only one God," Talia murmured.

"Then, something is wrong somewhere." Andrei was clearly attempting to moderate his zeal, but Yuri knew the attempt was for Talia's sake, not Yuri's.

"You could never completely throw aside your faith, Andrei," said Yuri.

"I'm not taking issue with the *existence* of God," Andrei countered, "as I admit many Bolsheviks do. Rather, I repudiate a certain *concept* of God. A concept based on superstition, repression, and ignorance. And it is in the name of that God, that concept of God, that the tsar practically worships that holy fool of his and places the fate not only of his family but also of the nation in the hands of that lewd, insane charlatan. How can any rational man do this?"

"You know only the propaganda those radical papers declare—half of which are completely biased, if not outright lies."

"I'll have you know I contribute to those papers! Are you calling me a liar?"

"Enough of this!" Talia interjected sharply. "You two be civil to one another or I shall leave."

Both brothers quieted and made an effort to calm their previous heat. Finally Andrei tossed a couple of rubles on the table.

"That should cover my tea," he said, rising.

"You're not leaving?" Talia's large eyes lifted beseechingly toward Andrei.

"It's better than ruining your party."

"It's as good as ruined anyway, if you leave."

"No it isn't." Andrei glanced back and forth between Talia and his brother. "You won't miss me at all. See you later."

Talia watched Andrei walk away with an odd sadness, almost a sense of loss, weighing her. She fleetingly wondered what would happen if one day Yuri actually returned her love and they—wonder of wonders!—actually married. Would she then lose Andrei's friendship? The two brothers seemed to grow more antagonistic toward each other as each day passed. If she did ever marry Yuri, there was a strong possibility that Andrei would stay away.

The prospect of that was more agonizing to Talia than even she could rightly explain. But Andrei was her dearest friend, perhaps even more so than Yuri was. Even with their busy schedules, she and Andrei managed to see each other at least once a week. They talked about practically everything, encouraging each other, and comforting each other when it was necessary.

Yuri was her friend, too, but they hadn't seen each other all summer. When Talia needed to talk to a friend, it was Andrei, not Yuri, whom she sought out. What did that mean? Did her love for Yuri—that romantic love—place their relationship on a different level? Or was his rejection of her a wedge between them? Was the relationship of marriage different, then, from that of friends? She had been too young when her father died to remember her mother's marriage to her father, but she still had a very vivid memory of Anna and Sergei's marriage. And it seemed to Talia that their relationship encompassed many different facets and levels. Friends, lovers, confidants, playmates.

Talia thought she'd have to marry *both* Yuri and Andrei to have all that! She smiled at the idea.

"What's the joke?" asked Yuri.

Talia reddened. She could never reveal what she had been thinking. Maybe to Andrei, but never to Yuri. Or could she?

"Oh, nothing. Just thinking about the future, I guess."

"It seems to be a bright and happy future you contemplate."

"I hope so."

"It'll only happen if you don't fall in love, Talia."

"It makes me sad to see you so cynical, Yuri."

"That's what love does to a person. It grinds a man's heart into the dirt, then brutally kicks it. I'll never love again."

"Just because one love doesn't work out doesn't mean you should give up completely. What if that person wasn't meant for you—and the right person is out there somewhere waiting?"

"You always were a romantic optimist, Talia. I suppose I used to be a bit of a romantic, too. That's probably why this has happened to me. And maybe that's also why I believe very strongly Katya is the person for me—the *right* person."

"Katya?"

The name almost caught in Talia's throat. Somehow it made it much more painful to have a name attached to what had before only been a gnawing fear.

"That's right. I never told you about her. It's just as well. I'll probably never see her again."

"Why?"

"That's the worst of it. I don't really know. I've never known anyone so mercurial. One minute she is warm and responsive to me, then the next she acts as if we are strangers. We had a huge argument, but afterward when I tried to analyze it, I simply couldn't put my finger on exactly what we had argued about. It was almost as if she picked a fight simply for the sake of picking a fight."

"Why would anyone do that?"

Yuri shook his head. "I can't figure it out for the life of me."

"Unless . . ." Talia paused. Was she going to act as counselor and matchmaker? The idea appalled her.

"What, Talia? If you have some insight, please tell me. I've always respected your opinion."

She couldn't deny him. "Maybe for some reason she is afraid of her own feelings for you. Maybe she is confused."

"She's hardly the 'confused' type. In many respects she is very self-assured. Yet there are times . . ."

"We all have times of doubt, even the most confident person."

"You may be right."

They were quiet for a few minutes, sipping tea, munching on sweet cakes. Then Talia said, "Yuri, if it turns out this Katya isn't the woman for you, will you promise not to give up on love?"

He shrugged. "It would really bother you if I did?"

"Very much. I mean, it might make you hard and bitter."

He smiled and reached across the table, taking her hand in his.

"Well, I'll always have you, Talia, won't I? You will keep me from getting bitter."

Talia sighed. The brotherly expression he wore, the dispassionate tone, were even more painful than the specter of a girl named Katya.

III

BROTHERLY DISCORD

Spring 1914

25

Yuri sat hunched over a microscope in the hospital laboratory. His eyes were red and sore. He had been awakened in the middle of the previous night for an emergency birth, which prevented him from getting back to his bed before his regular shift began in the morning. His shift lasted fourteen hours, and afterward he should have gone to bed, but he was too tense and keyed up from the busy day to sleep. Besides, he knew that the hospital laboratory would be relatively free that evening, and he wanted a chance to work at a microscope.

Since little Vasily's death, Yuri had developed something of an obsession with hematology. He realized physicians were not omnipotent, yet he hated the sense of utter helplessness he had felt at the child's deathbed. In this day and age, with all its vast medical advances, there ought to have been some way to save a poor child. Yet it might as well be the Dark Ages where Vasily's bleeding disease was concerned. There must be a cure for it—or, at the very least, some viable and successful ways to treat it. Toward that end, Yuri had been studying everything he could find, not only about hemophilia, but also about the blood in general. He had managed, in spite of feeling a bit like a ghoul, to get some blood and tissue samples from the boy's corpse. He was also making an extensive study of normal blood, hoping that in learning the properties of normal blood coagulation, he might discover a way to strengthen abnormal blood.

He rubbed his eyes. What a high opinion he had of himself! That he, a lowly intern, had even a prayer of making such a great discovery. Still, he was driven to try. Besides, it distracted his mind from his great disillusionment regarding Katya. He had felt so hopeful last fall. But he had not seen her since. The half dozen letters he wrote to her in Moscow had gone unanswered. He had hoped she would be in St. Petersburg for the social season, from Christmas to Lent, but as far as he knew she had stayed away.

Perhaps it was time to give up on her. Forget her. If only that were possible!

But he could not let go. It was almost as if he were under some kind of evil spell.

Even now, after so long, he could still clearly visualize her luminescent beauty, her disarming honesty, her childlike vulnerability. And, ironically, it became harder and harder to remember her mercurial personality and the way she had hurt him.

He slipped a new slide beneath the lens of the scope. It was a sample of his own blood, and he placed it beside a slide of Vasily's blood, increasing the microscope's magnification to its highest level. He didn't hear the lab door open and, thus, the intrusive voice startled him.

"I thought I'd find you here, my boy."

Yuri turned sharply, bumping his nose against the scope's eyepiece, almost knocking over the machine. He caught it in time.

"Didn't mean to startle you." It was Dr. Botkin.

"I was rather deep in thought. Perhaps too deep," said Yuri.

"Still studying blood, I gather."

"Yes, but to no avail, I'm afraid."

"Not *yet*."

Yuri gave a self-deprecating shrug. "Maybe I'll discover something, but at this point I doubt it will be regarding hemophilia. The greatest medical minds in the world have failed—"

"You don't give yourself enough credit, Yuri. The fresh insights of youth are often where great discoveries are born. And, in addition to that, you, my boy, have one of the finest medical minds in this country—"

"Please, Doctor, that is a bit much," Yuri protested, truly embarrassed by such words from his mentor.

"Well, I will concede that your mind now is green and unproven, but the potential is there. I have read your research notes. You have come to conclusions in a few months that seasoned veterans have taken years to reach. You have as much chance of making a new discovery as anyone." Botkin drew close, focusing intensely at Yuri. "Don't give up, Yuri! I will support you in any way you need."

Vasily had been Botkin's patient, too, but Yuri sensed there was more to the elder doctor's intensity than sympathy over the lost child. Yuri's studies had led him to some interesting insights besides the purely *medical*.

"I won't give up, Doctor, not soon, at least. I know there are other sufferers of that terrible plight, and even if they be high and mighty, they, too, touch my heart."

"What are you saying, Yuri?"

"It didn't take much for me to deduce the secret being kept at Tsarskoe Selo," Yuri answered, perhaps a bit more dramatically than was necessary. "In researching the disease, I discovered a definite pattern as I traced it through the royal houses of Europe. It first showed up in Queen Victoria's youngest son, Leopold. No evidence of it among British Royalty before that. But she had five daughters, all potential carriers of the disease. Of those, two, Alice and Beatrice, have had hemophiliac offspring. We know then that Alice, our tsaritsa's mother, was a carrier, and thus all of her daughters—five, to be exact—are potential carriers."

"It still seems a bit of a leap you are taking to draw conclusions about the tsar's family."

"Yes, it is. But what else would be crippling the tsarevich to the extent that he must be carried about in public by that sailor who is always with him? It could be a number of things. Still, I have heard rumors for years, and then there was that episode at Spala two years ago when the child came so close to death the public was at last notified. Yet no one has ever been told the exact nature of the boy's ailment. We are left but to wonder."

"And draw conclusions."

"Such an ailment as hemophilia could destroy the monarchy faster than any revolutionary. If the people knew there was no viable direct heir, it might well be the deciding factor in discarding the monarchy altogether. But, Doctor, I don't want to place you in an awkward position. I understand you are sworn to confidentiality in this matter. I don't even want you to tell me if I am right or wrong. But if the tsarevich might benefit from my research, it gives me that much more reason to continue to pursue it."

"You bear no ill feelings toward our rulers? I could hardly blame you if you did, after what happened to your father."

"I don't blame the tsar, and I especially don't blame a ten-year-old child. I think they are as much victims of a decrepit and twisted system as my father was. Did you know that several years ago my adopted sister had opportunity to have a private audience with Nicholas and Alexandra? She was quite impressed, especially by the tsar's gentle, humane nature. She felt them to be basically decent people, and I highly respect her judgment on such matters. I believe in judging people on their individual merits. Perhaps that comes of my apolitical nature. But, as a doctor, I don't see how I can do otherwise."

"You'd be surprised, my boy, at how many in the medical profession do just that. But we can only be true to our own selves. And, Yuri, because I feel as if we understand each other, I believe the secret to which you alluded earlier is safe with you."

"You can be certain of it, Doctor."

"It might well be, Yuri, that at some time I would call upon your expertise in treating my very special patient."

Yuri's stomach lurched. "I . . . I don't know what to say . . . I can't imagine what I could possibly do that isn't already being done."

"Always remember, Yuri, the importance of a fresh perspective. Now, if you would permit me, I'd like to change the subject."

Yuri nodded his consent.

"As you know, in a few days I will be departing with the royal family for the Crimea. All my regular duties here have been dispersed among my colleagues, but there is one thing that has slipped my attention until now. I had planned to attend a cardiology symposium at Moscow University. I would like to request that you go in my place. It will only take you away from your duties here for three days, but I think it would be quite valuable to you."

"I'd be honored to go, sir."

"Excellent! Now, one final matter. You look absolutely spent, Yuri. When was the last time you ate?" He paused a moment but didn't give Yuri a chance to tell him he'd last had some tea and a pastry at midday. "Never mind. I am under orders from my wife to bring you home for dinner tonight no matter how late the hour."

Yuri glanced at the microscope.

Perceiving Yuri's ambivalence, Botkin added, "Your efforts at research will be useless if you die of starvation. So, let's say in the interest of the national welfare you must take a break for sustenance."

"Putting it that way, sir, I can hardly argue."

As usual Yuri had a pleasant time at the Botkin home in Tsarskoe Selo. Yuri helped Botkin's young son, Gleb, with a science problem from school and listened to his daughter play a newly learned tune on the piano. The two doctors talked "shop" for a time, but nothing too seriously, and listened to Countess Botkin's stories of the daily happenings and gossip from the Tsar's Village—as Tsarskoe Selo was called because of the cluster of homes of nobility around the tsar's palace. The only topic of conversation that was in any way intense was when Botkin mentioned the current deliberations at the hospital over choosing a new chief of surgery. Yuri didn't hide his surprise when he heard that Karl Vlasenko was in the running. He had worked with Vlasenko on several occasions, and though his level of competence appeared to have improved since his military service, he was still little more than a mediocre doctor. In Yuri's opinion there were many on staff at the hospital who were far more worthy of the post whose names weren't even on the list of nominees.

"Unfortunately," Botkin explained, though unnecessarily, "politics has as much to do with these things as competence. But rest assured, Yuri, I doubt Karl has much of a chance. His name has been passed over twice before for this post. His medical skills aside, he greatly lacks in proper leadership qualities."

"That is a relief," said Yuri. "Did you know the Vlasenkos are distant relatives of mine? Our families have been at odds for years. I hate to think that colors my opinion of him, but—"

At that moment the telephone rang, the sound coming into the parlor from the alcove where the phone was located. A servant appeared at the parlor door within seconds.

"Sir, it is the palace."

Botkin cocked a perplexed eyebrow, then excused himself. When he returned, his face was lined with concern. "Yuri, I am needed at the palace. Please forgive my hasty departure."

"I understand, Doctor. I must be on my way also."

Yuri walked out with Botkin, and since the tsar was sending a motorcar for him, Botkin insisted Yuri take the carriage back to the train station. On the quiet carriage ride, he thought about the evening. He wondered what had happened at the palace to require a physician. He tried to imagine what he would do if called upon to treat the tsarevich. Had he learned anything that might lend, as Botkin called it, a fresh perspective? Sadly, he knew the answer was a negative.

Back in the hospital laboratory, he worked for several more hours before returning home in the early hours of the morning. He practically fell into his bed and slept for five hours, so soundly that his mother had to wake him in the morning. And he might have slept on except for the telephone call from Dr. Botkin.

26

Yuri dressed as quickly as he could, then hired a cab to take him to the train station. He arrived moments before the next train for Tsarskoe Selo was to depart. Only as he sat back on the train did he allow himself a chance to grow apprehensive about what lay ahead.

Botkin had made good on his offer to include Yuri in the care of the tsarevich much sooner than anyone would have expected. It was pure chance that a need for a physician had come so quickly on the heels of Botkin's offer. And Yuri's first impulse had been to flatly refuse. But his awe at being invited quickly overwhelmed that impulse. After all, one simply did not refuse an invitation to the Imperial palace, especially after Botkin had gone to some effort to secure permission for Yuri's presence.

Botkin explained on the phone, "When I was called away last night, it was to attend to the tsarevich, who had a toothache. He'd had it all day and it worsened to the point that the child was in tears. I believe he really feared it was another bleeding episode and that's why he was so upset. I determined that the tooth had abscessed and needed to be extracted. You can understand, Yuri, that in a hemophiliac this is not a procedure to be taken lightly."

"I doubt I would attempt it except as a last resort," said Yuri.

"Yes . . . and it has come to that point. I sat with the boy all night and the condition has worsened. His little mouth is swollen, and I fear a systemic infection should the abscess rupture. All are agreed, including the parents, that we must proceed."

"What do you wish of me, Doctor?"

"I have secured approval from the tsar that you be present for the operation."

"Me?"

"Professor Fedorov's assistant can't be here." Fedorov was one of the most respected physicians in the country and a renowned professor of medicine at the university. "Besides, when the tsar heard about your extensive research, he wanted to do anything possible to support you. If observing this procedure could somehow further your insights into the disease, then he was all for it. Also, it appears, he has a bit of a soft spot for the Fedorcenko name."

"He pardoned my father shortly before he was killed on Bloody Sunday."

"Well, His Majesty has a high regard for your family. Can you be here by nine this morning? I have already arranged for someone to cover your shift at the hospital."

A motorcar met Yuri at the station at Tsarskoe Selo and took him to the Alexander Palace. At the palace door, he was taken directly to a small sitting room, where Botkin met him a few minutes later.

"We are nearly ready," Botkin said. "Come with me, and I'll show you where to change and scrub up." He continued talking as he led Yuri through a door on the opposite end of the sitting room into a room with a wash basin, shelves of linens and various instruments and other medical equipment. The Imperial infirmary. Botkin indicated that this room led to a treatment/examination room that they had set up for the tooth extraction.

Yuri slipped off his coat and jacket, and Botkin helped him into a surgical gown. Then he scrubbed his hands at the wash basin as Botkin filled him in on his plan of action—Botkin was already wearing his gown, but he, too, scrubbed his hands. This done, they went into the treatment room, which Yuri found to be quite well-appointed and meticulously clean. Fedorov was already there, gowned, gloved, and ready for action. Also with him was Dr. Breit, a dentist. Introductions were made, and Yuri was pleased that Fedorov remembered him from the university.

"Yuri, would you help me with these gloves?" asked Botkin.

Yuri carefully picked up a pair of gloves lying on a sterile tray and held them as Botkin slipped into them. Yuri would not be gloved since he would mainly be observing and fetching supplies for the doctors.

"I've sent for our patient," Fedorov said.

Botkin nodded. "Everything appears in order."

The four doctors chatted a few moments until a servant came and announced the arrival of the tsarevich. Botkin went to meet them, and through the open door, Yuri caught a glimpse of the tsaritsa with her son. Her face was pale, her eyes ringed with dark circles from lack of sleep and worry. Botkin had a few words with her, then led the child into the treatment room while the mother waited outside. The tsarevich also showed signs of lack of sleep and his fine-featured face was red and swollen. He was seated in a wheelchair. He was also heavily sedated, for Botkin had administered a large dose of cocaine half an hour ago.

"Your Highness," said Botkin as he helped Alexis into a special dental chair, "as you can see, you are in very good hands. I believe you know all present except Prince Fedorcenko."

"Is he a doctor?" asked Alexis in a rather garbled tone from both his swollen jaw and the effects of the cocaine.

"Yes, and a very good one, too. He will be assisting us."

"Will it make me bleed, Dr. Botkin?"

"I should think a little, but we are prepared, Your Highness, with all the latest remedies. All we require of you, young man, is that you relax as much as you can. Think of your trip next week to the Crimea, and the warm ocean, and all the lovely sunshine."

"I'll try."

"You'll do very well." Botkin turned to Yuri. "Yuri, would you remove the cover from the instrument table? I believe we are ready to begin."

The doctors finished their final preparations, and Yuri uncovered the table as he was told. The instruments gleamed and were in perfect order. Obviously, this was no ordinary procedure. Their patient was the heir to the throne of Russia! That thought alone made Yuri's stomach lurch. And that unsettling sensation was only increased by the fact that one wrong move, one mistaken slip of the hand, could mean disaster. Yuri thought of his brother. He wondered what Andrei would think if he knew the future of the hated monarchy rested, for the next half hour at least, entirely in the hands of Yuri and the other doctors.

But Yuri didn't allow himself to dwell on such thoughts. This was only a ten-year-old child, in pain, suffering, afraid. Even Andrei would not be able to wish death on such a poor, helpless being.

As the operation proceeded, Yuri cleared all his wayward thoughts so he could focus on the task at hand. Dr. Breit had wedged an ice pack in the boy's mouth so as to lower the temperature of the area and hopefully retard circulation. The tsarevich was sitting quietly; in fact, once he was settled into the chair his eyes drooped shut. Hopefully the drugs would prevent him from feeling more than a little pain from the procedure itself.

Suddenly the treatment room door burst open, letting in a draft of cold air. Yuri was the first to see the intruder. It was Rasputin. Yuri didn't know what to say or if he should say anything. He knew that the *starets* had a certain amount of latitude with the royal family, but wasn't this too much? It was bad enough that the man was not garbed in proper surgical attire, but the reek of his body indicated he wasn't even washed.

Botkin was the first to speak. "What is the meaning of this?" His tone was even and calm. He apparently was willing to give the *starets* the benefit of the doubt.

But Rasputin answered defensively. "The tsaritsa called me to be here for this affair. And before you begin I insist you allow me to pray over the boy."

"This is a sterile operating theater, and you are not dressed properly."

"Do you think God incapable of protecting the child from a few germs?"

"I will not become involved in a theological debate with you, Father Grigori. But if you have real concern for the boy, you will leave so we can proceed. Your prayers are welcome, but say them in the waiting room."

"If I truly had my way, there would be no doctors at all digging and probing at the poor little one. The hand of God protects him and heals him. My prayers alone, not your precious, sterile instruments and scientific procedures, will ease the child's discomfort. But because the tsar wills it, I will allow you to proceed. Nevertheless, it is also his will that I pray over the child. Take it up with His Imperial Highness, if you wish to ignore his royal will."

Rasputin then strode all the way into the room and drew up within inches of the tsarevich. The doctors, needing to maintain their sterility, could hardly prevent him, nor did they wish for an altercation in the tsarevich's presence—or at any time, for that matter! Yuri might have been able to block the priest's approach, but that was the furthest thing from his mind at the moment, and, thankfully, the other doctors didn't expect it of him. Only when Rasputin drew a crucifix from his pocket and held it in his grimy hand directly over the instrument table did Yuri find some courage to comment.

"Father Grigori, can you withdraw your hand? The instruments . . ." Yuri's voice faded away lamely when Rasputin focused a chilling glance in his direction. None of the congeniality of their last meeting was evident in that look.

"Now I know why I have little use for doctors," said the priest. But in a minute, he did reposition his arm so that it was away from the instruments.

That was the only concession he made, however. As the doctors continued, Rasputin remained close by, mumbling prayers and breathing his fetid breath all over the sterile field.

The extraction went smoothly enough. The bleeding did not get out of hand, and Alexis was smiling an hour later. Of course, the credit for the success of the procedure went entirely to Rasputin. His prayers had guided the hands of the doctors and had miraculously closed up the child's blood vessels. Yuri had complete confidence that the operation would have been successful regardless. When he had first met Rasputin, he had been willing to give the man the benefit of his holy orders. But now he only wondered about a man, a mere mortal, who was so arrogant, so full of himself, that he would risk the safety of a child because he thought his germs were somehow exempt from natural laws. It simply did not seem right to Yuri. But more than that, he could never after that day shake the memory of Rasputin's cold, contemptuous look. There had been nothing at all saintly about it. It had even lacked the element of righteous indignation. It had simply been ugly.

27

Andrei was at last having his gallery exhibit. It had taken longer than planned—over a year since he had first heard about the opportunity. But it had turned into a more awesome commitment than he had anticipated.

Yuri would have said that was so typical of him, leaping into something without carefully looking about. In this case, he supposed it was true, as it was about his commitment to Kaminsky that he had never followed up on. But after his talk with Talia he gained a more realistic sense regarding his future. Nevertheless, producing twenty-four quality works of art had been no lark, especially when the realities of life were bound to intercede. In order to maintain his pride, he'd been forced to take on outside work, mostly grueling factory work from which he often came home so exhausted the last thing he wanted to do was paint.

But he had made it at last, and there was a fine turnout, too. Of course he had expected his family to be there. Even his grandparents had come up from the Crimea especially for the showing. Most importantly, however, Talia was there. The centerpiece of the exhibit was the painting of her as "Dawn." She had not seen it completed, and Andrei had worried that she would not make it because she was touring Europe with the ballet company, and the only date the gallery had available was a mere two days after her last show in Berlin. But miraculously, she had made it. Yuri had met her at Warsaw Station and brought her directly to the gallery.

No one thought much of it when Andrei strode exuberantly up to her, embraced her, and kissed her on her soft, pale cheek. Those observers couldn't hear his heart pound, nor feel the passion course through him as he held her close. But, then again, neither could Talia feel these things or even notice them. She couldn't know how hard it was for him not to press his lips against her sweet lips, tasting her, loving her . . .

Only Yuri gave Andrei a somewhat strange look after he welcomed Talia. But Andrei ignored it and tried to ignore his brother altogether. He tried not to notice how Talia was with Yuri almost exclusively when Andrei's attention, as guest of honor, was demanded elsewhere. But he couldn't deny the sickening fact that, even after months abroad and exposure to the créme de la créme of European society, she was still in love with Yuri.

Andrei made that much more of an effort to throw himself into the festivities of the evening, flitting among the other guests, shamelessly promoting himself and his art. If nothing else, maybe he could make a sale or two.

He sidled up to a heavyset man who was admiring a work entitled "Frosty Morning," an Impressionistic piece he had done a few years ago that captured a scene of a lone skater on a small pond on the Neva with the city-scape vaguely rising in the background.

Andrei found it was a singularly uninspired work and had included it in the show only as filler. But the man gazing at it as he leaned heavily on a cane seemed rather taken with it. He was obviously not a connoisseur of the arts.

"I painted that several winters ago," Andrei offered, not mentioning that he had been inexperienced and unenlightened at the time. "Do you know that was the coldest day in St. Petersburg for ten years before and since?"

"How interesting. I believe I recognize that pond." The man shifted his weight so that he could look at the painting from another angle. "Yes, it looks quite familiar—"

"It should," came a new voice from behind both men. Andrei recognized it immediately as belonging to his grandfather.

Both Andrei and the heavyset man turned sharply. "Grandfather," said Andrei.

"Grandfather. . . ?" The heavy man was truly perplexed, his flabby brow creasing.

Viktor seemed amused at the man's befuddlement. "Didn't you know, Count Vlasenko, that the great artist, Andrei Christinin, whose work you are so admiring is my grandson? A small world, isn't it?" To Andrei he added, "This is Count Cyril Vlasenko, Andrei, our distant relative. And I am not surprised that pond looks familiar to you, Count. The Fedorcenko Estate overlooks it."

Vlasenko rallied quickly from his surprise. "You, of course, must mean the *Vlasenko* Estate."

"Yes, of course . . ." Viktor said coldly.

Andrei knew well the Vlasenko name, even if he hadn't been able to immediately recognize the person. But before he could respond or attempt to diffuse the chilly atmosphere, Viktor spoke again.

"It's been a long time, Cyril. I believe I can be big enough to let go of the past, if you can."

Vlasenko shrugged. "What past, eh? And to prove how big I can be—figuratively speaking, of course—" He paused to chuckle at his wit, and Viktor managed a smile also. "I wish to purchase this painting. I think it will make an excellent gift for my son, who, by the way, is about to be made Chief of Surgery at the St. Petersburg Sisters of Charity Hospital."

"Yes, I've heard," said Viktor. "My grandson Yuri is an intern there."

"Is he, now? Well, perhaps one day he will rise to such heights."

"I don't doubt it a bit. He's already been called as a consultant at the Imperial palace." Andrei saw the proud gleam in his grandfather's eye and knew that, though the two men *spoke* of burying the past, they would always be rivals.

"Ah, yes . . . well, about the painting. Would you take thirty rubles for it?"

Andrei couldn't tell if Vlasenko was speaking tongue-in-cheek or not. He certainly appeared serious in his offer. Andrei tried not to show his affront—he wouldn't give the man the satisfaction. But thirty rubles would barely cover the cost of materials on a painting the size of "Frosty Morning." But he knew he had to make some response, and quickly, because he saw fire begin to flash in his grandfather's eyes.

"Count Vlasenko, I wouldn't dream of selling one of my paintings to a member of the family. Please, take it as a gift," Andrei said amiably. The look of surprise on Vlasenko's face and the approving look on Viktor's face was reward enough.

"Well, I . . . I don't know what to say."

"A mere thanks is plenty."

"All right . . . thank you."

As Vlasenko waddled away, Viktor grinned and put an arm around Andrei. "That was an inspired gesture, son. I don't think I've ever seen that old scoundrel at such a loss for words. But it is a shame he will now possess one of your paintings."

"That's a terrible piece of work, Grandfather. I think the Vlasenkos deserve it."

Viktor burst out laughing and was still chuckling a while later when Andrei saw him talking with his wife. And Andrei felt an odd sense of pride that he had struck a blow for the family honor. It almost made him regret abandoning the family name.

Later he shared the story of the incident with Yuri and Talia, who also milked a good laugh from it.

"But Vlasenko is in for a big disappointment," said Yuri, "if he thinks Karl has a chance at that promotion. He's already been passed over, and I have it on good authority that he doesn't have a chance this time."

"I'll bet you'd have the job, Yuri, if you weren't just an intern," said Talia, her girlish admiration obvious. "Andrei, did Yuri tell you about attending the tsarevich?"

"Of course," Andrei responded drolly. "He's been gloating about it for days. Next thing we know he will start behaving like Rasputin himself."

"Heaven forbid!" said Yuri.

"So, you've changed your tune about that charlatan?" Yuri shrugged, and Andrei knew it was hard for him to admit his mistake, but Andrei pressed relentlessly. "It wasn't long ago you were singing the Mad Monk's praises. Whatever happened?"

"I was not praising the man. I was merely countering your outrageous remarks about his importance in the government. And, no matter what anyone thinks of Rasputin, it is pure hogwash to believe the tsar is controlled in any way by him."

"So, now you are just a loyal monarchist, eh, brother?" challenged Andrei. "It didn't take much for them to get you to kiss their—"

"Here we go again!" Talia rolled her eyes. "But I'm not going to put up with it this time. I'm going to visit with your mother." And she turned as swiftly and gracefully as if she were on stage and strode away.

Andrei scowled at Yuri.

"What did I do?" Yuri protested.

"Nothing. I'll see you later, too. I've got business to do." Andrei turned too, wondering why he continued to put up with things as they were. He was a fool, and it was absolutely no comfort that Yuri was no less a fool.

Yuri tried to distract himself by studying his brother's paintings. But he made no pretense at understanding art, especially Andrei's modern interpretation of art. For example, the work in front of him called "Portrait of Pavlokov." He assumed it was supposed to represent their uncle Paul. Yuri did see a couple of eyes in the painting, one near the top and another about six inches lower and to the left of the work; there was also a hand—a very nice hand, too, long and fine, emulating intelligence and sensitivity, very obviously belonging to a man like Uncle Paul. Yet it was located somewhere in the vicinity of where a knee should be. And, other than those body parts, there was little else that hinted at the human form in the painting. If Yuri were a psychoanalyst, he might diagnose the creator of that piece of art as having serious mental problems.

However, even Yuri had to admit he was impressed by the painting of "Dawn." Knowing it was of Talia only made it that much more intriguing. It was a deeply moving work, even if the abstract presentation was hard to fathom. It occurred to Yuri that the artist could not have produced such a work without some intense feelings toward his subject. But then again, what did he know about the artistic process?

"Quite a fascinating work, isn't it?" came a voice at Yuri's back.

"Vladimir!" Yuri greeted his friend Vladimir Baklanov. "I had no idea you were a patron of the arts."

"Galleries are wonderful places to meet women of means, you know."

"Oh, you cad!" Yuri slapped him on the back. "It's good to see you. How long has it been?"

"Three months since I joined that law firm in Moscow."

"And so, are you now a converted Muscovite?"

"Are you kidding? I jumped at the chance to take a case here in the Capital. I only arrived yesterday, heard about Andrei's showing, and hoped to see you here."

"That's ironic, because I'll be going to Moscow in a few days—only for a medical conference, though. Just a brief stay."

"Well, I shall be here for a few weeks, so when you return from Moscow we can get together. I want to visit all the old haunts—The Bear, The Villa Rhode, you know, like old times."

"You act as if you've been in a social vacuum in Moscow."

"It hasn't near the attractions of Petersburg. But I can help you make a few social connections should you want some diversion while you are there."

"Really?" Yuri rubbed his chin thoughtfully. "Then, you do get around socially there?"

"Of course."

"Perhaps you are familiar with a certain family—the Zhenechkas."

"Yes, in fact our firm represents Count Zhenechka's business—what a tyrant he is! You'd think with all that vodka he produces he'd be a bit looser."

"Well, I wasn't exactly interested in the count."

"Ah, his daughter . . . now, I remember, you met her at Youssoupov's engagement party last year. Are you and she. . . ?"

"I'm working on it."

Vladimir's brow creased and the jovial glint in his eyes momentarily dimmed.

"What is it, Vlad?" It had never occurred to Yuri until then that perhaps Katya's failure to reply to his letters had been due to some tragedy in her life. Perhaps she was ill—or worse.

"How long has it been since you've seen or heard from her?"

"Months, I suppose. Is something wrong?" But when Vladimir hesitated, Yuri pressed, "Come on, Vlad, tell me."

"Well, Yuri, it's just that I have seen her on several occasions. We often travel in the same social circles, especially since there are such a limited number of social circles there, you know—but, of course, society in Russia is like that, isn't it—?"

"Vlad, get on with it! Tell me about Katya."

"You really care for her, Yuri?" Yuri only gave him a dark look that said he was losing his patience, and Vladimir continued. "Every time I've seen her, Yuri, she has been with the same man, a Count Pytor Prokunin. I heard a rumor that they . . ." He paused, licked his lips, and reluctantly finished, "Well, Yuri, that they are as good as engaged."

"A rumor, you say?"

"I know for a fact—and this is privileged information, and I am risking a great deal in telling you because of client-lawyer confidentiality—but Count Zhenechka has had our firm draw up papers regarding dowry and such for a match between Prokunin and his daughter. I tell you only because of our friendship."

Yuri nodded dumbly. Why should he be surprised? Katya had done little to encourage him beyond that glorious week in the Crimea. But that week had been so—he shook his head, trying to erase those sweet memories. He looked at his friend, hoping he appeared cool and aloof.

"Then, I guess that's it."

Vladimir's brow furrowed with concern. "You'll be all right?"

"Of course. Why not? It was just a whim, nothing more. We . . . we were practically strangers. She didn't mean a thing to me. I'm happy for her. I think I will send her a congratulatory note—yes, of course, I must wish her happiness and a long life with Count Prokunin—a happy marriage. She deserves it—"

"Yuri?"

"I've got to get out of here." Yuri ran a finger under his collar as if he were choking.

"I know just the thing for you. Let's go."

"I'd best tell my mother," Yuri said. "She came with me, you know."

"I'll meet you outside."

Anna, Talia, and Raisa were talking together as Yuri approached. "Mama, I'd like to leave now. Do you think Grandfather could see you and Aunt Raisa and Talia home?"

"I'm sure that would be fine, Yuri. Is everything all right?"

"Yes, of course." But his voice was thin, strained.

"Are you certain?" Talia asked.

"I'm not certain of anything." Why hide it? "Except that I have to get out of here."

"Andrei will be disappointed," his mother said.

"He'll understand."

Talia caught his arm as he turned. "Did you have another fight?"

"No," he answered shortly, then realizing she didn't deserve his ire, added more contritely, "Nothing like that. I'm just a bit mixed up right now, that's all."

"Do you need some company?"

If only Katya had reached out to him with such genuine concern. "I don't want to spoil your evening."

"We can explain to Andrei. As you said, he will understand."

The last thing Yuri wanted just then was to face Andrei again. His next words were completely selfish, but he didn't really care at that point. "He looks busy right now—" Indeed, Andrei was conversing with what appeared to be interested patrons. "Mama, would you let Andrei know as soon as he is free?" Then, without waiting for a reply, he grabbed Talia's hand and practically fled the gallery.

28

The boisterous atmosphere of the St. Petersburg nightclubs did little to numb Yuri's wounded heart. He moved in the midst of the noise, the music, the laughter detached and unaffected. He couldn't laugh; he could barely smile. He could hardly taste the wine. Even the gypsy music at the Villa Rhode left him unmoved. When, at some point during the night, Vladimir met an old female acquaintance and begged to be excused from Yuri's glum company, Yuri didn't protest.

Anyway, he still had Talia, though he had been as detached from her as from everything else.

"Are you ready to leave?" he asked her when they were alone. No sense dragging her down with him.

"Whenever you are, Yuri. I'm just here to . . ."

When her voice trailed away, probably unable to define just why she was there, Yuri patted her hand and managed a thin smile. "You're here to support me, Talia, just like always."

"What else are friends for?"

"And you are the dearest friend a man ever had!"

"Yes . . ." Her brow knit together and her eyes were sad.

"I'm sorry, Talia dear, for making you sad."

"It's not that, Yuri."

"What is it, then?"

"Do you still want to leave? I could use some fresh air."

They took a cab from the Villa Rhode back into downtown, then Yuri suggested they walk for a while. He didn't want to admit that the evening had drained his pocketbook and he couldn't afford a ride the rest of the way home. Anyway, it was a fine June night. The sky was clear, and though the air was crisp, the snow was all melted.

They walked for a while in silence. He hadn't even mentioned the cause of his mood to Talia, but the distractions of the evening had been no help. He decided perhaps he did need to talk after all.

"Talia, are you happy with your life—with the ballet and all?"

"Yes, for the most part. I enjoy dancing, but I don't think I will ever be a great dancer like Pavlova. Ballet simply doesn't consume me as I believe it does her. My contentment isn't entirely contingent on dancing. I want other things out of life."

"What do you want?"

"A husband, children—very simple things, I suppose."

"And have you a prospect in mind—for a husband?"

"Oh, Yuri," she sighed. "What a question . . ."

"I want you to be happy, Talia. At least one of us should be."

"And you are not, poor, dear Yuri." Her words were a statement of the obvious, not a question. She gazed up at him with those sweet doe eyes of hers, not with pity but with such an open love that it caught his breath. He tried hard to focus on her words, not on that disturbing look. "I want so for you to be happy, too," she said. "I want you to have only good things from life. If I could, I'd shield you always from pain and grief and . . . from anyone who would try to hurt you."

"I do believe you would." He smiled softly. "And I think you *could*, too, even with your delicate body." Impulsively, he put his arm around her. He felt a momentary tremor in her shoulders, then she seemed to relax and lean ever so slightly closer to him. "You've always taken care of Andrei and me, haven't you? Our little Talia, so strong, so caring."

"I've loved you . . . both."

"Andrei and I . . . we're very lucky."

She did not respond, and they walked again in silence. After a while they crossed the Senate Square. It was deserted now, and their shoes echoed against the cobbles. They paused before the bronzed statue of Peter the Great. He seemed so very lonely at this hour of the night. Yuri felt a knot rise in his throat as if he might actually start to weep for the lone tsar seated regally on his rearing mount, with no one to appreciate his awesome might.

Yuri and Talia came at length to the Nicholas Bridge. Then they noticed the lights in the sky. At first, they thought it was lightning, but there wasn't a cloud to be seen—it was clear and shimmering with the pale light of a white night. They paused at the mid-span of the bridge, finally able to discern the peculiar quality of the light. It was the northern lights—the aurora borealis. Ribbons of pink streaked across the night sky. As the heavenly show progressed, from green to blue to purple, Yuri's spirit began to be touched. His mood lifted a little and he felt safe and hopeful. Yet he knew those sensations had more to do with the woman at his side than some astronomical phenomena.

"Talia, I'm so glad you're with me now!"

"I wouldn't want to enjoy this with anyone else," she replied. Their voices had a hushed, dreamy quality.

"It's not just that. I feel so safe with you, Talia, so whole. How am I able to survive when you're not here?" He turned to face her, gazing down into her upturned face, plunging into her beckoning eyes, allowing himself to be embraced by her steadying presence. "Oh, Talia, I need you so!"

"Yuri . . ." she breathed.

And before he realized what he was doing—before he could think about or analyze his actions—he pulled her to him. When she didn't resist, he pressed his lips with urgent passion against hers. And the intensity of her response made him slightly dizzy. Katya had never kissed him so hungrily. Katya had never held him with such strong emotion.

"What's happening?" he murmured, still kissing her, but trembling now with both fear and longing.

"Don't you know?" she said. "I love you so much, Yuri. I always have."

"I've been a fool, my dear Talia. How could I have not seen the treasure in my own house?"

"I doesn't matter. You see now, don't you, Yuri?"

He let his kisses be his response. He didn't need the love of a faithless woman. He didn't need to torture himself any longer over something that would never happen. There was love and acceptance in his own backyard—in his own home!

The sound of an approaching carriage made them break suddenly apart. They were trembling and breathing hard. Yuri took Talia's hand—it was ice-cold. He brought it to his lips, gently kissing it.

"How thoughtless of me," he said, "keeping you out here in the cold."

"I hardly noticed. But it's just as well there was an interruption."

"Yes . . . I suppose so."

"We should get home. It must be very late."

"Then, let's not lose another minute." With her hand still in his, he broke into a run, and they kept it up for ten minutes, until, laughing so hard they could barely catch their breath, they paused under a streetlamp. Yuri had needed the exertion to help blow off some of his emotional energy and to clear his head.

They walked the rest of the way home. As they entered the flat, closing the door behind them, Talia said, "Yuri, did it really happen? Did you truly kiss me the way you did?"

"We couldn't have both been dreaming."

"It was wonderful."

"And, Talia, did you really say you loved me?"

She nodded, then stood on her toes and kissed him on the cheek. He responded by seeking out her lips again. Katya could not have tasted this good, this sweet. Katya could not have aroused in him such yearning, such hunger. He tried not to think of the Crimea, nor of the luminous eyes that had searched him with passion and vulnerability there on the balmy, sunlit beaches. That was a fading dream, with no substance, no hope.

Talia was reality. Talia wanted him.

The creaking of a floorboard stopped Yuri this time. He thought, somewhat guiltily, of his mother and what she would think of this display. Or worse, what of Raisa? But it was neither of their mothers coming down the hallway.

Andrei didn't mean to spy on Talia and Yuri. His mother had suggested he spend the night since they had returned home from the gallery after midnight. They had talked for a while, then his mother and Raisa had begun to worry about Yuri and Talia being out so late. Andrei had calmed them with assurances that all was well, and finally the two mothers had gone to their beds. His assurances, however, had not allayed his own worries. But he was less worried about their safety than he was about . . . other things. What if they ended up alone? Talia had looked so beautiful. How could Yuri not notice her? And what if he did? She had no reason to resist him—it would only mean all her dreams had finally come true.

Thus Andrei was awake when the front door opened. It seemed natural that he would come out to make sure it was them and they were all right. Wasn't it? And besides, they would probably be eager for one of their late-night talk sessions, like they had when they were children.

He regretted his curiosity—that's all it was—the moment he came around the corner of the hall and saw them in each other's arms . . . *kissing*. But before he could make a hasty retreat, he was caught. It was almost impossible to be stealthy when he weighed two hundred and twenty pounds and stood over six feet tall.

"Andrei?" said Yuri.

"I . . . didn't mean . . . that is, I—yes, it's me. Mama was worried."

An awkwardness hung among the three friends as it never had before.

"We lost track of time," Talia finally said. But she looked slightly away from Andrei. She couldn't look him in the eyes.

"Well, at least you're all right."

"Yes . . . we are . . ."

Then her eyes lifted and her gaze momentarily met his. And she looked more beautiful than ever. She was glowing. *Glowing!* All her present embarrassment and guilt couldn't conceal the joy coursing through her. But it was Yuri who had elicited that joy from her. Not Andrei. He only hoped she wasn't going to talk about it. He couldn't stand that.

"I think I'll go to bed," Talia said. "But I'll see you both in the morning." Her eyes, however, were only on Yuri as she spoke. She let go of his hand reluctantly and walked—no, floated—down the hall to the room she still shared with her mother when she was home.

The brothers watched mutely until she disappeared into the room, then Yuri said, "I'm going to bed, too."

Andrei hadn't wanted to talk to Talia about what happened, but he wasn't ready to let his brother off so easily. He stepped in front of Yuri, blocking his path. "And that's it?" he challenged.

"It's late, Andrei, and I'm tired."

"What happened, Yuri?" pressed Andrei. "A few hours ago you hardly realized Talia existed. Now, suddenly you are lovers!"

"Calm down, Andrei. You are behaving like an outraged father."

"Do you deny the implications of what I saw?"

"I deny nothing!"

"How *could* you?"

"Me? I don't believe I was alone. Talia was a willing participant—very willing, I might add."

"Why you—" Andrei lunged forward, grabbed Yuri's collar and shoved him up against the wall. "If you hurt her—"

"You have a nerve, Andrei, to even think I could do such a thing. If anyone else tried to make such accusations I'd answer them with a fist. But since you are my brother, I will try to respond with reason—heaven knows, one of us should! I would never hurt Talia. She is the dearest creature on earth to me. Now let go of me." He wrenched himself free of Andrei's hold before Andrei could respond.

"Just know this," Andrei warned, his voice shaking with passion, "I'll kill you if you hurt her."

"Don't be an idiot, Andrei!"

Andrei took a sharp breath. Yes, he must indeed sound crazy. He had to rein in his emotions. There was nothing wrong with what Yuri and Talia were doing. They had no idea they were ravishing his heart with their actions. Yet it was still inconceivable that Yuri could have changed so suddenly toward Talia. That simply was not in his character. Andrei could not keep from being suspicious.

"I don't understand, Yuri. Do you truly love her?"

"Do you think me incapable of love?"

"Of course not. But it wasn't so long ago that you were madly in love with that countess. What happened to her? How can you love someone so much one minute and then the next love someone else?"

"Andrei, life is never as simple as you would want it to be. Things happen, that's all. Things change. But you tell me something—why are you so outraged by what is happening between Talia and me?"

"Talia is my dearest friend in the world." *And I can't imagine how you can possibly love her more than I.* But he couldn't tell Yuri that. He could never reveal his feelings for Talia.

"She's my friend, too," Yuri said softly, earnestly.

"You won't hurt her?"

"How can you ask?" Yuri said. And Andrei knew he had wounded his brother with that question.

"Well, let's go to bed," Andrei said, making an attempt, even if half-hearted, to repair the damage.

They went to the room they had shared for so many years. Andrei could not remember the last time they had been there together. The room hadn't changed a bit, though now it was occupied only by Yuri. The things on the walls were the same—that handbill from a circus they had attended years ago when their father had still been alive. A few photographs of faraway places that as boys they hoped to see one day—one of the Statue of Liberty, one of the Great Wall of China, and one of a balmy, palm-tree-lined beach in the South Seas. Three drawings that Andrei had done, the one of their father in an especially prominent position. Yuri had changed the room little since Andrei had moved out. Had that been mere laziness on his part, or was it a pointed expression of how much their relationship meant to him? Yuri was not the lazy type. He was, however, extremely sentimental.

Andrei lay awake long after Yuri's steady breathing and soft snores filled the silent night. Nothing had changed . . . yet everything was different. And Andrei did not know how he would face tomorrow knowing that his brother and the woman he loved were now dreaming of each other and anticipating a future together.

29

The monk Iliodor had been a thorn in Rasputin's flesh for years. Once a close friend and confidant, Iliodor had quickly turned jealous at Rasputin's rise in Imperial favor. Rasputin knew for a fact that it had been Iliodor who had leaked his letters from the tsaritsa to the press, and he now realized he had been a fool to trust the man with something so personal. Since then, Iliodor had been actively trying to further discredit Rasputin. He wrote letters to the tsaritsa's friend Anna Vyrubova detailing Rasputin's sexual and social misconduct. He vigorously called upon the Synod of the Church to defrock Rasputin. But Rasputin responded with a barrage of appeals to the tsar himself.

And in the end, it was Iliodor who was expelled from his holy orders and sent under house arrest to his native village. Rasputin basked gloriously in his victory. Full of confidence in his Imperial standing, he followed the royal family that spring to Yalta and stayed in the best hotel, living like a king. It was now clear to his detractors that any who would attempt to disgrace him risked their own necks.

Sitting in a tavern frequented by many of the hotel staff with whom Rasputin had become friendly, he drank large quantities of Madeira while regaling avid listeners with boasts and sermons.

"Mama and Papa are lost without me," he said, wiping his silk sleeve across his mouth. "I cannot count the times Papa has looked to me for wisdom with regard to matters of state. Why, only last week he sought me out in the appointment of a railroad administrator. 'Grigori,' he said, 'please look into so-and-so's eyes and see if he is a man of honor.' Well, I did and found the man to be not at all satisfactory. He was filled with cunning and evil. I told Papa that Popugaev would be better for the job. You need not ask who now holds the position."

"Imagine that!" said a young woman, a barmaid, clinging possessively to Rasputin's side.

The *starets* leaned down and kissed her lips, pressing seductively close to her body. "Oh, my sweet little thing, your devotion isn't wasted on a nobody. I am the very voice of God in the Imperial ear. The tsaritsa loves me as a father. We are very . . . very close." He chuckled, then added, "So close, she can't live without her dear Friend."

"I never doubted for a moment your high esteem, Father Grigori. Look what I bought in the market today." She produced a photograph of the monk.

He grinned. The souvenir hockers were making quite a profit selling the photos. "Shall I autograph it for you, my dear?"

"Oh, please do! I shall hang it next to my most sacred icon."

"I'm not deserving of such an honor. I am only a humble man, a sinner whom God has chosen to use. Only through sin am I redeemed. The more the sin, the greater the salvation. Man must sin, you know, in order to have something to repent of. So, yield, I say, to sin—yield as often as God sends temptation. Do not resist. Then you will truly know the contrition of humility, and your penance will rise up to God as a sweet, sweet savor."

He continued on this topic for several minutes, then suddenly stopped and grabbed the girl. "Come," he said, his eyes penetrating her with open lust, "let me help you reach that true ecstasy of the spirit."

She didn't resist when he took her hand and they boarded his carriage, which drove them directly back to his hotel.

Later that evening Anna Vyrubova came to the hotel to visit Rasputin—one of her many calls on him since their arrival in Yalta. She often spent hours in his company, confirming to all who observed—and that was nearly all of Yalta society—that his boasts about his closeness to the royal family must have some validity. But Rasputin was on his best behavior when Anna was there. The moment his loyal spies informed him that her carriage was approaching, he chased out the barmaid he was with and made sure the samovar was replenished. The pious Anna might not understand his copious consumption of wine, and she most definitely would not understand his . . . other appetites. Besides, he couldn't have her bringing back unsavory reports to Mama and Papa.

The gossips were at it again. They were so cruel and spiteful. Alexandra was growing to hate them all. Didn't they have anything better to do than to spread their vile rumors about her dear Friend? And now they were whispering about Anna Vyrubova, too. How could they say such garbage about Alexandra's best friend? Just because she wished to spend time with a holy man, sitting at his feet, basking in his wisdom, the gossips chose to taint it with filth and innuendo.

The tsaritsa's confidant cavorting with the Mad Monk? What drivel! There was no more innocent, godly woman than Anna. Her heart was as pure as . . . as the gossips' hearts were evil. But the sad thing was that the rumors were beginning to get to Nicky. Alexandra tried to reason with him.

"Nicky, you know how jealous they are of Our Friend. They cannot understand true holiness. You know what is said about a prophet not being accepted in his own land."

"I know, Alix, but . . ." The tsar's voice trailed away momentarily. It was apparent he hated what he was about to say. "Even if the things they say might be lies—that is, they *are* lies, but they can be no less harmful to the esteem of the throne."

"And what about Alexis?"

"He has been doing quite well lately."

That was true. In the last few months there had been no more of his terrible spells. He had hardly bled at all after his tooth extraction. Alexis's color had returned fully, and he had even grown an inch. He was the picture of health. And Alexandra had allowed herself to hope that perhaps their holy Friend's prayers had at last brought about the long-sought-after *permanent* healing. Nevertheless, was it wise to cut off the provider of such a profound blessing? She said as much to Nicky.

"But, Sunny, dear," Nicky cajoled softly, "I'm not suggesting we cut Our Friend off entirely. But I think merely a brief *vacation* from the center of things for a short time is advisable. Only a short visit to his village . . . until the tongues stop wagging, you know. We have the matter of Olga to consider, too."

Ah, yes. The Minister of Foreign Affairs, Sazonov, had been working hard to cement a betrothal between Alexandra's eldest daughter, Olga, and the Crown Prince of Rumania, Carol. In a few days a trip was planned to Rumania, where a state reception was to be held, and where the romantic waters would be tested between Carol and Olga. Alexandra wanted a good match for her daughter, and though she completely repudiated the gossips, she realized what even a hint of scandal could do to Olga's matrimonial prospects. Still, wasn't their son's welfare more important than anything?

"But, Nicky—"

"I'm sorry, Alix." The tsar's voice was firmer than was usual when he spoke to his wife. "This must be done." Then he softened. "Grigori will be but a telegram away. Remember what he did from Siberia during the awful time at Spala? He will always be there for you."

So, with the resignation of a true martyr, Alexandra allowed fate to follow its course. But this time she made certain that Father Grigori understood that she in no way believed all the lies tendered about him and that she had done all she could on his behalf.

30

Once again, Yuri buried himself in his work—not a difficult thing to do, since the life of an intern was so hectic. Because of the lateness of his shifts, he often spent several nights in a row at the hospital. Talia never guessed that he was avoiding her. It would have been much more convenient if she had returned to her ballet tour, but the spring season was over and the company was on sabbatical.

That first morning after their passionate encounter, he had immediately realized what a mistake he had made. But when she greeted him with that glow of love in her eyes, he simply hadn't had the heart to say anything to her. And her confession that she had loved him for years only made it harder. Yuri had always considered himself a sensitive man, but apparently it wasn't true. If he had been, he would have noticed her feelings long ago. And he most certainly would not have taken advantage of her as he had that night on the Nicholas Bridge.

Or would he? He had been so caught up in the emotion of the moment and so terribly needy. Talia's love, the intensity of her affection, had filled the dark void left by Katya's rejection. For that moment, at least, it had affirmed to him that he was not completely worthless.

In retrospect, however, their encounter only proved how worthless he truly was. That night after he had fallen into a wretched sleep, his dreams had not been of Talia, but rather of Katya. Still he could not get her out of his mind—or heart.

What kind of man was he?

A coward.

Each time he saw Talia over the next several days, which amounted to only two or three times, he could not find the strength to tell her it all had been a mistake. It didn't help that in so doing he would also be proving his brother right.

But then an interesting thought occurred to Yuri. Did he really *have* to say anything to Talia? Why not accept her love? A man could do a lot worse. He did care deeply for her—even loved her, though only as a sister. But marriages had been built on far less. Why not accept a life with Talia? They could be happy—she was obviously happy now, basking in her love finally requited. He certainly should have no complaints when a woman as lovely as Talia was showering him with devotion.

Why not? he asked himself once more, as if he dared an answer to appear.

Yuri had made his decision. He would go to Moscow and use the time there to reflect further on the situation. If for some reason he reached a negative conclusion, he would talk to Talia. But he felt certain he could make things work. When he said good-bye to Talia the night before his departure, he kissed her for the first time since the Nicholas Bridge without sensing a shadow looming over them.

The cardiology conference in Moscow proved to be quite stimulating and informative. Yuri thought he might be bored between meetings, but there was a great deal of material to read and study. He almost declined an invitation from several of the younger doctors for an evening of recreation. But it was important for advancement in his profession to cultivate relationships with others in medicine. These were young men, hardly at the age where they wielded much influence, but two were sons of important men in the field. In the end, he went along.

Moscow's night life, in Yuri's opinion, was not nearly as lively as that of St. Petersburg, but it was not a desert, either. Still, he enjoyed it only half-heartedly. The complications that awaited him in Petersburg always lurked on the fringes of his mind. And then there was Katya. Before speaking to Vladimir, Yuri had actually entertained the idea of seeking her out during his trip to Moscow. He hoped that somehow in person he could appeal to her in a way his letters never had. Perhaps he actually had a chance with her. But now the shame of his folly goaded him. He wasn't about to make an attempt to see her again. Even Yuri Fedorcenko had only so much capacity for rejection.

Nevertheless he couldn't keep his thoughts from focusing on her. In a chic nightclub called The Caverns, he heard the familiar laughter and was certain he had imagined it. His heart nearly stopped when he saw her seated with a group of half a dozen others, three tables away. At the same instant, she glanced up and their eyes met. His chest constricted with an awful ache, partly because of his own sudden pain, but partly because of something in Katya's eyes. He must get control of his imagination. There simply could not have been sadness in her eyes, nor yearning, nor caring.

Oddly, Count Prokunin was not among her companions.

Yuri, you are a fool. Give it up.

Against everything that was sane and rational in him, he found himself rising from his chair and walking to her table.

"What a coincidence, Countess Zhenechka!" He listened to the casual tone in his own voice as if from outside himself, as if viewing an actor on the stage. His clicked his heels together and grinned, as he had observed his uncle Dmitri do on many occasions, and held out his hand to her.

"Prince Fedorcenko, this is a surprise." Her tone was equally casual, but as she took his hand, she lifted eyes to him that seemed disturbed. Were they both such incredible actors?

"I don't want to interrupt your party, but I did want to greet you at least—it would have been quite rude of me to ignore you, wouldn't it?"

"I can be a forgiving soul."

"Can you, now? A virtue I haven't acquired, I'm afraid."

Her cardboard smile faltered and momentarily died, then the

corners of her lips turned up once more in a very mechanical smile.

Yuri seemed to have no control over himself now; despite his better judgment, he pressed on. "And I understand congratulations are due you, Countess?"

"For what?"

"On your engagement."

Several of her companions responded to this with a flurry of surprised comments, which she immediately quelled.

"Whoever are your sources, Prince Fedorcenko?" she said with a little chuckle. "Those St. Petersburg gossips never could get anything right."

"It's not true?" The actor in Yuri faltered and his real self emerged, completely perplexed, confused, staggered.

She laughed. "Life is just too much fun to be spoiled with marriage." But there was something unreal about her laugh, something hollow in her words.

"Well, then, I will leave you to your party," Yuri managed to mutter, desperately looking for a fast escape.

"Why don't you join us?" It was more of a challenge than an invitation.

"I'm with friends."

"Then some other time, perhaps."

Yuri knew he would seek her out. He couldn't sleep that night for thinking of her. And he cursed the conference meetings the next day because his sense of duty required him to attend, even though it was the last place he wanted to be just then. When the final session ended, he left immediately. This was his last day in Moscow. It was now or never.

It wasn't difficult to locate the large Zhenechka Estate in town. But Yuri's zeal began to falter as his taxi pulled up in front. Was he really going to do this? He must be insane. What if she rejected him again? The idea brought an ironic grin to his face. That hadn't stopped him before, why should it now? Perhaps it got easier with each rejection. If so, by now, he ought to be able to shrug them off with a laugh.

He was still weak-kneed, however, as he walked up to her door. He pulled the bell cord and heard beautiful chimes within. As he waited, he entertained one frantic thought of leaving. He still had a chance to change his mind. He'd even told the cab to wait. Then he heard footsteps and knew it was too late.

To the butler who answered the door, he introduced himself, giving the man his card, and asked to see Countess Zhenechka.

"Are you expected?" asked the butler.

"I'm afraid not."

"Then, I shall see if she is available. But she usually doesn't take callers without previous arrangements."

Yuri waited awkwardly in the entryway. The Zhenechka wealth was quite evident even here with its hardwood floor of intricate inlaid wood designs, crystal chandelier overhead, and walls decorated with several pieces of fine art. He examined the art. There were no masters present, but they seemed to be originals of the Renaissance period. But he forgot all about the art when he heard her voice.

"Yuri." An electric charge coursed through him. She spoke his name with such familiarity. Images of the Crimea washed over him, and for a moment he was back there again, with her at his side.

He spun around, and his first glimpse of her left him breathless. She was so much softer than she had been last night. She wore a pale yellow day dress of a gauzy fabric that draped in delicate folds around her shoulders. But that delicate look came not just from her clothes, but from a kind of aura radiating from her very person. Her amber hair had grown since he last saw her and now fell in soft waves about her shoulders, wisps of curls framing her luminous face. Her lips quirked in a tentative smile, and her eyes glimmered. She looked like a Greek goddess.

"Hello, Katya." He tried to be cool and aloof as he had been at the nightclub, but it was impossible. "I'm sorry for not calling first."

"I have come to expect that from you, Yuri." There was amusement in her eyes and no reproach at all.

He wanted to throw his arms around her, but instead they just stood facing each other. "As long as you don't throw me out." He forced a chuckle from his tight throat. He was hoping for an invitation into the parlor.

Instead, she said, "No, I won't." But no invitation came.

Taking courage from her kind reception, he pressed, "Could we . . . talk?"

"I knew you'd come today," she began.

"Just like a loyal puppy."

"I don't want a puppy, Yuri."

"What do you want, Katya?"

"If only I had a simple answer to such a simple question . . ."

"Simple answers have never been good enough for me, anyway."

She smiled. "Would you like to walk outside?"

"I have a cab waiting."

"Then, take me somewhere."

She didn't stop for a wrap but just slipped her arm through Yuri's and led the way outside. Yuri followed, still feeling a bit like a puppy, but not caring. She could not look at him that way if she didn't care for him . . . just a little.

31

As they drove along Tverskaya Prospekt into the heart of Moscow, she said, "I'm afraid I will give you the wrong impression."

Straight ahead the red brick walls of the Kremlin gleamed in the silvery light of the summer gloaming. The steady clip-clop of the horses filled the silence that followed Katya's words. Yuri was afraid to respond. He had asked her if they could talk, yet he did not want to risk the sense of peace he felt between them at this moment. So he said nothing until the silence became as oppressive as a royal decree.

"How could you do that?" he said, then held his breath waiting for his fleeting happiness to be shattered.

"By coming with you tonight, by agreeing to talk. Yet I was too cruel to you before in Petersburg when I cut you off so coldly. I hope you can forgive me."

"I'm here, am I not?"

"Yes, but I don't think you came only to be told, though more kindly, that there can be no future for us. Still, I must tell you the truth. I care for you too much to hurt you again."

"Why, Katya? If only I understood *why*. You say you care for me, yet you push me away. Is there someone else? Prokunin? Is your father insisting that you marry him?"

She gave a petulant shake of her head. "Prokunin! He is nothing to me, and there is no way I would marry him, no matter what my father wants. Our families are trying to arrange a union. But I won't have it. I don't think I will ever marry. There are too many . . . complications."

"I don't care about that, Katya! You have referred to your past before, but nothing you could have ever done would bother me. I love you, Katya—"

"Hush, Yuri! Please, don't talk that way. It only makes things harder."

"Good. The harder it is for you to reject me, the better. I will only say it again: I love you—all of you, your past, your mistakes, your future—*all*."

"You would, dear Yuri," she said with a sad sigh. "And that is why I must take the initiative and set you free."

"I don't want to be free."

"I will not destroy your life."

With a sharp intake of breath he rolled his eyes in frustration. "You are a stubborn wench."

"Wench, is it?" she retorted with mock affront.

He grinned, hoping a bit of levity would steer them back to a better path. "Exactly! Shakespeare's Katherina comes especially to mind."

"Oh? And now I am a shrew, to boot. And you will tame me, Petruchio?"

"Why not? Better me than some other poor unsuspecting fellow. At least I already know the feel of your sting."

"And you like it?"

"I love it!"

Sighing, she said, "What will I do with you, Yuri Sergeiovich?"

"Marry me."

"I can't." The words were direct, but her tone lacked finality.

"Will you at least think about it?"

"You make this very hard, Yuri. I've tried to put you off with kindness but that hasn't helped. Perhaps I was justified in my previous cruelty. Yet I know I can't be cruel to you again."

"Do you love me, Katya?"

"Another question without a simple answer . . ."

"Then spend eternity giving me a complex answer! Tell me why you love me; tell me why you don't. Tell me why you are confused."

He sat back and folded his arms before him. "I have all the time in the world."

"I will think about it."

"About what?"

"Marrying you."

His mouth went slack.

She giggled. Then, more earnestly, "Don't take me wrong, Yuri. I won't be able to *keep* from thinking about it. But I can make no promises. You understand?" He nodded, still mute. "Now, no more talk of serious things. Let's enjoy the evening and have fun. Stop the carriage. I want to walk across Red Square with you."

Yuri was content. He didn't know what would become of him and Katya after this night, and he almost did not care. Let worlds collide, as he was certain they eventually must—it would not change the beautiful fact that Katya cared for him and would actually consider marrying him. He could live a long time on the ecstasy of that reality. He made a concerted effort not to think of Talia. Somehow he would make her understand.

Yuri did have a way of complicating Katya's life. But she couldn't blame him entirely. After encountering him at the nightclub, she had hoped he would come to see her. She had even considered ways of seeking him out in Moscow. Yet she hadn't. Her rational self reasoned that nothing could, or should, come of such impulsiveness.

Now she didn't know what to think or do. Had she really promised him she would consider marriage? What a foolish thing to do! But his dear presence had made her forget reality. She desperately wanted to believe that he would indeed be able to accept her completely. But even Yuri would be repulsed by the tainted woman that she was. How could he not be? Even she, with her modern ways, could barely accept it, and she had kept it a closely guarded secret.

Still, she wasn't certain she would have done so if her father hadn't insisted on it. Insisted? The man had practically threatened her with her life.

Yuri was a godly man, a man to whom spiritual things mattered. But it was too much to hope that he was saint enough to look upon her sin and still love her. Father Grigori, of course, had done so, but he was a *starets*, a man of whom such a virtue was expected.

She had decided long ago to bear her secret alone. But she had not reckoned on a man like Yuri entering her life.

Katya slowly climbed the stairs of her house. It was late. The lights were dim and the normal bustling presence of servants was absent. The corridors were chilly.

Her father, a great admirer of Alexander the Third, believed in an austere lifestyle and had fashioned his household after that of the tsar—a man so frugal that his children, little grand dukes and duchesses, often went hungry. Katya had been raised in the same way. Only when her maternal grandfather died and left her an income of her own did she begin to live a more extravagant lifestyle.

On the third floor, Katya paused at the nursery door. She had been reared in this nursery, but she had no memory of those toddler days when her mother was still at home and she had known some happiness. She had been abandoned by her mother long before she had been old enough to vacate this nursery, and, unfortunately, it was those lonely memories of abandonment that would always remain with her.

She opened the door. All the lamps were turned out, but the room was bathed in silvery moonlight shining through a crack in the partially open drapes. She crept in quietly and moved soundlessly across the room to the crib, which stood against a wall, right in the path of the moonlight.

"Hello, dear one," Katya murmured.

She reached into the crib and gently pulled up the satin coverlet over the sleeping form. The child stirred and blew a puff of air through her sweet little rosebud lips. Her eyes remained closed, but the long brown lashes fluttered once against her chubby cheeks. How dear and innocent she was, sleeping so soundly, so peacefully, with no bitter realities to disturb her dreams.

"I want it always to be that way for you, Irina. I want to make your life happier than mine ever was. My motives aren't completely selfish. I want to protect you, too. I don't want you haunted by scandal—"

Katya shook her head and shrugged. It was probably too late for that. How much longer could she keep Irina a secret? Even if the gossips never learned the truth, before too long Irina herself would be old enough to ask questions. Could Katya then continue with the lie her father had forced upon her—that Irina was the daughter of a relative and, left orphaned, had been taken in by the Zhenechka family?

Could Katya actually deny her own *motherhood*?

She ran a finger gently along the baby's smooth cheek. "You are part of me, little one, and I am part of you. I am your mama. Oh, I know I haven't been a very good mother. I leave you alone far too much. But . . ."

She couldn't admit her selfishness even to her sleeping daughter. But there were times when Katya wanted to forget that she was a mother burdened with responsibility. In those times it was not difficult at all to live her father's lie. She wanted to play and enjoy life as any nineteen-year-old girl would.

She must have a lot of her mother's blood in her, Katya mused. How easy it would be to run away and live in a Cossack village with those wild, uninhibited people. But, from the beginning, Katya had been determined not to leave her child to the fate she herself had known—growing up without a mother's love, hearing almost every day how her selfish mother had run away because she hated her child. Now, as an adult, the rational part of Katya knew her father had told her such things because he had been hurt and shamed by her mother and wanted Katya to hate the woman as much as he did. But part of her would always believe it and weep at the very thought of her rejection.

"I will try to do better, dear," Katya said. "Maybe I am wrong to deny you the chance to have a father—oh, and, Irina, Yuri would be such a wonderful father! But could he accept another man's child as his own? I don't know. I am afraid to take the risk. . . ."

Again the child stirred, but this time her eyes fluttered and then opened. The large brown eyes gazed up at Katya, and she couldn't resist the urge to lift the baby from her crib. Irina smiled and cooed, seeming to know she was in her mother's arms. Katya smoothed away a wisp of fine yellow hair and kissed the child's forehead.

"I do love you so. No matter what happens, we will survive together. I will never leave you alone—"

She stopped suddenly as she heard the nursery door open.

"I thought I heard you come in, miss," said the nurse.

"I'm sorry I woke her, Teddie."

"You don't look very sorry." The woman grinned.

Teddie was an American, more formally named Theodora Smithers. But she had been called "Teddie" for so long, her true name was all but forgotten. She was forty-five years old and not very attractive—in fact, with her broad, homely face, huge, bulbous nose, and disproportionately recessive chin, some probably would consider her downright ugly. But she had a heart as beautiful as a society diva and a huge capacity to love. She had come to Russia twenty years ago to marry a distant cousin, an arranged marriage to a man she'd never met. Unfortunately, he turned out to be a rather shallow fellow, took one look at his homely bride-to-be, and backed out of the arrangement. Not ready to go home to parents who wanted to control her life, she sought a "position" among the Russian upper classes and thus came to be employed by the Zhenechkas, who at that time were looking for a nurse for Katya. She had remained a loyal servant to the family all those years, even after her services as a nursemaid to Katya had no longer been needed and she had been shunted to other duties. Despite the shame surrounding Irina's birth, Teddie had been thrilled that her services as a nurse were called upon once more. And as she had loved Katya, she loved Katya's child. Too bad neither had been lucky enough to have Teddie as their mother.

"I need to spend more time with her," Katya said guiltily.

"You do the best you can, dearie. You're but a child yourself."

"Why must life be so complicated, Teddie?"

"Who can say? I think God intended it to be simpler. I suppose we are our own worst enemies." The woman sighed and put an arm around Katya with great affection. "And speaking of complications . . . your father spoke to me an hour ago and told me that when you came home, if it was a decent hour, he wanted to see you."

"Surely, it's too late now," Katya said hopefully.

"I've just come from the kitchen, and the light was still burning beneath his study door."

"Couldn't I just tell him I got home too late? He'd never know."

"When will you learn, dearie, that your father knows everything? A mouse can't sneeze in this house without him knowing."

"What was his mood like?"

Teddie rolled her eyes upward and shook her head. "Be brave, Katichka!"

"Oh, dear, this isn't going to be good."

Katya felt like a prisoner going off to her execution. Giving the baby a final kiss, she handed the child over to Teddie and exited the nursery. No meeting with her father boded well, but at this hour, and with him in a sour mood . . . it was, indeed, like walking to the gallows.

32

Count Lavrenti Zhenechka was a big man, six and a half feet tall and over two hundred and fifty pounds. Like most good Russian nobles, he had been reared to a military career. He had been decorated in the Balkan War of 1877, then gone on to win laurels in the Far Eastern conflicts. But when the family vodka business passed to him upon his father's death, he gave up his shining military career to enter the world of commerce. Under his stringent control—some called it tight-fisted—Zhenechka Vodka doubled its profits. He made more money than any Zhenechka could have dreamed possible, but he made no friends in doing so. He was feared and hated by many, and a good number of those adversaries were members of his own family.

He married at age thirty-six to a mere child of sixteen. Zinaida was a beauty, and her youth was appealing to a man like Zhenechka because she would be easy to control—or so he thought. But she proved to be too much of a free spirit for him. He worked hard to crush her will, and she fought back tenaciously. There was never any love in the marriage, and for most of its six-year span, contempt and hatred were the most prevalent emotions between the couple. Zhenechka wasn't entirely at fault, either. Zinaida engaged in several romantic affairs, which she publicly flaunted in her husband's face. To his knowledge, the affairs began after Katya was conceived, but he could never be completely certain the girl was really his daughter. He probably claimed her only because it would have been too humiliating to admit anything else. But on Katya's fourth birthday, Zinaida ran away with a Cossack to live as a barefoot peasant.

Sometimes Katya wondered if the worst thing her mother did was not merely running away, but doing so and leaving Katya behind to live her life under the same domineering rule that had caused Zinaida so much misery. Ironically, Katya had responded to her father's heavy hand in much the same way as her mother had—by constant rebellion.

In the spirit of that rebellious nature, when Katya reached her father's study door, she didn't bother to knock before entering. If he was going to insist upon spoiling her night, she would do what she could to defy him—short of refusing his summons altogether.

He growled at her brazen entry. "You are as ill-mannered as a peasant."

"How would you know, Father?" she retorted. "When was the last time you've had personal contact with a peasant?"

"I forgot you are an expert—from your relationship with that filthy peasant Rasputin."

"Careful what you say, Father. Rasputin has the respect of the Crown itself."

"Never mind that. It's late and, having waited up this late to see you, I am in no mood to spar with you. But it seems if I am to see you at all, it must be at this ungodly hour. Now, sit down and listen, for a change."

Katya toyed with the idea of remaining on her feet, in further defiance. But she was wearing tight shoes and her feet were sore. Standing would accomplish nothing and just make her miserable. With a careless shrug she flopped in a chair and kicked off her shoes. She knew such unladylike behavior would irritate him.

He lifted a paper from his desktop. "I have here a marriage contract—"

"Oh, Father," she groaned in disgust.

"Listen to me, young lady, you will marry, and you will do so soon. And since most decent families have tended to shun you because of your scandalous behavior, not to mention the stigma of your mother's wantonness, you should be thankful I have done as well with a match as I have. The Prokunins are a good family—not rich, but at least they are titled nobility. I have managed to convince the elder Prokunin that three-fourths of the rumors about you are not true and the rest is but youthful zest. The young Count Pytor is actually enamored with your, as he calls it, 'flamboyant behavior,' and thus is also pressing his parents for a match. I have committed a large dowry to the count and the promise of a share in the vodka business."

"No wonder he is willing to put up with my *flamboyant behavior*." She rolled her eyes and slurred the final words disdainfully. "If he marries me, he won't have to work another day in his life."

"Not a bad price, considering what he is getting—I doubt you will bring the poor, unsuspecting man anything but grief."

"And what of Irina?"

"I have suggested that since I am getting too old to care properly for the child, you and he adopt her."

"They have no idea of the truth?"

"There is no need."

"Sometimes, Father, I truly believe you live in a dreamworld. But regardless of that, you can just tear up that paper of yours. I have no intention of marrying the good count. I have already told you I have no interest in marriage at all."

"And you talk about dreamworlds?" he sneered. "I could have kicked you out on the street after what you did to me, to this family. But I protected you and that fatherless whelp of yours. I made it possible for you to maintain your place in decent society. You owe me obedience in this matter, or—"

"Or what, Father? You don't want the Zhenechka name smeared in the mud any more than I do. But I don't see why I must marry for further respectability."

"Because that is what proper, decent people do!"

"Well, I've already proven I am neither."

Zhenechka rose suddenly and abruptly from his chair, nearly knocking it over in the process. In three strides, he was standing over Katya menacingly. Katya's heart skipped a beat. It wouldn't be the first time she had felt her father's strong fist, but she glared up at him as if she didn't care.

"I can destroy you—and your child," he hissed, his tone as lethal as the hand clenched at his side. "Defy me and I will reveal to all that your precious daughter is nothing more than a misbegotten whelp of another misbegotten whelp. You will end up with not a penny to your name. Even your inheritance from your grandfather will be cut off, because I have final control over it."

"Maybe we'd be better off! No wonder the prospect of living among Cossacks was so appealing to my mother—"

The count's hand shot up, striking Katya's cheek with such force it felt as if her neck had snapped. Despite her dogged determination not to reveal weakness to her father, the pain brought tears to her eyes. He stood glowering over her, his hand still raised as if he were looking for the smallest excuse to strike again. Katya bit her lip. She couldn't give him that excuse. She had her daughter to think of.

"All right, Father, you've made your point." Her tone wasn't exactly contrite, but at least she managed to say the words. "But perhaps you would like to make a deal?"

"A deal?" He gave a dry, mocking laugh, but, nevertheless, nodded for her to continue. She knew he couldn't resist a business proposition.

"What if I made my own match?" she went on confidently. "Your main concern is to bring a titled, respectable name into the family, right?" He nodded again. "Suppose I could bring a name far more weighty than Prokunin. How does the name Fedorcenko strike you?"

"*The* Fedorcenkos? I served under Prince Viktor Fedorcenko in the Balkans and fought beside his son, Prince Sergei. But they fell from Imperial favor and disappeared from the face of the earth."

"Well, they are back. The tsar himself reinstated the family title to Prince Sergei when he was given a full Imperial pardon. They are no longer out of Imperial favor. Sergei's son Prince Yuri Fedorcenko is an assistant physician to the royal family. He has personally treated the tsarevich." Katya felt a surge of triumph as she saw an amazing transformation come over her father. His interest was visible even beneath his stoic, businesslike bearing.

"And you think *you* can make a match with this Prince Yuri?" He was blatantly challenging her.

"I know I can. All you have to do is tear up that agreement with the Prokunins and promise that my inheritance—and that of my daughter—is secure. That is a promise I will want in writing and properly witnessed."

"At times like this I can almost believe you *are* my daughter." He stepped away from Katya and leaned against his desk, folding his arms across his huge chest and gazing at her, if not exactly with pride, at least with respect.

"Well, what do you say?" she asked in the tone of a seasoned businesswoman.

"I agree. But I won't tear up this paper. I will give you three months to secure a marriage proposal. If none is forthcoming, this paper will take effect. You will marry Prokunin."

Katya agreed without hesitation. They shook hands on it like two businessmen. But somehow when she left his study, she felt dirty, as if she had made a deal with the devil. Only her father could have tainted what should have been a sweet, beautiful time in hers and Yuri's lives.

33

Yuri had parted from Katya with her assurance that she would come to St. Petersburg within a matter of days to see him and take up where they had left off on his last night in Moscow. Still, he left her with a great deal of trepidation. He kept telling himself that this time was different. Yet each time they had parted in the past, their reunions had been not only disappointing, but downright depressing for Yuri. If he could have remained in Moscow, he wouldn't have let her out of his sight. But duty called in Petersburg.

One duty he was anticipating less than all the others was that of talking to Talia. The day after his return to Petersburg he invited her out to dinner, selfishly hoping a public place would provide him some protection against what he knew would be an emotional scene. She looked absolutely radiant. He silently philosophized over the peculiarities of love. Here was a lovely woman, right under his nose, all his life. Yet it was to another, to a comparative stranger, that his heart belonged. Why was it that Katya stirred him so, made him feel alive, whole?

But he had to get his mind off Katya. He had to find a way to speak his heart to Talia without breaking hers. But when he looked into her shining brown eyes, gazing at him so expectantly, he realized he was seeking the impossible.

"So, how was Moscow, Yuri?" she said. "You've spoken so little of it."

"I'm sure hearing about the conference would only bore you."

"No, it wouldn't. Tell me about it."

"Well, I learned much that will help me with my research. There was a great deal of talk about the Price-Jones study of the size of red blood cells and the possible part their measurement plays in diagnosis." He talked for several minutes about this, until even he was bored. He knew he was merely postponing the inevitable. But there was no sense ruining their dinner.

Dessert was being served when he took a breath and plunged forward, "Talia, something else did happen in Moscow that I haven't mentioned. It's not easy for me to tell you about it. I wouldn't blame you if you despised me for what I've done. I only hope I can make you understand that I didn't intend to hurt you. It was stupid and insensitive, Talia, but never malicious—"

"I know you couldn't be malicious, Yuri." She took his hand and squeezed it with an affectionate smile.

"Your understanding only makes this harder . . . Talia, that night on Nicholas Bridge, I was hurting and confused. You were there—I'm afraid, in the wrong place at the wrong time. And when you reached out to me with such love, it staggered me, and it touched a terrible need I was feeling at the time. You see, I had just heard that the woman I loved was engaged to another man." Her hand went slack and fell from his. He avoided her eyes and forged ahead. "I saw her again when I was in Moscow. I learned the rumor of her engagement was untrue. I learned that she cares for me more than I ever hoped possible."

"I see . . ." Talia's voice was soft, strained. Still, Yuri could not meet her eyes.

"I have wronged you terribly, Talia. But I honestly didn't mean to."

"I know."

"I don't deserve your forgiveness. And I've probably ruined our friendship, as well—"

"You'll always be my friend, Yuri," she said firmly. Then she lifted her hand and turned it toward him. The little scar on her finger there was faded now, but still visible. "Remember, a three-fold cord isn't easily broken." Her lip quivered as she spoke, her emotions barely controlled.

Yuri dropped his head and covered his face with his hands so the sudden tears in his eyes were hidden. The memory of that childish, perhaps ignorant, act between him and Talia and Andrei had always been a pleasant memory—until now. The thought of their innocence brought a stab of pain to him. The worst of the pain was that he had to be the one to break that cord. For Talia's assurance was little comfort. He would always know how he had hurt her, and it would be a wedge between them. He didn't even want to think of Andrei's reaction when he found out.

"I hope that is possible," was all Yuri could say.

There was a long silence. The cake on the table was forgotten. Finally, Talia looked up. "C-can you take me home now, Yuri?"

When they reached their building on Vassily Island, Yuri thought it best to give Talia time alone, so he left her at the door, telling her he needed to walk a bit. She understood. She would also understand his decision to stay at the hospital rather than face the awkwardness of living in the same home. She was an understanding woman.

Talia had barely closed the door and started for the stairs that led to her mother's third-floor flat when the flood of emotion caught her. She swiped desperately at her eyes, but she couldn't stop the flow of tears. She climbed the stairs slowly, hoping that by the time she reached her flat, the weeping would have subsided. But it seemed impossible to control. She had been flying on a cloud this past week. All her dreams had come true. The man she had loved for years was at last hers.

She had flown too high.

She should have taken it more slowly, tried to cushion the fall. Instead, while shopping with a girlfriend yesterday, she had actually looked at clothes for a bridal trousseau. Worse still, they had gone into a designer's shop and looked at sketches of wedding gowns. She would have been better off spending her time wondering what had brought about the incredible change in Yuri.

Still, she couldn't hate him. She knew him well enough to know what he said in the restaurant was true, that he had acted more out of confusion and need than spite. But that insight didn't stop her tears, her pain.

As she came to the door of the flat, she hoped she could slip in and to her room without being noticed. But she had to walk by the kitchen on the way to her room and, unfortunately, her mother and Anna were there. And they weren't alone.

"Talia, come and hear the good news," said Raisa. "Andrei's sold a painting."

"In a minute, Mama. I want to . . . to . . ." But in her present state of mind she could not think of even one flimsy excuse. Her voice was shaky. Maybe they wouldn't notice.

"What's wrong, Talia?" It was the voice she least wanted to hear just then. Andrei's.

"Nothing." But a stupid sob accompanied the lie.

Andrei came to the kitchen door. "You're crying."

"I'm going to my room." She turned, but he laid a big restraining hand on her shoulder.

"Mama said you were with Yuri. Where is he?"

"Please, I just want to be left alone right now."

Anna now came and stood by Andrei. "Son, let her go."

"Not until I know what's wrong."

"You don't have to know everything," Talia retorted, her intended sharpness considerably dulled by her tears.

"He did it, didn't he?" Andrei accused. "He's hurt you."

"I don't want to talk about it."

"What happened? Did he find himself a countess or a princess he decided was better than you?" She sobbed again and he added angrily, "I'm right, aren't I? How could he?"

"You don't understand, Andrei. You always think the worst of him. He would never hurt anyone intentionally—"

"And still you defend him!"

"Please!"

"Where is he?"

"I . . . I don't know. Walking, I think."

"He was too ashamed to face his family."

"Don't talk that way, Andrei!" She pulled from his grasp and fled down the hall.

Andrei had been elated over the news of sale of a painting for five hundred rubles. He had gone home to tell his family—but especially to tell Talia. He had almost forgotten that she and Yuri had exchanged words of love. He tried to make the best of it when he discovered that she was not only gone but that she was out with Yuri. He'd had tea with his mama and Raisa and tried to maintain his enthusiasm. That was enough money for him to live on for some time.

Now it didn't matter at all.

He let Talia run away, even though he ached to hold her, soothe her, comfort her. He wanted to tell her that Yuri's love was nothing, that real love, *true* love, was still waiting for her. But she slipped from his grasp, leaving him there feeling her pain but helpless to do anything about it. Or was he helpless?

"I'll find him," he muttered. "I'll teach him!"

"Andrei," Anna warned, "don't leave this apartment."

"No, Mama. I can't obey you. We're no longer bickering children that you can pull apart and make us be friends again. He's gone too far this time."

"So, what are you going to do?"

"I don't know."

But he knew very well—he wanted blood. Not just because Talia had been hurt, but because Yuri's actions had also destroyed Andrei's chances with her. There was no way she would consider a relationship with either of her two best friends now. Andrei's hopes were destroyed, and Yuri would pay for that.

He started again for the door.

"Andrei, don't do this."

He ignored his mother and kept going.

34

Andrei figured Yuri would walk to the hospital. That's where he usually went to hide from life. But it wouldn't work this time. Andrei was going to have it out with his brother once and for all. He was sick of the prima donna, flaunting his successes, acting like such a saint, the caretaker of humanity. He was sick of Yuri's condescension, his phony show of gentility and sensitivity. The highborn prince. The holy physician.

Andrei fed his anger with each stride he took. And if all Yuri's past offenses weren't enough, all Andrei had to do to keep the fire burning within him was to conjure up an image of Talia's delicate tear-streaked face, her red eyes, her pale, devastated countenance.

He walked for ten minutes, his feet pounding, his visage mottled and dangerous. Passersby gave him a wide berth, for in his wrath he was an imposing figure indeed. Once or twice he wondered what he'd do if he didn't find Yuri. What if Yuri had decided to take a cab? But that only made Andrei more angry, that he might be robbed of a chance to vent his fury. Then, just as he came in sight of the spires of the Nicholas Bridge, he saw the lone man walking toward the bridge. He knew immediately it was Yuri. He would recognize his brother's walk anywhere.

"Yuri!" Andrei called.

Yuri turned. "Andrei? What in the world—?"

"You had to do it, didn't you?" Andrei panted, drawing closer to Yuri.

"What're you talking about?"

"I saw Talia."

"Oh. . . ? How is she?" Andrei ignored his brother's pained expression.

"You care, do you?" Andrei challenged. "I told you what I'd do if you hurt her."

"Come on, Andrei, you are being foolish."

"You heartless beast!" Andrei clenched his fist and sent it into Yuri's face.

Yuri staggered back but didn't fall, nor did he attempt to dodge Andrei's next blow, which landed him on his backside on the pavement. Yuri made no move to stand, but just sat there staring up into Andrei's red, twisted face.

"Defend yourself!" Andrei yelled, grabbing Yuri by the front of his shirt and yanking him to his feet. He lifted his fist again but stopped in midair as a sudden, unbidden image flashed through Andrei's mind. He wanted to curse it, to ignore it, but he couldn't. It was of his father. He dropped his fist.

"Go ahead, hit me again," Yuri said. "I probably deserve it—I *do* deserve it!"

"You make me sick," said Andrei, letting go of Yuri's shirt with disgust. "You're pathetic."

"Me? Maybe you should look at yourself, Andrei. It's so obvious you love Talia, and yet you haven't been man enough to admit it. You hate me for hurting her, but do you think you do her any good by keeping the truth from her? You are her best friend, and you lie to her every time you see her and say nothing of your true feelings."

"You don't know what you're talking about."

"All right, maybe I don't. Maybe you just want to kill me out of righteous indignation—not because I got from Talia something you'll never get—"

Andrei flew at his brother again, all restraint forgotten, all images of the past blotted from his mind. Yuri's words stung too deeply, and he had to react physically—for to respond in any other way he might have to admit the truth of those words.

This time Yuri fought back, but it was an uneven match. Yuri was slightly taller, but Andrei weighed fifty pounds more than his brother and had the strong, muscular form of a peasant accustomed to physical labor, not that of a scholarly physician. Neither brother, however, was a skillful fighter, for the only fights they had ever been in were boyish scuffles with each other. Andrei was clumsy, and if his big, powerful figure was intimidating it was also slow and lumbering. Yuri's hands were soft and slim and once, when he gave Andrei a good, painful clip on the jaw, Yuri winced with just as much pain in his fist as Andrei had felt himself. Andrei almost felt sorry for him.

Yuri was quick, though, and got in three or four good shots. But the final blow of the altercation was delivered by Andrei. His big fist plowed into Yuri's patrician nose like an anvil, the impact bringing tears to Yuri's eyes and blood spurting from his nose. Since the day their father was killed, Andrei had never had much of a stomach for blood. Yuri was well aware of his brother's squeamishness, and, perhaps out of spite, he did nothing at first to staunch the flow, which was substantial, running over his lips and down his chin. Andrei felt his own blood drain from his head. He staggered back and grabbed at a lamppost, which probably prevented him from falling over in a faint. Only then did Yuri pull out a handkerchief.

"You okay?" Yuri asked, his voice muffled under the handkerchief.

"Yeah. You?"

"I'll live, but I guess that's not what you want to hear."

Andrei shrugged. "It wouldn't help anyway."

"Now what?"

"I guess . . . the best thing is for us just to part company."

"You mean stop being brothers?" Sarcasm was clearly evident in Yuri's question.

"I don't know. Our lives are pretty much separate anyway. Let's just keep it that way."

"That's what you really want?"

"I wouldn't have said it if I didn't want it."

"I don't know, Andrei. You have been known to open your mouth before you've thought about what was going to come out."

"Not this time, Yuri. Something you said before is true—I could never stand being around you knowing you shared, even for a few days, an intimacy with Talia that I will never know."

"We weren't that intimate."

"It's enough that you held her in your arms, that she—" A lump in his throat forced him to stop. It was just as well. Nothing more needed to be said. "I'm going. But I'd appreciate it if you mentioned nothing to Talia about what's been said here. It would do more damage than good."

And he turned and walked away and did not look back even when his brother called his name.

"Andrei!"

Andrei's footsteps quickened, and Yuri resisted an urge to go after him. He'd give him a few hours, maybe a couple of days to cool off, then he would find him and try to mend the rift between them.

Yuri turned and walked in the opposite direction, back home. Heavily he climbed the steps to the flat. He had been on his way to the hospital when Andrei found him, and he should have continued in that direction, considering his bruises and bleeding nose. But that would have meant following Andrei. So, he returned home in spite of the possibility that he might have to face his mother and Talia. His stupidity had made quite a mess of his life. His beloved home was fragmented now, his dearest friend was brokenhearted, his brother was alienated. He couldn't even bask in the joy of his reconciliation with Katya. In fact, he was beginning to wonder if the love of a woman was worth the price he had paid for it.

As he entered the dark apartment, he hoped to have a reprieve from difficult encounters for one night at least. But he wasn't really surprised when he heard his mother's voice.

"Yuri." She was standing in the parlor door. No doubt she had been waiting for her sons to come home and hoping they would be together. How much did she know?

"Mama."

"Oh, look at you, Yuri." There was enough moonlight coming through the parlor window to illuminate the bloody handkerchief he held over his nose, which was still oozing blood. "Come into the kitchen so I can clean you up." She put an arm firmly around him and nudged him toward the kitchen.

"I . . . I . . ." He tried to protest, but then he glanced down into his mother's eyes and crumbled inside. "Oh, Mama! I've ruined everything!" He put his arms around her and wept.

"There, there, son." She patted his back lovingly.

They went to the kitchen, and Yuri sat at the table as his mother lit a lamp, then drew some warm water from the samovar onto a cloth so she could clean the blood from his face. He needed her gentle touch and her soothing words. If only he had gone to her when he had first heard the news of Katya's engagement instead of to Talia.

"It's still bleeding a little," she said. "I don't think it's broken, though. Just pinch your nose together with this cloth and hold your head back."

A half-smile invaded his misery.

Anna chuckled. "As if I need to tell you what to do, eh?"

"You'd be surprised, Mama."

"So, son, am I right in assuming your brother had something to do with your bloody nose?"

He nodded. "And I deserved it." Then he held back his head and couldn't speak for several minutes.

During the lull, Anna fixed them tea, then sat down at the table with him. "How are you doing?" she said.

He removed the cloth and there were no fresh stains on it. "It's stopped."

"And in here?" She held her hand over her heart.

"Andrei was upset, Mama. I don't think he ever wants to see me again."

"He'll get over it."

"I'm afraid not. I've never seen him like that before. It's all so complicated—the emotions that were vented, the feelings that were hurt, his and mine, but especially Talia's. She'll recover far quicker than Andrei. But I don't think things will ever be the same again. And that's the worst part. Facing the prospect of watching the bonds between us fall apart. Maybe it was bound to happen eventually, but for it to come about in this way—and for it to be my fault!"

"Yuri, I think that just *because* of those bonds between the three of you, your relationships will not die."

"I wish I could believe that."

"Can you have faith in the One who created those bonds, who brought you all together?"

Yuri knew his mother meant well, but this was an issue that only made things worse, not better. His mother had been patient with him, but in the last couple of years he had been rather careless about his faith. The intensity of finishing medical school and launching out on his career had been terribly time-consuming. But he had to admit it was more than that. His desire to be accepted among the nobility had also pulled him away from the simple faith he had learned from his parents. Not that the nobility were heathens, by any means. Yet too many of Yuri's society circle practiced only the form of religion, without the substance—the relationship that was the most important part. He had strayed far from the kind of faith in God he had always admired in his father and had at one time desired to have himself.

"Mama, I'm afraid my faith is kind of rusty these days," he admitted.

"Do you want it to be better?"

"Of course. I probably wouldn't have behaved so stupidly had I been stronger in my faith."

Anna smiled ironically. "Faith, my dear son, doesn't keep us from doing stupid things. Neither, I suppose, does God. But faith often helps cushion the blow of our mistakes, and God is always there to help us pick up the pieces."

"There are plenty of pieces now to be picked up."

Anna took Yuri's hands into hers. "Why don't we just let God know we are willing?"

"Yes, Mama."

They bowed their heads and Anna spoke to her God. "Father, please be with my children as I know you always have been. Heal the anger and the hurts; strengthen the special bond between them. Give Yuri the ability and the wisdom to forgive himself for the mistakes he's made. Let us never forget how much we need you and how much you love us."

When Yuri went to bed that night, he didn't exactly feel like a new man, but he did feel better. However, he still worried about his brother and Talia. What would become of them? Could God truly make things as they once were? Or perhaps God had something better in store for each of them. Yuri didn't know. But he hoped at least that somehow God would take away the ache and heal their hearts.

IV

WAR AND WEDDINGS

Summer to Fall 1914

35

The Duma had concluded its session for summer recess, and Paul was glad to have some time off from the political arena. Political tensions were strong in the Capital. Unrest had broken out among thousands of workers. Some in the working-class Vyborg District had even thrown up barricades to protect strikers. Paul had exhausted himself in the debates over labor issues and in attempting to mediate between workers and management.

When Kerensky invited him to join him on a speaking tour during the recess, Paul debated with himself about accepting. Mathilde convinced him that such a holiday would only refresh him and make him more effective when the new session resumed in the fall. As usual, she had been right. However, in the middle of the tour stunning news reached them.

They were in Samara, and Kerensky had just delivered a rousing speech to a packed auditorium. The town showed a great interest in politics, though mostly in internal affairs as opposed to international. The response, however, was heartening. The next morning, still basking in the successful evening, Paul and Kerensky took a walk down to one of the jetties on the Volga River. A steamer was leaving the dock and crowds of excited people on the deck were waving and shouting. None noticed the newsboy hocking his papers along the docks. They could not hear the boy's announcement of the latest news.

"Read it here!" the boy shouted. "Archduke Franz Ferdinand assassinated!"

Paul and Kerensky looked at each other. They both well knew the terrible implications of such news.

"This is it, Sasha," Paul said.

"It's no surprise, really."

That was true. Tensions in Serbia were always at the boiling point. That's why Ferdinand, the heir to the Austrian throne, had gone to the provincial capital of Sarajevo in the first place, as a gesture of friendship, or, in the interpretation of some, to cajole the Serbs into accepting his plan to reorganize the Austria-Hungary state as an act of benevolence rather than aggression. Serbian nationalists, however, saw it only as a threat to their existence. For years they had feared their Austrian overlords would absorb their little province, and so they would not be fooled by Ferdinand's phony gestures.

"War has been brewing in Europe for years," Paul said. "Bismarck was prophetic when he said, 'Some irksome, foolish thing in the Balkans will set off the next great war in Europe.' And that was years ago, before the present complexity of foreign affairs. I hoped, however, that it would wait a couple years more, at least, until Russia would be better prepared."

"When have we ever been prepared for war?" Kerensky shook his head dismally.

"And there is no hope we will be spared."

"Not with the tangle of alliances and treaties that immesh Europe. Germany will rush to Austria's defense—the Kaiser dreams of war and will not miss such an opportunity."

"And of course, Russia will be honor bound to scurry to the aid of little Serbia. Other countries will fall into line like so many tin soldiers." Paul sighed. "Why else are European monarchs so steeped in military tradition? They are bred to war."

"Not Nicholas, I'm afraid."

"No, for all his fascination with parades and uniforms, I seriously doubt he has the heart for it."

"Paul, I feel I'd like to find a church and light a candle for our country. Then, I believe we should immediately return to Petersburg."

The news, which came to Nicholas on his yacht, *Standart*, was all but eclipsed by two other far more personal disasters.

As the tsarevich was jumping enthusiastically aboard the yacht, his foot slipped on the ladder and his ankle twisted. His sailor-companion Derevenko caught him before any worse mishap occurred, and it at first seemed that would be the end of it. But, by evening, the ankle had swelled because it was bleeding into the joint. In addition to the pain, the injury was especially disheartening for the child. He had been doing so well lately and was very much back to being his normal, active, even rambunctious self.

Alexandra and Dr. Botkin tended the weeping, suffering boy all night. The tsaritsa toyed with the idea of sending a wire to Father Grigori. He should by now have arrived in his village in Siberia. It might upset Nicky and would probably set tongues wagging again. But what did she care? Botkin was a good man, but totally helpless to do anything to cure her son. Grigori was her only hope. Let people talk! Let Nicky sigh at her—she could handle him. Baby was all that mattered.

When the news arrived of the murder of Ferdinand, Alix hardly cared. She felt bad for Nicky's distress, but that was just politics. A few wires would fly back and forth, tempers would vent, agreements would be made, and the course of national life would progress as always. Nicky told her he didn't seriously believe this would erupt beyond the borders of Serbia and Austria. Russia need not get involved at all.

Alix returned to her son's compartment and found some writing materials there. She would compose a wire to be sent immediately by the ship's radio operator to Siberia.

Then Nicky brought her the other news.

"Sunny, dear one," he told her, drawing her away from Alexis's bedside. "A wire just arrived—this seems a most ill-fated journey we are on."

"What is it?"

He bit his lip and his sad eyes lowered. "It's Father Grigori . . ." He paused and tried to meet her eyes but couldn't. "He's been injured. Someone tried to kill him—"

"Dear God! No!" She felt her blood drain from her face and the cabin begin to sway—or was she swaying? How much could a woman take?

Nicky threw an arm around her and led her to a chair. She was shaking all over and it took a long while before she could form the fateful question. "Is he. . . ? Oh, please, don't let him be—"

"He lives," said Nicky quickly. "But it seems quite serious. He was stabbed by some woman."

Dropping her head into her hands, Alix wept. "What will we do, Nicky? What will . . . we . . . do. . . ?"

"You must be strong, my love. For Baby's sake. He needs you."

"How can I be strong? Our only hope was Our Friend. If we lose him, what else is there? This can't be . . ."

The tsarevich did recover from his injury in spite of the *starets'* absence. The boy could not walk for some time afterward, but at least the bleeding subsided. Alix did not recover as readily. She was a nervous wreck, barely able to communicate in public, barely able to appear in public at all. She spent more time than ever before in her bed, pale and afraid.

Anna laid the newspaper on the table and glanced up at Raisa. "What will happen now, Raisa? What will happen to our sons?"

"Maybe there won't be a war, Anna."

Since the news of the archduke's assassination days ago, Austria had issued an ultimatum to Serbia, which even Anna could see was aimed as much at Russia as at the little Balkan country. The world had sympathized with Austria in their outrage over the murder of their heir. Yet diplomats urged restraint. Still, Anna had listened to her brother expound often enough about world affairs to know the implications of events in Sarajevo, even if she didn't fully understand it all. The fact that things were daily heating up instead of cooling off only supported Paul's fears. Today's newspaper seemed to deliver the final blow. Hardly giving their ultimatum a chance to settle, Austria, in one swift motion, declared war on Serbia and launched a lightning attack on Belgrade.

Like the tsaritsa, however, Anna cared little for political affairs except where they touched her personally. And she, too, could only think of her sons, who were of conscription age. If there was war, they would certainly have to fight. Thirty-six years ago she had watched Sergei go off to war, and ten years ago, Mariana had answered her country's call. Would she have to face another parting laden with fear and uncertainty? Ten years ago, in Manchuria, her brother had been killed. Did more such sacrifice lay ahead?

"They should put mothers in charge of the world," Anna murmured. "There would be no war then."

Just then the front door opened. In another moment, Yuri appeared at the kitchen door where Anna had been reading the paper to Raisa.

"Mama, Aunt Raisa, have you heard?"

Anna held up the paper with little enthusiasm.

"You should see the Palace Square," Yuri went on. "There are huge demonstrations supporting Slavic brotherhood."

"It's the Balkan War all over again," said Anna. "How everyone cheered and supported it at first—then when things started to go sour, they turned quickly enough."

"That war never really ended." Yuri walked to the samovar and drew himself a glass of tea, then sat at the table. "The tsar is mobilizing our troops. They will need medical officers, and now that my internship is over, I'm sure I'll qualify." At least he didn't sound enthusiastic about that awful fact.

"Yuri, must you?"

"I may not have a choice."

"Yuri, promise me you won't go unless you absolutely have to."

"I don't know, Mama. We'll see . . ." He finished his tea, then rose. "I better go wash up." He sniffed the air, fragrant with the smells of dinner—borscht and fresh-baked bread. "I imagine dinner will be ready soon."

Anna had forgotten all about dinner, but Yuri had just worked a full day at the hospital and must be hungry.

"Yes," she said. "In half an hour or so."

He left, and she and Raisa began final preparations for the meal. There was hardly enough work for the two of them, but they were both anxious for a distraction. Anna wished some new houseguests would arrive; it had been several months since an orphan or needy person had come. She had never before had to go seeking them, but she was beginning to wonder how to go about doing so. The thought brought Misha to her mind. Would he be involved if there was a war? If he had a choice, he would. As an officer, his age would not be prohibitive; the army would need good, experienced officers such as he.

Where was he now? Did he think of her? She had heard from him no more than a handful of times during the last nine years. She wrote him mostly to keep him informed about the family. The letters at first had been personal and lengthy, but as time went by they grew more stilted, offering for the most part only information. His replies were fewer and very brief. Their lives had grown apart. Why should she have expected it to be otherwise?

In the past few years, however, she had begun to wonder what a future with Misha might be like, perhaps even fantasize about it. Time was loosening the strong emotional ties to Sergei. It was bound to happen. But did that necessarily mean she was ready for another marriage? She sighed, hardly realizing she had done so audibly.

"What is it, Anna?" asked Raisa. "Worry about the war?"

"Oh, I guess . . ." Anna began slicing a loaf of bread, then paused. "Raisa, why did you never remarry after your husband died?"

Of course, they had discussed these things before, but Anna wanted to talk about it again—*needed* to talk about it again.

"I suppose there was never really anyone who interested me—and no one I cared for who took an interest in me."

"I remember Yakov Alexandrovich called on you for a while. He seemed like a nice man."

"Yes, he was. But he was Jewish, you know, and it caused too much friction when talk of marriage was raised." Raisa turned from her work and leveled an intense gaze at Anna. "Can I be honest with you, Anna?"

"Feel free, please."

"I don't like change." Anna chuckled, for she had always known that about her friend. "Getting to know a new man," Raisa continued, "learning his ways, and possibly having to sacrifice some of mine . . . it's scary. I've got such a good life, and I am content. Why change anything?"

"Don't you ever get lonely for the company of a man?"

"Sometimes, but I guess that isn't strong enough to risk all the rest. I rather like being independent, taking care of myself, making my own decisions. I'm a modern woman!"

They laughed at this, for Raisa hardly looked the part, with the perpetual apron tied about her thick waist.

Then Anna said more seriously, "What if I married again, Raisa?"

"Is there someone?" Raisa was genuinely surprised. No doubt she thought she knew every detail of her friend's life.

"No . . . not really. But if there was, and I married, it would spoil the good life we have now."

"If I fell in love—as the modern women put it—I don't think it would seem to me as if anything was being spoiled. You haven't held back because of me, Anna, have you?"

"Not really. The memory of Sergei and my love for him has always held me back. But I've noticed more and more lately that those feelings are different. They don't hold me with the same intensity as they once did."

"And you think you'd like to marry again?"

"Not just for the sake of getting married, but if there was someone special . . ."

"You've been thinking of Misha again, haven't you?" Anna felt her cheeks turn pink. Raisa laughed and added, "Goodness, woman! I do believe you love the man!"

"I've always loved him in one way or another—"

"It's the *another* that's important now. Do you miss him?"

"All the time. But, it doesn't matter. I haven't heard from him in a year. I just could not bring myself to write him and say, 'Oh, Misha, I'm ready to marry now; please come running.' "

"Why not?"

"He's made his own life now. And, heavens! I'm fifty-four years old. I can't imagine starting a whole new life at this age. I'm sure he couldn't, either." She sighed again. "But I do miss his friendship."

"Well, Anna, with war coming, maybe our world will change enough to make marriage seem a small change indeed."

"You always look at the bright side, Raisa," Anna said with a droll grin.

But Anna feared that Raisa's words might turn out to be prophetic. In Russia, change vied constantly with stagnation for supremacy. There was never any middle ground, it seemed. And maybe some good could come from a bit of change. But Anna prayed fervently that change would come about by any way other than war.

36

"Anyone home?" Talia's voice rang through the flat.

Yuri was coming from his room just as Talia came in. He hadn't seen her since that night, less than a week ago, when he had told her he did not love her. She had decided to go live with some other dancers near the theater. Yuri felt bad, especially for Raisa's sake, that his actions had forced Talia from their home. He felt no better now as they greeted each other with a rather stilted formality that had never existed between them before.

"Good to see you, Talia."

"And you, Yuri."

"I hope you plan to stay for dinner."

She sniffed at the fragrant air. "Mama's borscht is hard to resist." But she hardly seemed enthusiastic. There was a strain in her voice that seemed—he hoped, at least—to stem from something other than their problems. "Maybe I'll stay for a little while, but I didn't come for a meal."

"Is something wrong? Is the news about Serbia troubling you?"

"Are Mama and your mother in the kitchen? I think I should speak to them, too."

Now really concerned, Yuri followed Talia into the kitchen. Anna and Raisa stopped their conversation and greeted Talia warmly, obviously thrilled at the unexpected visit.

"I'm afraid I'm not here for a casual visit," Talia said. "I've just come from Andrei's place. I went to see him, wanting to talk about events in Europe. But he wasn't there." She paused, worry etching her fine features. "I spoke to his roommate, who told me he'd moved out four days ago."

"Moved out?" said Anna. "But he's said nothing."

"You've seen him since then?"

Anna shook her head. "Not since—" She stopped and glanced at Yuri.

"I haven't seen him either," Yuri said. "I wanted to give him time to . . . you know, cool off." Talia probably knew nothing of his altercation with Andrei. This didn't seem a good time to tell her.

"Are you sure of this, Talia?" Anna asked. "I mean, he would have told me. Did anyone say where he moved?"

"The fellow I spoke with didn't know. He said Andrei was upset when he left. I'm worried."

Yuri tried to sound casual. "I'm sure there is no cause to worry. You know Andrei, how impulsive he can be at times. He's just sulking somewhere, probably intentionally trying to make us—"

"Yuri!" scolded Anna. "What a way to speak of your brother! You know as well as I that he had good reason to be upset."

"Why? What happened?" asked Talia.

Yuri hesitated. Was this thing never going to go away? Would he never have to stop paying for his stupidity?

He said with resignation, "Andrei and I had a bit of a row. He was upset about what I'd done . . . about how I treated you, Talia."

"Then, it's all my fault!"

"You know very well that's not so. It was my fault—all of it. And now it's up to me to do something about it."

"What can you do?"

"Find the little brat, that's what." He strode into the hall and snatched his coat from one of the hooks there. "Would you keep dinner warm for me, Mama?"

"Where will you go? How do you know where to look?" asked Talia.

"I doubt he'll be too hard to find. One thing he's not is devious."

"Well, I'm going with you," Talia said. "I know him better than anyone."

It was well past midnight before Yuri and Talia gave up their search. They had visited all his known acquaintances and none knew a thing—or were not telling. One of Andrei's Social Democrat friends, whom Yuri had never liked, seemed extremely secretive—but then all of those fellows tended to be that way. Andrei seemed to have disappeared without a trace.

Yuri thought it was rash behavior even for Andrei, a gross overreaction. It was hard for him not to be a little peeved at his brother—after all, he'd had nothing to eat in hours and had been on his feet all day, and now had been forced to traverse the city in this crazy search. Yuri was tired and grumpy when he and Talia paused in a little park to have a rest. They sank down on a park bench, both silent and moody. It was a clear, beautiful night, too, not unlike that night when he had exchanged thoughtless words of love with Talia. All but the weather was different now.

"What do you think he's done, Yuri?" said Talia.

"I don't know, but at least he could have let Mama know. It was thoughtless of him."

"I don't think he would do such a thing unless something was terribly wrong. More than just being angry at you. What if he's been arrested? He wouldn't be the first revolutionary to just disappear like that—oh, I wish I hadn't thought of that. Now I'm really worried."

"I'm sure it's nothing of the sort."

"Then, what could it be? What could make him just disappear like this? He isn't so heartless that he'd do this in retaliation for some little row."

"No, you're right, Talia. He wouldn't. But it wasn't really a little row—not to Andrei."

"What do you mean?"

"I promised him I wouldn't tell you . . ." Yuri shifted uncomfortably. This was presenting him with a mental quandary. Andrei would have scoffed at him for agonizing over this and probably would have blurted out what felt right at the moment. But whenever Yuri acted impetuously, it always seemed to backfire. He thought briefly of Katya and his frequently impetuous behavior with her. It seemed it was going to work out now, although he hadn't heard from her since seeing her in Moscow over a week ago. She had assured him she would meet him in St. Petersburg soon and that she would not turn cool as she had in the past. But he was getting a bit worried since she still had not come.

He shifted his thoughts back to Talia. What would be the benefit of telling her of Andrei's love? It seemed Talia had a right to know. Perhaps if she did, she would begin to view Andrei in a different light and realize that he was a desirable man for her. In addition to that, it would also help take her mind off her disappointment and hurt over Yuri's rejection.

And what of the harm? Well, it would make Andrei furious at Yuri—but then he was already mad as a wounded bear at his brother, so, what did that matter?

"I don't want you to break a promise to your brother," Talia said magnanimously, though her tone indicated that she wouldn't fight him if he did want to tell her.

"Now that I think about it," said Yuri, "I believe this is one promise that should be broken. Andrei can be so glib sometimes with his tongue, yet when it really might do some good, he has chosen to rein it in. He's been keeping a secret from both of us for years—not unlike the secret you kept from me, Talia. I guess it was inevitable that we three should have had such a complex relationship. Not bound by blood, yet we grew up practically as family. We've walked a thin line between different forms of love—"

"Are you saying it was wrong of me to love you as I did, Yuri?"

"Not at all. I mean, what woman could help falling for such a fine specimen of manhood as I." He chuckled in an attempt to lighten the conversation but only drew a perplexed half-smile from Talia. He began again more earnestly, "And neither is it wrong for Andrei to have fallen in love with you."

"What *are* you saying, Yuri?"

"Talia, I didn't think you were as dense as I am. But perhaps it's like scientific observation—you can get so close to a problem that you lose your ability to solve it. You have to step back and get a broad picture before you can see the small thing you missed before. Talia, dear, Andrei is in love with you. That's why he flew off the handle as he did the other day. When you and I were together, it killed him. Yet he was willing to accept that because he knew it made you happy—that's how much he loves you. Then, when I hurt you—"

"Oh! Poor Andrei!" Sudden tears rose in Talia's eyes. How well she knew the emotional torments Andrei was suffering—because of Yuri, she had suffered the same.

"I think he left," Yuri continued, "because he couldn't face either of us anymore. Me—well, he just plain hates me. You, because he could no longer face you and keep his secret."

"And he felt it was better to leave than to tell me."

"Was it, Talia?" Yuri gazed incisively at her.

"He's my dearest friend in the world. I suppose if I *had* to choose between the two of you, Yuri, I'd have to choose Andrei—for a friend."

"I've always known that. And it makes sense, too, because the romantic feelings you've held for me also held you back a bit from me. Not so with Andrei."

"I had no romantic feelings for Andrei." It was a statement that ended with a slight question mark. Talia sighed. "And now what?"

"Does knowing how he feels change how you think of him?"

"I'm confused. Earlier this evening when we were pretty certain he had disappeared, I felt so empty. I felt as if part of me would die if I never saw him again. There are things I want to talk to him about—a new routine I'm trying, a problem I'm having with one of the other dancers, the fear I have about the prospect of war. Not long ago we were talking about God, and I know if we could talk more, I could help him unravel his confusion about spiritual matters. I was walking through the Summer Garden the other day and I realized that he should paint some pictures of the lovely, old statues there before they crumble away. I wanted to tell him that, and—"

"Talia, if that's not love, what is?"

"Of course I love him, but—"

"I'm certainly not one to give advice on love," Yuri broke in, "but think about what you feel for Andrei and what you feel—or felt—

for me. What is more fulfilling to you? Which do you need more? How often did you think of me just when you wanted someone to share some little trivial aspect of your life with?"

She smiled. "I mostly dreamed of you as my husband, whom I would gaze at in awe—"

"But not one with whom you'd share all your innermost secrets."

"I was too busy *doing* that with Andrei."

"Exactly!" Yuri grinned. He was beginning to feel like cupid. "What do you want, Talia? A man to worship or one to share—really *share*—your life with?"

"Oh, the questions you raise, Yuri . . ."

"I know. They are rather unsettling, even to me. Will you give them some further thought?"

"How could I not think about them? But, Yuri, do you think it's too late to do anything about it? What if I don't see Andrei again?"

"We'll see him again. A bad penny, you know."

She gave him a playful thump on the arm. "You know you want to see him just as badly as I do."

Yuri nodded thoughtfully.

"Yuri, let's pray for him. That God would keep him safe and bring him back to us—soon."

Yuri prayed as fervently as he had in a long time. It felt good, and he was thankful that his spiritual bottleneck had been opened that night with his mother. How had he managed without his faith? Well, he knew the answer to that when he considered the mess with Katya. He hadn't managed very well at all. During a short pause as he and Talia prayed, he silently appealed to God to give him direction about his feelings for Katya.

37

In 1913 Lenin said, "A war between Austria and Russia would be a very useful thing for revolution, but it is not likely that Franz Joseph, the Austrian Emperor, and Nicholasha will give us that pleasure."

Shortly before that statement, the Bolshevik leader had moved to Kracow with the unofficial blessing of the Austrian government. It seemed he was being encouraged to be a thorn in the flesh of Russia's tsarist regime. Clearly, the enemies of Russia were using the country's internal and external foes in any way they could to undermine the tsar. And the Russian government was doing the same to their international foes by secretly backing Serbian nationalists to stir up dissention in Vienna. It was a political game, and Lenin was an expert player.

But it was more than politics that drew Lenin to Kracow. Lenin was a nationalist through and through, and he suffered greatly from homesickness for his beloved Russia. Kracow, in spite of the fact that it was part of Austrian Poland, was Slavic and as such held an ambiance similar to Russia. Lenin was delighted to be there, only an hour and a half from the Russian border, and incredibly, only an overnight journey on the express train to St. Petersburg.

Andrei, too, was glad his personal journey would only take him as far as Kracow. Andrei had desperately needed to get away from home, but he hadn't wanted to be so far that home was unreachable. Yet by going to join Lenin, he was going about as far from home and his loved ones as possible—emotionally if not geographically. Yuri, because of the monarchist that he was, would be cut off completely. Andrei's mother, as always, would try to be understanding, but she would cringe at the thought of her son consorting with such hardened radicals. Uncle Paul would be appalled and would blame himself that he hadn't been able to steer his nephew away from the Bolsheviks.

And Talia . . .

It wouldn't matter one way or the other to her. She would love him anyway—as a brother only, of course.

But he didn't want to think of Talia. That's why he was getting as far away as possible, from her and from all that threatened to spark a memory of her. It wasn't working very well at the moment, but he hoped that as time passed and as he threw himself into the movement with all the passion and zeal they required, he would soon be too preoccupied to think of Talia.

He could have just as well gone to Paris and joined an artist's colony there—he knew several artists who would have welcomed him. He supposed his present destination happened a bit as a whim, an impulse. He had moved out of his apartment the day after his fight with Yuri and had already made the decision to leave town, though he had no specific direction in mind. In the meantime he stayed with some Social Democrat friends and tried to get together money for a journey by selling off paintings. When news of Austria's attack on Belgrade arrived, everyone was concerned about the troop mobilization and the certainty that they would be called up to serve in the army. As a group, they swore they would not serve in the tsar's army, fighting an imperialist war for the ruling classes. Plans were bandied about for ways to leave the country in order to avoid the army summons.

Andrei saw no reason to wait for that. He had every reason to leave *now*. Another fellow, Semyon Ivanovich, was also anxious to leave the country, because the police were breathing down his neck for his part in several recent strikes. Semyon had procured forged travel documents and was going to Kracow to join up with Lenin. He invited Andrei to come along and was able to get the necessary papers for Andrei as well.

With war seeming so imminent, revolution might not be as far off as they had assumed. If Andrei joined up with Lenin, he might just be putting himself in the right place at the right time. It wasn't hard for Andrei to ignore his doctrinal differences with the hard-core Bolshevik Party line. To him all the political rhetoric was secondary to action—and Lenin, if anyone, represented action.

But Andrei was not entirely insensitive to the repercussions of his actions on his family. Before leaving Petersburg, he posted a letter to his mother telling her vaguely that he was leaving the country for a while, not indicating any particular destination. He promised to keep in touch and begged her forgiveness for not having the courage to say good-bye in person. She would understand, and since Yuri talked to their mother far more than Andrei did, she probably had some idea about the situation with Talia.

The melancholy that had hung over him since leaving home began to lift as his train crossed the Russian border and was almost entirely replaced with excitement as they neared Kracow. In the Polish city, however, they met a great disappointment. Lenin was no longer there. Apparently his wife, Krupskaya, had taken quite ill, and they had been forced to travel to Poronino, where they hoped the healthful mountain air would help her. When her health only worsened, they went to Switzerland for medical treatment. After her recovery from the surgery there, they returned to Poronino.

Andrei and Semyon arrived at Poronino in the Carpathian Mountains in late July and were greeted by balmy warmth and spectacular mountain vistas. Luckily Semyon was acquainted with Zinoviev, Lenin's close friend and right-hand man, so they were hailed as friends. Stephan Kaminsky, still Lenin's bodyguard, greeted Andrei with some hostility but mostly with a hint of triumph that the frivolous artist had finally seen the light. They met Lenin briefly upon arrival, but later, Andrei was invited to have a personal interview with the Bolshevik leader.

"Kaminsky tells me you are Paul Burenin's nephew," said Lenin without preamble.

He looked exactly as Uncle Paul had always described him, except the receding hairline of his youth had turned into full-blown baldness on the top of his head. He had also aged—in fact, he looked several years older than his forty-five years. His slanted, squinting eyes were still sharp and held very little warmth.

"Yes, sir, I am. I would have said so myself except I was certain Kaminsky would inform you."

"Tell me why you think I should accept you into my organization?"

"Because I believe in revolution and will do everything I can to help the cause."

"The Bolshevik cause?"

"Yes."

"You don't accept your uncle's prejudices? He did not try to dissuade you from the Party?"

"My uncle believed I had the right to choose my own path—"

"The path of betrayal?" Lenin's eyes squinted even more, and Andrei thought a thin, sharp blade could easily shoot from them.

Andrei swallowed but held firm in his convictions against the powerful presence. "My uncle never betrayed you, sir—not in his heart. He always spoke highly of you and even now greatly admires you." He wanted to tell Lenin that if he hadn't been so dogmatic and exclusive in his beliefs, he would never have lost a good man like Paul. Instead, he did what he could to be conciliatory—after all, he didn't want to harm his chances of working for the Party. "Sir, how else could I be here now, desiring to join you? My uncle was a great influence on me. He told me many times that he doubted revolution would happen in Russia without your leadership. I believe that, too, and that's why I am here."

"You are not even a Party member."

"I know. I—"

"Kaminsky says you lack the kind of fervent loyalty that makes a good Party member."

"At the time I was absorbed in my art career. Many artists are revolutionaries and have suffered under the weight of Imperial censorship. But the fact that I have a passion for this work doesn't mean I can't also have a passion for the cause. I've often used my talent to promote change in my country—from the time I was thirteen, when I first pasted a subversive poster on a public building, I sought to combine my two passions. I was put off from joining the Party by Kaminsky's attitude that I could not do both. Where would the Party be without a means to communicate its ideas to the masses?"

"You make a good point."

"I have contributed to several Party publications under the pseudonym of 'Little Soldier.' "

"Really? That is you? I am familiar with that name."

"I hope in a positive way?"

Lenin rubbed his chin, and a small light of amusement glinted from the slits of his eyes. "I would have a hard time accepting Burenin's kin. But *Malenkiy Soldat* . . . that is another matter. We can use him—*if* he were willing to join the Party."

"Show me how, sir, and I will do it immediately."

The days passed idyllically in the picturesque mountains in the sleepy village. It almost made Andrei forget about the modern world and all its modern problems. But they were bound to catch up with him, even there.

Word reached the backwater village of Poronino at the very end of July. Germany, incensed over Russia's mobilization and the threat it posed, had issued an ultimatum to the tsar to stand down. When Russia did not respond in the time limit given, Germany declared war on Russia. Two days later they also declared war on France, Russia's ally, and marched on Belgium simultaneously with another declaration of war on that country. Then, a week after Germany's declaration of war on Russia, Austria-Hungary also declared war on Russia.

This was unsettling news to the little group of Bolsheviks in the mountains. Beyond the obvious broader repercussions of war, the state of war between Austria and Russia now made Lenin and his comrades enemy aliens in a country at war with their country of citizenship. The Austrian Ministry of the Interior might have given covert consent to the presence of the Russians, but on the local level, Lenin and his friends were nothing more than aliens who spoke the tongue of Austria's—and Poland's—enemy. A war of such broad scope had not occurred in Europe since the days of Napoleon. No one was quite certain of what to expect—except perhaps the *unexpected*.

Andrei was in the village when he first sensed the air of hostility. A small group of women were standing at the village well as he passed on his way to the little house he shared with Semyon and several other single men in Lenin's entourage. The peasant women cast Andrei unfriendly looks, then began conversing in their native tongue. Andrei could not understand the words, but he easily discerned by their tone and sneers that what they were saying wasn't favorable. Then one of the women chattered something and spit into the dirt after shooting another piercing glance at him. He only understood one word they said, a word any revolutionary is quick to learn—*police!*

He headed as quickly as he could to Lenin's cottage. Everyone had been worried, of course, and with good cause, since Russia was already poised on the borders of Russian Poland for an invasion into Austrian Poland. But somehow they thought they might be spared because they, too, were enemies of the tsar. They should have known that Poland's peasant stock might not be able, or willing, to make such a fine distinction. Russians were Russians, and Poland's perpetual enemies and oppressors.

When Andrei reached the cottage, only Krupskaya and her mother, who had lived with her daughter and son-in-law throughout their exile, were there. Krupskaya was resting on a daybed in the front room. Her mother sat in a rocking chair nearby, knitting, and it was she who had answered the door. The old woman smiled warmly at Andrei. She had taken a liking to Andrei, and when sweets came into the house, she always saw to it that Andrei had a sample.

She informed him that Lenin was off hiking in the mountains—his frequent occupation these days, during which he took voluminous notes of his thoughts and plans for the future. Krupskaya immediately sent Andrei after him.

Andrei hiked for a half hour before he met anyone—specifically Stephan Kaminsky, who had accompanied Lenin on the hike as his bodyguard. Stephan pointed Andrei toward a spot where Lenin was seated on a stump, reading on an overhang of rock that formed a lookout over a fabulous panorama of the mountains.

Andrei hated to disturb the man, who obviously was enjoying himself and having a rare moment of relaxation. So he told Stephan the problem. They had been hearing rumors for days now, and fear was being spread among the locals of dastardly deeds done by aliens in their community. One village priest had been warning his flock that enemy aliens were poisoning the water. But this was the first time anyone had specifically mentioned the police. Whether or not it indicated an immediate danger, it did seem it was time for the Russians to act. Stephan concurred that they had to inform Lenin, and by the time the information was communicated and the three hiked back to the cottage, over an hour had passed.

As they approached within a hundred feet, they saw horses tied to the porch rail—by the insignias on the saddle gear, the horses were identified as belonging to the local constabulary. The three men stopped, covered by a stand of trees and bushes.

"Looks like they beat us to it," said Lenin.

"We can still get away," said Stephan.

"And where would we hide in this area? I doubt the situation is serious enough to take to the woods to live off roots and berries until the danger passes. No, the worst they can do is deport us." Lenin glanced at his young companions, not so much for approval, but to ensure that they were resigned to follow his lead.

But before they could make their move forward, a voice called from behind, "Halt! Don't move!" A uniformed constable approached them, pointing an ancient rifle at them. "Do you live in that cottage?" he asked, staring at Lenin.

"Yes."

"Your name?"

"Vladimir Lenin."

"Come along with me—and don't think about getting away."

"That is the furthest thing from our minds," Lenin said with confidence.

Andrei tried to take some encouragement from Lenin's voice, but it was still unsettling to have a policeman aiming a weapon at him. Nevertheless, he obediently followed everyone to the cottage, determined that, no matter what, he would acquit himself honorably and prove once and for all that he was to be trusted.

The man with the gun yelled into the cottage, and in a moment another constable, the chief, came out. Krupskaya followed him, looking quite nervous and pale.

"Ilyich, they are searching our home!" she said, wringing her hands together.

"It's all right, wife," said Lenin, "we have nothing to hide."

In truth, Andrei knew there were secret lists of addresses of Party members and other sensitive Party documents in Lenin's possession—things that, in Russia, would have had them all hauled summarily off to the farthest reaches of Siberia. He had no idea what the Poles would think of them. But, in fact, the constable had not even noticed them. Instead, he was holding one of Lenin's notebooks.

"Perhaps you have not heard the recent news," said the constable. "But you are at this moment an enemy national in our country. Do you realize this?"

"Yes," said Lenin. "But we have done nothing wrong."

"I will make that decision. What are these?" He held up the notebooks—all written in Russian so, even if the man could read, he would not be able to decipher them, not to mention the fact that many of the entries had been written in code.

"Journals and the like," answered Lenin.

"I know a little Russian," said the constable. "And these appear to be written in some sort of code. Why would you do that with mere journals? I have had reports from many citizens of seeing you roaming over the hills, taking notes in these books—in all likelihood gathering information on troop deployments, geographical landmarks, and so forth to send to our enemies."

"That's ridiculous," protested Lenin. "Those are simply my thoughts, notes for political articles I plan to write. Espionage? Bah!"

"And what about this—?" The constable now held up a pistol. "It was found among your belongings."

"A little protection. What's wrong with that?"

"You do not have a permit for it."

"An oversight."

The constable shook his head, not convinced. "I'm afraid I must place you under arrest for espionage."

"What? That is the last thing I would do. I am as much an enemy of the imperialist tsarist regime as you." That would have been the supreme irony, for Lenin to be shot as a spy for Nicholas the Second!

"This evidence says differently." The constable gave his booty a pointed shake.

Stephan made a move, but the other constable stepped up quickly and thrust a rifle under his nose.

Lenin said with a glance toward Kaminsky, "We will go willingly. You will see soon enough that you have the wrong men."

Only then did Andrei realize that all of them were under arrest. His eyes widened and his jaw went slack. All the years he had lived as an insurgent in Russia, he had never been arrested or even threatened! But the irony of an arrest outside of his oppressive country was hardly amusing. It was scary. He couldn't muster even a hint of Lenin's confidence.

Lenin said good-bye to his wife, who promised to get help from their contacts in the Austrian government. Lenin said they would be free within two days. Still, Andrei felt weak in the knees as the constable prodded them, on foot, back to the village.

"You've never been arrested before, have you, Andrei?" said Lenin. "I could tell by that strange mixture of fear and exhilaration in your eyes. There is nothing like the first time, knowing you are truly sacrificing for the cause!"

Andrei had felt something else in him besides fear, but hadn't been able to identify it until Lenin spoke. Now he realized that it *was* exciting. He had achieved an honor that placed him on a level with his uncle and his father. He had achieved something that Yuri certainly hadn't.

38

The news of war was greeted in Russia with wild enthusiasm. Workers gave up their strikes, and thousands of others, from prince to factory minion, all gathered at Palace Square to shout their support and praise their emperor. Where only nine years before, on Bloody Sunday, the armies of the tsar had shot down innocent Russians, fervent strains of "God Save the Tsar" now rose like a wave from the voice of the crowd. No one seemed to give a thought to the potentially destructive force of such a wave.

Yuri shouldered his way through the crowd on Palace Square. The blood that had been spilled there nine years before was long gone, but Yuri could still point out the exact spot on which his father had been killed. He couldn't get near it now—there were too many people there, cheering the tsar. But a lump formed in Yuri's throat as the memory of that awful day assailed him. He could almost sympathize with his brother's antitsarist sentiments. But, unlike Andrei, who believed he was honoring his father by hating his killer, Yuri always had the deep sense that his father would not have hated his own killers but would have forgiven them.

Yuri wished that godly compassion was his only motive for a forgiving attitude, but, to be honest, he knew his compassion also had roots in his desire to be accepted among the noble classes, who were by and large loyal monarchists. Still, it was never easy to come to Palace Square and not feel deep and conflicting emotions for the loss of his father.

He should have avoided it altogether today. He didn't need this to further clutter his already churning thoughts. But when the message arrived for him at the hospital, and he was compelled to leave, his destination took him past the square. He was curious. There might also be news about military conscriptions. He did not relish the idea of going into the army, but he knew he would go if he had to. Still, for the time being, he had a more immediate problem at hand.

Katya.

Since his talk a few days ago with Talia, he had been mentally agonizing over his relationship with Katya. He had realized that he wanted the same things with Katya that he had praised about Talia and Andrei's relationship.

He loved Katya passionately, thought about her constantly. His heart throbbed whenever he was with her—probably much as Talia had once felt toward him. But he had to ask himself the same question he had posed to Talia. Did he only want a woman to worship? Didn't he rather want someone at his *side*, whose passion and need equaled his?

His mother and father's marriage was a shining standard to him, and he wanted nothing less for himself. Thus, with that in mind, he had to ask himself if Katya was the woman to meet that standard? He had always sensed with her that there could be more. When their times together had been good, they had been very good, even excellent! But those times had been so fleeting. Her warmth and compatibility easily turned cool and distant. The pain of her rejection still hurt him. And always he had the sense that she was holding something back from him. Their last meeting in Moscow had been wonderful. But would it turn cool again? And even if it didn't, did he and Katya truly have that special *something* that made a marriage all it should be?

He loved her, and yet he also questioned that love. Perhaps, as with Talia and Andrei, he needed to be separated from Katya in order to evaluate his true need for her. But not separated as in the past when he had been rejected, and thus his yearning for her was mixed up with such an array of other emotions. Perhaps he needed to step back from the relationship while it was good, and of his own free will. Then he might be able to more rationally assess what was real and important in it.

Yet it was no easy thing to break off with this woman whom he had been pursuing for nearly two years—and to break off when he had finally won her! It seemed insane, but he knew no other way. If only he could break through those barriers that seemed to hinder them from achieving true closeness. Her distance undermined the kind of trust necessary for a permanent relationship to grow. He *felt* she loved him, yet she always kept him at arm's length.

What else could he do but back off? If he couldn't penetrate her barriers, then did he have any other choice?

All this reasoning would be moot, of course, if she had continued to stay away. It had been a month since their meeting in Moscow. True, she had written him, explaining about the unavoidable circumstance that required her attention. She said there was an illness in the family. But she had been rather vague about it, and he couldn't keep from wondering if it was just another excuse. Maybe it was her way of gently backing out of any verbal commitments she had made.

Thus, when the message was delivered to him at the hospital, he was torn. Katya had returned to St. Petersburg and wanted to see him. He had walked a good deal of the way, his steps taking him past Palace Square, to have a chance to sort out his feelings before seeing her. But all the activity on the Square had prevented that. When he arrived at her grandmother's house on Petersburg Side, he was no closer to understanding himself than when he had begun.

The meeting between him and Katya was difficult from the beginning. She had actually invited him in, an occurrence that had happened only twice before. This time he was escorted into the parlor, and a servant brought them tea. Katya seemed more relaxed and at ease with him than ever before. But even that worried Yuri.

"What a time I've had these last couple of weeks!" she said. "I've never had anyone close to me so ill before. It was difficult."

"Who exactly was ill, Katya?"

"Then there was the news about poor Father Grigori." She blithely ignored his question. "I haven't seen him for such a long time and felt so guilty. It has been almost a year since I promised I would see him, and I never did. I will make a point of seeing him now that I am returned to Petersburg."

"I was beginning to wonder if you were going to stay away forever."

"Not this time, Yuri!" She smiled radiantly, and he felt his heart race. "I thought constantly about you while I was gone—"

"When you weren't occupied with your worry over Rasputin." He regretted the caustic words. He was slipping into his old pattern, momentarily forgetting that this relationship no longer controlled him as it once had.

"Why, Yuri, it sounds almost as if you are jealous!"

"Not at all. I am glad the priest is better."

"You don't agree with all those who were wishing he wouldn't survive?"

"No." But he couldn't infuse his denial with enough enthusiasm.

"I think it's terrible, Yuri, that anyone, especially a doctor, would wish ill to any human being."

"Katya, I don't wish ill upon Rasputin, but I do hope you will think twice about seeing the man."

"Who do you think you are telling me whom I should see and whom I shouldn't—!" She stopped, her face twisting in frustration. "Blast you, Yuri! I didn't want to fight on our reunion. I wanted it to be special when I responded to our conversation from the last time we saw each other."

"What do you mean?"

"I told you I'd think about marriage. Well, I have, and—"

Yuri looked away. He could tell by the sudden glow in her eyes that she was on the verge of accepting his proposal. His mouth went dry. What irony!

"What is it, Yuri?" He could not meet her questioning eyes. "Oh no . . . you've changed, haven't you?"

"It's not that, it's—"

"How could I blame you?" On the verge of tears, her voice cracked. "I pushed you away so many times, treated your love so cruelly—"

"Katya!" Yuri broke in. "It's me as much as you." When she opened her mouth to protest, he said more firmly, "Listen to me. I haven't changed, not in the way you think. I still love you. But I have to be honest. Lately I've questioned that love. Have I loved *you* or loved an image I had of you and of what we could have together? Katya, I want to love a real person—someone I can trust and who can trust me, someone I can share my life with. We have passion, but is that all we want? I fear it is all we will ever have, as things are now. I feel that there is a wall between us of . . . I don't know what. Mistrust, fear? What is it, Katya? Unless we can overcome that barrier, even the passion we feel will diminish. I cannot enter a union with someone who occasionally touches my heart, then retreats again."

"It is my fault . . ." she murmured quietly. "I spoiled everything. I didn't trust you. Maybe your love was simply too strong for me to believe. God knows, I've never had anyone love me like that before. It was so fragile and beautiful—but I destroyed it like I do everything else." Tears rose in her eyes and she tried unsuccessfully to squeeze them back. "Love is so frightening, Yuri. I know so little about it. Maybe I'll never know . . ." The tears erupted, but she continued, "And . . . now it's too late!"

Yuri put his arm around her—he didn't know what else to do. She laid her head on his shoulder and wept.

"Maybe it's not too late," Yuri said after several moments. Was he just saying something to comfort her? Or was it really possible? He wished it was—*prayed* it was. He didn't understand it at all, but he still loved her.

"No, Yuri. If only I had told you before this. But now . . . you'd have every right to hate me for keeping my secret from you. I didn't trust you. It doesn't matter that I don't know how to trust, that I know nothing of the kind of love you want. I knew enough to be honest. But I couldn't do it . . . and now I've lost you . . ."

"What secret, Katya? I've always known there must be something."

"Don't you see, Yuri? If I tell you now, it's like I am trying to win you through sympathy. I'd rather have no love at all than that. But the crazy thing is, I was about to tell you everything. If only I hadn't waited . . ."

"Don't write me off, Katya. Can't you give me a chance? Didn't I give you many chances? Didn't I keep coming back, even when you hurt me? And maybe, after all, that's really what love is—giving each other the benefit of the doubt and never giving up on the other."

She lifted her head. How beautiful she was with tears streaking her pale face, so sad, so vulnerable. Her vivid eyes glistened with tears . . . and something else. Need. She needed him as much as he needed her.

She sniffed like a little child, and he gave her his handkerchief. She blew her nose and dabbed away some of her tears. Then, with a determined breath, she said, "Yuri, if I tell you, will you promise that you won't feel sorry for me? And you won't let it sway your feelings?"

"I promise."

"And I will trust you." She spoke the words with assurance.

He smiled. Her statement was so simple, yet infused with so much sincerity. It was all he really wanted.

"But this is something I need to show you rather than tell you." To his perplexed look she added, "Remember, Yuri, trust. Come, take my hand."

He took her hand in his and they rose from their seats. Much to his surprise, she led him up the stairs and down a long corridor.

Then they paused before a door. Katya knocked, and when it was opened, they were greeted by a middle-aged woman whose homely face was warm—in spite of her obvious surprise at their appearance.

"I've brought a visitor, Teddie," said Katya.

"Indeed you have!" A smile tugged at the woman's lips.

"This is Prince Fedorcenko. I want him to meet Irina."

Yuri looked over the woman's shoulder. They were in a nursery. But Katya strode into the room purposefully, and he could only follow. A child, about two years old, was seated on a blanket on the carpet. When she saw Katya approach, she quickly pulled herself up on a nearby rocking chair and toddled toward Katya with arms outstretched.

"Mama!" said the child as she reached her chubby little hands up to Katya.

Yuri thought he'd heard wrong. Surely the child must have mistaken Katya for someone else.

But no. The truth was obvious by the way the child snuggled close to Katya when lifted into her arms, and in the way Katya cooed and kissed the child. Then Katya looked at Yuri.

"It's your . . . child?" Yuri croaked.

She nodded. "My terrible secret," she said, then smiled lovingly at the child. "Terrible and beautiful and sweet."

"But, why a secret?"

"Time for all that later. First, let me properly introduce you. Yuri, this is Irina. And, Irina, this is the most persistent, most infuriating, most wonderful doctor you'll ever meet."

Irina giggled as if she understood, then reached out a hand to touch Yuri's nose, which she grasped with a strong grip. Yuri chuckled. "Just like her mother—thinks there's a ring in my nose." He took the little hand and shook it politely. "A healthy grip, too. Delighted to meet you, Irina. I wish I could have met you sooner. But now that I have, I think we will be great friends."

"Do you really, Yuri?" Katya's eyes filled with as much hope as any child's.

"It amazes me, Katya, that someone so tiny, so innocent, could have been such a huge barrier between two people. I don't completely understand why, but I do know it wouldn't be right to keep her in that place. It's much too ponderous a weight for a little child."

"If only I could truly believe that—"

"What happened to trust, Katya?"

"Perhaps it is time you heard the whole story."

They walked in the garden. It was warm and fragrant there, with roses in full bloom and honeysuckle and many other blossoms in rich flower. Katya left Irina in the care of Teddie, and Yuri held her hand as if they had nothing between them but sweet love. He didn't think anything she could say would alter how he now felt. Certainly seeing the child hadn't, and he could guess at what Katya's story might be. But she needed to tell him, and so he let her.

"I never married." She paused, the shame in her tone evident.

"We all make mistakes." The words were trite, perhaps, but he meant them.

"My father wanted me to go to someone he knew, a failed medical student, who helped women . . . get rid of such mistakes." She closed her eyes. Reliving that awful time was obviously still painful. "I couldn't do it. Instead, I ran away to a convent in the Caucuses—far enough away from everything so my secret would be safe. The nuns would have found a home for my baby. But I couldn't do that, either. Perhaps it sounds very selfish. I've told you a little about my own mother, how she ran away, but I've never expressed how horribly that affected me. I always believed it was me she ran away from, not my father, and that if I had been a better person, maybe she would have loved me enough to stay. I didn't want my daughter to suffer like that. Even if I turned out to be a terrible mother, at least she'd have me. She wouldn't have to grow up thinking her own mother didn't love her enough to keep her—" Katya broke off as a sob escaped her lips.

Yuri placed his arm around her and held her close. "My poor, dear Katya."

"I don't want sympathy, Yuri."

"Sympathy? You have it all wrong. It is because of love, Katya, that I want to comfort you. Trust me."

She nodded. "I wish I had trusted you sooner. From the beginning, I hated not telling you. But my father insisted no one be told—that our family shame stay within the family. I suppose there were times when I didn't mind keeping the secret. I wanted to be normal. I was so confused—I just didn't know what was best, and sometimes I didn't even care. When you came along, Yuri, I think I loved you from the start. But I was so afraid of what you'd think. What I did was a horrible sin, and most decent people would instantly shun me if they knew. At times I thought I could keep it a secret and still have you—at other times I knew I couldn't and shouldn't. Maybe you can understand why I vacillated so. Even now I feel you must think me a loose, brazen woman for what I did. Believe it or not, before Irina came along, I *tried* to be a brazen hussy. If you think I am wild now, you should have seen me before. I really shouldn't have been surprised when I discovered that my wild ways had caught up with me. But it did surprise me—it devastated me! I was on the verge of ending my life—and that of my unborn baby. That's when Father Grigori came into my life. Yuri, you may not think highly of him, but he saved my life. He helped me find God's forgiveness for my sins."

"Then I will try to think better of him," said Yuri. "I will remind myself that because of him I was able to find you."

"There is good that comes out of everything. And Irina is the greatest good. There are those who might say she is the punishment for my sins, but I will never believe that. She is pure goodness. If there was any punishment, it came in other ways, in the torment I experienced, the confusion, and in almost losing you." She paused and looked at him. He could tell she was not fully convinced that he could still want her.

"But you didn't lose me, Katya," he said with emphasis. "We have a God who brings joy to those who place their faith in Him. I let go of my own faith for a while, but I am beginning to find it again. My papa was fond of a Scripture that said, 'Delight in the Lord and he will give you the desires of your heart.' It is truly happening to me, Katya."

"I am the desire of your heart?"

"Oh yes. But the funny thing is, Katya, God didn't give me that desire until it was the right thing for me."

Her lips bent into an ironic smile. "It's odd, Yuri, that you have such a hard time accepting Father Grigori. He is a deeply spiritual man, perhaps not unlike your father was. I should think you two would have much in common."

She was right in a way—Rasputin was very spiritual. Yet Yuri was certain that Rasputin and Sergei Fedorcenko were worlds apart, especially spiritually. Just thinking of the *starets* made Yuri's skin crawl, but he didn't deem this a good time to detail his disquiet to Katya. Instead he said lightly, "I don't know what it is, probably just his smell."

"I know you are not that superficial, Yuri."

"Perhaps we ought to save this discussion for another time."

When she nodded, obviously relieved, he went on. "Katya, I do have another question about Irina. Your answer will not change how I feel, yet I guess I need to know. Please forgive me for asking . . . but, what about Irina's father?"

"I understand . . . and you have every right to ask. I can say without hesitation that he means nothing to me now. I thought I loved him, but I think mostly he represented a way of escape from my father's control. He is the son of a French diplomat and has now returned to France. As it turned out, he had no intention of marrying me, and since I didn't want to be the cause of an international scandal, I did not pursue the matter. He wanted no part of the child. I suppose at first I had hoped it would compel him to marry me, but I quickly realized that I didn't want any man who was forced into marriage. I have never revealed to anyone the man's identity. Perhaps one day Irina will want to know, but I will ford that river when I get there." She paused, sighing. "There you have it—all my dirty laundry. I have no more secrets . . ." Her voice trailed away and her brow creased. "Yuri, there is one other thing . . ."

He put his fingers to her lips. "Katya, I don't need to know anything else. I love you and want to marry you. If I have any hesitation now, it is only because of the war and all the uncertainty of it. But even that won't change how I feel."

"How am I so fortunate to have a man like you love me so?"

"Only by the mercy of God."

"Yes . . . truly!"

They returned to the nursery so Yuri could say good-bye to Irina. They played with her for a few minutes before Yuri had to leave for the hospital. He found it amazing how natural he felt around the child, especially for a man who had had little contact with children except in the hospital. When he married Katya, he would become an instant father. The idea was a little frightening, but he knew he'd have no trouble at all loving Katya's child.

39

Katya was understandably nervous about meeting Yuri's mother. Yuri joked that it could not possibly be as daunting as his upcoming meeting with her father would be.

A little shadow flickered across her face, then she chuckled. "You're right. I'm sure this will be a lark by comparison."

Yuri also knew Katya was uncertain about what to say to her prospective mother-in-law about Irina. But they had both agreed to put an end to secrets, though they weren't quite certain yet just how they would handle questions about Irina's origins. Yuri thought his mother would have wisdom for them because of her peculiar situation with Mariana.

Yuri was thrilled to present the woman he loved to his mother. It had been difficult keeping that relationship quiet. In the past, he'd made one or two vague references to Katya, but their status had always been so uncertain that he had never felt confident enough to make serious mention of her. Now, as he and Katya traveled by cab across Nicholas Bridge to Vassily Island, he felt his first touch of nerves. He wondered what his mama would think of Katya. She was quite different from Talia and also from the domestic types Anna and Raisa were accustomed to. His mama had probably always pictured her conservative son with a flower of Victorian womanhood rather than with a modern woman such as Katya.

Yuri felt the differences most strongly as they entered his plain, working-class flat. Katya was wearing a lovely silk summer dress, pink and white stripes, perfectly suited to the warm August day. She looked like a breathtakingly beautiful flower growing in a poor alley. The dress was the latest spring offering from Paris, and even Mariana and Talia had never looked so absolutely chic.

Katya gave him a weak smile. "She won't think I'm putting on airs, will she? I tried to dress simply."

Yuri knew she was dressed as simply as she could. There was nothing in her wardrobe, after all, that was not a Paris original. He gave her an encouraging smile. The moment his mother appeared, Katya would be put at ease. Even Yuri himself felt no sense of hesitation at bringing someone like Katya into his poor home. And even if he did, all he had to do was remind himself that his mother was a princess of Russia who *chose* to live a simple life.

"Mama!" he called as he closed the door behind them. Katya squeezed his hand tighter.

Anna stepped from the kitchen, drying her hands on the clean white apron she was wearing. "Goodness! You're early." She smiled, not in the least put out by their surprise appearance. She quickly took off her apron. She was wearing her best also, a tan linen two-piece outfit, with brown buttons down the front. Mariana had sent it to her two years ago for Christmas, and she wore it only on special occasions. This was as much an important event to Anna as it was to Yuri and Katya, and Yuri thought his mother might be feeling a touch of nerves also.

Anna draped her apron over the telephone table in the corridor, then strode to her guest with her hands held out.

"Katya! It is such a pleasure to finally meet you."

There was a momentarily awkward pause before Katya took Anna's offered hands. But, as their hands touched, the two women appraised each other carefully with their eyes. Yuri held his breath, his confidence wavering slightly.

Then Katya said, "Princess Fedorcenko, the honor is mine, believe me! Yuri has sung your praises to me often, and now I see he has only spoken the half of it."

Anna grinned and winked at her son. "Yuri, why don't you take Katya into the parlor. I have one or two more things to do for dinner in the kitchen—"

"Please, Princess, may I help you?" asked Katya.

This truly amused Yuri because, to his knowledge, Katya had never set foot in a kitchen. But it endeared her to him even more.

"Come along, then," said Anna. "There's not much to do, but we can visit. However, before we do anything else, I must confess to you that I can't abide being called 'princess.' My son bears his title well, but mine has never quite fit me. Please, just call me Anna."

Yuri had almost forgotten how his mother had moved among the nobility in her youth, how she had come to be dearest friends with a princess. It showed now in how graciously she put Katya at ease.

He had also nearly forgotten how much Katya longed for a mother. Now, it seemed, she had finally found one.

After dinner the three sat in the kitchen with cups of tea and homemade sweet rolls. Raisa was gone for the evening, attending one of her daughter's performances. Both women had felt that one mother figure at a time was quite enough to subject Katya to, so it was just Anna, her son, and her daughter-in-law-to-be.

The prospect of a new daughter in the family came easily for Anna. Yuri was ready for marriage, and she had been expecting it to come anytime. The idea of losing him never occurred to her. She was only gaining another daughter. And a granddaughter, it seemed, as well.

She was already a grandmother three times over, of course, from Mariana and Daniel. Mariana came to Russia once every year or two, so the children were not complete strangers to her. But Anna had not yet seen the newest addition to their family. The children, and even Mariana, were beginning to seem a bit foreign, adopting American ways. Nevertheless, she loved them dearly, and she knew she would come to love Irina. That none of these youngsters were her blood grandchildren was simply not an issue to Anna.

As they sat at the rough old table, Anna could tell that something was troubling Katya. Through dinner they had talked mostly of trivial things or, at least, introductory things—likes, dislikes, experiences—nothing too deep or difficult. But now Katya obviously wanted to move into more sensitive areas, but she seemed to be having difficulty finding the proper approach. Anna was proud of her son who, seeming to sense the strain, stepped in to pave the way.

"Mama, I've told Katya something of our family's peculiar history, but I thought she might like to hear a woman's perspective, especially about how you came to adopt Mariana."

"Mariana. . . ?" It took a moment before it dawned on Anna what Yuri was leading to. Then she remembered a passing remark he had made when he first told her about his engagement to Katya. At Katya's request, he had told Anna about Irina so it wouldn't come as a complete shock when they met. Yuri had mentioned that Irina might one day have an experience similar to Mariana's. "Ah, yes, Mariana. She was the daughter to Princess Katrina Fedorcenko, to whom I was a maid."

"Yes," said Katya, "Yuri mentioned that. But I was never quite clear about the reason for the secretiveness surrounding her."

"I must admit it is complicated," Anna replied. "There was a madman who wanted to kill Mariana's parents and Mariana, too, for that matter. When Katrina died in childbirth, we decided it best that no one know the child survived. Her father was forced to leave the country, so I raised the child. I think that Katrina wanted her daughter raised simply, away from the pressures and intrigues of the nobility. Perhaps she had a rather romanticized view of the peasantry, probably fostered by my own stories of my parents, who were rather extraordinary. Nevertheless, she knew no one could love Mariana as much as I, and Katrina had no other family left with whom she felt she could entrust her child."

"So you claimed her as your own?"

"Everyone in the village drew their own conclusions. At first there were rumors and whisperings because I wasn't married, and it was very difficult for me not to speak up and set everyone straight. Then Prince Sergei and I married, and soon everyone just came to accept us and our child. People are basically like that, you know—short on memory, long on forgiveness. Not all people, I suppose. Basil Anickin, the madman I spoke of, had a *long* memory, but he was unusual in that area."

"It's apparent you told Mariana about her origins, but may I ask when?" asked Katya.

"Practically from the beginning—that is, we told her about her real parents. I wanted her to know about her mother and love her as she deserved to be loved. But Mariana always understood it was something to be kept within the family."

"But how can a child understand such a thing?"

"Children don't care to be different, so they are not likely to speak about things that may make them seem so. We didn't want to teach her to be deceptive, nor did we want her to fear—for, of course, there was still danger involved for some time. We simply let things evolve naturally. If she felt compelled to tell someone, we asked her to discuss it with us first, but if she didn't—well, we just prepared ourselves to bear the repercussions. Secrets are as demanding and hurtful at times as the worst truth. We never told her about her nobility—not until her father showed up when she was sixteen. I still don't know if that was the right or wrong decision. God saw that our hearts were seeking to do the best we could, and I believe He honored that in our lives and in Mariana's life."

"You know why I am so curious about this, don't you, Anna?" said Katya.

"Yes, I do."

"My situation is a little different from yours in that true scandal is involved. Sometimes I feel I could bear the scandal. You may as well know that in society, I am considered rather a wild one—"

"My Yuri would not love you so if your heart were not made of gold."

"I want to be worthy of that love." Tears glistened in Katya's eyes. She bit her lip and tried to continue calmly. "Anyway, most people wouldn't be surprised by anything they heard about me. But I fear what would become of Irina—and even Yuri. It is enough I made a terrible mistake and nearly destroyed my life; I don't want to ruin their lives, too. Wouldn't it be best to keep things as my father arranged it? Why does anyone need to know?"

"You wouldn't mind going through life as your daughter's aunt or, at best, adopted mother?"

"Even now, I haven't had the heart to prevent her from calling me 'Mama.' But that is only in the privacy of the nursery. I have never gone out with her in public." Katya paused, her lip quivering. "I want to be her mama. But I don't want her to be hurt again by my selfishness."

"People may hurt Irina no matter what you do—"

"You just said they were forgiving."

"Yes . . . sometimes. But people are . . . well, people. We human beings are a complex breed. Which is the best argument I can think of for living your own life, by the standards that best suit you—and hopefully, if you have a true heart toward God, those standards will also please Him. Either way, it can be self-defeating to constantly try to please other people. You'll never be able to do it, Katya. There will always be someone out there demanding something different from you."

"Well, I think it would be best for Irina to have her mama."

Anna smiled. "So do I. She has a fine mama, too."

Katya's cheeks flushed. "I try to be." Then she looked at Yuri. "What do you think about all this?"

"At last, a man's point of view!" he quipped. "Seriously, I believe that we will weather whatever is hurled at us *together*. The Fedorcenko clan are expert at surviving rumors and scandal. In fact, I think we have thrived on it and become rather more noble from it all."

"Then, I am marrying into the right family!"

"You are indeed, Katya!"

Anna was warmed by the intensity in Yuri's and Katya's voices. She knew about the rocky beginnings of their relationship, but now she saw nothing but the makings of a strong and true union.

40

Nicholas basked in the initial support of his people for the war. For those first weeks, he felt like the autocrat he was supposed to be. But more than that, he felt like the benevolent *batiushka*, Little Father, he so longed to be. Even the Duma, for years a thorn in his side, overwhelmingly supported the war, with only the Bolshevik contingent dissenting. He could almost feel the streets throb with excitement as thousands of soldiers marched daily to Warsaw Station and on to the Front. Nearly five million soldiers were ready with the initial mobilization to go to war. Another ten million would be available should the need arise. They were truly, as the British press had dubbed them, "the Russian steamroller."

Sitting atop his mount now at Mars Field, reviewing the troops, he could believe those who declared that all the Russians would have to do to defeat the Germans was to throw their caps at them. He knew better of course. It would take guns and bombs and railroads, all of which Russia was in poor supply. Yes, they had an awesome contingent of personnel, but putting guns into all those millions of hands was another matter completely. Before the end of the year, half of his mighty army might well go to war without rifles in hand. But at least they would march to the Front sober.

One of Nicholas's first acts of the war, while he was still riding high on the people's good will, was to institute prohibition against the sale of vodka. And in another zealous moment, Nicholas issued a decree changing the name of his capital from the decidedly German-sounding St. Petersburg to the more Slavic Petrograd.

As long as he had the support of the people, Nicholas felt invincible. He even felt he could dismiss Rasputin's criticism. From his hospital bed in Siberia, the *starets* had implored the tsar to stay out of the war. One telegram had the ominous ring of prophecy to it: "Papa, you must not go to war, for it will mean the end of Russia."

Nicholas had never wanted war. In fact, he had been fairly certain that his cousin Willy, the Kaiser of Germany, would dissuade Austria from rash actions. When that had not happened and Willy had betrayed Nicholas, the tsar moved forward into war with righteous confidence. He still felt that confidence despite Grigori's pronouncement of doom.

Now word had reached the tsar, via the agents assigned to keep Rasputin under surveillance, that the Mad Monk had returned to Petrograd. Nicholas received the report with mixed feelings.

To his secretary, Fredericks, he said in a candid moment, "Better to face one Rasputin than ten fits a day of my wife's hysterics."

In truth, his feelings toward the priest ran the entire emotional gamut from utter disdain to near devotion. After all, Nicholas had seen Rasputin heal Alexis with his own eyes. He had watched his son go from near death to health. Alexis was everything to Nicholas, his heart, his soul, his hope, and the man who could restore all this to him must be revered.

Yet Rasputin's behavior—at best crude, at worst supremely vile by many reports—was an intense embarrassment to the tsar. Alix didn't believe any of the reports, but when they came from trusted officials, men of honor, it was difficult for the tsar to dismiss them so easily. In Nicholas's eyes, however, Rasputin was a *family* concern and, thus, ought not to be anyone else's concern.

Sometimes Nicholas forgot that he was not merely a country squire, who had the prerogative to *have* family concerns. Rather, he was the ruler of the mightiest nation on earth. His life, his family, even their most intimate details belonged to a whole nation, perhaps even the world.

When he returned home to Tsarskoe Selo in the late afternoon, he was still feeling exhilarated. He was ready himself to go to the Front, and he would, too, even if his commanders had talked him out of taking the reins as commander in chief of the army. He went to his study and was about to read the latest mail when the door to his study opened. Nicholas looked up sharply, a bit annoyed at being so rudely interrupted. He was about to rebuke the intruder until he saw it was his daughter Tatiana.

"Papa! I'm so glad you are home. Mama told me to watch for you and fetch you quickly when you arrived. Alexis is bleeding again."

"Dear Mother of God, no!" He rose. "Has Dr. Botkin been called?"

"Yes, Papa. He and Dr. Fedorcenko are there now."

Nicholas hurried with his daughter through the corridors of the Alexander Palace to the tsarevich's bedroom. The moment Nicholas entered, his wife rushed to his side.

"I hope I wasn't wrong in waiting to call you, Nicky," she said. "It seemed a small incident at first. A nosebleed that started with apparently no cause. It just . . . started. And it hasn't stopped since this morning. He's so weak now." She was wringing her hands and on the verge of tears. He put his arm around her, and together they approached the boy's bedside where the doctors were bending over their patient.

"Dr. Botkin," said Nicholas, trying to instill calm into his voice, "what do you think?"

"We are trying something new," Botkin replied. "I've packed the nasal passages with gauze soaked in a solution Fedorcenko has concocted—"

"What solution is that?" Nicholas knew his tone was sharp, suspicious. But this was his son, the heir to the throne, and he didn't like the idea of him being used as a guinea pig.

Fedorcenko replied, "Nothing that would be harmful, I assure you, Your Highness. A simple mixture of groundsel leaves to which I've added alum root. Both have been used for generations on bleeding in the mucous membranes. I've been experimenting with several herbal folk remedies, Your Highness."

Nicholas leaned close to his son and, gently stroking the boy's warm forehead, said, "How are you Alexis, dear?"

"My pillow is wet, Papa." The child's reply was barely above a whisper. He was so pale.

Then Nicholas noticed the puddle of blood under his head. He looked at Fedorcenko. "How long do you expect before this takes effect?"

"I was hoping by now. I believe it has abated somewhat, but—"

"Not enough, though?"

Both doctors shook their heads in a grim negative.

"There is nothing else to be done?" asked the tsar. How many times had he asked that question over the years—always hoping.

"Sir," said Fedorcenko, "I would like your permission to try another medication. It has been patented in America and has been on the market for nearly ten years. It's called hydrastine. It's been used with success in cases of uterine bleeding."

"Do whatever you must," said Nicholas. "As must I."

He then turned away from the bedside and from the doctors, took his wife's arm, and led her to the back of the room. "Alix, I've had a report that Grigori is back in Petrograd—"

"Nicky! When?"

Nicholas was unable to meet his wife's eyes when he said, "Two or three weeks. Forgive me, Sunny, but—"

"How could you?" she raged. "Our son might never have had this happen had you told me earlier. You are cruel, Nicky."

"Alix, he confuses me so. I never know what is the best thing to do about him. There are so many disturbing reports. I don't know what to believe. Can't you give me some credit that I am telling you now?"

"Now? When it may be too late?"

"Sunny, you have my blessing to call him."

Saying no more, Alix spun around and rushed from the room.

Two hours later, leaning heavily on a roughly hewn walking stick, Rasputin burst into the sickroom. His sudden appearance was a shock to the subdued quiet that had been hanging over the room. Yuri noticed that the monk was much thinner than when he had last seen him. Under the scruffy, greasy beard, his face was gaunt and pale. He was dressed in a wrinkled, old cassock, a pectoral cross—which many said he had no right to wear because he was not a real priest—hanging prominently about his neck.

Alexandra rose from where she had been seated at her son's bedside and strode to the *starets*, taking his grimy hands in hers.

"Father Grigori! At last."

"I came because I bear you no grudge for so cruelly snubbing me. I am God's servant and must do *His* bidding. He has called me to be the tsarevich's savior, and so I must ignore the sting of betrayal—for the salvation of Holy Russia! And so I come to you."

She knelt before him and tearfully kissed his hands. "I didn't know you were here. Anna Vyrubova and I—"

"I know about you and Anna. You've had a falling out with her.

And you let that come between *us*? Between me and the salvation of your son? Oh, Mama! You are a petty woman!"

"Forgive me, Father Grigori! I beg of you! Heal my son. I will do anything!"

"Oh yes, you will, Mama. Believe me, you will!" Then he turned his back on her—on the empress of Russia!—and walked to the bed. Before he focused on the boy, however, he leveled a glare at Yuri and Botkin. "So, the worthless doctors have failed again! They call you first, but it is I—only I!—who can heal. Someday they will learn. Now get out of my way."

When Botkin stood firm, Yuri, following his lead, also stayed put.

"I said, get out of here!" shouted Rasputin.

"Please," said Botkin, "this is a sickroom."

"Only because of inept fools like you!" raved the *starets*.

A tense moment passed as the two doctors and the monk seemed to face off. Then Nicholas, who had been quietly sitting in the shadows, said, "Please, Dr. Botkin, Dr. Fedorcenko . . ." The tsar was beseeching them, not ordering them as he certainly had a right to do. "Let the priest in."

Despite the tsar's less-than-compelling command, Yuri knew they could not ignore it. They stepped back. Rasputin bent very close to Alexis. Yuri cringed when the man roughly pulled out the gauze packs. The bleeding had slowed, even if just marginally; yet the abrupt removal of the gauze could irritate the tender membranes and bring on a fresh hemorrhage.

"Alexis, look at me," demanded Rasputin.

The tsarevich's eyes fluttered open. "Father Grigori . . . you have . . . come to save me. . . ?"

"Have faith in me and in the Holy Virgin . . . and God will intercede."

"Yes . . ." Alexis murmured. His eyes drooped closed.

"I said, open your eyes!" Rasputin's tone was harsh. Yuri wanted to thrash the man for his insensitivity. Then Rasputin grabbed Alexis's shoulder and gave it a hard shake. "Look at me, boy! Keep your eyes on me . . . I am your salvation and the salvation of Russia."

"I am so tired, Father. . ."

"Do you want to get well?"

In response, Alexis forced his eyes open once more. Rasputin's face was an inch from the boy's.

"Good. It won't be long before you will be walking and running in your favorite places," Rasputin said, this time in a soothing, sing-song tone. "You and I will walk by the balmy shores of the Black Sea. Remember when you made castles in the sand? And your sisters will be there, too. You'll swim and play tag . . ."

Rasputin went on for several minutes in this vein, describing trips the tsarevich had been on or ones he hoped to take. He took the boy on imaginary strolls in the woods, chasing butterflies, or driving under a summer sky with salt air in his nostrils. Then, when Rasputin finished, using his stick for support he straightened. "Now, you can sleep, little one. You will be whole again."

Finally, Rasputin crossed himself and the tsarevich, and he intoned, "In the name of the Father, and the Son, and the Holy Ghost!"

Alexis's eyes dropped shut as if they were mechanical, operating by the sound of Rasputin's voice. When the *starets* moved away from the bed, his whole body was shaking. His face was twisted with pain as he took a hobbled step. He was obviously spent. And Yuri was almost certain this was no act. The man had expended a great effort in what he had just done. Of course, the fact that he was barely recovered from a near-fatal injury was most likely the reason for this reaction.

But any pity Yuri felt was clouded as the priest brushed past him, then, pausing, turned and spit at Yuri's feet.

"You will kill the little one someday," Rasputin said, "with your concoctions and remedies. God curse you and your kind!"

The utterance was not spoken glibly, but rather with an unsettling power. Yuri hated himself for it, but he was shaken by the man's words.

The tsar and tsaritsa followed the *starets* out of the room. Yuri and Botkin were silent for some time. Yuri had almost forgotten about the tsarevich. But Botkin had gone back to the bedside.

"Yuri, come here," said Botkin.

Yuri came up next to the elder doctor and gazed down at the child. He was asleep—not just asleep, but his breathing was regular and relaxed. The lines of fear etched into his youthful brow were gone. And, even with the gauze packs removed, no more blood oozed from his nostrils.

Yuri's mouth went dry. "Dr. Botkin . . ."

"Don't think it, Yuri! You know as well as I that it is common for the bleeding to stop as spontaneously as it began. That fraud comes when the crisis has peaked, speaks his incantations when natural physiology is about to take its course anyway, then leaves, taking all the credit."

"But so quickly . . ."

"You saw how he hypnotized the child."

"Yes . . . the effects of relaxation upon the blood vessels, which hypnosis could induce, can be remarkable." Yuri sighed. "We can see the marks of scientific fact in what has happened, Doctor, but, unfortunately, the empress never will."

"Too true. God forgive me, but I despise that man."

"Even if he can heal," said Yuri, "it isn't right the way he uses his power. I cannot see God in him, and I have tried, Doctor—for my own reasons, I have tried."

41

It was a chilly and gray day as Yuri looked out the window of the train that took him away from his grueling session at Tsarskoe Selo. Fall was still very much evident, but winter was not far away. Yuri wondered what winter would bring. The war was not progressing well. After two initial victories over the Germans at Gumbinnen and Galicia, the Russians, at the end of August, had suffered the stunning defeat at Tannenberg in which over a hundred thousand Russian troops had been lost. Yuri counted his presence in Petrograd—would he ever get used to that name?—by minutes and hours. He fully expected his summons for military service to come soon. The need for doctors at the Front was growing with each bloody defeat.

After the exhausting session at Tsarskoe Selo with the tsarevich, however, Yuri almost thought a posting to the war might seem a lark. Every time he encountered Rasputin, it left him drained and confused. He was glad Katya had not pursued her old acquaintance with the man. He knew she desisted, however, only because he had asked her not to. She felt a loyalty for the priest, perhaps even a tenderness, because he had helped her in the past. She was completely blind to Rasputin's dark side. And that worried Yuri. Several of Katya's friends were devotees of Rasputin, and her ambivalence toward him might cause her to be easily swayed into the circle of women, the *Rasputini*, who always seemed to surround the *starets*.

Yuri didn't know what they saw in the man, and this morning's episode didn't help Rasputin's cause in Yuri's eyes. It especially disturbed Yuri to see how the tsar and tsaritsa behaved around him. Alexandra had actually knelt before him! It would be different if Rasputin were a venerable elder, a true saint, but Yuri was becoming more and more convinced that he was, at the very least, a crass opportunist, using a helpless child to further his own ambitions. At worst, Rasputin might well be truly evil. One thing was certain to Yuri—the *starets* was no holy man. If he did indeed heal the tsarevich, his powers could not possibly come from God.

Yuri's troubled mood did him no good when he arrived back at the hospital to find a letter from the military induction board. His hands trembled as he opened it. The dreaded words inside were no surprise, but they made him cringe anyway.

His first thought was to find Katya. But he had to work. If doctors were needed at the Front, they were no less needed here. Wounded poured into the city daily, not to mention the civilian cases that continued at their normal rate. Yuri telephoned Katya several times, but she wasn't at home. He worked until about ten that night on two serious emergency surgeries. It had been impossible for him to get away. Then, not five minutes after he sent the second case to the recovery room, a third arrived, a man who had extensive shrapnel embedded in his abdomen. It was hard to believe the man had made it this far from the battlefield. Yuri scrubbed, and a nurse was helping him don clean surgical garb when he felt himself sway.

"Are you all right, Doctor?" asked the nurse.

Yuri squeezed his eyes shut in an attempt to make his blurry vision clearer. He had been on his feet since six that morning, with the exception of the train ride to and from Tsarskoe Selo, and he had eaten nothing. "Who else is on call?" It was foolish to keep going in his present state, risking his patient's welfare.

"Dr. Vlasenko is, sir."

He grimaced. But even Vlasenko would be more competent than Yuri at the moment. "I think you'd better call him."

He went to the doctor's lounge and tried to rest but was too keyed up. He tried Katya again. Perhaps it was late enough for her to finally be home.

"I'm sorry, Prince Fedorcenko," said the servant on the other end of the line. "Countess Zhenechka did come home earlier, but then left again two hours ago."

"Did no one tell her I called?" he asked sharply.

"That is possible, sir, because she was only here a few minutes before an urgent call arrived for her and she left again."

"Where did she go?"

"To . . . the *starets*."

"Rasputin's?"

"Yes, sir."

Yuri hung up the phone. By now he was functioning on pure grit and instinct. He didn't even debate what he would do. It incensed him that Katya was with Rasputin when *he* needed her, and when he had expressly requested that she not do so.

He hailed a cab outside the hospital and went directly to 64 Gorokhavaya Street. Having not been to the place in months, Yuri was amazed at what greeted him. Outside the building and trailing up the three flights of stairs that led to Rasputin's flat was a mob of people. Yuri talked briefly to one of them and learned that they were all there to petition the *starets* for a favor—a promotion, clemency for a loved one, exemption from military service—any number of boons that could be granted by the tsar if Rasputin would but say a favorable word.

For the first time in his life, Yuri was truly frightened for his country. All the revolutionary unrest in the world could not be as terrifying as so much power dwelling in the hands of a dissipated, twisted holy man. And a sudden panic began to grip Yuri as he raced up the steps.

A young woman, about Katya's age and obviously of noble birth, answered the door. She was Katya's friend Countess Olga Rybin.

"I'm looking for Countess Zhenechka," Yuri said, dispensing with any preamble or polite pleasantries.

"Well, I don't know—"

"Is she here?" When the woman still hesitated, Yuri continued with a more concerted effort at propriety. "Perhaps you don't remember, Countess Rybin, but I am her fiancé, Prince Fedorcenko. I was told she might be here. It's . . . urgent that I see her."

"Yes . . . I suppose it would be all right. Follow me."

Yuri glanced around the flat as he went. It hadn't changed at all. There were bouquets of fresh flowers everywhere and a dozen or so women milling about the place. The word *harem* occurred to Yuri, and that only heightened his panic, not to mention his disgust. Would others think that of Katya if she started seeing Rasputin?

Started? She was seeing him now. How did he know she hadn't been doing so all along, secretly? All their promises of trust fled from his mind.

The mere idea of Katya being part of this perverse scene made him sick. Somehow he had to make sure she didn't get involved with the man. Yuri knew she had deep needs and insecurities that he himself might not be able to help. Rasputin, on the other hand, was probably expert at exploiting such vulnerability.

Yuri passed through the dining room where there were more flowers and several baskets of fruit. It looked as if everyone was paying court to royalty. Then they paused at a closed door. His guide knocked. Katya answered.

"Yuri!"

"So, here you are." He couldn't think of anything else to say. His voice shook, a poor mask of his ire.

"I hope it was all right, bringing him here, Katya," the woman said.

"Yes, thank you, Olga," said Katya. The woman left, and Katya continued. "Father Grigori is ill. He went to Tsarskoe Selo today to help the tsarevich. He has only recently been allowed out of bed. He exhausted himself. Perhaps you can do something for him, Yuri?"

"Me?"

"I believe he needs a doctor."

"Can't the healer heal himself?"

Now she first seemed to notice his sour attitude. "Yuri, what's the matter?"

"I've been trying to reach you all afternoon. How do you think I feel, finding you here?"

"I don't know . . . I shouldn't think it would matter."

"Well, it does matter. I asked you not to see him."

"Yuri, let's talk about this another time—"

"Of course, we don't want to disturb the holy priest!"

She stepped into the hall, closing the door behind her. "I don't understand you, Yuri. I knew you didn't approve of him, but I saw nothing wrong in ministering to a person in great need."

"He simply couldn't survive without your attention?" Yuri asked caustically.

"It's not that. I feel I owe him—"

"Does that mean you'll continue to see him?"

"I don't see why I shouldn't."

"Even though I don't want you to?"

She hesitated a moment. "If it means that much to you . . ."

Yuri wondered if he was asking too much, but before he could speak again, there was a noise inside the room.

"Wha's all the commotion?" rasped a coarse voice as the door swung open.

Rasputin stood there dressed only in a clean, white nightshirt—probably the cleanest Yuri had ever seen the man. His beard and hair, however, were still filthy and oily, and he reeked of alcohol.

"Can't a man res' in his own home?" slurred the *starets*.

"Is this what you call sick, Katya?" said Yuri with disdain. "He's not sick, he's drunk." Then to Rasputin he added, "Where did you go after you left the palace? To some brothel?"

"Yuri!" exclaimed Katya in dismay.

"Wha' do you know . . ." Rasputin said, "you sanctimonious imbecile!" He swayed and Katya caught him.

"There, there, Father," she said gently, placing her arm tenderly around him. "Come back to bed."

"Oh, my sweet, pretty Katichka! When I am well, I will reward you properly." He cast a leering covert glance toward Yuri, then pressed his moist lips against her forehead.

Yuri shuddered at the intimate gesture.

Katya led the *starets* back into the room and to his bed. Yuri watched as she helped him gently between the covers, pulling the red fox coverlet over him as she would a little child. She straightened to leave but he grabbed her arm.

"Please! Don't go," Rasputin said. "I don' feel the pain as much when you are here."

"Let me just see Yuri to the door."

"Never mind," Yuri said. "I can find my own way out."

"Don't go like this, Yuri."

"You give me no choice." He turned to go.

"Yuri!"

He paused. He couldn't walk out on her like that. They had talked so much about trust. Wasn't this a perfect opportunity to really practice trust? They were engaged. They had committed to *marry*, to spend their lives together. It was a hollow commitment if something like this could so easily shatter it.

Rasputin said, "Go, Katichka. Attend to your doctor . . . he is so needy . . . we must be godly toward him, mustn't we?"

"Thank you, Father."

Yuri and Katya walked together to the adjacent dining room. There was no one there at the moment, and they sat at the big table in the high-backed chairs.

"I'm sorry for the way I behaved," Yuri said contritely.

"I should have been more sensitive. I didn't know you felt so strongly about him."

"It's just hard for me to understand—" He stopped abruptly. "Let's not talk about him now."

"It seems to be enough of a problem that we should—"

"Katya, I've been inducted into the medical corps."

"Yuri! No!"

"It was bound to happen."

"When?"

"I have to report for duty in a week."

"So quickly? How can they do that, Yuri? We need more time."

"The powers that be care little about that when there is a war on."

"Yuri, I'm sure that if I asked Father Grigori, he would intercede on your behalf to the tsar—"

"No! For one thing the man has little use for doctors in general and, I'm certain, for me in particular. I won't lower myself to make such a request. Besides, I must do my patriotic duty. Heaven knows where Andrei is—but it is certain he will never do his service. I must go. Do you know that a Fedorcenko has been represented in every major war for two hundred years?"

"I almost think you want to go."

"I don't want to, but I won't shirk my duty. You couldn't expect that of me."

"No, I don't."

"We have a week." Even as he said it, he realized how paltry it sounded. He wanted a lifetime with her. Then a wild idea occurred to him. "Is that enough time for a wedding?"

"Why, Yuri, I didn't think you could be so impulsive."

"I have my moments. What do you think?"

"A week? You haven't even met my father. But he will be so glad to get me married off, I doubt he'd mind." He could see her mind was racing. "Can we do it? *Could* we do it? A small, intimate wedding is all I'd want anyway. We could have it at my grandmother's. There is a little chapel there. She is fond of you, Yuri, and would be thrilled."

"Then let's go tell her now, and my mother, too!"

"But Father Grigori . . ."

"The other ladies can tend him, can't they?" He made an effort to speak sensitively.

"Yes, I think so. But before we leave I must tell him the good news." She jumped up, then paused. "It's a good omen, Yuri, that it happened here. Don't you think?"

Yuri only smiled in response, hoping that in her excitement she didn't notice what a forced smile it was. If he had his way, he would have wanted this decision to be made anywhere but here. Still, he refused to think about such things as omens, good or bad.

42

Yuri and Katya weren't the only young people to plan a hasty wedding in those uncertain days of war. Anna did not try to talk them out of it. She still remembered when Sergei had marched to war, how he had proposed to her days before he departed. What might have become of them had they married then and there? The thought had crossed her mind, as she was sure it had also crossed Sergei's, even if they had never spoken of it. It was a natural thing to want *some* security when the rest of the world seemed to be exploding in turmoil.

Anna understood. Yuri and Katya sought a small island of peace and security in their love and commitment.

The wedding was small, attended mostly by Yuri's family and friends—Raisa and Talia, Viktor and Sarah, Paul and Mathilde, Vladimir Baklanov and his new wife, Dr. Botkin and his family, and two or three other associates from the hospital. Andrei was conspicuously absent, a void perhaps only Anna felt the strongest.

For Katya, there was only her grandmother, her American nurse, Teddie, and little Irina. She wanted it that way, she said. She had no close friends, and her father said that the unstable state of the vodka business made it impossible for him to leave Moscow at that time. Katya didn't seem to mind.

The ceremony was brief, performed by an Orthodox priest in the small chapel at Katya's grandmother's estate. Rasputin was not an ordained priest of the Church, and thus could not have performed the marriage sacrament. But he did show up at the wedding, though Anna did not recall his name on any guest list.

Katya looked beautiful in a simple pale pink satin gown. And Yuri radiated love. He looked so much like his father, Anna wanted to weep. She missed Sergei most in moments like this, even though the painful ache of the past was gone now. She allowed herself only a momentary flutter of sadness that he was not present to share in his son's special moment. Then she concentrated on the lovely ceremony.

"Yuri Sergeiovich, will you take this woman to be your wife, to have and to hold until death do you part?"

"I will," answered Yuri, his voice trembling with intensity.

"And you, Katya Lavrentinovna, will you take this man, to cleave unto him in sickness and health, for better or worse, until death do you part?"

"I will." Katya's voice was breathless, as if she could not believe such joy was possible.

Anna felt a tingle course through her as the priest announced: "Then I pronounce you husband and wife. What God hath joined together, let no man put asunder. In the name of the Father and the Son and the Holy Ghost."

For the next half hour a photographer took pictures, then the group went to the large parlor where a splendid reception had been laid out. The general gaiety of the group was slightly tarnished, however, by Rasputin's intrusive presence. Anna had heard conflicting reports about the *starets* and had read about him in the newspapers, but none of that prepared her for seeing him in person.

Anna was a peasant herself and thus had no prejudices against that class. But as with any group, there were all kinds of peasants, and she could only think that Rasputin came from the lowest end of the scale. He wore an embroidered silk shirt and shiny new boots, but he smelled horribly, and his manners were even worse than his stench. She would have thought that mingling among the noble classes—even the royal family itself!—might have improved upon his peasant upbringing. But he literally guzzled champagne and grabbed food from the refreshment table with his dirty hands and even declared at one point that "a man with a beard didn't need a napkin."

Anna overheard Yuri's friend Vladimir whisper, "Is he a friend of the bride's or groom's?"

"Neither," said Yuri sourly.

"Then, who invited him?"

"I don't know." Yuri cast a quick glance at Katya, who was busy talking to another guest.

With a chuckle Vladimir said, "I guess you can't kick the tsar's personal friend out, can you?"

Rasputin might have spoiled the affair by stealing all the attention with his drunken laughter and his preaching. But he left the reception early. And everyone, even Katya, seemed to let out a sigh of relief.

Just as the monk was departing, another guest arrived. Anna glimpsed the fine red cloth of his uniform out of the corner of her eye, but before she could turn to fully assess the newcomer, Yuri's exuberant voice identified him.

"Uncle Misha!" Yuri hurried up to him and embraced the Cossack. "What a surprise!"

"Do you think I'd miss your wedding, son?"

"The mails wires are so jammed up with the war, that I didn't know if you got my telegram. I'm so glad you came."

Yuri introduced Katya to him, and there was a flurry of attention around Misha for several minutes. But Anna hung back, her old shyness suddenly gripping her. She felt a bit silly, like that shy young girl of many years ago, but her heart had actually leaped when she saw him. And she felt a little pang of jealousy toward Yuri for being free to embrace Misha so warmly. She longed to embrace him too, but her feelings went deeper than those of a friend.

At last the welcoming clamor around Misha seemed to quiet, and he turned toward her. Their eyes met, and Anna rebuked herself for her shyness. Had she acted quickly, an embrace would have seemed quite natural. Now she felt constrained, as if her emotions would be obvious to everyone.

"Anna!" Whether Misha gave it any thought or not, Anna

couldn't tell, but he strode up to her and threw his strong arms around her, lifting her off her feet as he held her. When he set her down, he gave her a good appraisal. "Anna, you're all pale, just like the frightened maid who didn't know enough to bow before the tsar."

"I'm just a bit shocked, that's all. It's been so many years." She had not, in fact, included Misha's name on the guest list. Apparently Yuri had noted the omission and, thinking it only an oversight, had taken the matter into his own hands. But when she glanced at her son, he was grinning.

"I thought it would be a grand surprise, Mama."

She frowned slightly, trying to interpret the meaning of that grin and the glint in his eyes, then she laughed. "It *is* a grand surprise! Now come, everyone, let's continue to enjoy these fine refreshments."

Misha's hand on her arm gently restrained her.

"Anna, are you faint with hunger?" Misha asked.

"Not really."

"I don't need to eat right away, either."

"Why don't we try to catch up on lost time. . . ?"

"That's what I was thinking."

"I am told there is a nice garden in this house. Would you like to take a look at it with me?"

He smiled and took her hand, and they slipped out of the parlor. After asking a servant for directions, they eventually found the garden, shrouded in darkness and chilly, with a slight breeze penetrating the garden wall. The sky was full of stars, far away and tiny, and although there was no moon, several lanterns lit the garden path. Anna's initial shyness wore off quickly, and within minutes she was chatting easily with her old friend. She filled him in on everything that her stilted letters had so poorly conveyed, and she wept a little when she told him about Andrei.

"I think he is all right, but Paul heard a rumor that he is with the Bolsheviks. It wouldn't be so bad if I knew he was happy, but I think he is where he is because he was running away, trying to escape things that hurt him. You and I know that never works." The words were out before she realized what she had said, then she brought her hand to her lips and let out a little gasp. "Oh, dear."

"No, Anna, it doesn't work. Not when the things that hurt us are also the things we love."

"I wish you hadn't stayed away so long, Misha."

"I didn't know you felt that way, Anna."

"I could have said it many times in a letter, but . . ." She shook her head sadly. "Letters can be so inadequate."

"I could have come back," said Misha. "It was stubborn of me to stay away like I did."

"That's a side of you I've never really known."

He shrugged, obviously flustered.

"What brought you back, Misha?"

"Weddings," he said, "are so romantic, don't you think?"

She smiled. "Perhaps for young people. But I am an old grandma."

"And I am an old Cossack."

"What a life we've had, Misha! Together we have traveled a long, long road. You were part of everything important that ever happened to me. It's mind-boggling when I think of having a friend like you. We've been as close as any husband and wife."

"As close as you and—?" He stopped and shook his head in frustration. "That was an unfair remark."

"A remark you *didn't* make."

"I said enough."

"Misha, Sergei will always be a fundamental part of who I am and of the memories I hold most dear. But Sergei is gone now, and the hold he has on me is no longer the death grip it once was. Do you understand?"

"I . . . I think so."

"Tell me, Misha, do you think a couple of old folks like us could really find romance? Wouldn't we feel just a little silly?"

"I do feel a bit ridiculous, Anna. But I can't help it. I love you as if I were a twenty-year-old boy. As a matter of fact, a twenty-year-old could never feel the extent of love I feel for you, because it has only been made richer and deeper by the years of experiences we've shared." He gazed down at her with all the intensity of his fierce Cossack nature. And in his eyes she saw the glow of young love, despite the crow's-feet around his eyes and the gray in his hair and beard.

"I'm feeling a little silly myself," she said. Silly, and lightheaded, too, she thought, rather bemused by it all. "I do love you, Misha!" It was the first time she had ever said those words to him, and she meant them in *every* way.

"It's amazing, isn't it?"

She nodded, grinning and still light-headed. "Now what?" she breathed.

"I'm going to war myself, you know. In a few days. Yuri and I will probably travel together."

"I feared you would be going. I do feel a bit better, knowing you will be there to look after Yuri."

"I do, too."

They walked in silence for a few minutes. Anna hardly noticed the beautiful plants surrounding them. She was too intensely aware of Misha's presence. She had almost forgotten what it was like to be close to a man—a man she loved. It stirred things within her that she had thought long dead.

Misha spoke, "Anna, to be honest, it is the war that really brought me back. I couldn't go without seeing you once more. If I die now, I can be completely content."

"Completely, Misha?"

His lips slanted into an ironic smile. "I should have said, I *thought* I could be completely content. It doesn't really work that way though. Seeing you only makes me want more. God knows, I am ready to die for my country, but I don't *want* to die—not now. Still, we both know it could happen."

"Let's leave it at that, then."

"Anna, I want to marry you."

"Before you leave?" She said it with a teasing tone.

He laughed. "Why not?"

"Because I couldn't face losing another husband."

"I'll have to die eventually."

"Maybe I'll die first."

He touched her cheek and ran his finger along the line of her jaw. "I don't think you will ever die, dear Anna. You are ageless, immortal."

"My, this wedding *is* bringing out the romantic in you," she said lightly.

He slipped an arm around her waist and nudged her close to him. "Can you blame me? I have loved you for thirty-five years. I long ago gave up the hope of ever having you feel the same about me. So I don't care if I do appear a love-struck fool now. To finally have you . . ." He closed his eyes, and she saw moisture seeping through the corners. "It's more than I could have ever hoped would be possible."

"And now I'm asking you to wait even longer," she said. When he said nothing, she added hopefully, "But a marriage ceremony wouldn't change the bond between us—"

"Don't be naive, Anna."

He wrapped his powerful arms around her and bent down so that his face was a fraction of an inch from hers. Anna closed her eyes, and when his lips met hers, it was like the fulfillment of dreams she didn't even know she had. She felt the passion that had simmered within him for over three decades. But that was not the most profound sensation in that explosive moment. What was truly incredible, truly miraculous, was the power of the *love* she felt.

"Misha . . ." Anna murmured. "There is a priest at our disposal for the rest of the evening . . ."

He threw back his head and laughed. "My! When tentative little Anna makes up her mind, she does it with a vengeance. But I can wait until tomorrow so Yuri and Katya can have their day all to themselves."

"Dear, patient Misha!" She took his hand. "Well, let's at least give everyone the shock of their lives and make our announcement."

43

They weren't the only lovers saying farewell that day at Warsaw Station. Everywhere men in uniform said their good-byes to teary-eyed women. Anna was not ashamed of her tears, not when she had to part with both her son and her new husband.

Her husband!

It was still nearly inconceivable that she and Misha should actually be married. And even more remarkable was that she had found in her lifetime *two* men to love her so deeply and completely. But she had a new ring on her left hand, and a glow in her heart, as incontrovertible proof. The wedding had taken place four days ago, and since Misha insisted on a honeymoon, they spent their last days together at the Astoria Hotel in downtown Petrograd adjacent to St. Isaac's Cathedral. Anna balked at the expense, for it was the most opulent hotel in town.

"I have the money," Misha said. "In thirty years I've had nothing else to do with my money but save it!"

Anna felt like a true princess. Keenly aware of the fact that it must soon end, she let herself enjoy every minute. And now it was time to part at Warsaw Station.

"Misha, we did the right thing, didn't we—marrying suddenly like a couple of crazy kids?"

"Unlike young people, Anna, we know how fragile and fleeting life is. Our mortality clings to us like ill-fitting clothes. We part knowing full well what may lie in our future."

"It makes it no easier."

"I never said it would."

"Well, you must come back to me, Misha. I didn't marry you just for four days in a fancy hotel."

"We will have the rest of our lives together."

He said it with such confidence that she choked back a sob. If only she could feel the same way!

"Take heart in this, my dear wife," he added. "When I return, I will not leave again. I plan to retire from the military. For better or worse, you will have me around every day, all day."

"That's why I married you."

He bent down and kissed her. "It is real, then? We are *married*!"

"Until—" She paused, unable to say, *until death do us part*. Instead, she murmured the word she wanted to believe: "Forever!"

Yuri had hardly let go of his new wife since their wedding day, and now he held her even closer. They were an island in the midst of the busy train station, but they were not a calm island. Katya clung to him, weeping. And he felt close to tears himself. It did seem too cruel that he and Katya should finally come together only to be separated once again.

"I'll just be in the Medical Corp," he tried to comfort her. "I won't be at the front lines."

"I'll be counting on that. Please, don't be a hero, Yuri."

"Me? Never! I tremble at the thought of getting too close to a bullet."

"I don't believe that for a minute."

"Believe this, then, Katya—that I love you, and I will do nothing to jeopardize our future together." He kissed her again . . . and again. It was the only way to keep their minds off their fears. "It could be worse," he said as he glanced over to where his mother and Misha were saying their good-byes. "We could be like my poor uncle Misha who waited thirty-five years to marry the woman he loves, only to be parted from her after four days."

"Yes . . . that is too bad." She seemed relieved for the distraction. "What a surprise their announcement was! At least, I was surprised. I didn't think people that old could still fall in love."

"Just wait until *we're* that old! I will fall in love with you again and again! But those of us who know Mama and Misha shouldn't have been surprised. They have been friends forever. In fact, when Papa died I remember thinking that maybe Misha would someday take his place—not that anyone really could take Papa's place, but you know what I mean. I thought when the period of mourning ended, he would certainly marry Mama. Instead, he left. Mama just told me that back then she wasn't ready to remarry. Her love for Papa was too strong. When she finally was ready, Misha was already gone."

"You didn't get your persistence from your mama, then," chuckled Katya.

"That is definitely from my papa."

"But they loved each other all that time and did nothing . . . it's hard to comprehend."

He shrugged. "I suppose old folks are not as impetuous as the young."

"Thank goodness for impetuosity!" For the first time that morning, she smiled.

A ripple of warmth ran through Yuri as he saw the glow in her eyes. That's exactly how he wanted to remember her.

The train whistle shrieked loudly, and instantly their smiles vanished.

"All aboard!"

For a brief moment the entire station seemed to freeze, like a still frame of a moving picture. Not a soul in that place was immune to the fateful call.

In another moment, the celluloid started moving again, and the station erupted in a frenzy of activity.

Yuri wanted to fight it. He wanted to keep still, keep holding his wife. He did not want to be a part of the dreaded flow toward the waiting cars. But people continued to shove past them, jostling them. He lost his hold on her, and for a terrible moment they were forced apart.

"Katya!"

He pushed against the movement of the throng reaching out his hand. A soldier stumbled between them, and Yuri almost knocked the man down. Finally, his and Katya's hands clasped, he held on as if to a life preserver. In another moment, the pressing crowd pushed them so close together their noses touched. Their panic turned to laughter at the irony. Arms around each other, they let the crowd propel them along.

But they reached the open door of the car too soon. Yuri only had a brief instant to kiss his wife before he was forced to climb the steps of the car. He twisted around trying to see over the heads of the other soldiers that pushed in after him, but the crowd had swallowed her up.

"Yuri!" came a familiar voice.

"Misha?"

"Come with me."

With Misha's big body, in the intimidating uniform of the Imperial Cossack Guard, shouldering a path through the packed railcar, Yuri followed silently. The passengers gave way before them, and they reached the back of the car, where they had a clear view from a window of the platform outside.

Anna and Katya were standing side by side, waving toward the car. Misha lowered the window and shouted, drawing their attention. It was such a small thing, but Yuri could not express how much it meant to have those few more moments of eye contact with his wife as the train lurched into motion.

"Thank you, Uncle Misha!"

"I told your mama I would look out for you."

Yuri kept his gaze fixed on the window. He didn't want the mighty Cossack to see the tears welling up in his eyes. Then, in the reflection from the glass, he caught a glimpse of Misha's ruddy, tear-stained cheeks.

V

SCATTERED BONDS

Winter to Fall 1915

44

The war brought separation, but it also brought a very special reunion for Anna. Her daughter, Mariana, returned to her homeland from America. When her husband, Daniel, was dispatched to the Front to cover the war for his newspaper, Mariana, to be nearer to him, traveled to Russia with her children.

Anna had not seen her grandchildren since Yuri's graduation from medical school. The two oldest, John, now eight, and Katrina, five, were no longer toddlers. John was a studious boy whose strong resemblance to his father ended with external appearance. He was quiet and thoughtful, without that mischievous glint his father always had in his eyes. Katrina, even at five, was a tall beauty with wavy auburn hair and matching eyelashes. She was more talkative than her brother and—like her maternal grandmother and namesake, Princess Katrina—far more self-possessed. The baby, two-year-old Zenia, whom Anna had never seen, was a chubby bundle of energy with a thick mop of yellow curls and a happy-go-lucky personality.

Mariana arrived in time for Christmas, turning a holiday that otherwise would have been quite dreary into a festive time. The Holy Synod had banned the use of Christmas trees because it was a German custom, but nevertheless the four children—Mariana's three and Katya's little Irina—filled Anna's flat with delight. The adults let themselves forget, for a time at least, the war that constantly hung over them. And Katya brought even more joy to the day when she announced that she was expecting Yuri's child.

"Have you told Yuri?" asked Mariana.

"I just wrote him. He probably hasn't gotten my letter yet."

"How I wish I could see his face when he hears of it! Imagine, Yuri a papa!"

"I can't wait, but August is such a long way off," said Katya. "This stupid war had better be over in time. I want Yuri here when the baby comes."

No one commented. But soon the women were chatting about babies and telling stories of their pregnancies. Mariana enlightened them on the different medical practices in America and the social differences in how Americans treated their children.

"I don't know how many times I've heard, 'Spare the rod, spoil the child.' And, 'Children must be seen and not heard.' Many of our American friends think little Katrina is an absolute tyrant and Zenia totally incorrigible."

"All American children are sedate and well-behaved?" asked Katya, astonished.

"Hardly!" laughed Mariana. "It's all just talk."

Anna was pleased to see how well Mariana and Katya were hitting it off. They had many similarities—both strong, modern women. But Anna hoped some of Mariana's deep faith could be transferred to Katya. In many ways, Katya was very spiritual, and especially since her engagement and marriage, she had indicated a deep desire to please God. Each time she and Anna saw each other, Katya was full of questions about faith. But because of their age difference, it was sometimes hard for Anna to relate to Katya. Anna had grown up in a simpler time, with simpler questions.

Mariana, on the other hand, seemed naturally suited for this role in Katya's life. Mariana was fourteen years older, but she understood the complexities of modern life.

Unfortunately, Mariana's friendship with Katya didn't have a chance to grow. Shortly after the New Year, Mariana went to Moscow to spend some time with her father, Dmitri, and his family. Anna would just have to trust God to work in her daughter-in-law's life.

February of 1915 closed with a freezing snowstorm. The short days were growing dreary and depressing. Katya tried to cheer herself by shopping, but the war was making it difficult for the new fashions to make it to Petrograd, and decent maternity clothes were even harder to find. She was starting to show now and wanted more than ever to look stylish, not fat and frumpy. If she couldn't find things for herself, the least she could do was buy clothes for Irina and a layette for the new baby. One day, when it had warmed up a bit—to ten degrees!—she went out with Teddie and Irina. The sun was trying to shed some light in the pale winter sky.

As Katya climbed into the motorcar, she felt a small stitch in her side, but she ignored it and proceeded with the shopping excursion. A hour later, she was seated in a salon that specialized in children's clothing when the pain began stabbing at her once more. Now it was sharper and came in regular throbs.

"Princess Katya, is something wrong?" asked Teddie.

"I . . . I'm not sure. Some pains in my stomach. Perhaps I need something to eat."

"What kind of pains?"

"I don't know—sharp, throbbing—"

"Regular throbs?"

"I guess so."

"I think we best go home."

"I'll be fine," Katya protested, but another pain gripped her at that moment, far worse than the others.

They managed to get home—to Katya's grandmother's house, where she and Irina now lived all the time. But as she started up the stairs she collapsed, and a manservant had to carry her up to her bed. *Hold on*, Katya kept telling herself. *Hold on*.

But a few minutes later, she lost the baby.

"Oh, Teddie!" she wept when it was over. "Why did this happen now that I *want* a baby?"

"I don't know, dearie, but don't fret over it. You need to get some rest."

"I was so happy, Teddie. I forgot to ask God to protect my baby. How could I be so selfish!"

"God was protecting your baby long before you knew you were with child."

"Then, why did I lose it?"

"I don't understand God's ways, Katya, dear. There must have been some reason."

"How can I bear it, Teddie?"

"Katichka, why don't I call your mother-in-law?"

Katya nodded weakly. "Anna always knows the right thing to say. Maybe she can help." But deep down, Katya doubted that even Anna could make this situation all right.

Anna had spent several hours with Katya, but Katya was too despondent to get any benefit from the visit, especially after the doctor arrived and made his grim pronouncement.

"It may be best for you not to have any other children, Princess Fedorcenko. It may not endanger your life, but I cannot guarantee there would not be another miscarriage."

It was simply too horrible to consider that she and Yuri would have no children of their own. Katya had so hoped to repay Yuri's loving acceptance of Irina by giving him children. But her despair went far deeper than that. Since she first realized she was expecting, Katya had believed that this child was God's way of once and for all absolving her of her previous sin.

Now what was she to think? Was it possible that even God could not forgive her?

When her friend Olga came the next day to console her, Katya almost refused to see her. She was in no mood for visits. But she had so few friends her own age—so few friends at all—that she could not turn away such a gesture of friendship.

Olga had recently married and had a child of her own, so she had some understanding of what Katya was experiencing—though she couldn't, of course, comprehend her grief. She was truly saddened when Katya confided what the doctor had told her.

"Oh, Katya! How awful! But doctors don't know everything—that is, some doctors . . . I mean, of course, your Yuri is different . . ."

"I don't know what I'd do if he was really right."

"So, you don't fully accept his prognosis?"

"I don't know . . . I desperately want to have a baby for Yuri."

"Katya, have you spoken to Father Grigori?"

"No . . ."

"Didn't he help you once before? You mentioned that you had some problems and he prayed for you and such."

"That was a long time ago."

"He can help now, Katya! I'm sure of it. Why don't you call him?"

"Olga, my husband doesn't want me to have anything to do with him."

"I thought you were more liberated than that! Anyway, Yuri is far away at war. What can he do to stop you? Besides, I don't know Yuri well, but from what I do know, I think he would give you anything you wanted."

"I'd still feel like I was betraying him."

"Would you feel better never having children?"

The question lingered in Katya's mind long after Olga left. What if Father Grigori *could* help her bear children? Wouldn't Yuri understand her dilemma and forgive her? He might even applaud her. Grigori was a healer. Katya had heard many stories of his miraculous powers. Perhaps she could be one of those stories.

Katya was still debating her moral quandary when a servant came to her door and announced the arrival of Rasputin. Apparently Olga didn't trust Katya to make the right decision and had taken the matter into her own hands . . . unless the *starets* had prophetically deduced Katya's need.

Anna arrived at Katya's home as soon after she received Teddie's call as possible. She had never much liked having that telephone in her house, but Yuri had needed it for his work. Now, she saw its definite advantages.

"I didn't know what else to do!" Teddie fretted, wringing her hands together. "I could not stand to have that priest here, and Countess Elizabeth was also at a loss at what to do about it." Teddie spoke the word "priest" with revulsion. "If only her husband could be here. Curse this war!"

"Can I see her, Teddie?"

"He's with her now."

At that moment, Katya's grandmother appeared. "Princess Fedorcenko, how good of you to come." She held out her hand, and Anna took it with a thin smile. "I fear it will start all over again," the countess murmured.

"What's that, Countess?"

"Before, when—you know all about Irina, don't you?" When Anna nodded, the countess continued. "Katya nearly took her own life because of her shame. Then Rasputin came. Maybe he did help her. I suppose it was he who prevented her from that terrible act. But I never felt he could be trusted. I worried terribly each time she went to see him. In those few weeks she was involved with him, she began to change. She became almost too mystical, too spiritual. I believe I have a deep faith in God, Anna, but I could never be entirely settled about the changes in Katya. I couldn't quite identify what disturbed me, however—except the involvement of Rasputin. I thanked God when she went away to the convent to have the baby. When she returned, she seemed more interested in worldly pursuits than in the mystical. I am ashamed to admit it, but I was somewhat relieved by that. I've always felt so inadequate because I couldn't help her in a more—how shall I put it?—conventional faith."

"If you failed, Countess Elizabeth, I don't know what I can do."

"I know she thinks highly of you. Perhaps she couldn't hear from me because of her natural inclination to rebel against an authority figure, as I was forced to be in her life."

"May I see her?"

"Of course. But that Mad Monk is there now."

"Perhaps we can just be nearby offering the *presence* of some balance, if nothing else," suggested Anna.

"I tried to go in a few minutes ago, but he chased me out—imagine the gall! Chasing me out of my own house. But he can practically get away with anything these days, now that he has the full blessing of the tsar. Nevertheless, Anna, you are welcome to try. Teddie, please take Princess Anna up to Katya's room."

"Yes, madam!" The nurse spoke with enthusiasm. Teddie seemed to have more faith in Anna than Anna herself did.

Nevertheless, Anna followed the nurse upstairs. When they reached the door, Teddie knocked, then stepped aside. There was no response. Undeterred, Anna boldly opened the door. Katya could throw her out, but she had to make the attempt. The *starets* could bully her, and she had to admit to a little fear of the man, but she reminded herself that he could not really hurt her. She had faced up to worse enemies than he in her lifetime.

Actually, no one noticed her quiet entry. Rasputin, boldly sitting right on the bed, was talking, and Katya, grasping his hand, was focused only on his face.

"Only humility brings salvation, little Katya," Rasputin was saying. "Turn from your prideful ways! Rejoice in simple things. Don't you know pride goes before a fall? It is the greatest sin of all. Cover your head and bow humbly before the Lord. Only then will He look upon you and bless you and open your womb. You must—" He stopped suddenly. Anna had taken a step farther into the room, and a board creaked beneath her foot. Rasputin turned sharply, glaring at her. "What do you want?"

"I've come to see my daughter-in-law," Anna replied, trying to infuse grit into her tone.

"Go away—!" Then as an afterthought, he added, "Wait! She is your daughter-in-law? You are *his* mother, then."

"If you mean, am I Prince Yuri Fedorcenko's mother? The answer is yes."

"He'll bring ruin on her yet."

"What on earth do you mean?"

"Because of him she is in this prideful state. I knew no good would come of such a union."

Briefly Anna wondered why he had come to the wedding. If his consumption of food and champagne was a measure of his approval, he certainly hadn't indicated any opposition then. But this wasn't the time to voice such thoughts, instead Anna said, "What's done is done . . . Father—" She didn't quite know how to address the man and felt awkward using a term of holy respect. "Now, we must love Katya and support her, not lay recriminations upon her."

"Love? What do you know of love?" He turned his gaze back to Katya. "You know I love you, don't you, Katya?"

"Yes, Father . . ."

Then, to Anna, he said, "Who told you to come here? I am a busy man. I can't be wasting my time repairing the damage of such misplaced good intentions. You see, I give you that much—that your intentions are good—"

"And I'll do the same for you, Father," said Anna curtly.

He laughed. "A sharp-tongued woman! You need some humility yourself. Don't you know the tongue is an unruly, evil instrument, full of deadly venom. It defiles the whole body. It can't be tamed, especially a woman's tongue. Only by the purifying fires of God can there be redemption. Trust me, woman, and I will pray for you and petition God to show His mercy upon you. But not now—I am too exhausted. I need some wine. Go fetch me some wine."

"You will have to ask a servant to do that, sir." Anna heard the pride in her voice but she made no apologies.

"He that is great among you must become a servant—ah, well, I am spent, I must go, anyway. I will return, Katichka. Rest now. God be with you!" He rose and bent over Katya and kissed her forehead and both cheeks, then he made the sign of the cross over her. He turned and strode from the room, passing very close to Anna. Their eyes met briefly and a chill coursed through Anna. It was as if they both read each other quite thoroughly, neither much liking what they saw.

"Do you feel up to another visitor?" Anna asked Katya when they were alone.

"Yes. I feel stronger now, like I can go on. Oh, Mama Anna! It is so terrible! I lost Yuri's baby. I wanted it so bad. Why can't I do anything right? It's because I lived such a wicked life before—"

"No, no . . . dear," Anna cooed assuringly. "Father Grigori didn't tell you that, did he?"

"He said to have faith, to humble myself before God. I want so much to please God. I could never please my own father, so I hoped maybe I might do better with God. I just didn't try soon enough, I suppose, with my awful, wild ways. But I was afraid . . . afraid if I did truly try, I would botch it as I have everything else. Since I met Yuri, I wanted to do better—I've tried! But look, I've still messed it up. Why is it the thing I want most, I can't have? Pleasing God . . . babies . . . maybe I'll even lose Yuri if I can't be better. Maybe I'll never be good enough!"

"Katya, you mustn't speak so. God looks at your heart, not at what you *do*. He knows we can never be perfect, not here on earth, anyway."

"Then, why did He take my baby?"

"God didn't take—"

"I have to try harder. I have to be humble. My pride killed my baby—Yuri's baby . . ."

Anna realized then that Katya was not in a place to hear her answers—if indeed she had any answers at all for the young woman's anguish. And she wasn't about to badger her in her present state—Rasputin had done enough of that. Anna just sat quietly and held Katya's hand, praying silently that God would let His truth prevail in the girl's heart. It was all she could do—but, as Anna's papa used to say, it was also the most and the best she could do.

45

Tsar Nicholas loved the atmosphere found at Stavka, the Russian command post located in a Polish forest. The camaraderie of men, the regimented rigors of the military life—a hard cot to sleep on, no-nonsense meals, marching and drilling and plotting strategy.

He loved his Alix, but the air around Alexander Palace could be so cloying with perfume and flowers and that hideous mauve everywhere. It was decidedly a woman's world, with Alix and four daughters and all their ladies-in-waiting and such. Not to mention the opulent furnishings and the fine china and . . .

Not so here. The air was fresh and clean, with a fine hint of gunpowder to make it complete. He was going to have to bring Alexis here soon—it would be good for the boy, also, to get away from the influence of women.

Nicholas visited the camp as often as possible, yet he was careful not to interfere with his cousin's command. That wasn't always easy, because he still deeply desired to be commander in chief himself. He never voiced it, but he was jealous of the man. Who wouldn't be? The Grand Duke Nicholas Nicholavich, at six feet six inches tall, towered over the tsar. He *looked* like a real warrior. And the men all but worshiped him. There were rumors that Nicholas Nicholavich, or Nicholasha, as the tsar referred to him, had said he would one day reign as Nicholas the Third. The tsar chose not to believe the nasty rumors.

Such minor disturbances could not possibly interfere with the tsar's enjoyment. Nevertheless, he was less than pleased when he saw a copy of a telegram sent by the grand duke to Rasputin. Apparently the *starets* had telegrammed the grand duke offering to come to the Front to speak a blessing to the troops. The grand duke had replied in his impetuous, bombastic way: "Yes, by all means, come. I will hang you!"

That took gall, even for the commander in chief, and as much as the tsar hated to do it, he had to confront the man over the issue. Alix, of course, had been livid when Rasputin showed her the message and had immediately wired the tsar. Now Nicholas wouldn't hear the end of it if he didn't say something to his cousin. He requested that the grand duke come to his private railway car, and as soon as the man arrived, the tsar handed him the copy of the telegram.

Nicholasha quickly scanned the brief sentences, then lifted his eyes to squarely meet the tsar's. "I cannot have some fake priest underfoot at the Front," he said bluntly. "We have enough problems, don't we?"

"Grigori Rasputin is an Imperial friend," the tsar protested. "I cannot have him spoken of in such a manner. If it were not for him—"

"I think we'd all be a lot better off!" the grand duke interrupted.

The tsar winced slightly at such cheek—no one interrupted His Imperial Highness! "Nicholasha, tread lightly on this matter. If I recall, it was you who recommended Grigori to us in the first place."

"An act I will never cease to regret."

"Even you cannot deny what he has done for the tsarevich."

"I make no comment on matters of spiritual content. I am only concerned about the military. And I say it would not be beneficial for our army to have that man here. You aren't going to override me on this, are you, Nicky?"

"I don't think it would be appropriate for him to be here either, but for different reasons altogether." The last thing the tsar wanted was to have his delightful military world intruded upon by anything to do with the Imperial Court back in Petrograd, especially Rasputin. At the very least the man was . . . a necessary evil. Still, the tsar tried very hard to see the monk with Alix's eyes. There must be good in the man for her to adore him so.

The tsar was very much relieved when the grand duke asked if he might digress to a new topic. They spent the next hour discussing the new spring offensive aimed at Galicia, where they had known such loss last fall. Both men seemed to relax. The deep creases on the tsar's face receded and a glow of excitement appeared in his eyes.

Unfortunately, Yuri could never find enjoyment in things military. Even if he hadn't been constantly surrounded by blood and death, he would have found army life stifling and tedious. But, if there was any glory at all in the military, Yuri saw none of it as a doctor. Serving in a frontline dressing station, he knew only the aftermath of glorious charges and heroic deeds—usually in the form of severed limbs and shattered bodies.

A million Russian soldiers had already been either killed, wounded, or taken prisoner. Yuri worked twenty hours a day trying to save the wounded ones. Sleep and food became luxuries to him. He functioned by grit and willpower. No wonder the news of Katya's miscarriage had shaken him so. The telegram from his mother said she was physically all right, but it wasn't hard to read between the lines. They both wanted children, but, to Katya, having a child represented God's absolution for her mistake.

Then last night he had received a letter from Katya mentioning

Rasputin, how he had come to see her and had ministered to her at her bedside. She made a point of saying that he had come on his own, not at her bidding, but she certainly hadn't made the man leave. Yuri's greatest fear was that in this time of loss, she would turn again to the *starets* for counsel. He worried constantly about what distorted ideas Rasputin might feed her poor, distraught mind. He desperately wanted to be home, both to comfort his wife and to steer her away from Rasputin. But his request for a leave had been turned down.

The refusal made no logical sense, either. The influx of casualties had slowed over the winter months, and there were a few weeks yet before the spring offensive was to begin. He could easily be spared now—at least more so at this time than later. But, then, the army rarely operated on logic or common sense.

Yuri turned his attention back to his morning rounds. It didn't help to think about home and his new wife and the life the war was robbing them of. In the next hour, he examined twenty patients and gave half of those papers for transfer back home. The lucky ones! Of the other half, six would be returned to the line, while the rest were too critical to be moved anywhere.

He was writing notes in a patient's chart when he heard his name called.

"Yuri."

"Daniel!" Yuri dropped the chart and strode to his brother-in-law, giving him a big bear hug. "I wondered if you were over here."

"Are you kidding? Let them try to have a war without me reporting it!"

"I'm finished here," said Yuri. "Why don't we find the mess tent and get some tea? You have time, don't you?"

"You bet! I've been looking for you since I arrived."

Yuri told a nurse where he'd be, then he and Daniel trooped through the ankle-deep mud of the compound to the mess tent. Their timing was perfect. The midday meal was being laid out. They both piled plates full of food.

Yuri motioned to his plate. "Usually by the time I get here, if I do make it at all, there's nothing left but the dregs."

"Well, eat hearty, brother—it looks like you can use it."

Yuri laughed self-consciously. He had lost so much weight that his clothes had begun to hang on him. "Please, don't say anything to Mama. She has enough worries."

"I wouldn't think of it."

They concentrated on their food for a few minutes, then Daniel said, "I heard about Katya. I'm sorry, Yuri."

"She'll recover, and there will be more babies. But I think it's been much harder on her emotionally than anything else. You haven't been to St. Petersburg—I mean Petrograd—have you?"

"No, I came directly here. But Mariana and the children are there now."

"I'm glad for Mama's sake."

"I'm kind of surprised to find you here now, Yuri. I said I'd been looking out for you, but I was not looking for you right now. I thought for certain you'd be in Petrograd with Katya."

"Believe me, that's where I want to be. I've tried to get a leave, but for a long time there was a shortage of doctors, and my superiors didn't feel Katya's condition warranted a leave."

"Things have been quiet lately. If you don't get away now, who knows when you'll get another chance."

"I know . . . I know." Yuri gave a weary shrug.

"I've been assigned to General Headquarters," Daniel said, "though I try to get away as often as possible to observe the situation in the trenches with the regular soldiers. Anyway, I rub shoulders with a lot of brass. If you'd like, I could put a bug in someone's ear on your behalf."

"I'd be in your debt forever, Daniel!"

"Hey, we're brothers—no debts between us." Daniel paused, seeming reluctant to progress, then added, "Speaking of brothers, have you heard from Andrei?"

"Nothing. And the little nitwit is risking a thrashing next time I do see him if he remains in hiding much longer."

"At least he's out of the war. With the horrendous casualty rate, his chances of being killed, wounded, or captured by the Germans would be pretty strong. I was present a week ago when the tsar was reviewing troops, and he asked how many had been here since the beginning. Precious few hands were raised."

"You don't have to tell me. I've seen enough blood to swim in it. So, I guess it is just as well that Andrei, with his tender stomach, did what he did. But who knows if he is any safer where he is? We heard a rumor he was with the Bolshevik exile community, perhaps even with Lenin himself."

"There's a man I'd like to get close to. An in-depth interview with the Bolshevik leader—front-page stuff!"

"Find Andrei, and maybe you'll find Lenin."

"I might just work on that. At least until the spring offensive begins."

"What of America, Daniel? Will they come into the war?"

"So far, there's strong support for the President's declaration of neutrality. But this latest German threat may just push us over the edge."

"I'm afraid I don't hear much news. What threat?"

"Germany declared they will actively patrol, by U-boat, all waters surrounding Britain and Ireland, including the English Channel. They will torpedo any enemy vessel. This will seriously endanger U.S. shipping in the area, not to mention Americans who might be passengers on British or French vessels. If any American lives are lost—well, you can imagine how quickly public opinion will turn against Germany."

"Germany will back down. They don't want the U.S. in the war against them—"

Just then a nurse appeared at the table. "Dr. Fedorcenko, I am sorry to intrude, but several new wounded have just arrived, and you are needed."

"Thank you, Sister. I'll be right there." Yuri turned back to Daniel. "How much longer do you plan to be here, Daniel?"

"I'm to hook up with Colonel Dolgich this afternoon for a tour of regimental headquarters. I'll drop by after that, and maybe you'll be free."

They rose and Yuri gave Daniel another hug. "It's been great seeing you. I hope we can talk again; there's so much to catch up on. But if not—"

"Never mind that!" exclaimed Daniel. "We will catch each other again—I'll see to it."

They did see each other again for an hour that evening, then not again for several weeks. Within a week of their meeting, Yuri received a pass to return home. He believed his brother-in-law to be a true miracle worker. And who knew? Maybe Daniel might even be able to find Andrei. If he did, Yuri hoped he'd be able to talk some sense into their wayward little brother.

46

Paris in springtime. What could be more inspirational? Andrei could not resist taking an hour from his work to sketch the sights along the Champs-Elysees. He had so little time for his art these days, not to mention that his comrades always made him feel frivolous for indulging this passion. Hadn't Lenin given up many of his pleasures in deference to the cause? But Andrei still felt he could do both. So, seated on the edge of a brick planter across the street from a cafe, he was intent on drawing a waiter who had caught his interest. The man was middle-aged, short and plump, and looked far too intelligent for his job. He was a veritable chameleon in his relations with the customers—to pretty women he was a suave charmer; to a romancing couple he was a jolly matchmaker; to a businessman he was a discreet servant. As evidence of his success, his pockets bulged with tips.

Andrei was not as fortunate financially. Besides enjoying the Parisian scenery, he hoped he might earn a few francs selling sketches. Tourists thought it chic to patronize sidewalk artists, and even in wartime, Paris had its share of tourists. Yesterday, Andrei had picked up twenty francs, but today the trade was slow. But at least he was not alone in his poverty. Most of his Bolshevik associates were also experiencing a financial slump. The war had taken some of the edge off revolutionary zeal. And many socialists had turned away from Lenin, whose appeal to turn the war into class war along international lines was received with distaste.

At least Andrei was free. After his arrest with Lenin last fall, he had been imprisoned only for two weeks. The worst of it was that he had been isolated from his comrades and put in with petty thieves and the like. At times he feared that even if Lenin did get released, he'd forget all about Andrei. But the Bolshevik leader knew how to take care of his loyal followers. Two days after Lenin's release, he had used his contacts to procure the release of Stephan and Andrei. The group then immediately moved to Switzerland, a neutral country where they had no fear of a repeat of the incident in Poland.

But because of the war, they were isolated in the Swiss town of Bern. Lenin was too well-known to risk travel outside its boundaries. He was forced to use his comrades such as Andrei to travel to other parts of Europe, gathering information and making contact with other Socialist organizations. Using a false passport and traveling with another of Lenin's associates, Inessa Armand, Andrei had gotten into France. Their task was to make contact with the French antiwar Left. Andrei had been assigned mostly as a bodyguard, since he knew little about being an *agent provocateur*. Inessa, however, was quite good at it.

"So, my young Monet," came a voice from behind Andrei, "have you made your fortune yet?"

Andrei turned toward the familiar voice and smiled. "I'm afraid I shall always be a starving artist—but aren't they the best kind?"

Inessa Armand gave a throaty, lusty laugh that left the hearer with the impression that she knew how to enjoy life. She was a tall, willowy woman with thick auburn hair pinned up on her head in a sensible style. Her gray eyes were sharp, intelligent, witty, and thoughtful. She could have been a chameleon herself, except her striking presence made that impossible. Her beauty, youthful even at age forty, resided in the vitality and passion of her character as much as in her striking physical features.

Inessa had long ago thrown aside all pretenses to what she called "bourgeois hypocrisy." Her marriage to Alexander Armand, a Muscovite of French extraction, had ended—though not legally—when she fell in love with her brother-in-law, Vladimir. When she was exiled to Siberia, he followed her there, but he contracted tuberculosis and was forced to move to Switzerland. She escaped from Siberia and joined him shortly before his death. A year later she became a Bolshevik and an ardent follower of Lenin. Rumor had it that she was Lenin's mistress. She had four children by her first husband, but she never returned to him. Still, his continued financial support made her flamboyant and revolutionary lifestyle possible.

Andrei had never known such a worldly woman. He was, to say the least, a bit uncomfortable traveling with her—especially since they were posing as husband and wife and had to share the same hotel room. He wondered at Lenin's wisdom in setting up such an arrangement. Perhaps he believed his paramour would be safe in the company of a young man seventeen years her junior. Andrei had no intention but to honor his leader's trust. But it wasn't going to be easy. Since their arrival two days ago, he had sensed from Inessa subtle advances toward him. Maybe it was just his imagination. After all, what could a woman like that see in a mere boy like him?

She now came up behind him and leaned down, peering over his shoulder to view his work. The smell of her perfume was distracting at best, downright intoxicating if he allowed himself to think about it.

"You won't be starving long, *mon chéri*," she said, her breath tickling Andrei's neck. "You have talent." She said it as if she *knew* such things, and Andrei wasn't about to argue with her.

"I look forward to when the revolution comes and artists will be free to truly express themselves."

"Yes, of course that will be so. But isn't the struggle, the oppression you fight, an integral part of the art and of the passion within you? It is possible the creative process may suffer a bit under government sanction."

"It almost sounds like you are saying the struggle toward the goal is more to be desired than actually achieving the goal itself."

"The struggles, the fighting, make life worth living. I'm a little afraid of what will become of us when we are finally victorious. I suppose many of us will die of sheer boredom. I hope the revolutionary movement is spawning a generation of bureaucrats to take up after us."

"Well, I doubt we will have to worry about that anytime soon." Andrei scooted over to make room for Inessa to sit rather than having her continue to lean over him in such a disconcerting way. "Have you had any luck making your contacts?"

"I'm getting close. I must be discreet. I believe the *Surete* has me under surveillance."

Andrei was surprised at her calm tone. He thought it no small matter to have the French secret police on their trail. Two weeks in jail was quite enough for him. "Do you think we should abort our mission?"

She laughed again. "You are taking this little excursion too seriously, *cher ami*. We are Russians visiting an allied country. No one will arrest us, unless of course they learn of our political affiliations."

"That's what worries me!"

"You are such a child, Andrei." She put her arm around him. "But don't get me wrong, *cher ami*, that's one of your greatest assets." She focused her eyes on him, and her magnetism was so strong, he could not turn away. "A sweet boy, but so handsome and powerful." She rubbed her hand along the broadness of his shoulders as if she were completely oblivious to the fact that they were sitting on a public street. "I'm surprised it is taking you so long to succumb to my charms, *cher*. Perhaps I have been too subtle, eh?"

"No . . ."

But before he could say more, she pressed her lips against his, engaging him in a kiss of such passion he could not have fought it even if he had wanted to. For a minute, he didn't want to at all. She drew away just when he was beginning to regret that they were in public.

Laughing, she said, "That is more like it, *cher*—my sweet 'Little Soldier'—" She squeezed his muscular arm. "But not so little, eh?" She took his hand. "Come, let's go back to the hotel."

Without thinking, he rose and started to walk away with her. This beautiful, compelling older woman wanted him; *Lenin's* mistress wanted him. It was simply too overwhelming. Perhaps it was time he, too, cast aside all his "bourgeois morals." Anyway, he wasn't going to muddy the spontaneity of the moment with debate. Leave that to people like Yuri.

He let Inessa hail a cab. They had driven a couple of blocks when something outside the vehicle's window caught Andrei's eye. It was a large poster that, though slightly faded, was still striking in design and color. But it was more than the artistic appearance of the poster that drew Andrei's attention. In large letters across the top were the words: "Ballets Russes." Beneath the heading was a drawing of a dancer, ensconced in tulle.

Andrei quickly tapped on the window dividing the driver from the backseat of the vehicle. "Please stop!"

The driver pulled up to the curb; they were close enough to the poster now for Andrei to read the smaller print: "Performing at the Theatre des Champs-Elysees, beginning May 5, 1914." Andrei's initial surge of excitement was immediately deflated. Of course, it was an old poster. Talia wouldn't be in Paris now, not with the war on.

"What is it, *mon chéri*?" asked Inessa.

Suddenly, everything snapped into focus for Andrei. What was he thinking? He must indeed be every bit the fool his brother took him for. If he followed his present impulse he would forfeit all his years of devotion to the only woman he ever loved. He had been faithful to her for this long, and Inessa was not the first temptress to come along—even if she was the most compelling. Yet he knew he wasn't ready to give up on Talia. Not if his reaction to that poster was any indication. The mere hint that she might be near had gripped him in a way that even Inessa's closeness hadn't. The thought of Talia touched Andrei in a place so deep it transcended mere *physical* sensations.

He looked at Inessa and shook his head. "Inessa, this is a mistake."

"What do you mean?"

"Do you love me, Inessa?"

She chortled an ironic chuckle. "Love, *cher*? What has that to do with anything? We are living in the age of unrestraint, don't you know? It is time to throw aside the Victorian bourgeois rules of morality. We are free to indulge our passions without the constraints of such outmoded ideas as *love*."

"Do you love Lenin?"

"Of course! With my soul, my body, every particle of who I am. But that has nothing to do with other liaisons I might engage in. We are free, Andruska!"

"I suppose, then, that I am not as free as I always thought I was," Andrei replied. "I don't believe faithfulness is a bourgeois idea at all. But even if it is, I'm afraid it's not an idea I wish to abandon. I love someone, Inessa, and sometimes I feel all I have to offer her is my faithfulness. If she ever returns my love, I want to know—"

"What? This is a one-sided affair you are having?"

"Yes, but I haven't given up hope yet."

She gently brushed her hand across Andrei's cheek. "Ah, you *are* a boy, aren't you? A sweet, naive little boy. But—" She shrugged casually and winked. "I am enough of a romantic to understand true love. Still, I hope you don't waste away your youthful good looks on unrequited love. There must come a point when you say, 'enough is enough.' "

"Maybe . . . but I don't know when . . ."

He thought about that for quite a while—and never arrived at an answer. Maybe he would never see Talia again. With a war on, anything could happen.

"Tell me, *cher*, who is this girl who has imprisoned your heart?"

asked Inessa. "And what has it to do with your stopping the cab so suddenly?"

Andrei nodded toward the poster. "She is a dancer with the Ballets Russes. Seeing that poster brought me back to my senses."

All at once, Inessa jumped out of the car and ran up to the wall where the poster was tacked. Then, to Andrei's astonishment, she pulled it cleanly from the wall and brought it back to the cab. "Here, *mon chéri*." She grinned. "Keep this in case you should forget yourself again."

Andrei laughed. "You know, it was rather fortuitous that this appeared when it did."

"Quite a coincidence, eh? Fate, perhaps."

"Perhaps more."

"Well, Andrei, it may well be that fate, or perhaps even God, is looking out for you."

"Because of the poster?"

"Not entirely. I read an article recently that Diaghilev has begun an artistic colony in Switzerland."

"What does that have to—" Suddenly awareness dawned on Andrei. Diaghilev, of course, was the director of the Ballets Russes. "In Switzerland, you say?"

Inessa nodded, a conspiratorial glint in her eyes. "Where you happen to reside these days when you are not traipsing about in other countries on Ilyich's business."

"But I don't know what good it will do—"

"Just like a man!" she thumped her head. "Such a thick skull."

What if Talia were in Switzerland? Just to *see* her would be wonderful. Yet it might also be excruciating. Could he bear further rejection from her? Could he stand looking at her, even talking to her, knowing she was thinking of Yuri, aching after Yuri, longing for Yuri—as Andrei longed for *her*?

No . . . this was one decision he could not make impulsively. He had to think about it. It might, after all, be better just to keep things as they were.

47

"One, two, three, four—that's terrible extension! Come, girls! You are professionals—act like it!"

Talia brushed a bead of sweat from her brow. The dancers had been practicing for two hours without a break. She was getting a cramp in her leg. She didn't think driving the dancers like serfs was going to make them any more professional, but she certainly didn't have the nerve to say as much to the coach. One of the other dancers finally protested.

"Vera," the bold girl said to the coach, "I am ready to drop. We must have a break."

"If that is all the stamina you have, then perhaps you should stay behind when the rest of us go to America, eh?"

"We can only take so much."

"Is that how the rest of you feel?"

Emboldened now, the other dancers readily agreed.

The coach threw up her hands. "With that kind of attitude, we will be a monumental flop on our tour." Then she shrugged. "All right, take a five-minute break."

Talia limped to a table where a pitcher of water and glasses were laid. She poured herself a drink and a second for another girl who approached.

"I'm so excited about going to America," said the girl. "I suppose it's worth the extra practice."

"I suppose," said Talia without matching enthusiasm.

"Surely, Talia, you want to go to America?"

"It's so far . . ." Talia sipped her water.

"I think it is just as well to get away from Europe while the war is on."

Talia had joined the company of the Ballets Russes last season. It had been a difficult decision because the company did not perform in Russia and probably never would. But the chance to work with the great Diaghilev had been too marvelous for her to pass up. When she rejoined the company after her summer sabbatical, it had been far easier. During that summer, her life had been turned upside down with Yuri's whirlwind declaration of love and just as stunning rejection. After learning of Andrei's love and his subsequent disappearance, Talia had found some relief in distancing herself from Russia for a while. The grueling discipline of her work had been quite welcome. But it hadn't prevented her from thinking about Andrei. And the more she thought about their friendship, the more she realized how much Andrei meant to her. This separation from him also made her acutely aware of the truth of Yuri's words: *"If that's not love, what is?"*

She wondered constantly what would happen if she saw Andrei again. And often she would actually ache with yearning for him. But he seemed determined to stay away from his loved ones. Her mama wrote that Andrei had sent his mama one letter shortly after the war started asking her to understand and forgive his need to leave. There had been no word since from him. But there was a rumor that he had joined the Bolsheviks in European exile.

At least he was out of the war, or so she hoped.

During her performances she always fantasized that she would gaze out into the audience and see his face. But she was to depart for America in two days. Hope of seeing him again soon was dwindling to nothing.

Still, if she did see him . . .

She certainly wouldn't let him go away again. And she would love him—yes, love him! She'd not let him go another minute with his love for her unfulfilled. Since Yuri opened her eyes to Andrei's feelings, Talia's feelings for Yuri had simply faded away. She had been clinging to a childhood dream for too long. Now she thanked God for Yuri's rejection, for only when the flimsy bubble had been burst had she been able to truly see how insubstantial it really was.

If only Andrei had waited a little longer. But patience never was his best quality, she thought with an affectionate smile. She couldn't be angry at him, though. They had all behaved foolishly and blindly. She just hoped they could soon set everything right. She was tempted not to go to America, but the tickets were bought and all the arrangements were made. Besides, if she stayed here, she'd go crazy hoping for him to appear around any corner or in any crowd. The tour to America would only be for a few months. Perhaps by then Andrei would have come to his senses and returned to Russia.

Andrei and Inessa planned to take the four o'clock train from Paris to Bern. But before they departed for the station they had a meeting with the French Bolsheviks, whom Inessa had finally contacted. The meeting went on far longer than Andrei's store of patience. His grasp of French was adequate enough to follow the conversation, but it was so much tedious political debate that at times he wanted to scream. Part of the source of his impatience, of course, was a growing anxiety to return to Switzerland. Since learning that Talia might be there, he could think of little else. He tried logically to debate the positives and negatives of seeing her—just like a hardened Bolshevik! But all the while he knew that no matter what logic told him, he *would* see her.

Once he and Inessa got under way, the trip to Bern was maddeningly long. Inessa tried to distract him by reading several essays she had written on free education, one of her pet causes. They arrived in Bern only to learn that Krupskaya's mother had died. The old woman had been practically a mama to all of the Bolsheviks, and she had been especially kind to Andrei. Andrei could not turn immediately around to go off after a woman. He had to remain at least long enough to attend the funeral.

Two days later he began his pursuit of Talia.

Talia took one last backward glance at the villa where she had lived and practiced for several weeks. It was a lovely place, but she wasn't going to miss it. The only misgivings she had about leaving were lodged in the knowledge that she would soon be farther than ever from Andrei. But it was impractical to stay in one place forever in a futile hope that he would miraculously appear on her doorstep.

Her career might not be everything to her, but it was important. She loved to dance, and she had made close friends among the other performers. And the opportunity to travel to America was just too much to give up, especially for a romance that might never happen. Besides, Diaghilev had promised her two or three small solo appearances, and to be so honored was no small thing. With Nijinsky and Pavlova no longer with the company, Talia's chance for larger roles was even greater. Surely Andrei, who had always supported her in the past, would not want her to turn down such an opportunity.

Still, it was not easy to drive away. It was still harder to board the train that would take her a world away. But the tour would not last forever. By fall she would return to Europe—and maybe by then Andrei would also be in Russia.

The Villa Belle Rive, overlooking the Rhone River, was in a beautiful setting, especially with spring blossoming all around. Andrei thought it a perfect locale for a reunion with the woman he loved. He had procured a ride to the isolated colony from a farmer who was returning from town after selling a wagonload of hay. Andrei offered the man a coin to pay for the ride, but the farmer would not take it, so Andrei thanked him and jumped from the back of the wagon.

Bits of hay clung to his wool jacket and trousers, and he spent a moment brushing them away before he strode up the dirt path that led to the villa. He emerged from a thick stand of trees that fronted the villa, and the view left him breathless. How quiet and peaceful the place was! Almost too quiet. There had to be a large entourage connected with the Ballets Russes, from dancers to stagehands. But there was not a soul to be seen about the grounds. It was late afternoon; perhaps they were napping or something. But all of them?

He walked up to the door and knocked loudly. A minute or two passed before he heard footsteps approach inside. A woman in a plain dress and apron answered the door.

"May I help you?" she said in French.

"Yes," said Andrei, aware of his heavily accented and rough French. "I'm looking for one of the performers in the ballet company."

"The company left yesterday on tour."

"Yesterday?" Andrei quickly deflated, then just as quickly he thought of something and hope sparked him again. "Where did they go?" Perhaps he could catch up with them on the road.

"They're off for America."

Now he was truly deflated. "America . . ."

She must have perceived his disappointment because she added brightly, "But they will return in the fall."

"Did they all go?"

"Yes. There's just my husband and myself left. We're the caretakers."

"Did you know any of the dancers?"

"Some I did. But others were a bit snooty, you know."

"There was one dancer—sweet as a spring blossom, and delicate as a bird. She hasn't a snooty bone in her. Perhaps . . ."

"What was her name?"

"Talia Sorokin—"

"Oh yes, I spoke to her several times. A very kindly girl. I'm sorry to tell you, but she also left with the American tour."

So that was it, then. She was gone. Perhaps she would return in the fall, but who could say where he'd be? With shoulders slumped and hopes dashed, he walked away. The five-mile walk to town didn't improve his spirits.

Maybe there was no such thing as fate, after all. Worse still, if there was, it appeared as if it was stacked against him ever being with Talia.

And God?

He tried to think what his mama would say about God in such a situation as this. That God's timing was perfect. That He was the giver of good things. That they who wait on the Lord would be blessed.

Maybe if he were closer to God, such words would help. But he was too confused to see God clearly, much less trust Him or even wait for Him. He might have thought differently if God had come through for him now—if Talia had been there to affirm his love and devotion. But now there was a void in Andrei's heart even larger than before.

48

At the beginning of the war, Lenin had been disgusted with the large majority of socialists who gave over to patriotism, supporting the defense of their various countries. To Lenin, this was nothing short of treason to the socialist cause. The "imperialist war" of the ruling classes, he believed, should be manipulated into an opportunity to bring about collapse of the present rulers on an *international* scale—a vision to be achieved not by sabotaging the war, but rather by a massive propaganda attack among soldiers as well as civilians. In short, Lenin was calling for civil war.

"Guns should not be turned upon our brother socialists and the working classes," he wrote, "but rather against the Imperialist and bourgeois governments of the world."

The defeat of Russia, in Lenin's estimation, would be a lesser evil than the defeat of Germany. Still, he refused to enter into negotiations with the Imperialist government of the German Kaiser. But as the war progressed, the expediency of some kind of dialogue with Germany became more and more evident.

The prevailing political intrigue almost helped ease Andrei's despondency over Talia's departure. He eagerly accepted any work Lenin offered him. His comrades jokingly referred to him as the "Little Soldier, but the *big* workhorse," and his work went a long way in strengthening his Party ties and smoothing over his ideological differences.

Andrei, however, was especially ambivalent about the talk of dealings with the Germans. Now he more fully understood his uncle Paul's struggles before he finally broke with the Bolsheviks. Andrei loved Russia, and it grated against his inborn patriotism to be in any kind of collusion with its sworn enemy. On the other hand, the Russia that was at war with Germany was the tsarist regime, which he hated and wanted to see defeated at all costs. He thus convinced himself that peasants and workers, his own people, were being driven like slaves to die for a cause from which they would in no way benefit. The only way to help them would be to scheme against the *tsar's* war.

He still felt odd when Lenin encouraged him and Stephan Kaminsky to meet with German socialist Alexander Helphand, code named Parvus. Parvus had worked closely with Trotsky during the 1905 Russian Revolution and had contributed several articles to *Iskra* in those days. But he was also a German patriot and in close association with the German government.

"He is first and foremost a Social Democrat," explained Stephan in an attempt to allay Andrei's suspicions. "But he has no qualms against working any side he must in order to obtain his political ends."

"I've heard he made a fortune profiteering during the Balkan War two years ago. Sounds like a capitalist to me."

"An opportunist," corrected Stephan. "And I am not saying I like the man. Lenin himself won't even see him. But he is curious to hear what Parvus has to offer. Lenin would be willing to agree to an armistice with Germany should he gain power in Russia. Yet he knows he can't achieve power without money—"

"And Parvus has money?"

"More than you or I will ever see. In addition, he has other resources to draw from."

"A German bankroll, perhaps?"

Stephan shrugged. "We'll just see what the man has to say."

They traveled to Zurich, where Parvus was staying in the fashionable Hotel Baur au Lac. He was in Switzerland ostensibly to organize the Institute of Science, an operation supposedly for the purpose of translating and disseminating socialist literature. It was, in fact, a venture solely dedicated to bringing about the Russian Revolution—and covertly funded by the German government. Parvus was recruiting exiled revolutionaries to work for him.

Andrei and Stephan met Parvus in a cafe near the hotel. Stephan had described the man to Andrei, saying, "He's got the body of an elephant and the head of Socrates." And the part about the body was accurate. A huge man, both ponderous and powerful at the same time, Parvus appeared to be in his mid-forties. Dressed fastidiously and expensively, he was obviously a figure to be reckoned with. Five minutes of conversation with Parvus confirmed the second part of Stephan's description. He was intelligent, articulate, and quite devious.

"And how is Ilyich these days?" asked Parvus after signaling for a waiter. "It's been years since I last saw him."

"He is very busy," said Stephan. He and Andrei had agreed that Stephan would do the talking. Andrei had no argument with that, for he immediately felt out of his league with Parvus. Stephan was also out of his league, but better to let him make a fool of himself than Andrei.

"We all are, aren't we? The war consumes everything." The waiter arrived, and Parvus ordered a meat pie and wine. He nodded toward his companions, "You would like to order, no?" When they hesitated, he added extravagantly, "Please, be my guest . . . or shall I say, the guest of my very generous client."

"Who might that be?"

"Come! Food and pleasure first, eh?"

It took no more prompting than that. Andrei and Stephan, like all the exiles, were very low on funds. Both were big, muscular men with large appetites that had not been fully satisfied in months. Though it was three in the afternoon, they ordered full meals. Parvus laughed, delighted.

"I see the cause plods along in its usual penury," he said, "while the ruling classes wallow in luxury."

Stephan cocked an eyebrow and appeared on the verge of making a rather undiplomatic comment about Parvus's hypocrisy. Andrei quickly interjected, "Why don't you tell us about your new organization?"

Parvus went on for a few minutes, describing the bogus "institute" as if it were real, detailing its many lofty goals. Then he spoke passionately about its real purpose, changing instantly from the urbane gentleman to the fervent revolutionary. Parvus seemed to enjoy playing a "part," and Andrei could easily picture the man fitting in as smoothly with high German government officials as with revolutionaries. All things to all men, Andrei thought, that's Parvus.

After five minutes of explanation, Parvus shifted to the part of the cunning businessman. "I am offering substantial salary to my employees, and I will pay all the expenses of their journey to Copenhagen."

"Copenhagen, you say?" said Stephan.

"Yes. We will be based there. The Danes have a strong socialist movement."

"It's also pro-German."

"Stephan Alexandrovich, this seems to bother you a great deal. But I have been given to understand that Lenin himself recognizes the fact that a German victory would not harm his cause in the least."

"Germany is still a monarchy, ruled by bourgeois imperialists."

Parvus shrugged, but before he could respond, the waiter arrived with their food. The conversation waned a bit as the three men concentrated on the hot meal. Andrei savored his meat—an item that was especially absent from his diet these days. It was a delicately roasted chicken in a savory garlic sauce. He ate slowly, chewing each bite as if it might be his last. He hadn't come here with any intention of working for Parvus, but his lucrative offer was looking better and better.

"Tell me," Parvus continued after a few minutes, "am I correct in my understanding that Ilyich has already made subtle overtures toward the German government?"

"You are quite *in*correct," said Stephan emphatically. Andrei knew, however, that Lenin had in fact met a couple of times with an Estonian patriot who was in direct communication with the Germans. Stephan added, "And that is, you understand, the *official* line and will continue to be so."

"I understand fully. It was foolish of me to ask such a tactless question. But . . . let's say, just for curiosity's sake, if Ilyich *were* to consider a, shall we say, *Teutonic* liaison, what might his conditions be?"

"Aside from complete Russian autonomy from German influence in the newly formed Russian republic, I believe he would insist that Russia would not be required to pay any war indemnities to Germany, nor to cede it any territory. He would want Russia to have a free hand in India. And he would agree to evacuate Turkey."

Parvus cocked an eyebrow. He had every right to be impressed by this kind of commitment. It indicated that Lenin *had* given careful thought to an alliance with Germany, and that he was willing to be quite cooperative, especially in giving Germany an unimpeded hand in the Middle East. But also, if Russia were to invade India, it naturally meant that she would become an ally of Germany *against* Britain. It could mean a whole new balance of power in Europe.

"This is quite interesting," said Parvus with great control. "For a purely imaginary offering, that is." Parvus glanced at his pocket watch. "Well, it appears as if I must be off. This has been a most stimulating conversation." He rose with incredible grace for his size. "I hope we will meet again. And do give some thought to my institute." When Andrei started to rise also, Parvus held up his large hand. "Sit and finish your meal. Now, good day, gentlemen." He strode away with confidence.

Andrei and Stephan did indeed continue with their meal—they weren't about to allow such food to go to waste; in fact, Andrei also finished off Parvus's half-eaten pie and the rest of his wine.

49

Paul saw signs of a different kind of anti-German sentiment in St. Petersburg—he doubted he'd ever get used to the new name of Petrograd. Even the Russians who were throwing rocks through the windows of merchants with German-sounding names often slipped and called the city Petersburg. And the hostility was worse in Moscow, which was far more "Russified." Earlier in the summer, businesses and homes of residents with German names had been burned and vandalized. Now Paul felt the tension strongly in the Capital.

As Paul walked along, he felt an oppressive pall hovering over the beautiful St. Petersburg. It made him long for his papa Yevno's clean simplicity more than he had in a long time. It made him wish he had never left Katyk. Yet Paul knew that the decay and sense of hopelessness was just as bad in the country. His mama and papa's home had been but a small haven in all the rot that seemed now to have penetrated all of Russia. He could almost smell it wafting up from the sidewalks or carried on the fetid wind like a plague.

Ah, Russia!

Paul loved this land. He had once been willing to die for its freedom, even to kill for it. Was he still? Was it worth dying for? With its corruption, its apathy, its Rasputins, its decadence? He thought of the thousands of men at that very moment dying on the fields of battle, not even knowing why, and worse, not even questioning it. He recalled an inane article he had read the other day in the newspaper that opened: "Our brave Russian men know how to die! Their staunch courage is a shining example to the enemy."

Perhaps death in battle was the only way they knew to give their wretched lives meaning. Or, probably nearer the truth, the article had been the voice of a government-sanctioned paper trying to glorify such total and complete waste. Surely even Russians must question the slaughter eventually. He had heard that more and more soldiers were taking "French leave"—that is, deserting. But even that twisted ray of hope increased Paul's growing sense of despair for his country. Russia, and *Russians*, deserved far better than they were getting from their government. And they shouldn't have to resort to dishonorable acts in order to get it.

Thus, Paul had very little sympathy for the empress. There was a growing outcry against her, the public even going so far as accusing her of being a German spy. Paul doubted it was true.The empress might be German by birth, but she had been raised by no less than Victoria of England herself. Yet the people had never liked Alexandra, and her dealings with Rasputin had alienated her even more. Her German heritage was simply another convenient reason to ostracize her. Rumors were rampant that she was harboring spies in the palace, giving secrets and money to the enemy cause. The public called for her to be locked up in a convent—a typical so-very-Russian method of disposing of unmanageable empresses.

Things might be different, of course, if the war were going better for the Russians. But defeat was following defeat. In August of that year, 1915, Warsaw fell and the Germans overran Poland. More than half the Russian army was destroyed. When Yuri came home on leave in the spring, he said medical supplies were, even then, scandalously low. But the depletion of ammunition was worse. Reports had it that half the Russian soldiers were going to war without rifles. They dotted the field of battle like clay pigeons before the well-equipped German enemy.

Paul turned into the Tauride Palace, where the Duma met, and climbed the stairs to Kerensky's small office. He wished he could shake this mood he was in; his meeting with his friend would only make it worse. He had received a telephone call from Sasha, asking to see him that morning before the daily session began. It couldn't be good news—there was no good news these days.

"Good morning!" Kerensky said as he opened the door. As usual, he was full of energy, but his eyes showed the strain of the last year in which he had frequently found himself butting up against the implacable attitudes of the majority of the Duma. He had been furious when the Duma, almost to a man, stood in unreserved support of the war. He had called for support only if the tsar would agree to a few basic demands, such as ceasing persecution of Jews, Poles, and the like. But only a handful of members, including Paul, were with him on this. Kerensky was a patriot, but he believed the best service to his country was to be a vocal critic of the government, warning it against folly, exhorting it to higher aims. The majority of the Duma, unfortunately, saw patriotism as silently accepting whatever the government said.

Paul recalled a speech Kerensky delivered a few months ago at an Imperial reception for the Duma—in the Winter Palace, no less.

Kerensky had said, "You have no enemies among the working classes of our enemies. This war would never have happened if the governments of the world would have faithfully upheld the sacred principles of 'liberty, equality and fraternity.' But now you must strengthen your hearts for the trial that lies ahead, to fight the terrible war that was not of your choosing. But I say this. After you have defended your country, *liberate* it!"

No wonder one of the Bolshevik members of the Duma had written to Lenin suggesting that they join forces with Kerensky. But, since all five of the Bolshevik members of the Duma had, not long ago, been arrested and exiled, few voices remained to speak out in opposition to government injustice. Kerensky's voice was being heard more and more. He was practically becoming an icon among Petrograd's working masses. Paul regretted that he himself was not a charismatic speaker, though he was greatly encouraged by Kerensky's boldness to be more outspoken.

"You're early. That's good. We have a lot to talk about. Sit down, please. Would you like tea?" said Kerensky.

He drew two cups of tea from the samovar that was wedged in between books and papers. They sat in the only two chairs in the office—Kerensky behind his desk, and Paul on the other side.

"There are a couple of items on today's agenda that I thought you should be aware of, Pavushka," said Kerensky.

"News from the Front?"

"In a manner of speaking. We've received word that the tsar

plans to take command of the army."

"I'm not surprised. He's wanted to do it from the beginning."

"And certainly our army can do no worse."

"The real problem lies in the repercussions this will have at home, not at the Front. He's a poor leader, but I shudder to think who might be in charge when he's gone."

Kerensky looked at Paul intently. "He has given the tsaritsa power as a dual monarch."

Paul closed his eyes and sighed. "And we know who controls the empress."

"Which brings me to the other matter I wanted to inform you about, since, no doubt, it will be a topic for discussion at today's Duma session." Kerensky shuffled through some papers, found the one he was looking for, and handed it across his desk to Paul. "This is a current police surveillance report on Rasputin. It makes for rather lurid reading, I'm afraid."

Paul scanned the sheets. They contained the highlights of the man's activities for the last two months. It read like the escapades of a first-year university student, or worse, an officer in the Guards. Visiting prostitutes, engaging in drunken orgies in his home and in the homes of friends, frequenting the public baths, and all-night calls upon various females. But the final entry was the most scandalous of all. As he read it, Paul shook his head in disgust and despair.

For propriety's sake, Rasputin had been assigned his own private room at the Villa Rhode. The police thought this the best way to keep his sometimes outrageous behavior from the general public. But on the night in question a small crowd had gathered in his room—some, including journalists, by Rasputin's invitation, others who simply found their way past the loose security. Cyril Vlasenko never got the whole story.

When he arrived, the police and proprietors were frantic. The noise and music from the room was deafening, penetrating throughout the entire gypsy nightclub. But the police couldn't very well evict the tsar's personal confessor, could they? They hoped that Cyril, with his past ties to the police, his place in government, and his acquaintance with Rasputin, might somehow mediate the delicate situation.

This is no place for a seventy-three-year-old man, he thought as he wearily approached the room. He had been roused from his bed at well past midnight, and now the rowdy din was making his ears ring. Suddenly, from inside the private room, there was a crash of breaking glass, followed by a woman's scream and the roar of laughter. Cyril gripped the door latch, but the police who were accompanying him held back. The cowards! he thought. He could handle the *starets*, though the man was strong as an ox. His own fortitude bolstered. He opened the door.

The gypsy band was playing some loud, shrill tune Cyril didn't know and hoped he'd never hear again. Rasputin was in the center of the group, dancing wildly to the music. Around him ranged a diverse crowd, including titled gentlemen, some whom Cyril knew, society ladies—if any woman visiting a place like this could be called a *lady*—and more common-looking sorts, no doubt Rasputin's friends from the streets. The crowd was yelling encouragements to the dancing monk, who had a woman in each arm. Another woman ran into the circle and placed a champagne glass on the floor and, with a bloodcurdling yell, Rasputin stomped the glass to pieces. The throng screamed with delight. Then someone passed a bottle of vodka to him. Cyril hardly gave a thought to the presence of liquor when there was supposed to be a prohibition on—everyone knew it was still readily available, especially to the rich. The priest set the bottle to his lips and, dribbling some down his beard, guzzled a good deal. He was obviously quite drunk, but he didn't miss a beat of the dance.

Laughing, Rasputin kissed the women in his arms. "If you're good, I'll show you real kisses later, eh? Like I do with the *old woman*." He winked, and everyone, even Cyril, knew to whom he was referring.

"You don't know the empress that well!" called someone in the crowd.

"I know her better than even her husband knows her!" Rasputin yelled. "Look at this!" He grabbed his satin embroidered shirt. "The *old woman* made this for me with her own hands. She kisses my feet. I do anything with her that I please."

"Aw, I'll bet you're not even the real Rasputin," challenged one of the onlookers.

"Yeah!" said another. "You're an imposter!"

Rasputin took another draw from the bottle. "How dare you! Questioning me! I am the tsar's confessor. I am the tsaritsa's lover. I am—"

"Prove it!"

Suddenly with a violent swing, Rasputin threw the bottle against a wall where it dented the plaster before it shattered and fell to the floor. "I'll show you!" he cried. Then he tore open his trousers.

An uproar rose from the throng—a mixture of shock, glee, and outrage. For a brief moment, Cyril stared in stunned silence. His first thought was: *How are we going to get out of this one?* Then he sprang into action.

"Let's move!" he ordered the police. And, with them behind him, he strode into the room, parting a way through the gathering with his cane. Cyril threw his own great coat around the *starets*, covering the fool as best he could, then placing an arm around him, he said soothingly, "Come, Father, I need to see you alone."

"Why, my old friend Cyril Karlovich!" slurred the priest. "I am always at your service." He turned to the crowd. "Duty calls. But save some vodka for me. I'll be back."

"Not if I can help it," muttered Cyril under his breath as he led Rasputin away.

Cyril got the man safely home, where he saw him crash on his bed in a dead stupor. He'd sleep until noon. Now Cyril had to do what he could to repair the situation, or at least doctor it a bit, before it reached the ears of the tsar. It was two in the morning now, and no doubt news of the incident had already spread to Rasputin's enemies, who would be quick to use it against him. Cyril had to be faster.

Very early the next morning he made a telephone call to the minister of internal affairs, Prince Shcherbatov, making a complete report of the incident—his watered-down version, of course. Cyril could have written the report himself, but he deemed it more advantageous for it to be in someone else's hand. Let Shcherbatov, who was openly hostile to Rasputin, bear any Imperial displeasure that might descend from it. This was a prime opportunity for Cyril to use masterfully to his advantage.

50

News of the events at the Villa Rhode spread like a ravenous fire through the city. The public devoured it eagerly. Rasputin was doomed for certain now. No one could survive such a shameful, public disgrace of the empress. Surely she would finally see the light and put the debauched priest where he belonged—where the snow and ice never melted.

Not if I have anything to do with it, Cyril swore to himself. When Rasputin was sobered up the next day, Cyril made sure the *starets* knew his version of the story.

"That's all the tsar needs to know about last night," Cyril said. "A little more to drink than usual, the noise and such got a bit out of hand. Nothing more, do you understand?"

"I don't need to lie. Papa will forgive me." Rasputin looked a complete wreck after the night's debauchery—a man to be truly pitied. Cyril prayed that would work in the man's favor when he was called before the tsar to answer for himself.

"No one is suggesting that you should lie, Father Grigori. Heaven forbid! Only that you protect the royal family from . . . ah, sordid details. The tsaritsa's delicacy must be protected at all costs."

"Ah yes . . . Mama is so fragile. I am her protector, her savior."

"And it wouldn't hurt to save yourself while you're at it." *And me, too*, Cyril added to himself.

He was tiring of the agriculture ministry, and he feared the ministry was going to end up a scapegoat for war shortages and the like. Critics were already talking about mismanagement and poor planning in allowing so many peasants to leave the fields for the Front. He didn't want to be around when things crashed in. The ministry of the interior might not be any safer haven, but that's where the real power was inside Russia, and Cyril still coveted the top post in that ministry. He'd been hinting to Rasputin about this for the last two years. Shcherbatov's days had to be numbered, and the Villa Rhode incident might just be his undoing—there was always a way to make such a scandal reflect on the Minister of the Interior. Cyril was determined to milk this thing to his personal advantage.

Hat firmly gripped in hand—both literally and figuratively—Rasputin, an abject and repentant man, stood before the tsar, who was home from the Front for a visit.

"Can you deny this report, Grigori?" the tsar asked angrily, waving a sheet of paper, now crumpled, in his fist.

Several weeks had now passed since the incident. The tsar had overlooked the first report sent to him, which had been skillfully watered down by Vlasenko. It had seemed such a trifling matter at the time, especially with a war on. That report said the *starets* was drunk in public, dancing and making noise. However, yesterday he had received a new report. Shcherbatov said he had later personally investigated the matter when further details had reached him concerning the evening at the gypsy nightclub. This second report revealed all the gory details.

"Oh, Papa!" wheedled Rasputin, head bowed. "I never claimed to be a saint. I am truly a sinner, perhaps even the worst of sinners. I am human. I am weak and lowly, not worthy to be called of God. Please, Papa, forgive me."

"You have brought disgrace to the Crown!"

"Curse the evil liquor!" cried the priest. "The pain from my wounds forces me to turn to the vodka for relief. Then sometimes I lose my head. Pray for me, Papa, that I can be strong enough to refuse it, that it will never touch my lips again." Suddenly he fell on his knees before the tsar. Tears spilled from his eyes. "Save me, Papa! Save me from myself. Lift up my wretched plight to God!"

Nicholas felt a bit awkward with the *starets* whom he had so venerated now bowed before him, seemingly broken and contrite. For a moment he didn't know what to do. Then he lifted his hand and laid it on Rasputin's head.

"You are forgiven," the tsar said. What else could he say? Grigori was a friend, and to turn his back on the man now would have been too callous and vindictive for a man of honor to do. God himself instructed that a man should forgive those who have wronged him seventy times seven. Yet, as the Little Father, Nicholas also knew it was expected of him not only to forgive his wayward child but also to discipline him. "Grigori, you must return to your home in Siberia for a time. It simply would not be good for my other subjects if I did nothing to censor you for what happened. Do you understand?"

"Oh yes, Papa. You are more merciful than I deserve."

The tsar's next undesirable task was to face his wife. He was glad he'd be leaving in a few days for the Front in order to take command of the army. She was so pleased about his new status as commander in chief that she might not be too upset about Rasputin.

He was wrong.

"Nicky! How could you?"

"I had to do something, Sunny, dear."

"Sometimes you let them walk all over you. Don't you realize when they attack Our Friend, they attack the dynasty itself? By sending Grigori away it's as much as saying those horrible stories are true."

"We've been over this ground before, Sunny."

"Yes, we have . . ." She gave a long-suffering sigh. "And someday you will actually raise your voice to naysayers like that awful Shcherbatov and maybe even pound your fist on the table once or twice. You must be firmer with them. They just don't fear you enough, Nicky. Especially when you give in so readily on issues like this. You are the tsar. And you are now commander in chief of the whole army. You *must* make people fear you, or they will crush you."

"I will try to do better in the future, my dear. But I only did what I felt was best. Please try to understand. It was an untenable situation."

"I've heard that the man at the Villa Rhode was nothing more than an imposter—someone our enemies hired to behave so and bring disrepute upon Our Friend's name."

Nicholas sighed. Let her have her fantasies, he thought. What harm could it do? "Nevertheless," he replied, "people are going to believe what they wish even if we were to prove them to be lies."

"They want to think badly of him—of us. It kills me when I think about what people are saying, the awful accusations. They wouldn't say such things if this were a real autocracy, as it was meant to be."

"I'm trying to maintain as much power as I can, Sunny."

"I know, dear." She moved close to him on the divan and put her arm around him. "My poor Nicky." She laid her head on his shoulder, gently stroking his beard with her hand.

"I wish it could be like this always, my Sunny one. Just you and me—and the kiddies, of course—in our own little cottage, perhaps on the Black Sea. No affairs of state, no wars. Just sunshine and sand and the smell of salt and fish in the air."

Nicholas sighed. That's the life he was suited for. His father had known it all along, had not even tried to prepare him for leadership. He had been born a *second* son—with good reason, he was certain. Only the cruel hand of fate had thrust him into a position he not only loathed, but feared as well. He was doing the best he could for the good of the kingdom. That would have to be enough. "And tomorrow I must return to Stavka," he added. He had to face reality.

"Come, my love," said Alexandra, "I will make your last night here one that will carry you through many days of hardship."

He reveled in the sudden passion burning in his wife's eyes, almost forgetting his distressful lot in life.

Cyril's plan was working beautifully—almost as if it really *were* a plan. In truth, it was merely that events were finally falling into place in such a way that at last favored him.

Rasputin was gone to his village in Siberia, but Cyril knew it wouldn't be for long. And so did the public. Before, he had been sent to Pokrovskoe, only sixteen hundred miles from Petrograd, and always returned. The public, especially the Duma, was outraged that Rasputin had received nothing more than a slap on the hand for his shocking conduct. Cyril gloated at their dismay, ignoring warnings that this was the last straw, that the tsar would regret thumbing his nose in such a way at the Duma.

In the meantime, during the weeks of Rasputin's absence, Cyril kept in close contact with the *starets* and with the detachment of agents sent to protect and spy on the man. In turn, he also kept in contact with the tsaritsa, passing on to her innocuous news about Rasputin, his state of health, etc. At the same time, he made certain Alexandra did not hear other choice tidbits about her favorite monk, such as his drunken behavior on the trip to Siberia, or the row he'd had with the ship's captain, or the fact that when Rasputin arrived at his home village of Pokrovskoe, he was so dead drunk his daughters had to carry him home.

But the Minister of the Interior seemed bent on undermining Cyril's work at every turn. The man even leaked a story to the press that strongly linked Rasputin to the Germans. On top of that, Shcherbatov also joined with eight of the tsar's ministers to sign a letter opposing the tsar's taking over command of the army and urging him to reconsider. As a result of the letter, four ministers were immediately dismissed, including Shcherbatov. Cyril couldn't have been more delighted. The time was right for men such as himself to attain power.

Cyril kept Rasputin informed of these events, making certain the *starets* understood that Cyril was the man for the vacant ministerial position. Rasputin thus sent a telegram to the tsaritsa. Cyril never saw its contents but he could guess at the gist of it: "Count Vlasenko is a man who thinks like us. He is a loyal subject. He will protect and uphold the honor of the Crown. He is deserving of a promotion." Perhaps the *starets* might even have gone so far as to say, "God told me that Count Vlasenko should be Minister of the Interior."

When the telephone call came, Cyril tried to be as reserved as a minister was expected to be. But the grin plastered across his face remained there for two full days. His lifelong dream was at last realized. He was Minister of the Interior. He had arrived. Let old Viktor Fedorcenko top that! It didn't even bother him when a member of the Duma approached him and said, "Your appointment more than ever convinces me that the dynasty is doomed. If you truly cared about Russia, you would resign."

Cyril had laughed. Resign, indeed! The only way anyone would extradite him from this office was to drag his dead body away.

He threw himself immediately into his work. There were bribes to collect, kickbacks to arrange, revolutionaries and Jews and foreigners to harass. And, of course, the name of the Duma member who had spoken so indiscreetly to him was put on the police list to be closely watched. Cyril was, at last, a truly happy man.

After the ministry of the interior fell to Vlasenko, other key ministry positions toppled in quick succession. All went to Rasputin followers, devotees, or lackeys—depending on one's frame of reference.

Alexandra sent daily letters to the tsar at the Front, frequently containing hers and Rasputin's suggestions and opinions about political matters.

"Dear Lovey," she wrote once, "I don't like that Minister of War, Polivanov. You know he is Our Friend's enemy. He protested giving Grigori a war office car, saying it was too fast. He's afraid the police spies won't be able to keep up with Our Friend. The nerve! You must get rid of the man, Hubby. Don't dawdle in making up your mind."

Some believed all the power of the government was now in the grimy hands of the Mad Monk, the peasant *starets* from Siberia—he and that German woman, the tsar's wife. Probably closer to fact was that the government was in no hands at all. The tsar was happily and blindly tending to the war; Rasputin and Alexandra were haphazardly following their emotions; the ministers were either looking out for their own interests or simply too ignorant to know what interests to look out for. And the Duma, in the interest of patriotism, was standing back and letting it all happen.

Russia was tottering on a precipice. And no one did anything. Some citizens were looking in the wrong direction. Some were gaping into the hole, stunned to silence. Some didn't believe the precipice existed, and others firmly believed they would never fall in. Still others saw the inevitable and deemed it in the hands of fate.

But there was yet another group of Russians, poised and ready to *push* the country toward its calamity.

VI

Momentous Decisions

Fall 1916

51

Anna read the letter from Misha again. She had it all but memorized now. It might be the last letter she'd receive from him for a while. Shortly after this letter had arrived four months ago, she had been notified that he had been taken prisoner and was in a POW camp. Part of Anna was glad he was out of the war, yet she had heard that conditions in the camps were terrible. And more than that, she knew Misha well enough to know that he would make every attempt to escape. Anna could never be entirely at peace—not until this war was over and he was at her side.

"I won't let you go again, no matter what," she said to the pages she held in her hands.

It was difficult to believe she was really married to Misha—two years! She wanted to have a life with him before they were too old to enjoy it. He had taken one leave since the war began, and it had been far too short. But at that time he promised her, once again, that he would retire from the military when the war was over. Now that they were married, he was anxious to be a family man.

"Oh, God, please let it happen," she murmured.

She thought about last Christmas. It seemed so far in the past now. If the Christmas of 1914 had been festive with Mariana's arrival, the Christmas of 1915 had been a full-blown celebration. Everyone had been there—except Andrei.

Yuri and Misha had been home on leave, and Daniel was there, though he did manage to get to Petrograd far more often than the soldiers. Talia was home from her tour of America, and Viktor and Sarah came up for the holiday from the Crimea.

What a time they all had together! It had almost been as if the war did not exist, and for a whole week they all pretended that there would be no more partings. But the day after New Year's, Yuri and Misha left, and Daniel followed a few days later. Yuri had managed another leave before the spring offensive in May. Now it was less than two months before the Christmas of 1916; Anna did not expect a repeat of last year's celebration.

At least Mariana and the children were still here. She should have returned to America, but it was hard for her to leave her mama. She did consider sending the children back without her, but she had never been separated from them before. Still, it was risky staying in Russia. Unrest, due to widespread strikes and shortages, was the rule now. Little food could be found in the markets, and there were long lines to get what food was available—at hideously inflated prices. Basics such as meat and flour had risen in price nearly three hundred percent.

Part of the problem was transportation—the railroad rolling stock had been commandeered for the war. But fewer crops were being planted, too—there were simply no men to work the fields. Anna had heard from her sister, Vera, that the Burenin plot in Katyk was lying mostly fallow because her sons were at the Front and her husband was in poor health. After the crisis of 1905, Anna and Raisa had always kept a small stockpile of staples, but even that was becoming seriously depleted. Katya sent what she could from her grandmother's larders, but those supplies, too, were getting low. No one looked forward to the approaching winter.

Anna wondered where it would all lead. Paul said the Duma was finally waking to the surrounding chaos, but he feared it was too late. They had demanded the resignations of the premier, Stürmer, and Cyril Vlasenko. Many moderates and even staunch monarchists were openly discussing deposing the tsar. But there was little agreement on who to replace him with. Some favored the tsarevich with the Grand Duke Nicholas as regent, others supported the tsar's brother Michael. Other rumors had it that the Grand Duke Nicholas would stage a coup d'etat. And those who wanted to get rid of the Romanovs completely were growing more and more vocal.

Amid all this uncertainty, Anna wished more than ever their men could be with them. She was not so independent that she did not feel acutely the need for Misha's protection. And she knew Katya was feeling this even more lately. She was six months pregnant—a gift from Yuri's spring leave. But she wasn't doing well. Actually, the doctor was surprised she had carried the child this long. Katya had been bleeding off and on throughout the pregnancy. A week ago, she had taken to her bed with premature labor. Anna spoke to her yesterday and there had been no improvement. The poor girl was scared.

Mariana had gone to visit Katya a couple of hours ago and should be home soon. Anna prayed the news would be good. Mariana had taken a midwifery course in America, mostly because when she had been expecting her first child she had been curious and wanted to know all she could about the process. It was a godsend now. Doctors were scarce in the city, and when Katya could see her doctor, he was very impatient and told her as little as possible about her condition. Mariana's medical training was a great comfort to Katya—and to Anna, too! When the time came, if a doctor could not be reached, Mariana would be more than capable to handle the situation.

Suddenly Anna heard the noise of children in the hall. Mariana was back. Zenia tumbled first into the parlor where Anna sat. She ran up to Anna and jumped into her lap.

"Kiss, Gamma!" she said, then planted her wet lips on Anna's cheek.

Glad to have a diversion from her thoughts, Anna grinned and returned the gesture, adding a loving hug to it. Then Katrina strode into the room, so pretty in a royal blue dress, trimmed with blue and white ribbons, and more blue ribbons tying back her auburn curls.

"Hello, Grandmama," she said in such a grown-up tone for a six-year-old. She slid with the fluid grace of a ballerina onto the sofa next to Anna. Anna kissed her cheek and gave her a squeeze with her free arm. "Aunt Katya was feeling better today. She had lunch with us. But Zenia spilled her milk on Aunt Katya's bed—"

"Now, Katrina, don't be telling tales," Mariana said as she entered with John close behind.

"I was only going to say, Mama, that it didn't upset Aunt Katya, but rather she just laughed. And I haven't seen her laugh in a long time."

"That is true." Mariana took a chair adjacent to the sofa. John stood behind her, seeming to take up the position of man of the house.

"I'm so glad to hear it," said Anna.

"I play wif Reena," said Zenia.

Anna noted that the children's Russian was excellent, even Zenia's, with its childish lisp. Mariana had worked hard to make sure her children didn't lose their heritage, but there was a marked

American air about them, too. They spoke both English and their Russian with unusual accents.

"They're getting to be great friends," added Mariana. "It's so good for Irina to have children around. Before we came, she had no playmates."

Mariana paused and reached into her handbag and withdrew a folded paper—a newspaper by all appearances, but small like the underground pamphlets Anna often saw being handed out surreptitiously on the streets. "Mama, look at this." She handed the paper to Anna.

Anna unfolded it. Its name was *Freedom*. She glanced up at her daughter before looking further. "Mariana, perhaps you've been in America too long, but here it is not a safe thing to take such material."

"I know, Mama, but look closely at the front page and you will know why I had to take this."

As Anna studied it, her eye was immediately drawn to a cartoon drawing. Central to the drawing was a large, almost Bhuddalike figure, obviously intended to be Rasputin with his long, dark beard and evil, piercing eyes. In his arms, nestled like children, were the tsar and tsaritsa. The caption read, "Who rules Russia?" But it was the signature of the artist that Anna really noticed. *Malenkiy Soldat*.

"Andrei . . ." breathed Anna.

"I knew you'd want to see it, Mama," said Mariana. "We can burn it when we're through."

"At least he's alive. It's a mixed comfort, however, knowing what he's doing."

"It's not that much of a surprise."

"No . . ." Anna glanced again at the drawing, trying to visualize Andrei working on it. She hoped he was happy—and safe. "Do you think he is in Petrograd?"

"I don't know. Daniel said he has been trying to locate him through some of his European sources. He hasn't said anything to you because so far he's been unsuccessful. But I hope he's not in Russia, Mama. With everything that is going on here now, he'd be certain to be in the middle of it."

Their conversation was cut short by the ringing telephone. John went to answer it. He returned with a grim expression.

"That was Aunt Katya's grandmother," he said. "She is sending a car here. There is an emergency with Aunt Katya, and you both are needed."

They arrived in time for Mariana to deliver Katya's baby. There was no doctor present, and most likely none would get there. But it probably wouldn't have mattered. The child died ten minutes after it took its first labored breath. It simply had not been strong enough or mature enough to survive. It was a boy.

Katya was despondent, but when the priest—thankfully not Rasputin—arrived and asked for a name with which to baptize the child, she did manage to tearfully give the name she and Yuri had decided upon should they have a boy—Sergei Yuriovich.

Anna, Mariana, Teddie and Countess Zhenechka sat by Katya's bedside the rest of the day, though Katya offered no acknowledgment at all of their presence. But the four women prayed over her nonetheless. They prayed out loud together, and they prayed silently.

All Katya could say was, "How will I tell Yuri?"

52

The artillery fire was close. Closer than it had been an hour ago—so close it made the ground under Yuri's feet tremble. The sound of the incessant explosions was making his head throb, too, but he had to ignore it and concentrate on the frantic activity in the dressing station compound. People were scurrying around everywhere, not a soul was standing still. Supplies were being hurriedly packed into cartons, tents taken down. Men bearing stretchers were moving patients from the tents still standing. All this with a freezing wind howling through the compound. Chaos appeared to reign, but Yuri understood the order to it all—well, at least to most of it. The army was in retreat, and the dressing station had to retreat with it.

However, as Yuri paused for a brief moment in the compound, he sensed something had gone wrong. The artillery was closer than it should be. He could even hear rifle fire. The army was being pushed back too fast. The dressing station had not been given the order to evacuate soon enough. In less than an hour, the ground where he now stood could well be overrun by Germans.

Yuri grabbed the arm of a passing feldsher whose arms were loaded with cartons. "Forget the supplies," Yuri said. "We have to get the patients out."

"But, sir, we can't leave all this to the Germans."

"Listen, Corporal." Yuri paused. "That's German artillery. We don't have enough shells to be firing that often. We haven't time for supplies."

"I'll do as you say, but it won't matter much if the trucks can't get through."

He was right, of course. So far only two trucks had arrived to assist in the evacuation, and they were now nearly full. They would need ten more trucks to complete the move and accommodate all the patients. As a matter of course, they expected only five trucks to be allotted to the hospital. Yuri would be happy if three arrived. And to make matters worse, new wounded were constantly pouring in. He began to wish he'd learned German in school instead of French.

Yuri returned to one of the two hospital tents left standing. He'd just been to the supply depot to see if, by some miracle, more morphine was available. He had already sent two orderlies who had returned empty-handed. Deeming it was time to throw around his weight as an officer, even a prince if he had to, he had marched to the depot to confront the supply sergeant himself. Even in the Russian medical corps there had to be some morphine, and he'd heard a rumor that the sergeant was hoarding it to sell on the black market.

Yuri was still shaking over the scene he had created in the supply tent.

"I want a case of morphine," Yuri had demanded.

The sergeant laughed. "I've got a little laudanum, that's all."

"I've got men with their guts spilling out, with arms and legs missing! I may as well give them aspirin. I know you have morphine, and I want it."

"I don't know how you know that . . . sir. You can come in and look for yourself—"

Yuri grabbed the man's shirt and shoved him harshly against the flimsy tent wall, nearly knocking it over. He didn't realize until then that he had such nerve, such strength.

"I don't have time to fool around!" Yuri yelled into the sergeant's face. "In less than an hour, I have to move a hundred wounded men over rocky, rutted terrain. They're going to be sedated first, do you hear?" But he suddenly realized he wasn't much of a threat. How could he make this burly, hardened soldier obey him?

While the man was completely distracted by Yuri's uncharacteristic violence, Yuri took the sergeant's service revolver from its holster. It was a crazy act, and from the look of shock on the man's face, he would agree. Yuri aimed the gun at the sergeant's head.

"Morphine," Yuri said, his voice discordantly calm and matter-of-fact.

"I tell you—"

The revolver shook in Yuri's hand as he pressed it into the man's temple. "Now!"

"I'll take one more look."

"That's more like it," said Yuri. He followed the sergeant into the tent.

The place was a maze of cartons and crates. The sergeant had been busy packing up. Yuri prayed he could find what he wanted quickly. The man made a show of searching through several crates, then said at last, "I found it!"

Yuri wasn't surprised. But when the sergeant handed him only three boxes of medication, Yuri raised the revolver once again. "I want the rest."

"What do you mean? This is all there is."

Yuri cocked the revolver.

"All right! All right! I'll look again."

"Make it fast. We're running out of time."

Yuri left the tent with a day's supply of morphine in a box tucked under his arm. There was probably more but he had lost his patience, and since he had no intention of shooting the sergeant, he couldn't really force the issue further. He still couldn't believe the man could be so heartless. But it was common knowledge that handling supplies in the army was a lucrative business. The sergeant was just doing what others before him had been doing for generations.

As Yuri entered the hospital tent, he had already forgotten the unsavory incident. There was too much to do to dwell long on moral issues.

He got his two feldshers busy administering the morphine while he circulated among the patients, seeing that they were secured for transport. He was nearly shaken from his feet as a shell exploded dangerously close to the compound. Then someone came to the tent.

"We've got new wounded!" the man yelled.

Yuri rushed into the compound where carts were arriving. He wasn't on triage duty, but the other two doctors didn't seem to be around. Nevertheless, there would be no surgery until the station moved, so he might as well do what he could in the compound. One of the doctors joined him, but the third, Grekov, was nowhere to be seen. "Where's Grekov?"

"Killed, less than a half hour ago. Didn't you hear?"

"No . . ." Yuri shook his head, but instead of feeling grief over his colleague's death he only thought, *How are we going to manage with just two doctors?*

But what choice was there?

He began examining the new wounded.

A shoulder wound . . . the man could wait. Didn't need morphine either, though the patient was crying in pain.

A shattered fibula. He'd lose the leg. A quarter grain of morphine until the camp was relocated and surgery could be performed.

Shrapnel in the abdomen. He'd make it if he received immediate surgery. A half grain of morphine.

A crushed chest. Bleeding profusely. He'd never make it. No morphine. Ignore his screams of pain.

Frostbite. He'd lose half his toes, but he could wait.

Head injury. Part of cerebrum visible. Pupils fixed and dilated. No hope.

And on it went. Yuri pronounced men's fates with all the detachment of a machine. Earlier, he had thought of Mariana's experiences as a nurse in the last war and how she had once saved a man's life who had been pronounced hopeless. But for once in Yuri's life he could not moralize over his actions. There wasn't time; there wasn't enough personnel. He could not waste time in a possibly futile effort to save a single life when three more had a better chance of survival in his place. He had to be a machine. It was the only way to survive the mental ordeal himself—that and not making eye contact with a patient during triage duty. Think of the man only by the nature of his wounds, not as a person.

More wounded arrived. This must be the bloodiest retreat in history, Yuri mused to himself. He lost track of time and place. He forgot how cold it was; he forgot to be afraid of the barrage of explosions. Germans could have marched right into the compound and he wouldn't have noticed—or cared. Even the artillery fire seemed to diminish. But that was only his imagination, for they were as close as before, if not closer. Then one sound did penetrate his senses.

Trucks!

As he was trying to stop a hemorrhage, Yuri looked up to see four trucks rumble into the compound. He wanted to cheer, but if he moved his hand, his patient would bleed to death. The man had a damaged femoral artery, but the wound itself wasn't too severe, and the man could be saved if only the bleeding could be stopped. Acting by pure instinct, Yuri had pressed his hand to the artery before assessing that the patient might be beyond help, at least, considering the backup of other wounded. Even a machine breaks down occasionally. And now he was committed to the task, because by removing his hand too soon he would be *actively* dooming the patient to death. It was a fine distinction, he knew, but one that for the moment gripped him.

Then someone shouted from across the compound, "Doc! We need you!"

A man on a stretcher was writhing about convulsively while two feldshers were attempting to hold him down. Yuri glanced around for the other doctor, but he, of course, was busy also. Yuri gave the feldshers a helpless shrug.

A nurse hurried past. "Sister," he called. "I need a dressing tray."

"Yes, Doctor," she said, as if she didn't have a hundred other things to do at the same time.

To his surprise, she returned rather quickly but with only a few bandages. "This is all I could find. Most of the supplies are being loaded into the trucks."

Yuri took the bandages. Maybe in the Russian army supplies *were* more precious than men. Why else would they be using the trucks for those instead of for the wounded?

Lifting his hand from the artery, he was gratified to see the hemorrhage had slowed. A pressure bandage should take care of further bleeding, though if this man did get loaded up into a truck, the ride over rough terrain would probably start the bleeding all over again. But if Yuri learned nothing else during this war, he at least knew for certain that he was only human, and there was a limit to what a man could do. The rest he had to leave in the hands of God.

Then, without warning, the dressing station became a target for enemy artillery. Several blasts hit the compound—one a direct hit on the supply tent. By then, most of the supplies had been removed, but the supply sergeant wasn't so lucky. He was found in the rubble and Yuri attended him.

"I guess I got what I deserved, Doc," the man said.

"Shut up!" Yuri snapped as he worked desperately over him. "Save your strength."

"I'm a goner—"

"Not yet, Sergeant."

But a piece of shrapnel had practically eviscerated the man, and his intestines were peppered with fragments. Those needed surgical removal. There were at least a dozen other pieces of metal imbedded in his skin. Frantically Yuri removed what he could, but, with bombs blasting in his ears, men running everywhere and yelling, his hands weren't steady enough for such delicate work. He needed an operating room, instruments, disinfectant. . . .

Suddenly another shell hit the demolished supply tent. As it impacted, debris flew in all directions, and Yuri threw himself bodily over his patient to protect the man. He felt something hard strike his back, then deflect away. Then there was silence. Complete silence.

"You okay, Sergeant?" he asked as he lifted himself away from the man.

"Yeah. Thanks, Doc."

"Doctor Fedorcenko." A feldsher came up behind Yuri. "You're bleeding on your back."

Yuri hadn't felt a thing, but when he reached behind him, his back was soaked. The feldsher taped him up while he continued to work on the sergeant. When Yuri had done as much as he could for the sergeant, he gave him an injection of morphine and instructed the feldsher to get the patient onto a truck.

"Hey, Doc," said the sergeant as Yuri turned to go, "I'm sorry, you know, about before. If I make it, I won't do . . . that again. I promise."

"Good, Sergeant." Yuri didn't have the energy to muster more enthusiasm than that.

Somehow the dressing station completed its move to a location about five miles down the road. It took the rest of the day to get everything set up again. At least the bombardment had stopped and all was quiet on the Front. But the only benefit Yuri gained was that he now had an operating room—or rather, an operating tent—to work in. There was no chance to sleep. He and the other doctor were in surgery through the night. In the morning a new doctor arrived, and Yuri got a couple hours of rest before the battle resumed three miles away and wounded started coming in again.

Around three in the afternoon, there was a short lull in the flow of wounded. When Yuri finished his current operation, there was no new patient waiting. He looked around, rather dazed, and the nurse said there would be about fifteen minutes before the next batch of wounded were prepped for surgery. Yuri stripped off his rubber gloves and his blood-smeared smock, then stepped outside the O.R. for a breath of fresh air. He didn't care about the wind and cold—anything was preferable to where he had been. A feldsher was standing nearby having a cigarette.

"Want a smoke, Doc?" he asked, handing Yuri a pack of cigarettes.

"No, thanks." Yuri took a deep breath. The air was filled with dust and the reek of gunpowder, but at least that sickening odor of blood was gone. They never mentioned in medical school that blood had an odor, and under normal circumstances it wasn't noticeable. But when there was so much of it, it became pungent and cloying. He'd never get used to it, and he prayed he would never have to.

"Doc," said the feldsher whose name Yuri now remembered was George, "I heard a rumor that we were finally pushing back the Germans. What do you think?"

"I hope so. I don't want to move again." But the sounds of artillery in the not-so-far distance didn't offer much hope of that.

"Yeah, that move was a real nightmare, wasn't it? You ever get any sleep?"

"I tried this morning. Closed my eyes, but I couldn't sleep."

George held out the pack of cigarettes again. "Take a couple, Doc. They'll relax you."

"Yeah, but what do I do when I *have* to have one and there aren't any?"

"Two things the Russian army has in plentiful supply is cigarettes and vodka. There'd be mutiny if those ever ran out."

"I'm afraid not even that's helping . . ." Yuri's words were followed by a brief silence. Neither man wanted to comment further on the distressing state of the army, with desertions and mutiny occurring daily. Officers were taking leaves whenever they wanted, going home for extended periods, some not returning to the Front at all. For a brief moment Yuri cursed his wretched sense of honor.

"When was the last time you were home, Doc?" asked the feldsher, almost as if he had been reading Yuri's thoughts—but that wouldn't have been too difficult, since home was what everyone thought of most around here.

"Last spring. My wife is expecting a baby soon, but I doubt I'll get back for that."

"Well, congratulations. I've got four children myself. I miss them terribly."

"This'll be my first."

The man laughed and slapped Yuri on the back. "Well, if I was giving out leaves, you'd be at the top of my list. A man ought to be present that first time, at least. You should do what everyone else is doing. Take a French leave." He laughed.

Yuri shrugged and managed a half-hearted chuckle. He knew it wouldn't happen. His sense of responsibility was too strong. And Daniel couldn't be expected to procure leaves at will. For now, Yuri was stuck where he was. Pregnant women were a low priority during wartime. But there was always the vague hope that the war would be over by the time the baby was due. However, if that were to happen, it would be a sure bet that the Germans would be the victors.

Then a nurse poked her head outside and said, "Dr. Fedorcenko, we're ready."

"All right, Sister," said Yuri. When the feldsher also moved to follow, Yuri added to him, "Finish your smoke, George. You probably won't get another for a while."

"Thanks, I'll do that."

Yuri turned and walked back into the tent. As he did so, he vaguely heard a familiar sound. He was trying to place it as he stepped toward the nurse, who was holding out a clean operating gown for him. Suddenly it came to him.

The whistle of an incoming bomb!

But the realization came too late. The explosion struck in the very spot where he had only moments before been talking to the feldsher.

"George!" he screamed. Then the force of the explosion propelled Yuri several feet into the air before he fell in a heap on the floor. In another instant, something landed on top of him. It took a moment in the dust and mayhem before he identified it as a stretcher with a wounded man on it. He tried to move out of its way, but an excruciating pain shot through his body. Screams and cries went up all around him, but he couldn't see what was happening, and every time he tried to move, the pain only got worse. Then the surrounding noise grew dimmer and dimmer, and Yuri sank into a numb, black silence.

53

Yuri was coming home!

Although she would never wish harm to her husband, Katya found herself glad he had been wounded. Maybe it would be serious enough so he would never have to go back to the Front again. When she had received word—both, thankfully, in the same letter—that he had been wounded and was returning to Petrograd, for the first time since the death of her baby, she felt a spark of life and joy.

She desperately needed Yuri. She felt as if she were hanging on to her strength, even her very sanity, only by a thread. Olga had been encouraging her to go see Father Grigori, but Yuri had mentioned subtly several times in letters that he didn't want her to see the *starets*. And so far she was respecting that request. But she could not keep from wondering what might have happened had she followed up on that last visit from the *starets* when she lost the first baby. Maybe she wouldn't have had the second miscarriage. What if he had the power to heal her, to make her womb whole and able to carry a child to term?

Olga told her that only a few months ago, Father Grigori had healed Anna Vyrubova, the tsaritsa's friend. Anna had been in a terrible train accident and had been near death. Her legs had been crushed, and her head and spine had been seriously injured. The doctors had given up on her. But Father Grigori arrived at the hospital and, like Jesus himself, had commanded Anna to wake up and rise. She opened her eyes and even tried to speak and get up. Grigori said she would get well but would be an invalid for the rest of her life. The woman did indeed recuperate, though she now used crutches or a wheelchair to get around. Olga knew Anna personally and had no doubt of the truth of those events. Grigori had healed her.

Could he not do the same for Katya? Several times in the last two weeks she had come very close to going to 64 Gorokhavaya Street in spite of Yuri's warnings. She couldn't understand what Yuri had against the man. And Teddie and Grandmother and Mama Anna, too—they seemed to want to believe the worst, lies that had no doubt been fabricated by Rasputin's enemies.

And even if some of the things *were* true, he said himself he was not a saint, but a sinner saved by the grace of God. He was fallible. That's what gave him the ability to reach others.

But in a few minutes, Yuri's train would be arriving, and she would be able to feel him and hold him and hear his dear voice. Perhaps that would be healing enough. She stood in Warsaw Station waiting, surrounded by Anna and Mariana and the children. She would have liked a private reunion—just her and Yuri—but the others, especially Anna, could not be denied. They were almost as anxious and excited as Katya. And she would have plenty of time alone with her husband later.

That prospect worried Katya as much as it thrilled her. After two failed pregnancies, she was afraid of it happening again, afraid to face more disappointment and grief. Yet at the same time she desperately wanted to give Yuri a child.

Katya's conflicting emotions confused and frightened her. Perhaps if she talked to someone about them, maybe Anna or Teddie . . . but she hated to admit her selfishness. Father Grigori told her she must trust God; Anna would say that, too. Everything was sure to work out as soon as she was with Yuri. The confusion would melt away, and the fear would vanish. Everything would be perfect then.

The screech of the train whistle made her jump. Anna took her hand and squeezed it affectionately. The train roared into the station and, with a mighty huff of steam, braked to a stop. The passengers, mostly soldiers, streamed out with slings on their arms or bandages around their heads, hobbling on crutches or canes. Some were missing legs or arms. Yuri, at least, had not been permanently disabled. His broken leg would heal. She scanned the crowd, focusing especially on the men on crutches.

Then she saw him! He was exiting a car, having some difficulty maneuvering his crutches down the narrow steps. She left Irina with Anna and Mariana and ran toward him. The moment he touched the station platform, he saw her, and the sudden grin on his face warmed her. He dropped a crutch as she embraced him. But she held him steady.

They kissed, but it was the embrace, the feel of his arm around her and hers around him that made her feel secure and protected. Despite their problems in the past, feeling him near assured Katya of the inexplicable connection between them, something that went to the depth of their souls.

"You feel so good!" he said huskily.

"I could hold you like this forever."

He smiled, then suddenly his brow creased with perplexity. "Katya, you've had the baby!"

All at once her joy was spoiled. "I'm sorry I didn't tell you. I . . . I didn't want to worry you while you were in the hospital . . ." Her lips trembled as she spoke.

"What happened?"

"He died, Yuri . . ." Her voice disintegrated into a choked sob.

"Oh, my love! And you had to face it all alone."

"I named him after your father, Yuri, as we had discussed. Did I do right?"

"Of course. A son . . ."

"I'm so sorry!" she sobbed.

"There, there. You know it's not your fault." He ran his hand over her hair and held her closer. She didn't deserve a man like this, Katya thought, but she clung to him nevertheless.

Suddenly little Irina ran up and began tugging at them.

"Papa!"

Yuri grinned when she called him "Papa," and he bent down and scooped her up into his free arm. "Hello, Irina. What a joy to see you!" He kissed her cheek and she kissed him back. Their interaction had been brief before the war, but Irina hadn't forgotten Yuri's tender affection.

"You stay home, Papa?"

"I hope so. I don't want to leave my girls again."

He did love Irina, Katya thought, perhaps as much as if she were his own daughter. Maybe that would be enough for him. Maybe he didn't need to have his own child.

But Katya still could not shake the feeling that somehow she had failed the man she loved.

Yuri's injured leg slowed him down, but it didn't completely incapacitate him. He spent a week resting and enjoying his family, but was soon restless to work. The war was still going on and wounded continued to flood the city. But conditions in Petrograd hospitals were vastly different than in a dressing station a few miles from the Front. At the Front, speed had been more vital than delicacy—quickly patch up as many wounded as possible so they could be transported farther back behind the lines to a field hospital or, if they were lucky, to hospitals in Russia. But here in the city he could indulge in more exacting work. And, once the wounded made it this far, the death rate dropped dramatically.

At the Front, he had begun to hate his chosen profession. But now he learned to love it again, and to feel confidence once more in his fitness for it. One positive effect had come out of the ordeal at the dressing station: it had honed and perfected his skills as a surgeon, confirming to him that this was the facet of medicine he wanted to pursue. His colleagues began to recognize his excellent skill and to call upon him for tricky cases. While he was on crutches he mostly acted as a consultant, but a couple of times he donned a surgical gown and gloves and, with a nurse helping to balance him, actually took a scalpel in hand.

One day while making rounds, he ran into an old acquaintance. He had not seen Prince Felix Youssoupov since the war began, and before then only a few times. But at Youssoupov's engagement party, Yuri had met Katya, and he had never forgotten the man's gracious good humor.

"Yuri Sergeiovich," said Youssoupov as he strode into the ward, where Yuri was examining an amputee he had operated on the previous day. "I was told I could find you here."

"Prince Youssoupov—"

"Remember, it is Felix to you."

"Ah, yes. It's been a long time."

Youssoupov rubbed his chin thoughtfully. "Four years since we met at my engagement party."

"I won't forget that day. I met my wife at your party."

"Yes, I do recall hearing you and Countess Zhenechka had married." He added with mock affront, "But I wasn't invited to the wedding."

"Nor was I invited to yours," said Yuri with a sly grin.

"We are even, then. And I hope still friends."

Yuri handed the chart he was holding to a nurse, giving her a few instructions, then turned back to Youssoupov. "Let's walk into the corridor. I'm sure you had a reason for finding me."

They left the ward, and Yuri led them to the end of the hall where there was a small waiting area by a window.

"You've been at the Front," said Youssoupov.

Yuri had heard that Felix had escaped the army under a law that allowed an exclusion for a family's only son. Some had criticized the man for it, hinting that he was a coward. Yuri held no such judgments. If there had been a way for him to avoid the army honorably, he probably would have taken it.

"Yes, I have. And I'm very happy to be home."

"I can imagine—well, I suppose I can't really, never having been to war myself." He sighed. "It's not something I'm proud of. You know, my older brother was killed in a duel a few years ago, and the thought of losing another son nearly drove my mother mad. Some think it's merely an excuse, and perhaps it is. The idea of violence sickens me."

"I doubt I could harm another man, either. I'm thankful I was in the medical corps and could do my part by healing rather than killing."

"I never had that option. I've tried to do my part with hospital work."

"Yes, I heard you have turned several of your homes into hospitals." Yuri smiled. "Very commendable."

"It's not enough, though. I've joined the Corp of Pages—"

"You will go to war, after all?"

"I will when I finish my training. Honor has finally compelled me to ignore my mother's pleas and take up my country's banner. The problem is, I've already failed the final exams once. I've simply not the aptitude for the military." He paused. "But I have another matter I wish to discuss with you. As you mentioned, I have been involved in setting up hospitals to treat the wounded. I'm in the process of converting another one of my townhouses into a facility to treat especially serious cases. I'm recruiting the best I can find to staff it. And I would like you to take the post of Chief of Surgery."

"Felix, I'm flattered but—"

"You must do it, Yuri. I've heard from several different sources that you have become one of the finest surgeons in Petrograd."

"And, have you also heard that I am less than four years out of medical school? I'm only twenty-six years old, Felix! I couldn't take such a post."

"Granted, you are young, but that is the nature of war, isn't it? Battlefield promotions and such."

"The war has stretched our pool of doctors to the limit. Nevertheless, there must be someone available more qualified than I."

"You are not merely a last resort, Yuri. You *are* qualified. How long were you at the Front?"

"Almost two years."

"That's equivalent to about ten years of normal experience."

"Well, I can say it probably *aged* me ten years!"

"Will you consider my offer? And, in the meantime, will you come work in the hospital just as a surgeon? I realize your injury won't permit you to take on a full load of work."

After giving it a moment's thought, Yuri said, "Yes, to both requests."

"Splendid! And, to seal our venture, will you and your wife join my wife, Irina, and myself for dinner tonight?"

With not a little apprehension, Yuri accepted, hoping Katya was up to social engagements.

54

It was odd how society seemed to continue to function, regardless of the fact that the world as they knew it was crumbling by degrees. But as Yuri stood in the Youssoupov parlor, surrounded by thirty or forty of Russia's social elite, he had the impression that they were more like the shell of a bombed-out building, ready to crumble with the least wind or earthquake. They were functioning out of mere habit, he supposed. They simply knew of no other way to live. They went to the opera or ballet, played faro, danced, drank champagne. Their jewels sparkled, their expensive clothes shimmered. What else was there?

For years, Yuri had dreamed of being a part of this society, but now he could feel nothing but pity for them. What was he thinking? He *was* part of all this. He was here. He had arrived.

He was to be pitied, too, he supposed. Maybe everything Andrei used to say was true: the depravity of the ruling classes, their oppression of the masses, their irresponsible use of wealth, the—

"Yuri, you seem so distant." Katya came up next to him and slipped her arm around his. "Is everything all right?"

"Oh yes, I suppose . . ." He glanced at her. A peasant family could live for a lifetime on the diamond necklace she wore. Her gown of white satin trimmed in white rabbit fur was one of Worth's latest designs. But he was not garbed as a pauper either. His tuxedo had been tailored by a Frenchman whom Felix Youssoupov himself patronized, costing several hundred rubles. There was no bread in the city, but the rich, of course, could get anything they desired.

Suddenly he sobered. Katya, his own wife, was one of the wealthy. This was the life he had always longed for. And because of his contacts he was truly able to do good with his medical training. Was it all wrong, then?

"Do you want to go home, Yuri?" asked Katya solicitously.

"Am I spoiling the party for you, my love?"

"I thought I might enjoy socializing a bit," she said. "It has been such a long time. I thought it might help me shake the sadness I've felt since . . . well, you know. But, Yuri, it's not the same. Maybe I've grown up a bit, do you think?"

He smiled. "We both have. It's something to truly thank God for. I wouldn't want to be here completely oblivious to the darker side of life, dancing and laughing as if I were not at all aware of what is happening a few hundred miles away."

"Do you think that's how everyone else is?"

"Some, but I pray not everyone. *We're* here, aren't we? Trying to put the best face we can on pain and loss. Most of the men here are in uniform and have been to the war. They know."

"I can name at least four families present who have lost sons and brothers and husbands. The war has touched the upper classes."

"You're right. God forgive me for my judgment of them. I guess it comes from my own sense of guilt for being here in comfort and ease knowing how much I am needed at the Front."

"Yuri, you've done your part." There was more than a hint of scolding in her tone.

He wished he hadn't said anything. But his leg was getting better. He was using only a cane now to get around. He was working a full load at Youssoupov's hospital. There was no reason why he couldn't function at a dressing station or a field hospital. Surely Katya realized that he wasn't home permanently. But he didn't have the heart just then to pursue the subject.

"Yes . . ." he sighed.

Then Youssoupov came up to them. "You will dance with me, won't you, Katya? You need not be a wallflower just because your husband is incapacitated."

"Thank you, Felix, but—"

"Go on, Katya, if you like," said Yuri. "You've hardly danced at all this evening."

Yuri watched Katya dance away and wondered if his marriage were a mirror of the Youssoupov party. On the surface all seemed well. Yet often he had the distinct impression they were merely acting out a marriage. When he talked to his mama about it—at least sharing the little he felt comfortable expressing—she assured him that they were still newlyweds in spite of the fact that they had been married two years. It would take time for them to adjust to each other and to marriage in general. And, she said, he must be patient and persistent.

He did not pursue the discussion with his mama. He couldn't admit that there seemed to be more to it. He would not have been able to explain it, anyway. He and Katya were kind and considerate and loving to each other. They never argued or disagreed as they used to do before they were married. But that was it—there was no life or passion. Of course it was physically too soon for them to be intimate after Katya's pregnancy, but it seemed to Yuri that if they were newlyweds, there should be an energy to their relationship on many different levels.

Maybe he was expecting too much.

Then there was the matter of Father Grigori. Katya had hinted several times that she would like to see him. She believed he had the power of healing and thought—or hoped—he could prevent her from having another miscarriage. Yuri had seen Rasputin at work, and even he had wondered if miraculous powers had been responsible for the tsarevich's inexplicable recoveries. Even a scientist like Yuri could believe in a God of miracles. What he questioned was that God would use as a vessel a man like Rasputin.

What was most disquieting about his and Katya's brief discussions about the *starets* was that they hadn't really argued over it. The tension between them was repressed, but he could almost feel the pressure build up inside them. Was it ready to blow? He couldn't tell. Perhaps it was just newlywed insecurity. He didn't know what to do about it.

In spite of his growing disquiet about the Rasputin situation and his marriage in general, Yuri nevertheless agreed to Felix Youssoupov's invitation to meet with some friends to discuss Rasputin. To be invited to join with a clique of Russia's highest and finest appealed to Yuri's ego, and he pushed aside his apprehensions.

He should have known he was in for trouble when Youssoupov gave him some rather suspicious instructions for the meeting. A waiter named Martìn would be looking for him and would take him to Youssoupov's private room in the restaurant. The secrecy seemed overdone and a bit ominous, but curiosity prevented Yuri from bowing out.

Yuri entered Felix's private room, to find a small group already present. Yuri recognized only one man besides Felix—the Grand Duke Dmitri Pavlovich, the tsar's young cousin. He was about Yuri's age, a handsome man surrounded by a definite air of royalty. He was, in fact, in the line of succession to the Crown. Yuri knew Dmitri and Felix were best friends, and he also knew that, until a few months ago, Dmitri had lived in Alexander Palace with the tsar's family and was considered by them to be practically a son. Dmitri's father, the tsar's uncle, Paul Alexandrovich, had been exiled some years previously because of his second marriage, an ill-advised union with a commoner. And, thus, the tsar had taken the young Dmitri under his wing. But Dmitri recently moved out of Alexander Palace because the tsar and, especially, the tsaritsa disapproved of Felix, whom they believed was a bad influence on the younger man.

Yuri was introduced to the others in the room. A Captain Soukhotin, who was on leave from the war, recuperating from a wound. And a commoner named Pourichkevich, who was a right-wing member of the Duma, and though a fervent monarchist, an outspoken critic of Rasputin.

"So, Yuri Sergeiovich," said Felix lightly, "you must be wondering what this little clique of conspirators is all about."

"Conspirators, eh?"

"I hope that doesn't scare you away."

"I am only here out of curiosity."

"That's well enough. I can assure you that we are concerned only with the welfare of Russia and the monarchy."

Dmitri Pavlovich added, "I know for a fact that you care about the welfare of the tsarevich."

"I do," said Yuri. "And the tsar. I am a loyal subject."

"As are all of us!"

"So, what is this all about?"

"Grigori Rasputin," Felix answered.

"Yes. . . ?" Yuri wondered at the meaning of the peculiar tone of Youssoupov's voice.

"My aunt Alexandra has criticized you, Yuri Sergeiovich," Dmitri said.

Yuri raised an eyebrow. "I'm sorry I have displeased her," he said cautiously. "Can you say what I have done to offend Her Highness?"

"She knows you disapprove of the *starets*. She believes you have requested that he be removed from Court."

Yuri smiled at the preposterous statement. "Your Highness," he said to the grand duke with barely controlled amusement, "I am just a physician. I hardly have the nerve to look the empress in the eye, much less make demands about how she runs her Court."

"So you don't disapprove of the Mad Monk?"

"I didn't say that. I can't lie even if it incurs the disfavor of Her Highness. I highly disapprove of the man. I have looked into *his* eyes, and I have been appalled at what I've seen in them."

"For that very reason," put in Felix with excitement, "we'd like to ask you to join us—"

"Join you in what?"

"It is time for that man's reign of evil to end!" Dmitri Pavlovich interjected passionately. "It is time to take back the monarchy."

"Can he really have as much power as people say?"

"I have been there, Yuri," said Dmitri. "I have been in the middle of it all. I have seen him give counsel to the tsaritsa, not only on personal matters—that might be tolerable—but on issues of state, on military matters, for heaven's sake! It must stop!"

"Dmitri," said Felix, "tell him about your suspicions about the drugs."

Dmitri shook his head with disgust and dismay. "While I was at Stavka I noticed the tsar was taking some medicine. I asked him what it was, and he casually said it was something Grigori had given him, just something to relax him, that's all. But I fear it is more than that."

"I had a conversation with Rasputin about this," said Felix. "He freely admitted that he is supplying the tsar and tsarevich with medicine. Some of it, he says, causes divine grace to descend upon them—imagine that! But some is intended to—and these are Rasputin's words—'fill the tsar with peace, so everything appears good and cheerful to him.' "

"Sounds like mood elevators, perhaps narcotics and the like," said Yuri. "I wish I had some samples to test."

"The point is, Yuri, that even if you proved Rasputin is drugging the tsar, it wouldn't matter. They would find a way to rationalize it, to defend Rasputin. While they are under his power, there can be no reasoning with them."

"So, you propose to eliminate the man? To exile him—?"

"Exile, be hanged!" said Dmitri. "He's been made to leave many times, but he always returns. And now nearly everyone in power is a tool of Rasputin's, handpicked by him, and so they would never agree to exile him. Look what happened after that deplorable incident at the Villa Rhode? Absolutely nothing! We are left with only one recourse—to assassinate him!"

Yuri gaped at the men, shocked.

"Certainly, you can't be surprised, Yuri," said Felix. "We're not the first to suggest such a solution to the Rasputin problem."

"You must be the first of the tsar's own family to suggest it. You are hardly Bolsheviks or Social Revolutionaries."

"And that is the exact reason why we are the best suited for the task. The Revolutionaries don't want to kill the man—Rasputin is playing right into their hands. Give the *starets* a little more time and the government and the monarchy will crumble completely. But if they were to kill Rasputin, it would only place power right into their hands instead of ours. Only if a loyal subject does the deed will there still be a chance to save the Crown."

"But you are talking about *murder*!"

"Political assassination," put in Pourichkevich. "There is a difference."

Yuri shook his head. "I am a doctor, sworn to uphold life, not destroy it—for any reason."

"Tell me, Yuri, that you wouldn't kill to protect your family, your loved ones!" said Dmitri.

"I suppose I would."

"And that is what this is all about."

"If you put it that way, then my only response is that it is your family, Dmitri Pavlovich, not mine."

"It will be your family soon enough. If the Crown falls, do you think any of the nobility will be spared? Do you think Russia will escape its own Reign of Terror? Either we take action now or we might as well resign ourselves to watching our loved ones march to the guillotine. Are you prepared to sacrifice your wife and daughter, your mother and sister, in order to spare the life of one evil, vile monster?"

Yuri swallowed, suddenly uncomfortable. He couldn't refute Dmitri's argument. It was the age-old dilemma: sacrifice the one to save the many. He had already practiced that very thing at the Front. And, to further support the medical metaphor, Rasputin was a malignant growth. Cutting him out would save the rest of the body.

But could Yuri be a part of such a thing? Call it political assassination—it was still murder.

Yuri decided to skirt that issue for a moment. "What do you want of me?" he asked. "Surely the four of you can adequately handle eliminating a single man."

"We need a doctor," said Felix. "We'd need you to obtain poison and to instruct us on the proper dosage. Also, we'd want you to . . . uh . . . pronounce the man dead. We don't want any slipups."

"I just couldn't do such a thing. The sanctity of life is just too deeply ingrained in me."

"I am not a violent man either, Yuri," said Felix. "The thought of all this repulses me. But I am bound by honor and duty. If I don't do this, no one else will. I could not live with the repercussions of that. I don't expect an immediate decision from you. Think it over. We have a little time, which I will use to curry a friendship with Rasputin so that when the time is right he will not be suspicious about coming to my house. That will be the best place to . . . do the deed. Think about it, Yuri—please! We need you."

55

Yuri thought of nothing else. Of course he wouldn't do it. But he couldn't keep from thinking that it needed to be done. Did that make him a hypocrite, then? Let others do the dirty work, while he kept his hands clean—sterile? But, didn't just knowing and remaining quiet about it make him an accomplice of sorts? Yet he didn't know the time or the place, nor did he know just how serious Youssoupov and his friends were. It might have been just talk.

Nevertheless, the whole matter put him into a terrible state. And it didn't help that he felt like such a scoundrel every time he saw Katya. She admired the man, and if Yuri hadn't disapproved, no doubt she'd be one of his followers. And now her husband was part of a scheme against the man. He did not tell her anything about his meeting with Youssoupov—he didn't dare.

But soon his dilemma over the Rasputin matter paled in comparison to another problem that was looming larger and larger. Two weeks after his unsettling discussion with Youssoupov and his friends, the time came for Yuri and Katya to be intimate once again. They had agreed to take certain precautions against conception, yet the risk remained. Still, since Yuri saw no physical risk involved to Katya, and Katya said she wanted to try again to have a child, he saw nothing standing in the way of them being together. Yuri naturally assumed that she was anticipating that moment as much as he.

He chose an evening that had been especially relaxing and pleasant. Katya's grandmother had gone to the opera with friends. He had left the hospital early, and he and Katya had dined alone.

Katya sighed with contentment as she rose from her place at the dining table.

"Are you tired, sweetheart," Yuri asked solicitously.

"Not really. I suppose I just feel rather lazy. I'm glad we didn't go to the opera with Grandmother."

"So am I. Would you like to retire early?" He asked the question with a suggestive smile.

"Perhaps so."

"Might I . . . join you?"

He tried not to read anything into her slight hesitation. "Yes . . . of course. Give me a few moments, first, all right?"

She left the dining room, and five minutes later, he followed. First he went to his room and changed into his dressing gown. In Katyk, he and his whole family had slept in the same bed, and even in Petersburg, when Yuri and Andrei had their own little room, his mama and papa always occupied the same bed in their own room. But the rich did not live thus. The husband and wife each had their own rooms, their own beds. It seemed to him to be very cold—very safe, but not in a good way. He never much liked the arrangement and complied with it only because Countess Zhenechka had been rather scandalized when he suggested otherwise. As soon as he felt more secure in his new home he determined to alter the arrangement.

When he judged he had given Katya enough time, he went to the door adjoining their rooms. He wished he had some gift to give her, a small romantic token. Then he recalled the bouquet of roses on the dining table. At dinner, he had thought them terribly decadent, considering they had come from the south, an early Christmas gift from one of the countess's friends. Roses on the table, when many people didn't even have bread. But now he saw them in a new light. He hurried downstairs and plucked a beautiful red bud from the bowl. Back in his room, he caught his breath, then knocked softly on the adjoining door.

"Come in."

She was lounging on a velvet daybed. She, too, was in her dressing gown, and there seemed no doubt that they both had the same expectations. He held out the rose with a grin. He was a bit nervous, almost as he had been on their wedding night. The quick, almost tentative smile that twitched upon her lips did nothing to calm his anxiety, but it was not forbidding, either. She took the rose, and he sat on the edge of the daybed.

"You are so thoughtful, Yuri." She brought the rose to her nose and smelled the delicate fragrance.

"It's not hard when I love you so!"

"You do, don't you. . . ?" It seemed an odd thing for her to say.

There was such a sadness in her voice.

"You don't doubt it, my love? Not after all we've been through?"

"No, of course I don't. But doesn't it ever worry you—I mean, to love someone so much?"

He smiled, trying to lighten the moment. "With all that is happening in the world right now, that, Katya my dear, is the least of my worries. In fact, I believe it is actually what soothes those worries."

He moved close and wrapped his arms around her. Did she stiffen ever so slightly, or were they just a bit rusty? After all, it had been months since they had been together. He forged ahead, carried along by his growing passion. He kissed her, murmuring words of love in her ear.

"Katya, I love you so!"

"Oh, Yuri . . ."

"How I have longed to be with you."

He took her hand and led her to the bed. In his excitement he was oblivious to all but her nearness. Gently, he nudged her into the bed, sliding in beside her. His heart was pounding as he showered her with loving caresses.

Then he felt her tenseness. Even he couldn't mistake it this time.

"Katya, what is it?" But he kissed her again, thinking that might help.

Her response was the last thing he expected. A choked sob broke from her lips.

"Katya?"

"Yuri . . ." she said between sobs. "I . . . I . . . can't . . ." She pushed away from him.

"What's wrong, my love?" He tried to be gentle, understanding. He wanted nothing more than to be a good husband to her.

"Please, Yuri, I'd like to be alone for now . . ."

"What have I done?" His voice shook with confusion and disappointment.

"I'm just not ready."

"But, I thought—"

"Can't you just leave me alone!" she snapped.

"The least you can do is tell me what I've done."

"I'm sorry. Forgive me." She turned her back to him and, burying her face in a pillow, began to weep again.

"Katya! You have to tell me what's wrong. You have to talk to me."

"I don't want to!"

"That's not good enough!" He was losing his patience.

"*I'm* not good enough. I don't deserve you."

"That's not true. I love you! I am committed to you, heart and soul. Why can't you believe that?" He put a hand on her shoulder, but she shrugged it away.

"Please . . . go," she said tearfully.

"You can't do this to me, Katya." Ire mixed with agony in his tone. His world was collapsing, and he felt like a shorn Samson, helpless, impotent to do anything to save it.

She lifted her head and turned to face him. In the dim light of the single lamp that was burning, she looked vulnerable, desperate.

"Yuri . . . please don't come back to my room. It's . . . best this way."

"You don't know what you are saying."

"I do."

"Why?" he pleaded.

"You should know why."

His anger and frustration got the best of him. "How can I know why," he yelled, "when you haven't told me?"

"Don't make me say it. I feel bad enough."

"All right!" he exploded, throwing off the covers and jumping from the bed. "I should have known this was how it would be. You haven't changed at all from that spoiled, thoughtless woman I first met. I've given you everything I could. But you still find it so easy to throw it back in my face. Fine! I will leave. You need not worry about me entering your inner sanctum again!"

He spun around and stalked from her room, slamming the door as he left. Then, as an angry afterthought, he locked the door. That, of course, was a silly gesture. She would never come after him. She didn't want him. But even as he turned the latch, he hoped to hear her call his name, entreating him to return.

But there was only silence.

He stood in his room, shaking all over. He paced about but could not calm down. What in the world had happened? How blind and stupid was he that he had not sensed this coming? He thought they were in love, that their hearts and spirits were one. He thought all was well. But he shook his head, remembering his attempt to talk to his mother. He had known something was amiss. But he had tried to minimize it, thinking it was just because of their wartime separation, and, of course, their grief over the loss of their newborn son.

Perhaps he had been insensitive, not fully understanding how deeply that loss might have affected Katya.

Yet, wouldn't his comfort, even his physical comfort, be just the thing to help her over her grief? It certainly wouldn't help for her to push him away. She had done just that before they were married—backing off from the very thing she wanted and needed, retreating from his love when she longed for it most. He had responded by being persistent, but that wasn't as easy now. They were married now. He shouldn't have to pursue her like a love-struck lad.

Why did she have to be so confounded complex? But wasn't that the very thing that had drawn him to her? He was not the most simplistic of men either, and, thus, she had been able to reach him and touch him in all the ways he needed.

He loved her so much. Too much? Was that what she had hinted at earlier when she asked if it worried him to love someone so much? Did it worry her? Did it frighten her? She'd often said how she had never been loved like that before. Her mother ran out on her when she was a little child. Her father was a cold, ruthless man. Irina's father had been looking for everything but love. Poor Katya.

And now when she was confused and uncertain again, what had he done, her husband who claimed to love her, heart and soul? He had yelled at her, accused her, then walked out on her. He had given up on her when she needed him most. But she had told him to leave. What else could he do?

He turned back to the adjoining door. Perhaps she had just spoken in the heat of the moment. Now that a few minutes had passed, she was probably calm, perhaps even hoping that he would return. Anyway, one of them had to make the first move. He didn't mind that it was him. So he unlatched the lock and turned the knob.

It didn't budge. It was locked from her side!

He knocked several times, but there was no answer.

"Katya, please let me talk to you," he said to the door. "Don't be like this."

When there was still no answer, frustration consumed him and he kicked the door. "Okay! Be that way. You can't say I didn't try."

He strode to his bed, took off his dressing gown, pulled back the covers, and flopped into bed. He wasn't going to lose any sleep over her—she didn't deserve it. She had no right treating him in this way. He yanked up his covers, turned off the bedside light, rolled over, and closed his eyes.

But he didn't sleep.

56

Katya lay in her bed for ten minutes weeping. She heard Yuri knock and call to her. She wanted him desperately. Yet she could not bring herself to answer. How could she invite him in when she couldn't give him what he wanted, what was his right as a husband to have? It only made it worse that she knew Yuri would not demand intimacy, that he would be patient with her as he always was.

Maybe if she could just talk to him.

But what if that didn't help? What if, by that concession, she raised his hopes only to realize that she still could not be with him? What if she could never be with him again?

Oh, God, she wept, what am I to do?

Just when she thought her life had finally started going right, when she believed happiness was possible, everything had crumbled once more. She would have been better off never to have let Yuri into her life—they both would have been better off. She should have kept to her resolve to live her life alone, just her and Irina. It had been foolish to take the risk she had. Why couldn't she have left well enough alone?

Why, indeed?

Because she had ached for love. Was that so wrong?

Yuri had loved her in all the ways she had longed for, and she had known his love was truly eternal. He would never run out on her or turn cold on her. He assured her of that constantly. Yet she was always a little afraid of that happening—and maybe that fear would never leave.

Yes, she longed for love—and she feared it, too.

Wasn't that enough of a burden? Why did God have to inflict upon her another one as well? It was bad enough to fear receiving love, now she must fear giving it also.

Where was the God of love and compassion? Why was He toying with her so?

She tried to think of the things she'd heard others say about God—Father Grigori, Anna, Teddie. But her mind went suddenly blank, as if her spirit was a vast, empty vacuum. All she could think of was that she had somewhere gone terribly wrong. It had to be her fault. It couldn't be God's. But what had she done wrong? Did she have to be punished for the rest of her life for her one mistake? Grigori had told her something about pride. What was it?

Dismally shaking her head, she happened to glance at the clock on the mantel. Was it only nine o'clock? It felt as if hours had passed since Yuri had come to her room, and it hadn't even been half an hour. Suddenly she remembered that Olga had invited her to come to the *starets* home tonight—at this very hour. She knew he kept late hours. And he often received visitors late in the evening. If he went out for the evening, it was usually not until after ten at least.

Why am I thinking about this now?

But the answer was clear. She had fought it long enough. She had been the obedient wife, and her life was in as much of a shambles as it had been four years ago when she had almost committed suicide. Did it really matter if Yuri would be furious at her? Could he possibly be more angry?

Father Grigori had helped her once. Maybe if she had gone to him sooner, her marriage—her life—would not have turned so disastrously. Perhaps he could help her. He could pray for her. Perhaps there was still hope for her marriage—if Grigori prayed for her. She might find the courage to risk being with Yuri again. And more than that, Grigori might also make it so her body could be able to carry another child.

She jumped from her bed and quickly dressed. Then she went to the maid's room next door.

"Helga, go quickly and find the chauffeur and tell him to get the car ready. I'll be going out."

"Alone, madam?"

Katya started to flare at that question and its impudent implication, then she answered more calmly than she felt, "What is that to you? Just do as I say."

"Yes, madam."

The girl scurried away, and Katya returned to her room to get her heavy coat and muff. It had been snowing all day and was freezing outside. As she turned to leave her room, she noticed the rose

Yuri had given her. It had fallen on the floor. She picked it up and brought it to her lips, kissing it and laying it tenderly on the daybed.

Yuri, dear, what have I done to you?

Her resolve deepened as she walked quietly down the hall with only a brief glance at the door to Yuri's room. He had never liked the idea of separate rooms. Perhaps when she returned from her errand, she would be able to make up for her previous behavior.

Oh, Father Grigori, you must help me. If you can't, I don't know what I'll do.

At number 64 Gorokhavaya Street, she had the driver stop. The usual horde of people was lined up in front of Rasputin's building and up the stairs that led to his flat. Even at this hour there were fifty or sixty people of every kind and class, all hoping to see the *starets*, to ask for some boon or favor. Like it or not, Rasputin was one of the most influential people in the country now. He had the ear of the tsar. If he asked for something, it was bound to happen. At least those who braved the freezing night hoped so.

Katya confidently walked past the line to the front door. She was obviously a lady of quality and no one really expected her to wait with the hordes. The maid, Rasputin's only servant, opened the door.

"Countess Zhenechka—"

"It is Princess Fedorcenko, now, Akulina."

"Oh yes, I am sorry."

"May I see Father Grigori?"

"Well . . ."

"It's urgent, Akulina."

"I . . . I'll see . . ." The maid turned back into the flat, then paused. "Please come in, Princess. Forgive my rudeness."

The girl seemed hesitant, reluctant. But Katya was too desperate to heed that or to care. She followed the maid into the flat and was directed into the parlor as Akulina went to find Rasputin. There were several women already in the parlor. All were ladies of quality like Katya, of varying ages. Some were chatting quietly together, others were sitting, not interacting, seemingly absorbed in their problems. Olga said there was always a group of women in Grigori's flat. They were very much like a sewing circle, only here, instead of sewing, they fawned on the priest, ministering to him in any way they could while listening to his wisdom. Katya had sometimes envied Olga that camaraderie she had with the other women. Perhaps now I will join them on a regular basis, Katya told herself.

Katya greeted the women she knew in the group, then sat in a vacant chair and waited.

Soon there were voices outside the parlor. One was obviously Father Grigori's.

"Another time, child, eh?" he said.

"I don't know why I must wait," replied a woman's voice.

"I am not my own man, Countess. I cannot shun the urgent needs of others."

The parlor door opened. Grigori looked in. Behind him, the countess put her arms around him.

"Oh, Grigori . . . don't make me wait!"

"Be off with you now. Come back tomorrow afternoon. Emergencies don't usually happen in the daylight."

She hesitated a moment, then let go and walked away, buttoning the top buttons of her tunic as she left. But all that took only an instant, and in the next moment, Grigori saw Katya and grinned.

"Ah, Katichka! I knew you would come to me," Rasputin said.

"Father Grigori, I should have called first perhaps?"

"Nonsense. You are always welcome in my home."

"Thank you, Father."

He took her hand. "Come with me so we can be alone."

"But the others—" She glanced at the other women, knowing they wouldn't be happy about her receiving preferential treatment. But she was too desperate to argue strenuously on their behalf.

"They can be patient," he said. "Eh, ladies? An exercise in patience is good for the soul. And this *is* an emergency."

He led her from the parlor through the dining room, where there were a few more women sipping tea around the big table. And then to his bedroom. When she hesitated at the door, he smiled benignly at her.

"Do not fear, little one," he said. "Can I do anything but purify you? Surely you don't wish to discuss personal matters within the hearing of others?"

Katya followed him. After all, she had been in this room when Father Grigori had been ill. It did appear to be the only place in the five-room flat where there would be privacy, and she certainly did not want to discuss her intimate marital problems in front of others. The bedroom was filled with the odor of incense from the candles that burned before the icons in the Beautiful Corner. It made her feel a bit more comfortable, for it gave her the secure sense of being in a church.

There was, however, only the bed to sit on.

She sat, somewhat stiffly, on the edge, then said, "Father, you said you knew I would come. What did you mean?"

"The time of your confinement is over, isn't it?" She was surprised that he was privy to such information. But no doubt Olga had confided to the man her worries about Katya. She nodded. "I feared it would be hard for you."

"What am I to do, Grigori? I'm so afraid!"

He sat on the bed next to her, quite close, and put his arm around her. "Katichka, you must trust me."

"Yes, Father . . ."

"Will you do whatever must be done to find healing?" He focused his gaze on her, and she could not help but lift her eyes to meet his. And the intensity of his eyes, as in the past, held her.

"Yes, Father Grigori."

"Make any sacrifice?"

She only nodded, her mouth suddenly too dry to speak.

"What an innocent you are, little one!" He caressed her cheek with his hand. "So beautiful, so innocent."

She swallowed and managed to say, "I thought I lost my innocence four years ago."

"You lost your virginity, then, dear one, not your innocence. That is why I held back—your innocence touched me so. But it is time for us—yes, both of us—to make the supreme sacrifice."

"What is that?" she breathed, every word an effort as she became more and more lost in the power of his gaze.

He lay his hand on her thigh, gently caressing her as he spoke. She tried to ignore the discomfiture this caused in her. After all, he was a man of God and must be judged by a different standard from other men. There must be a higher purpose to whatever he did.

"It is time to get rid of your pride," he said.

"Will that give me peace?"

"It's the only way."

"How . . . do I do that?"

"Come to me, Katichka, I will help you." His other arm encircled her, and he kissed her head as he had often done in the past. "You must yield to the will of God, dear one. Only then will you find peace. Don't you want to be close to God? Don't you want to find His peace? How can you draw near to God if you do not repent? But how can you repent if you have not first sinned?"

"But I *have* sinned, Father."

"Not enough to break your prideful spirit. The more you sin, the more opportunity for repentance."

His breath now came in quick pants as if he were in a race. She felt her own heartbeat quicken, too. She could not quite identify the colliding emotions within her, but they weren't all pleasant. She thought of rumors she'd heard of the *starets* taking women into his bedroom and seducing them. And, regardless of what Grigori had said about her innocence, she had been around men enough to not be completely ignorant of these things.

Yet wasn't Grigori just trying to help her? He must know what he was doing. What if by running away she spoiled forever her chance for healing? What if she only had to submit to him to find peace, to find happiness at last with her husband? Grigori was a man of God. He should know, shouldn't he?

A voice inside her head said, "No! Fight it." But she couldn't make herself obey that voice. Not only was she confused, but she was also physically unable to make herself move. She suddenly felt sapped of strength, of will. There was only Grigori, his eyes bidding her to submit, his lips speaking words of God.

His kisses became more intense and soon found their way down her neck.

"Love me, child," he murmured. "Love me as the woman who anointed Jesus loved Him and gave her all for Him."

"I . . . I don't . . . know . . ."

"Don't let your pride keep you from God."

His hands moved over her in ways she knew only a husband should touch a woman. But she was so weak.

"Please, Father . . ." She tried to protest, but even she could barely hear her own weak voice.

"I must have you now!" He groped for her clothes.

"No!"

57

Yuri didn't know why he even pretended to sleep. It was a ridiculous ruse. He'd not sleep until he could see Katya and make her talk to him. He wanted to understand her, help her. But he couldn't do that from his bed. Somehow he had to make her see him. He didn't care if he had to wake the entire household. This wasn't the time for reserve, not when his marriage, his very life hung in the balance.

He jumped out of bed and once more threw on his dressing gown, but this time with an iron will. He would not return to his room until he and Katya had talked.

He pounded on the adjoining door, and when there was no response, he went into the outer corridor and started pounding on the door that faced that hall.

"Katya!" he yelled. "I know you can't be sleeping."

He had never before entered her room without a welcome from her, so he didn't try the doorknob at first. Besides, in all likelihood it was locked also. Then his desperation got the better of him, and to his surprise, when he turned the latch, the door opened.

"Katya, forgive me for coming unbidden, but I didn't know what else—"

Only then did he see her bed was empty. His first thought was that she had gone to the kitchen for tea, and he quickly left the room with the intention of going there also. But his yelling and pounding had aroused the attention of the servants. Katya's maid and two footmen had come running.

"Your Excellency!" said one of the footmen, out of breath and obviously distraught. "What is it?"

Yuri was suddenly embarrassed to have his marital discord brought to such public attention.

"Well . . . I . . . uh . . . nothing really." Then he added lamely, "I just wanted to see if the princess would join me for a cup of tea."

Both footmen raised their eyebrows skeptically but said nothing. The maid, however, said, "I didn't think Her Highness would be back so soon."

"Back?"

"She had me order up the motorcar for her about half an hour ago."

"Where did she go?"

"I don't know, sir."

At that moment Teddie joined the group. "What's wrong? I heard yelling and thought maybe a revolution was starting."

"It's nothing, Teddie." Yuri sighed, adding, "Do you know where Katya might have gone?"

"I didn't know she had gone anywhere. Usually she tells me if she is leaving in case there are instructions about Irina."

"I know . . . I believe she left suddenly." Yuri glanced awkwardly at the servants. "You may go," he told them. But to Teddie, he said, "Please stay. I'd like to talk with you a moment."

"Yes, sir."

The others hurried away, no doubt glad not to be involved in what appeared to be a delicate situation.

Yuri turned to the nurse. "Teddie, Katya was upset. I'm afraid she was extremely distraught. We . . . that is, I think we had an argument."

"You *think*, sir?"

"We did, I'm just not entirely sure what it was all about. Teddie, I hate to bother you with my personal problems, but I . . . don't know what to do. Have you any idea where she might go if she were upset?"

"I think you probably know as well as I, Prince Yuri."

"Why would she go to *him*? She promised me she wouldn't. Why can't she talk to me? God knows, I've tried to be understanding. I've tried to talk to her. But she won't tell me what's wrong. She thinks I should know. But, blast it all! I don't know!"

"If you would like to talk about it, Prince Yuri, I will listen, and perhaps I know Katya well enough to help."

"It's all so terribly personal. But . . . yes, help me, Teddie."

Teddie led Yuri into Katya's room and they sat, Teddie on the chair by the dressing table and Yuri on the daybed. Yuri idly picked up the rose from where Katya had laid it, fingering it tenderly and sadly as he spoke. "Teddie, she refused me tonight," he blurted out, hoping he wouldn't have to go into further detail. Teddie nodded as if she understood, so he continued, "I don't know what I did. She was very upset."

"Have you considered, sir, that it is not something *you* did, but rather something within Katya that . . . holds her back?"

"Do you think. . . ?" Yuri felt almost relieved at this new idea. "But why won't she talk to me about it?"

"My poor Katya has always been so afraid of being close to people."

"But isn't she close to you, Teddie?"

"More than anyone else, I suppose, but not always on such a deep level. I've tried, but I am too much like a mama to her."

"Well, if she chooses Rasputin over those who truly love her, then there really isn't anything to be done about it."

"Do you actually believe that, Prince Yuri?"

Yuri shrugged, confused.

"In a way, Rasputin is safe. She knows he won't reject her. And even if he did, I doubt it would hurt as much as if you turned away from her."

"But I've told her a hundred times I wouldn't do that. What must I do to prove myself to her?"

"I don't know what it will take, dear boy. Persistence, patience—and you have shown all those. I suppose you just need to show more. I know it is a hard thing to ask of one as young as you are—"

"I'll do whatever I must to keep her."

"Prince Yuri, of one thing I am certain. She must be kept from the *starets*. I fear she is very vulnerable to him."

"Teddie, you don't mean—?" Yuri's stomach churned with fear and loathing. "I don't want to say it. I don't want even to think it . . ." He closed his eyes, but he knew it must be said, for Katya's sake. "Teddie, you know the rumors as well as I about Rasputin's women, the *Rasputini*."

Teddie gasped. "Never!"

"How can you be so certain?"

"She would never be unfaithful to you."

"They say he hypnotizes them, bends them to his will—"

"Not Katya!"

"I wish I could be as certain as you," Yuri said miserably.

A silence of several moments followed, then Teddie said urgently, "Prince Yuri, you should go after her."

"If that's where she wants to be . . ."

"Don't you know your wife better than that?" Teddie said with reproach.

"I'm simply not sure anymore."

"She is a frightened little girl, Prince Yuri. She was upset this evening?"

"Very."

"Don't let Rasputin have her."

"I'm afraid of what I'll find if I go."

"Have faith in her, young man, and especially have faith in God. She needs you, Yuri, to protect her from—our God only knows what! Rasputin is a devil, but, in Katya's eyes, he is dressed like a lamb. How can she fight an evil she can't see? We must fight for her."

"She'll hate us if we do, and I don't think I have the courage to face her hatred."

"Then, she is lost."

"Oh, Teddie!" Yuri groaned, dropping his head into his hands.

Teddie moved to the daybed and put a motherly arm around Yuri. "It's all right, dear boy. We can still pray for her. God is merciful."

Yuri raised his head, wiping a hand over his moist eyes. A new resolve washed over him—a strength to do what must be done. He hardly knew where it came from. Perhaps he didn't need to speak his prayers before God answered them. "You pray, Teddie. I must go into the lion's den."

Teddie smiled. "I will sit right here and pray until you return victorious."

From somewhere deep within the depths of her soul, Katya found the strength to stand. She rose from the bed, but Grigori was instantly on his feet also. He put his hands on her shoulders—hot, heavy hands. He fixed his gaze on her.

It struck Katya all at once, like the kind of spiritual revelation Rasputin himself often spoke of.

The spirit of God cannot be in this man.

Perhaps it had been at one time, and fragments of that occasionally continued to spill over into the present. Four years ago he had accepted her when no one else would. He had loved her as even her father and mother hadn't. He had taught her spiritual truths. But whatever had driven him in the past, whatever had drawn

Katya to him, was not present now. It could not be. What he was doing was wrong.

Terribly, terribly wrong.

He was breathing hard. Lust glinted from his compelling eyes. "Take off your clothes," he ordered.

"What?" She shook her head, trying to clear her muddled senses.

"Do you think I degrade you, Katichka? I purify you." He caught her gaze once more. "Give yourself to me, and you will give yourself to God. Only then will you find the grace of God."

She closed her eyes to try to break the power he seemed to have over her. But he began to push her back onto the bed. His physical strength was too much for her.

"Please . . . Father Grigori . . ."

"Don't fight it. This is for you, Katichka."

"Oh, God . . ." she cried.

"Yes, Katichka!"

She felt sick and empty. She had once loved Father Grigori, *revered* him. How could she be such a poor judge of character? But what did she know? She was confused. He was a man of God. The rumors couldn't be true. Could they?

It's wrong . . . it's wrong, the voice in her head chanted silently.

But what if by cutting him off, she cut off her only hope?

Then she thought of Yuri, his tender love, his gentleness. Even tonight, when he had every right, he had not forced himself upon her.

What Rasputin was doing was nothing like that. She felt no love, no tenderness. Only . . .

Lust.

Selfish desire.

He said it was for her, but it wasn't what she wanted. He said it would make her close to God. But at that moment, she could not have felt *further* from God. She felt dirty, sick.

He held her firm with one surprisingly strong arm while he fumbled at her clothing with the other.

"No, Father Grigori!" she said, trying hard to infuse force into her voice. She struggled to gather back her will. She tried to push him away, but by now he was so absorbed in his deed that he seemed not to be aware of her at all.

58

Yuri drove the carriage himself, whipping the horses, driving them as fast as possible through the city streets. He, too, was driven with an urgency he didn't understand. But a voice in his head kept saying: *Hurry! Hurry!*

Something told him Katya was in danger. He couldn't explain it, and for once in his life, he didn't try. Maybe he'd feel foolish if he arrived at Rasputin's all hot and lathered only to find that Katya was not even there. But a terrible knot in his stomach, a twisting of his heart, told him he was right. He *knew* she was with the *starets*. She had been wanting to go for weeks now. It only took a crisis like tonight to push her to defy Yuri and make that visit.

About a block away from Rasputin's, he slowed the carriage. He knew the place was watched by police and, thus, it would be unwise, under any circumstances, to make a scene. Some of the police were there to inform on Rasputin, but some were there to protect him. Yuri didn't want to be arrested for threatening the man—unless the *starets* needed threatening, in which case Yuri would take the risk of arrest. He'd do whatever needed to be done to protect Katya.

There were people petitioners and the like, milling about outside the place and more people lined up on the steps leading up to the flat. Yuri threw down his cane and raced up the three flights of steps, two at a time, ignoring the pain in his leg, and ignoring the looks and comments of those he hurried past. He was not about to wait in line. That urgent voice in his head still throbbed.

Only when he reached the door did a modicum of propriety afflict him. He paused and knocked. The servant girl he had seen before answered.

"Is Princess Fedorcenko here?" he demanded.

"I am not at liberty—"

"Tell me now!" He glowered at her with the same menace he had once turned upon a burly, thieving sergeant. The young girl wilted under his force.

"I . . . I . . ."

He shoved past her, striding into the house with all the authority of an Okhrana raiding party.

"Katya!" he called, looking into each room as he came to it.

He came to the dining room. She had to be there, for she was nowhere else. The women in the room, sitting placidly around the table, sipping tea, looked up, startled at his abrupt entry. But Katya wasn't among the ladies.

Now, he was starting to feel foolish. His little voice had been all wrong.

"Dr. Fedorcenko," said a woman he knew from the hospital.

"Countess Petrov."

He was about to apologize—until he noted a peculiar look cross the woman's face followed by a skittish glance toward a door that led off the dining room. Rasputin's bedroom. A new panic seized Yuri. He started toward the door.

The countess ran up to him. "You can't!" She grabbed his arm to restrain him.

"She's in there, isn't she?"

"He will purify her," said the countess.

"No!" Yuri groaned as he wrenched his arm from her grasp.

He flung open the door. In an instant he took in the awful scene. They lay on the bed, Rasputin on top of Katya, apparently fumbling at her clothes. Katya was struggling—thank God!—fighting.

The *starets* was trying to rape her!

Yuri's experience at the Front, when he had attacked the sergeant, was the first time he realized he was capable of violence. But that incident was nothing compared to what he was feeling now. He could never have pulled the trigger and killed the sergeant. But, if he had a gun now, he knew he would have killed Rasputin. What the Grand Duke Dmitri said about protecting loved ones was true. He would kill to protect his wife.

But he had no weapon, only his bare hands—the hands of a surgeon, hands devoted to saving lives. They were primed for murder now.

He raced up to the vile monk, grabbed him by the shoulders of his dirty cassock, and yanked him from his prey.

"What the—?" Rasputin grunted, still panting from his sexual frenzy.

But Yuri smashed a fist into the man's face, not giving him a chance to say more. The *starets* stumbled back and fell to the floor. Yuri took that moment to appraise Katya. Her blouse was torn open; her other clothes were askew; she was sobbing and shaking.

"Katya, are you all right?" Yuri said.

She couldn't speak, but she nodded her head. He prayed that meant he wasn't too late. But a fear gripped him that it might not be so.

"What did you do to her?" he screamed at Rasputin. He grabbed him by the collar and yanked him to his feet, then drew back his fist to deliver another blow.

"You would raise your hand against God's servant?" said Rasputin.

"You are nothing but a lecherous beast!"

"You fool! You speak your own doom—"

Yuri let his fist fly. But this time the *starets* ducked with amazing agility. Yuri attempted a quick follow-up to the missed blow. He raised his hand but never got further than that.

He had not heard the approach of the police. They rushed up behind him and threw restraining arms around Yuri almost before he realized what was happening.

"That'll be enough, now!" ordered one of the police.

Yuri, his body still pumping with fury and violence, struggled against the hands that held him.

"What's going on here, Grigori Efimovich, sir?" The gendarme sounded far too sympathetic toward Rasputin for Yuri's liking.

"The boy lost his head—" Rasputin began.

"He tried to rape my wife!" Yuri yelled. Oh, God, please let it be that he only *tried*! Katya was still sobbing on the bed, unable to allay his worst fears.

"He doesn't understand," said Rasputin.

The gendarme cocked his eyebrow as if he didn't understand either, but he said to Yuri, "Assault is a serious crime."

"You fool!" cried Yuri. "He's the one who should be arrested for assault!"

"You want me to arrest the priest?" The man actually laughed.

And Yuri now understood all Felix and his friends had meant. Rasputin was above the law, above punishment. He had free rein—with everything in Russia and *everyone*. No one was safe. If he wanted to have his way with a man's wife, then, so be it. If he wanted to dispose of an adversary, then the enemy was as good as dead.

"You are going to do nothing?"

"So, Father Grigori," said the gendarme, ignoring Yuri's question, "shall I arrest this man? Do you intend to press charges?"

Rasputin focused his steely gaze at Yuri, but, amazingly, Yuri was not affected. He stared back with more hatred than he thought himself capable.

"Let him go," said the *starets*. "This man will destroy himself. He doesn't need me to do it."

The two policemen holding Yuri dropped their hands. Yuri rushed to Katya's side. "Come, Katya, let's get out of here." When she did not immediately respond, he placed an arm around her. "Katya," he entreated.

Slowly she moved her hands from her tear-streaked face. She gazed at him vacantly, as if he were a stranger. Renewed panic clutched at Yuri. He *had* been too late! Then a glimmer of light fluttered through her wasted eyes. She seemed to slowly come to herself—at least a small shadow of herself. But it was enough for her to recognize Yuri and look upon him with need, if not love. With his help, she rose from the bed. But she was so shaky that she had to lean heavily upon him in order to move.

They had to walk past Rasputin to get to the door. Katya averted her eyes from the man. But Yuri could not help giving him a final glare.

"Katya Larentinovna," said Rasputin, his tone shaking with the intensity of an Old Testament prophet, "you have sealed your doom. You have turned your back on God's anointed. You will never have children. You will lose one more prematurely, then you will have no more."

Only then did Katya look at him. Her eyes were stabbed with fear and pain. Yuri jerked her forward. That man would have no more hold on her if he could help it.

Yuri could physically protect Katya from the *starets*, but he had little control on the emotional effect of the man. Days after the attempted rape, Katya was still sullen and silent. Yuri had hoped, now that Katya saw what the man's true motives were, she would be better. He hoped that in rescuing her, she would come back to her husband.

What Yuri soon realized was that though Rasputin had not violated Katya physically, he had still raped her soul. And there could be no lower crime than that. He twisted spiritual things to fit his vile lusts, causing his poor victims so much confusion they didn't know what to do. It was possible they might even heap recriminations upon themselves for thinking ill of the priest. Yuri didn't know if Katya felt that way. He didn't know what she felt at all! She said very little about that or anything else.

Yuri's mama came often to see her, but mostly just sat by her, holding Katya's hand. Katya hardly left her bed in the days following the encounter with Rasputin. Yuri had hoped that seeing Irina would help pull Katya from her silent depression, but the moment she laid eyes on her daughter she broke down in uncontrollable sobbing.

All of this only made Yuri think more than ever of Felix Youssoupov's plan to do away with Rasputin. And, after three days of Katya's silent despair, Yuri had no problem at all with going to an apothecary with his personal prescription for a sizable amount of potassium cyanide.

"Got a rat problem at the hospital, doctor?" asked the pharmacist.

"A very large rat," said Yuri grimly. Then realizing how ominous his words sounded, he added, "but not in the hospital, in my home. A terrible problem. This should take care of it."

"I should hope so!"

Next, Yuri went to see Felix.

"Do you know what we talked about a few days ago?" Yuri asked.

Although he and Felix had had several conversations since then about professional matters, Felix knew exactly to what Yuri was referring.

"Yes . . ."

"I've gotten what you wanted me to get."

"You have?" Felix smiled solemnly. "So, you are in?"

Yuri nodded. "I've come to see that the man's reign must end and that because of his power there is only one way to see that it happens."

"I know this isn't easy for you, Yuri. It isn't for any of us. But it is a truly noble cause. It is the only way to save Russia."

"I suppose you are right, but I won't attach an aura of nobility to it. We are going to murder a man—there is no other way to put it. God only knows if it is the right thing to do. I just have to do what

I feel must be done and pray God will forgive me."

"Personally, I am willing to live with eternal damnation, if it will save Russia," said Felix with passion.

"Felix, I must confess something to you—"

"Save it for a priest, Yuri. I lay no judgment upon you."

"It's nothing like that, really. It is just that I can't have you thinking my motives are purely altruistic. I have a personal vendetta against the man. You see . . . three nights ago, he tried to rape my wife."

"Yuri, I am so sorry."

"I'm afraid what he did to her damaged her, not physically, but in her heart, her very soul. God only knows if she will ever be mentally well again." Yuri's voice trembled as he expressed for the first time his deepest fear. "The man must be stopped before he harms anyone else. Do you know, when I suggested to the police that he be arrested, they just laughed in my face. They know they can do nothing to stop him. No one can."

"Except us," said Felix. "Everyone else *talks* about it, the Duma, the nobility, the tsar's own family. But they still think there might be an alternative, some way to get rid of him and still remain clean and safe. Our passion for the cause makes us beyond fear of repercussions."

Yuri nodded. "How soon can we do this? I want to get it over with before I find my fear again."

"After Christmas, December twenty-ninth. Dmitri's social schedule is quite heavy, especially with the holidays, and that is the first day he has free. We feel it might arouse too much suspicion for him to cancel a previous engagement."

"That's less than a week away."

"Yes."

Yuri gave Youssoupov the packet of poison. "Keep this," he said, "just in case I lose my nerve."

59

Christmas of 1916 was a dismal holiday in the city. No one felt like celebrating. For Nicholas, tsar of Russia, it was especially demoralizing. He had never felt more isolated. It had been bad enough when he felt the sting of criticism from his subjects, but now it had spread to his own family. His mother refused to come to Tsarskoe Selo while Alexandra was there. Nearly all the grand dukes had come to him with passionate appeals to form a government acceptable to the Duma—a true constitutional monarchy, with ministers they had confidence in. To them he had replied, "When I ascended the throne, I solemnly promised to pass on an autocracy to my son. And that I will do."

Alexandra had been more pointed. "This talk of pleasing the Duma is ridiculous," she said. "My husband is an autocrat. How could he even consider sharing his divine rights with a parliament?"

Hardest on Alix had been the confrontation with her sister Ella. The saintly Ella, who had joined a religious order after the murder of her husband in 1905, had come from Moscow specifically to appeal to her sister. But Alix was incensed that Ella believed all the lies about Rasputin. In the end, Alix coldly asked her sister to leave.

One by one, the tsar's family was abandoning him. The Grand Duke Paul, Dmitri's father and the tsar's only surviving uncle, had summed up probably what they all were feeling. "Must we all suffer for your foolish stubbornness? You have no right to drag your family down with you!"

They did not want to go down with a sinking ship. But Nicholas had to cling to the belief that the ship of his reign was not imperiled. He must never lose hope that he would pass the Crown on intact to his son. Not an easy thing to do with everyone conspiring against him.

Just before Nicholas was to return to the Front, Rasputin came to dine at Tsarskoe Selo. It was not the send-off the tsar would have chosen. The *starets* seemed uncharacteristically moody and preoccupied. He spoke so much of death and approaching misfortune that the tsar finally sent the children to bed. No sense in subjecting innocents to such depressing talk. But Grigori wouldn't let it go. "I have seen a river of blood and my ears are filled with cries of pain and suffering. Darkness surrounds me, like the night, like a shroud. I will suffer a great martyrdom, but I will forgive my tormentors. If the hand that is raised against me is of my brothers, the Russian peasantry, then you, my tsar, need have no fear. You and your son and his son will reign in Russia for hundreds of years. But woe to you if my blood is shed by nobles and by your own relatives! Then neither you nor your children nor any of your family will remain alive for more than two years."

Nicholas was glad the children hadn't heard *that*. The man was in a strange mood. Nicholas and Alix tried to console him, assuring him that no such thing would happen. Nicholas poured Grigori another glass of wine to try to lift his spirits. But it didn't help much, and when the *starets* rose to leave, his shoulders were slumped and he walked with shuffling feet, like a man about to be executed.

Making another attempt to cheer the man, Nicholas said, "I will be leaving for the Front in the morning, Father. Please bless me."

"I cannot do it, Papa," Rasputin replied dismally. "It is I who needs your blessing."

In the Duma the uproar against the present government had risen to fever pitch. Paul could remember the days when such attacks against the emperor would have been the surest path to exile, perhaps even execution. But now they continued even after the tsar resolved to replace several members of the Progressive Block of the Duma with right-wing conservatives, and failing that, to dissolve the Duma altogether.

Although the idea shocked Paul's sensibilities, he was not surprised when several army officers approached Kerensky with a plan to assassinate the tsar by nose-diving an airplane into the tsar's motorcar. The most persistent plan, however—and perhaps the most sensible—was to force the tsar to exile Alexandra to the Crimea.

Paul could not guess what would come of all this. One thing was certain—change had to be implemented at the highest level of the government or collapse was inevitable. Everyone believed this except, unfortunately, the tsar. Some still hoped that change might possibly come without violence, but Paul believed the country had come to the point where change would only come by uprising. There had never been any middle ground for Russia, after all, so why should anyone think it would happen now?

Paul went to see his sister Anna, to warn her to prepare for the worst.

"Stockpile whatever food you can," he suggested. "I'm afraid it's inevitable that this conflict will escalate into violence."

Anna smiled. "We barely have enough for our daily needs."

"Find a good hiding place for your valuables and money."

Mariana and Raisa listened intently. "Do you really think money will do us any good?" Mariana asked. "Even now, I couldn't buy a loaf of bread with a hundred dollars."

"You'll need it for bribes and payoffs, not food," Paul replied. "And, Mariana, you would be wise to wire Daniel's family to send you cash immediately. If you have any valuable jewelry, sew it into the linings of your clothes."

"Paul, you sound like you are preparing us for the end of the world," Anna said.

Mariana frowned. "You are frightening me, Uncle Paul."

"I'd rather you be frightened and prepared than ignorant like our emperor will be when doom falls upon him."

"Is it really so bad?"

"It couldn't be worse." Paul shook his head. "I have worked all my life for the end of the Romanovs, the end of the monarchy. Yet, even if such a thing were to happen, I'm not certain that the immediate results will be good. Perhaps in the long run the outcome will be beneficial, but at first there will be chaos and violence, not unlike the 'Time of Troubles' following the demise of Ivan the Terrible."

"I may be old-fashioned," said Anna, "but it will be too bad if everything that makes up Russia is destroyed. I know the monarchy is not perfect, isn't even close, yet it has given a kind of security to us. The benevolent Little Father image is a comforting one—"

Paul grimaced. "A fantasy!"

"Perhaps," sighed Anna. "But couldn't we keep the good and throw out the bad? They have a good system in Britain."

"The same thing could happen there if a Rasputin came into power."

"What about the Magna Carta?"

"A Rasputin would find a way to poison it as he has poisoned whatever might have been decent in our monarchy—not that I believe anything was decent about it!"

"I wish he would go back to Siberia. The way he hurt poor Katya, he deserves some punishment."

"Is she recovering?"

"Yes, she is, but slowly. She placed her trust in him, and he abused it terribly."

"Well, there are many who wish more than exile upon that beast," said Paul. "And some are doing more than *wishing*."

"What do you mean?"

"Each day I hear two or three plots against him. Some are even discussed openly in the Duma. Even Rasputin has begun to fear for his life. I've heard he hardly ever goes out in the daylight now."

"I agree he is an evil man, but to kill him—" Anna shook her head.

"What if that were the only way to get rid of him?"

"Paul, are you involved in such plots?"

"No, but I cannot say I wouldn't support a viable plan were it to be presented to me."

"Paul, no!"

"I remember how Papa always used to try to see the best in life and in people, Anna. I never was able to do that, not when I was young and, unfortunately, not now. I have matured to some extent from those terrible days when I tried to kill Alexander the Second. I know now that such acts of hatred will only turn against the one who performs them. It nearly consumed me. But acts of patriotism, acts of expediency, are another matter . . . in many cases they are no different than the killing that occurs on a battlefield."

"And that is what you think the murder of Rasputin would be?"

"He is a traitor, Anna. Many believe he is in direct collusion with the Germans. In time of war, traitors are shot."

"Ah, Paul, but I feel so very sorry for the one who ends up pulling the trigger."

"That man will be a hero of Russia."

Anna gazed at Paul with great sadness and no condemnation. "But he will also be a murderer."

60

The conspirators met one final time to discuss the plan they would set into motion that very night. By the time they finished, Yuri was trembling. How could he be involved in such a plot? He was a doctor. He had sworn a solemn oath to uphold the sanctity of life. How could he kill a man, even a monster like Rasputin?

Now that Katya had begun to recover from her ordeal, Yuri's initial fury at the man was fading, and for that, at least, he was thankful. It seemed far worse to kill a man out of hatred than it did out of "political necessity," as his accomplice Pourichkevich would call it. But even at that, Yuri had debated frantically to convince himself of the necessity of the deed. What kept him going was the realization that he knew in his heart it *must* be done.

He had considered leaving the matter in God's hands. But he couldn't decide if that was merely a convenient excuse so he could remain clean, or if it was truly a spiritual principle. The Rasputin problem wasn't going to remedy itself.

The Bible said, "Thou shalt not kill." But thousands upon thousands of good Christian men were at that very moment killing other human beings upon the field of battle. Were all those soldiers doomed to eternal damnation? He didn't think so, and he didn't think he had a right to try to remain above that himself. This was his moment to take a stand for his country . . . and for his tsar.

Still, even if war was morally no different than political assassination, killing a faceless enemy was a long way from luring an unsuspecting man to your home—in this case, Youssoupov's home—and offering him wine and cakes laced with poison. Then, if that were not enough, wrapping the body in a rug and carrying it off to an isolated bend in the river to dump it under the ice. That's what made Yuri shake with fear—the *personal-ness* of the affair. Granted, in the plan they had concocted, Felix would be the one to entertain Rasputin and feed him the poison. The others would wait upstairs and be in charge of disposing of the body—after Yuri had pronounced the man dead.

The whole thing was gruesome, appalling.

But necessary.

How else to rid the country of an enemy more dangerous than any German?

"Yuri?"

Katya's soft voice intruded into his grim thoughts.

"Yes, my dear." He smiled benignly, reaching out to take her hand.

It was good to have her back, even though she still was wounded in her heart and in her soul. Rasputin had seriously undermined her budding faith. Because in her mind he was so wrapped up with her belief in God, she no longer knew what was right and true. She was back to groping around in spiritual darkness. But at least she hadn't given up. She was still trying to seek the real truth. She and Yuri and Anna had had several discussions about faith since that awful night. Katya had many questions, and she was not going to be satisfied with easy answers. If anything, her experience had made her more determined than ever to understand true Christianity.

Perhaps I should be thanking Rasputin rather than trying to kill him, Yuri thought. But his commitment to the deed had gone far beyond anger over his wife's ordeal. He knew now it had been growing in him since his first encounter with the man, and especially since that first time he had seen him with the tsarevich. This was his destiny.

"Yuri, you seem so far away," said Katya. "What are you thinking about?"

She had no idea what he was planning to do. In her delicate state, he hadn't wanted to trouble her with his decision. But now that she was better, he didn't want to lie to her. The last thing she needed now was for someone else close to her to lie and damage what trust she had. But he couldn't tell her the full truth. It was best, for her sake, that she not know. The conspirators had sworn themselves to secrecy, although Yuri knew Pourichkevich was not being very discreet, and that there were vague rumors afloat about the plan. Nevertheless, it was best to keep it as quiet as possible. However, because of the possible repercussions to him, he wondered if it was fair to keep it from his wife. Shouldn't she have a chance to be prepared for his possible arrest?

"I've been thinking about the future, Katya," he said finally.

"Sometimes it doesn't look very good, does it?" she said. "All the uncertainty about the war and the growing unrest at home—it can be frightening."

"You've been through so much, my love."

"Yes, but remember when we talked a few weeks ago about maturing? I thought I was mature then, but I was so very wrong . . ."

"We both were a bit ignorant, weren't we?"

She nodded with a slight smile. "At least I am now mature enough to see how wrong we were. Your mama said something the other day that really struck me as true. Each trial we experience, each of life's scars, can only mature us if we allow them to do so, if we don't let them stop us in fear and panic. I'm trying hard to look at things that way. She said our lives are like a big chunk of marble, and the sculpting process is long and tedious. Each little chip doesn't amount to much, but, chip by chip, it will eventually turn into a beautiful work of art. The saddest thing would be for the sculptor to tire of the process and quit too soon, leaving a half-carved piece of stone that resembles little or nothing at all. I don't want my life to be that way, Yuri. I want to keep moving ahead. It scares me, but the alternative is even more frightening."

Yuri looked at her as if he were seeing her for the first time, and what he saw left him breathless. Her little-girl tenderness was still present, but there was so much more depth to her than he had ever remembered—around her eyes, the curve of her mouth, the set of her jaw. Was it possible that her suffering had made her more beautiful than ever? She *had* matured. He saw it in the way she gazed at him with the understanding of a woman—yes, a *woman*—who was truly letting her trials work for good in her and not ill. She was stronger, perhaps, than he gave her credit for.

"I want to be able to say the same thing of my life, Katya."

"You already can."

"We have so much further to go."

"What's troubling you, Yuri? Even though I've been wrapped up in my own problems lately, I can't help but see there is something wrong with you—something more than concern over me. I doubt I can help you much, but maybe just talking about it will help."

"I didn't want to involve you, Katya. But I see now that if we are truly one, then you *are* involved. I can't tell you everything—for your own safety—but I will say that I am about to do something dangerous, something that could well get me arrested. I am totally convinced, however, that it is for the good of Russia."

"What are you going to do?"

"I'd rather not tell you any more."

"Will your life be in danger?"

"I don't think so." A half-hearted smile twitched at the corners of his lips. "Actually, if we are successful, I may well become a national hero." But his attempt at levity faded. "That's not why I'm doing it, though. It's not a heroic act, but it is necessary."

"I wish you wouldn't be so vague. Why can't I—?" Suddenly she stopped, and all the color drained from her face. "You're going to kill Rasputin, aren't you?"

"Don't ask any more questions, please."

"Dear Lord, no! Yuri, you can't."

"I know how you feel about him, Katya, and for that reason my decision has deeply grieved me—"

"I don't care about that, Yuri. I care about you and what could happen to you."

"I've gone too far to turn back—*if* I wanted to. But I don't."

"Are you doing this to avenge what happened to me?"

"I was approached long before that, and I've been thinking about it for some time. What happened to you only solidified in my mind the absolute necessity of . . . it. If he continues to reign, Russia will be destroyed. Not a single informed soul in this country doubts that."

"But why you, Yuri?"

"I've asked myself that many, many times. I don't know why fate led Felix to come to me. But now I believe it must be done and that it is Russia's only hope of survival. To dump the dirty task on another would make me the worst kind of coward, Katya. I couldn't live with myself."

"But how can you do this thing and live with yourself?"

"It won't be easy, not for any of us who are involved. I suppose it boils down to a choice between evils. I'd rather face the suffering that might come of doing such a deed rather than pass it on to another. At least I can lean upon the strength of mind that God has given me. But if you cannot bear what may come of this, I will back out. I don't want you hurt further."

"I have no idea what I can bear—no, I suppose I have a better idea today than I did a week ago." She took a breath. "It would be so easy to use that to stop you. But I won't. I will bear what I must bear. I've learned I can do that, if nothing else."

"And you truly have no problem with the fact that he was someone you once cared for?"

"My eyes were opened the other night, and I saw the evil in him. But I feel very sorry for him, too. I think at one time he truly was a man touched by God. But he abused his anointing. He brought his own doom upon himself."

"That's what he said of me."

"His prophecy ended up being for himself."

"I hope so."

"We must both be strong."

Yuri tentatively held out his arms, and Katya came swiftly to him. It was the first time since that night with Rasputin that she had allowed Yuri to be so close.

"I just thought of something," Yuri said, "something that has been important to me all my life. My brother and Talia and I recited it over a little ritual we once did so we could be blood brothers. 'A three-fold cord is not easily broken.' Katya, together, you and I will be far stronger than we ever were separately."

"I have always sensed that, Yuri."

"Even when you were running away from me?" He smiled.

"Especially then. Why do you think I ran?"

"I love you so, Katya!" He kissed her fragrant hair. He could feel their hearts beating almost as one. Thoughts of Rasputin faded. In her arms he could forget his fear of what lay ahead, basking only in her love.

61

Yuri tried to carry those final hours of love with him. He had assured Katya that his life was not in danger, and they had both chosen to believe it. But nothing could be certain. He did not know, when he told her good-bye that night, if he would see her again. Any number of things could go wrong, not the least of which was his capture after the crime was committed.

He arrived at the Moika—Youssoupov's house on the Moika Canal in Petrograd—at eleven in the evening. Dmitri was already there, and Soukhotin and Pourichkevich came soon afterward. Felix took them to the basement apartments of the palace, and the five conspirators stood around a bit awkwardly. Everyone seemed acutely conscious of the fact that in these rooms Rasputin would spend his final moments.

The large main room was divided in two by an archway so that one half was a sitting area and the other, the larger half, a dining room. A stairway led up from the sitting area to private quarters, and halfway up this stair was a door that led to the courtyard. Felix had been in the process of refurbishing the apartment, but he had taken great pains to make sure the place was finished, or at least convincingly furnished, tonight so it would have a lived-in look. It was well lighted, a samovar was steaming on a sideboard, and the dining table had the appearance of a recently finished meal.

"I told Rasputin," Felix explained, "that when we had guests, we took our meals here."

He didn't need to explain. They had been over these details many times. He had also told the *starets* they would be coming there tonight to meet Felix's wife, who was actually in the Crimea, and that she might be entertaining upstairs when they arrived. But Felix was nervous and repeated it all again.

Then he showed them a beautiful cabinet of inlaid ebony, with delicate bronze columns backed by mirrors. It was quite unique—and quite deadly. He had stored the poison in it. As Felix opened it, Yuri noted the crystal and silver crucifix that stood on top of the cabinet, an expensive piece of Italian Renaissance art. It seemed an appropriate sentinel to stand guard over the room.

Felix's hand shook as he gave the packet of cyanide to Yuri, and Yuri's shook no less as he took it. He carefully put on rubber gloves and ground the poison into a fine powder. The others watched as if in a trance. Yuri was certain that, like him, none of his companions felt a sense of reality. It was as if they had climbed aboard a train and were proceeding along a set track, unable to stop, unable to veer from the predetermined path.

A plate of cakes sat on the table. Yuri opened each one and liberally sprinkled them with cyanide. The poison in one cake would be enough to bring down several men. Yuri would mix more poison with liquid and put it into three glasses, but he would wait twenty minutes after Felix left to get Rasputin. He did not want to take the chance of having the poison evaporating away.

Yuri took off the contaminated gloves; he had an extra pair for later. Without thinking, he tossed them into the fireplace. The hot fire immediately melted the rubber and sent awful smoke and fumes into the room.

"What have I done?" Yuri groaned.

Everyone ran around opening windows and the door to the courtyard to air out the room. Yuri kept thinking it was a bad beginning. Someone even voiced that thought.

"No harm done," Felix said. "Just be sure to close the windows before I return so the place doesn't freeze."

Finally everything was ready. The fire in the hearth was once more burning cheerfully, and the rooms looked very inviting. Felix had done a fine job in getting the apartment ready. The innocuous appearance of the place helped dull the impact of what was about to happen there.

Soukhotin put on a chauffeur's uniform in order to drive Felix across town to pick up the *starets*. They wanted everything to appear as normal as possible, but of course didn't want the real chauffeur to be involved. Rasputin must suspect nothing. Yuri, however, could not help wondering if the holy man's reputed "second sight" would come to his rescue tonight. The scientist in Yuri wanted to write off the man as a total charlatan, yet, as a spiritual man he knew the mystical, the miraculous—even the occult—did exist. As Katya had said, it was possible that at one time Rasputin had indeed been anointed of God. He might have been a true healer, even a prophet. But down deep, Yuri thought that if the man had ever had any power, it very likely had *never* been from God. Perhaps he was even a type of Antichrist.

Once again Yuri tried to console himself. He was ridding not only his country of a great evil, but perhaps even the world.

After Felix and Soukhotin had gone, Yuri prepared the wine, then he, Dmitri Pavlovich, and Pourichkevich went upstairs to wait in Felix's private sitting room. Dmitri turned on the gramophone, playing "Yankee Doodle Dandy." They were supposed to play lively music and give the impression that a party was going on. They tried to talk, but every attempt at conversation fell flat. They would have to do better than that when Felix returned with his guest if they were going to be convincing.

It was a long wait, and Yuri began to wonder if something had gone wrong. He almost hoped it had. Perhaps the *starets* was too suspicious and refused to come. He had been quite cautious lately—after all, he knew half the country wanted him dead. But just as Yuri was thinking they could all go home with the sense that at least they had *tried*, he heard the courtyard door open and the sound of voices. A few moments later Soukhotin joined them.

With the music blaring in the background, they had to raise their voices in order to question him about what had happened. Now it did sound like a party.

"What took so long?" asked Dmitri.

"He kept trying to get Felix to go to the gypsies instead. Felix had to do some smooth talking to get him here. Then we drove a roundabout way here to ensure we weren't followed by the police."

"I've got to see what's going on," said Pourichkevich, opening the door and creeping out to the landing.

The others followed, but they could only hear a dull murmur of voices. They returned to the sitting room. Dmitri put on another song. They tried to talk, they tried to laugh as if they were having a good time. Soukhotin poured them wine, but Yuri took one sip and felt sick. His stomach was in knots. The others seemed a little calmer. But Dmitri and Soukhotin were both soldiers, trained to have nerves of steel. Pourichkevich, the oldest, had never showed any faltering of his zeal for this task.

But all the men paced; no one could sit still. Someone produced a deck of cards, and they tried to play for a while. Someone else kept pouring wine. Before long the noise level had risen. It seemed to Yuri to be more like a horrible nightmarish scene—the incessant, cheerful notes of "Yankee Doodle Dandy," the bantering voices of card-playing men, the clink of glasses. Suddenly the room began to close in on him.

"Yuri, are you all right?" said Dmitri.

Yuri felt the blood drain from his head, and his insides churned. He jumped up from his seat, and the room started to spin. Dmitri caught him. When he was steady, he rushed out into the courtyard, and thus no one had to watch him lose what little there was in his stomach.

Yuri was still trembling when he returned to his coconspirators.

He felt like a fool but took a little comfort in noting that Dmitri looked rather pale as well.

On his way back to the sitting room from his ordeal in the courtyard, Yuri heard Felix singing down in the basement. What was happening down there?

While the others played cards, Yuri paced and watched the minutes tick by on the mantel clock. An hour passed.

After a while Felix came up. "He wouldn't eat the cakes. I forgot he doesn't like sweets. He finally had one and nothing happened!"

"What about the wine?" Yuri asked.

"I made the mistake of pouring it into a clean glass, then he wouldn't take a new glass when I changed the variety of wine. I had to drop the glass to get him to take one of the poisoned ones. But still there has been no effect!"

"Give him more wine," said Pourichkevich.

"This is taking too long," said Dmitri. "He's sure to get suspicious."

Felix returned to the basement, and another hour and a half dragged by. They were all nervous wrecks now. Yuri felt wretched. He had to hurry out to the courtyard once more. Something definitely must have gone wrong. They had failed. But why was Felix staying away? Maybe the *starets* had hypnotized Felix. Maybe Felix was dead. They began to discuss whether they should take matters into their own hands. Taut nerves and short fuses quickly turned the discussion into a lively argument.

Then the door burst open. It was Felix. He, too, was a wreck, wild-eyed, shaking, pale.

"The poison isn't working!" he exclaimed, only by great effort keeping his frantic voice down.

"That can't be!" said Yuri. "How much has he taken?"

"Several cakes and all of the wine!"

"But the dose was huge," Dmitri said.

Yuri frowned. "Even if it lost half its potency, that much still should have . . . killed him instantly."

"But he still sits there," Felix said, "smiling, laughing, getting drunker and drunker. He seemed to have difficulty swallowing at one point, and some shortness of breath, but that's all. And now he's getting impatient. He wants to meet my wife."

"What can we do?"

"Let's all go down there," Pourichkevich suggested. "Together we can take him down and strangle him."

"You must be crazy!" Yuri protested. "We've had our chance and we've failed. I say we give it up."

"Yes," agreed Dmitri. "I've had enough for one night. I'm ready to go home."

"We can't leave him half-dead," declared Pourichkevich. "We have to finish the job or we are all doomed—not to mention Russia! We must all swear together not to leave this place until the deed is done. There is no turning back."

They looked around at each other. No one looked the least convinced. And they hardly looked like dangerous saviors of Russia. Yuri was sure he looked and felt far worse than Rasputin with his gut full of cyanide. He might yet have to make another dash to the courtyard. And if he did that, he would just keep on going. Honor alone held him back. He couldn't run out on his companions—unless they all agreed to give it up.

That was not going to happen.

Felix said, "Well, we can't all go in there. It would surely make him suspicious, and then he might escape. I'll go myself." And, to Yuri's horror, Felix took Dmitri's sidearm, a Browning revolver, and returned to the basement.

The others, unable to stand another moment waiting in that room, quietly descended the steps after Felix and waited, out of sight, at the courtyard landing. Yuri could hear but not see what happened next.

"The party is breaking up," Felix said to Rasputin. His voice was stilted and hollow. If that didn't arouse Rasputin's suspicions, nothing would.

"Good . . ." came Rasputin's reply in a gravelly, dull-sounding voice.

"Are you not well, Grigori?"

"I don't think I am," said the *starets*. "My head hurts and my stomach is burning. Give me another glass of wine. That will help."

There was the sound of clinking glass as Felix obviously tended to the *starets'* request.

In a few moments Rasputin said, "Ah, that's better."

Two or three more minutes of silence passed. The four conspirators, listening with very little remaining patience, held their breath so as not to risk being discovered in the silence.

Finally Rasputin said, "Let's go visit the gypsies."

"It's so late."

"Not for them. I often go after I've spent a late night at Tsarskoe

Selo. It's a release for my poor, tired body. The thoughts in my mind truly belong to God, but my body is my own. And the flesh must be appeased, don't you think, Prince Felix?"

Felix mumbled something in reply. Yuri couldn't believe that a man who had ingested such a massive dose of poison could be sitting there reflecting on religion! Perhaps the pharmacist had given Yuri worthless stuff. There had been no way to test it beforehand. But there might be other plausible reasons for the *starets'* resistance to it. Yuri tried, but couldn't think of any just then. Instead, what flitted through his distraught mind was the awful fear that maybe Rasputin *was* a messenger of God, after all, and God himself was protecting the holy man.

Yuri groaned. Dmitri, jabbing him in the ribs with his elbow, hissed at him to be quiet.

Finally Yuri heard a chair being pushed back and someone rise. After a moment, Rasputin asked, "Why are you staring at that crucifix?"

"It's one of my favorite pieces," Felix said.

"It must have cost a lot." Another chair pushed back, and feet, much heavier than the first, shuffled across the floor. "I like this cabinet better," Rasputin added.

Both men had to be standing by the cabinet now.

Then Felix said, "Grigori Efimovich, I think you would do well to look at the crucifix—and say a prayer, too."

"What—?"

Suddenly a shot rang out, followed by the thud, hopefully, of a body falling to the floor. Yuri swayed on his feet and clutched Dmitri's shoulder for support, but his companions left him and dashed down the stairs into the room. By sheer instinct, Yuri hurried after them. But he took only a few steps when suddenly the place went dark. Someone had accidently bumped into the light switch.

There was a mad scrambling of noise and fumbling until, a moment later, the lights flashed back to reveal Felix standing over the fallen form of Rasputin, holding Dmitri's revolver.

"Is he. . . ?" said Soukhotin.

"He better be," said Pourichkevich. "Well, Doctor, what do you say?"

Rasputin was not Yuri's first corpse, but it was certainly the first he'd had a hand in causing. He didn't want to look at it; he didn't want to touch it. It took all the courage he possessed to bend over the body and lay his trembling fingers on the man's neck. He did so quickly. It was really unnecessary. There was a bullet hole in the man's chest.

"He's dead," Yuri said.

And Russia was saved. Oh, God, please let Russia be saved! Yuri didn't want to consider the possibility that this gruesome patriotic deed might be for nothing.

62

Yuri would never know how he managed to complete the remaining part of the plan. He and Dmitri Pavlovich, with Soukhotin dressed in Rasputin's coat and hat, returned to Rasputin's flat, so it would appear as if the *starets* had come home, thus buying time for his assassins before Rasputin was discovered as missing. Then they had to return to the Moika in order to dispose of the body.

There, they were greeted by Felix and Pourichkevich and the most chilling tale yet. Apparently Rasputin had not been as dead as Yuri thought. While Felix was alone with the "corpse," it had tried to attack Felix. A struggle had ensued in which the very-much-alive *starets* had been able to break free, get up the steps, and out into the courtyard. Pourichkevich grabbed the gun and chased after Rasputin, shooting him two more times. But these shots had roused the attention not only of a couple of servants but also of the gendarme who was making his regular nightly rounds in the neighborhood. Felix was trying to convince the policeman that the shots were merely horseplay among some of his partying friends when Pourichkevich, no doubt having had too much strain for one night, appeared and began to brag to the officer about killing Rasputin. Fortunately, the policeman was sympathetic and swore he would tell no one.

Yuri, his confidence all but gone, once again examined the body, which had been moved from the courtyard to the landing on the stairs, and verified that there were two new gunshot wounds in it. It seemed incredible that Rasputin could have survived the previous wound, much less tried to evade his pursuers. He appeared quite dead now, though Yuri had had so much wine and was so unnerved that even he did not trust his medical judgment. Still, there was no pulse, no breathing. He had to be dead! Nevertheless, Yuri was glad when they finally wrapped up the body in a rug to take it away.

Felix had been so distraught by the final struggle with Rasputin that he went to bed, nearly in a faint. It was left to the remaining four to complete the task. Yuri's three comrades suggested that he, too, forego the job. His wounded leg was aching, and he was limping badly, and he looked decidedly green in complexion. But Yuri was determined to finish what he had begun. So, together they loaded the body into Dmitri's motorcar and drove it to an isolated bend in the Neva, where they lowered it into a hole in the ice.

After all was finished, Yuri returned home. Yet he knew that would not be the end of it. Whether Rasputin had come back to life and attacked Felix, he did not know. But he did know that man would probably haunt them all for the rest of their lives.

It was six in the morning when he got home. Katya was awake and appeared not to have slept all night. When he knocked on her door and entered her room, she jumped from her bed and ran to him, but Yuri put up his hand to stop her.

"Don't touch me," he said. "I feel too dirty."

"I'll have a servant draw you a bath."

"That might help," he said without enthusiasm.

In another hour, after a soothing bath, he did not feel better. But he was able to hold Katya, and that was a tremendous help. A few days ago she had been the needy one, leaning upon his strength—now the tables were turned. And she rose up to meet his need, to comfort him, to love him. He wanted it to be enough. He wanted to lose himself in it. But his mind kept replaying the awful events of the night. The cold, dead face of Rasputin would not leave him alone. And, as if that were not bad enough, he kept thinking about all the mistakes he and his accomplices had made. There was blood in the Moika, blood in Dmitri's motorcar in which they had transported the body, witnesses who had seen Rasputin leave his flat with Youssoupov, servants who could not all be trusted to be silent. They had forgotten to weight the body with the chains they had brought along before dumping it into the river. A shoe had been left in the boot of the car. . . .

How much more incriminating evidence had they left behind?

Yuri's worrying did not make it easy for him to receive his wife's comfort—not when he feared that at any minute a troop of police would be beating down his door to arrest him.

"What have I done, Katya?" he murmured over and over.

Alexandra refused to believe her Friend was dead. But the report that the *starets* was missing bore such ominous tones. He had been last seen leaving his house the night before with Alexandra's nephew, Felix. Then there was a report of a drunken orgy and shots being fired at the Moika. Pourichkevich had been there bragging about killing the *starets*. Somehow Dmitri Pavlovich was involved as well.

Alix was amazingly calm, though she knew it was the calm of hollow emptiness rather than peace. Anna Vyrubova was with her and the children, but she longed for her husband to return to her. She had written him a letter and then sent him a telegram. He asked her to keep him apprised of the situation. Of course he had the war to tend to, but did he fully understand what the loss of Grigori would mean?

Even she did not want to think of that. It was simply too awful to contemplate. For if her dear Friend was dead, it might also mean a death warrant for her son. . . .

Cyril Vlasenko had assured the empress that he would personally direct the investigation of the *starets'* disappearance. He doubted the man would be found alive, but he didn't tell the tsaritsa. Evidence was piling up quickly, all implicating—of all people—that effeminate milquetoast, Prince Felix Youssoupov!

The Chief Commissioner of Police delivered an updated report shortly after lunch on December thirtieth.

"Your Excellency, I personally questioned Youssoupov," said the Commissioner, General Balk. "He denies that Rasputin ever came to his house last night. He says he entertained some friends and things got a bit out of hand. The Grand Duke Dmitri was toying with a pistol and shot one of the dogs."

"What about Pourichkevich's confession?"

"The prince says Pourichkevich was drunk and had been likening the dog to Rasputin, with regret that it was the dog instead of Rasputin that was dead."

"I know Pourichkevich—we are both involved in the Union of Russian People. The man never drinks. In fact, I believe he belongs to a temperance organization."

"Believe me, that is not the only hole in the prince's story. Witnesses saw him leave Rasputin's flat with the *starets*. But Youssoupov refused to divulge the names of his guests last night. And he refused to allow a search of his home, claiming that the law forbids the searching of the homes of members of the Imperial family without an order from the tsar."

"I'll get an order. You have no idea about accomplices?"

"I have some names gleaned from witnesses and indiscreet servants. Besides Youssoupov and Pourichkevich, the Grand Duke Dmitri was almost certainly at the Moika last night. I am all but certain there must be others involved, but I have no leads."

"Well, keep all of them under close surveillance. Can't have any of them slipping away. Besides, they may inadvertently lead you to other conspirators."

Later in the day, Cyril obtained from the tsaritsa an order to have the known suspects, that is, Youssoupov and the Grand Duke Dmitri, placed under house arrest. In actuality, she wanted to have them shot. Of course none of it was legal because only the tsar could have members of his family arrested. But the suspects cooperated with the arrangement, nonetheless.

Anna came to the Zhenechka home later in the day, completely ignorant of her son's involvement in the death of Rasputin. Yet there was no way he could hide from her the fact that something dreadful was wrong. Had he tried, she would have known by his wasted appearance. But he had no strength to hide anything just then.

The moment he saw her he crumpled into her arms.

"Oh, Mama! I've done a terrible thing!" She embraced him and he wept in her arms. "I killed him, Mama—!"

"Say no more, son," she said softly. "Confession may be good for the soul, but there are other things to consider right now as well."

Yes, of course. He had to gather his wits about him. If his loved ones knew nothing, they would never be placed in the impossible position of testifying against him. He was, however, still amazed that no one had yet implicated him in the crime. He supposed it helped that he had never been a close associate of either Youssoupov or the grand duke. No one would dream that someone of his social level would be involved in a conspiracy with members of the royal family.

When Yuri heard that the whole city was cheering the demise of Rasputin and toasting the conspirators as heroes, he was not in the least bothered that his name was unknown. But it was hard to live with his continued freedom after he heard of Felix and Dmitri's arrest.

Then Uncle Paul telephoned with news that the body had been discovered. The police had found blood on the railing of the bridge where it had been dumped. They had also followed tire tracks in the snow that led from that location, three miles away, right to the Moika. The terrible roads in Petersburg proved hazardous once again.

Upon hearing the news, Yuri had to excuse himself so he could be sick in the privacy of the washroom. He still feared that a carelessly forgotten clue would lead to him. But getting caught weighed least on his mind. At times he even considered turning himself in, but was dissuaded from that by Katya's and his mother's tears. What weighed heaviest on him as the hours passed was the awakening realization that he had made a terrible mistake. He had taken a man's life; he had destroyed his Hippocratic oath. Even if he never was arrested, he'd have to live with that.

Each successive day brought new evidence against the conspirators, but none more shocking, more demoralizing to Yuri than when the autopsy report revealed there was water in the *starets'* lungs. Rasputin had still been alive when they dropped him in the river!

Finally, the legal repercussions came. No matter what the tsar may have felt about Rasputin, he could not let his murderers off scot-free. Youssoupov was exiled to his estate in Kursk. The grand duke was ordered back to the war to the Persian Front. Yuri was finally vaguely connected to the crime, but because no solid evidence implicated him, he never faced charges. However, Yuri's involvement was known well enough—probably thanks to the loose-tongued Pourichkevich—so that when Yuri was out, strangers often came up to him and patted him on the back. Yuri wondered if there could be a worse consequence for him. Soukhotin, too, was not implicated and returned to the Front—perhaps enough of a sentence for any man. The police had no doubt of Pourichkevich's complicity, but he was spared judgment. Even the tsar knew better than to touch a member of the Duma under the present political climate.

All in all, the five conspirators were let off easy, indeed. But Yuri felt no relief at all. He knew that every one of them would suffer in ways the tsar would never imagine.

Worst of all, nothing really changed in Russia. Rasputin's murder brought a flurry of passion and excitement in the country, but in less than two weeks, all the fervor had died away and life continued on the same corrupt, miserable path as always. That, to Yuri, was the most defeating blow of all. What a fool he had been to think that Russians could change so easily! He should have seen that things had already gone too far. Maybe if Andrei had been around, he would have set Yuri straight.

Suddenly Yuri had a strong desire to see his brother. Andrei represented a kind of security and stability to Yuri, the idyllic past, a time when they had been young with dreams and hopes . . . and a papa to guide them on the path to manhood.

Not even on the day of his father's death had Yuri ever felt the truth more strongly: All those things were gone forever.

VII

ENDS AND BEGINNINGS

Winter to Spring 1917

63

Andrei had never been more homesick in his life. How he wished he had been faithful about communicating with his mother! At least then he might have a letter or two from her with which to console himself. But he'd let too much time elapse after that first and only letter he wrote her. Now he was too ashamed to write.

Perhaps he would feel better if there was something stimulating happening where he was. A bit of vital activity would help keep his thoughts from straying to home . . . to his dear Russia . . . and his family. But life in the emigre community had taken on the quality of—how had Krupskaya once described it?—a "dog-trot" existence. He had moved to Zurich with Lenin a few months ago. Lenin had preferred Zurich because the libraries were better there; Andrei had stayed with Lenin, hoping to be nearer to the center of activity, as paltry as it was. But still *nothing* happened. Andrei had not left his home and loved ones for this. Those who had been in exile for years tried to console him and instill patience in him. But Andrei wasn't a patient man, and he longed for action.

Those enjoying more scholarly pursuits, like Lenin, could find diversion in the well-stocked libraries. Out of sheer desperation Andrei had done a lot of reading, but where others of his circle were pursuing Voltaire, he had discovered Mark Twain. He defended himself with the fact that Twain had been a great supporter of Russian revolution. In Twain's books, the ruling classes were always the villains, and the protagonists were always simple proletariat types.

Andrei had hoped the Zurich Youth Rally would offer some excitement. Many revolutionary-minded young people from countries all over Europe were now in Zurich fleeing conscription in imperialist armies. Perhaps there might even be a new Russian face among them with news from home. Wartime made current news difficult to come by.

Lenin gave a rousing speech that day at the rally, exhorting the youth to stay the course of the revolutionary struggle. He stressed the importance of an international revolution freeing all the proletarian masses. Exile and the lack of progress in Russia had greatly broadened Lenin's outlook. He was talking much more these days about the incompetent Swiss government than about Russia.

Lenin concluded his speech with a statement that Andrei knew was weighing on the Bolshevik leader more and more.

"We of the older generation may not live to see the decisive battles of this coming revolution. . . ."

Yes, even Lenin was despairing of the "dog-trot" life of an exile. Was he spending most of his waking moments thinking of ways to get home? Andrei was. It was, in fact, becoming an obsession. Inessa had gone home once and been arrested and exiled again. But Andrei was beginning to think it was worth the risk. What if Talia were there? What if there was another man in her life? He couldn't stand the thought of losing her without even a chance to express his love to her.

As Andrei left the meeting, pulling up the collar of his shabby overcoat against a gust of icy February wind, he wondered how much longer they could stand this life. How had Plekhanov and Zasulich and so many others done it, exiled for *decades*?

The wind almost carried away the voice calling Andrei's name. Uncertain that it had been his name he heard, but anxious for any diversion, he turned and was greeted by a face he had not seen in years.

"Daniel!"

"I knew I'd find you eventually!" Daniel laughed as he embraced his brother-in-law. "It's my lot in life to keep my wife's two little brothers in tow."

"I can't believe it's actually you. But then, I shouldn't be surprised to find you a few miles from a war."

"What a reputation I have!"

"Well, I can tell you right now, you'll find little news in Zurich. It's the dullest place on earth." Then he added with a grin, "But the Swiss do have remarkable chocolate, and there's a place near here where we can satisfy even the most stubborn sweet tooth."

"You're the one with the fondness for sweets, if I remember, but lead the way. I want something warm, whether it's sweet or not."

They went to a little bakery two blocks away, a place Andrei frequented and where he was well known. The wife of the baker, Madame Fortier, greeted him cheerily and immediately poured out two tall mugs of hot chocolate. Daniel also ordered several pastries and insisted on paying.

"I won't argue," said Andrei. "My budget allows one glass of Fortier chocolate a month. Occasionally I get a little more by working in the bakery."

Daniel squeezed Andrei's muscular arm. "I'm happy to see poverty isn't wasting you away."

"I get a little more than chocolate when I work in the bakery," Andrei said sheepishly.

"It would appear!"

"Tell me the news from home, Daniel!" Andrei asked eagerly as they seated themselves in a corner of the bakery. "We know next to nothing about what's going on in Russia. And I know even less about Mama and everyone."

"You could have written, Andrei—"

"Please, Dan, I don't need to be browbeaten. I know I am a rotten son. And I know Mama would forgive me all my rottenness. But . . . I don't know . . . writing never did come easy for me. I love them all no less."

"I'm sorry. We've all been really worried about you. But, okay, enough of that. Now for news. Are you ready? There's a lot."

"I've been ready for two years."

"Let's see . . ." Daniel rubbed his chin, obviously searching back in his mind two long years so he wouldn't leave anything out. "Your mama married Misha; Yuri married a countess named Katya, and he also helped to assassinate Rasputin—"

"Wait a minute!" Andrei shook his head. "Maybe there's something wrong with your Russian—or I didn't hear right."

"My Russian's perfect," said Daniel. "And I am sure you heard right."

"Mama and Uncle Misha got married! That's a shock enough. But what's this about Yuri and Rasputin? I can't believe it."

Daniel explained all the details he knew, but still Andrei found it hard to fathom.

"I would never have thought Yuri capable of such a thing."

"He isn't, Andrei. It has torn him apart. Not only the act itself, but the fact that it has done no good at all. He convinced himself that it was for the good of Russia, that it would save Russia and the tsar. But now, weeks later, the tsar continues in his dreamworld, convinced he can continue in the autocracy as a benevolent 'Little

Father.' He won't give an inch to the liberals."

"Good! Neither tsar, nor liberals, nor even poor Yuri's sad act of patriotism will save Russia. The savior of Russia is here in Zurich, Daniel, if only he is given a chance."

"Zurich is a long way from Russia."

"We know that only too well. Did you hear Lenin's speech today?"

"Yes. Even he is beginning to doubt if he'll have a part in what is to come."

"Would you like to talk to him, Daniel?"

Daniel grinned. "Do you think I looked you up just to gaze on your pretty face?"

"But I doubt he'd talk to an American capitalist named Trent."

"I can be somebody else, Andrei. Just get me in to see him. Exposure in a mainstream American newspaper could only help his cause."

"I didn't know you were such a champion of the socialists."

"I'm not. Neither am I a capitalist—not at heart. I can only promise to write an objective article. No one can, or should, ask for more than that."

"I'll speak to him. But in return, I want more details about the family. Tell me about those weddings. Tell me about Mariana and my nieces and nephew. Is my grandfather still alive? What about Uncle Paul and Raisa and . . . Talia, that is, if she is still in Russia." He tried to be casual about his final words but Daniel seemed to read a great deal more into his slight hesitation.

"Talia returned to Russia around Thanksgiving—that is, about the end of November. Last I heard, she decided to remain there until the end of the war."

"What about her dancing?"

"She's more concerned about her family. She couldn't bear to leave her mama and Anna once she got home."

"So, she is . . . uh . . . unattached?"

"It sounds like that would matter to you, Andrei. But, yes she is—as far as I know."

"Will you be going home, I mean to Russia soon?"

"I haven't been there in three months. You can thank Mariana's detailed letters for all I've been able to tell you. She was able to get delicate information, such as about Yuri, out by way of the American Embassy. I'm very anxious to get back. Things are bad there—shortages of food and fuel, not to mention the situation with Yuri."

"Was he arrested?"

"The tsaritsa wanted to have Rasputin's murderers executed—two were members of the royal family. But they received fairly mild discipline instead. And, thankfully, Yuri was never implicated. He's suffering nevertheless."

"The poor fellow," said Andrei with real sympathy.

"Anyway, I'll be on my way back soon. I would have left a week ago but I met a fellow, a socialist, who knows Lenin and was able to tell me how to find him. I had hoped that in finding him, I would find you, too."

"I wish I could go with you."

"What's stopping you?"

"For one thing, I am a Russian national. I can't be traveling around as freely as a cocky American."

"It hasn't been so easy for me either with relations between the U.S. and Germany steadily heating up. I'm sure the States will enter the war at any moment. But there are ways of getting around, Andrei—many I've used with great success."

"Daniel, if you do get home, would you. . . ?" Andrei paused. What was he thinking? Would he pass words of love to Talia through another? It was stupid of him to even consider it. Yet his greatest fear was that if he ever did see her again, he would find her married, surrounded by a passel of children. But he couldn't very well express his love and ask her to wait for him through Daniel. For one thing, it was assuming too much—even for him. She had a life that he had not been part of for years. He was the only one clinging to a past that was probably gone forever.

"Never mind," he added. "Just tell everyone I'm well and love them. That's all."

"I still think you can tell them yourself."

"If only . . ."

"What if I could get you papers, Andrei? The capitalist steel tycoon, Daniel Trent, might be good for something, you know. I have a few connections in the right places."

"That would be selling out my convictions." But even as Andrei said the words, he knew they were just words. Even Lenin believed in expediency, to a point at least. Still, Andrei knew that loyalty could never bow to expediency.

But, to Andrei's surprise, when he approached Lenin with the possibility of returning to Russia, he received a positive response.

"If you get through, you can smuggle in some copies of *Pravda*.

It's been months since we've been able to get anything into Russia," Lenin said.

Lenin also gave him the task of making contact with the small Bolshevik contingent in Petrograd. The organization there had all but collapsed in the last few years. There was little or no communication with those small numbers who remained active. Andrei was glad to have some purpose besides his own personal reasons for returning.

64

Cyril Vlasenko approached a meeting with the tsar with only a fraction of his usual confidence. His short tenure as Minister of the Interior was in serious jeopardy. The Duma was crying daily about forming a "ministry of confidence," that is, a ministry approved by them, which innately meant a wholesale purge of any and all Rasputin "appointees."

The mood in the city was tense, old bitternesses rising to the surface to converge with the many newer problems. In recognition of the anniversary of Bloody Sunday, a hundred and forty thousand Petrograd workers went on strike. The garrisons of soldiers in the city were comprised mostly of new, young recruits who simply could not be counted upon to react decisively against civilians. If there were serious outbreaks in the city...

Well, Cyril hated to consider the consequences. But the workers were growing more and more militant. They were calling the tsar the "Butcher of Bloody Sunday" and the husband of a traitor, if not a traitor himself. Everywhere there was talk of plots against the dynasty—and supporters of that dynasty.

That left-wing insurgent Kerensky was openly and fearlessly attacking the regime. His speech for the opening of the Duma had blatantly called for "the immediate overthrow of the medieval regime at all costs." The man ought to be sent to Siberia for such words. The empress had an even better idea.

"Kerensky should be hanged for such a speech. There ought to be martial law in the city," she had declared.

If only her poltroon of a husband had the backbone for such measures. Cyril remembered fondly the days when as chief of the Third Section he could slap irons around dissenters at will. But members of the Duma were untouchable these days.

When the Duma opened for its new session in mid-February, Cyril, expecting trouble, did authorize the arrest of several labor members. He also ordered a large and intimidating showing of police and Cossacks at the Tauride Palace. But there were no demonstrations that day, and his premature move backfired on him. The public accused him of *trying* to provoke a clash with the workers.

How the tsar could think of leaving the city now was beyond Cyril. And therein lay the purpose of Cyril's audience with the emperor. He must convince him to stay. Cyril did not want to face what might come alone—that is, he did not want to take full responsibility for it. But the tsar claimed that the war needed his attention. That was as good an excuse as any for running away. Poor deluded man—he still thought the war could be concluded victoriously in three or four months!

Nicholas greeted Cyril with his usual warm formality. But he seemed vague, detached throughout the interview. At one point his gaze wandered toward a window, and he was completely distracted from what Cyril was saying. Cyril had to repeat himself. The tsar had never been a strong or confident man, but now he appeared absolutely lost. His fatalism was in full bloom. He was prepared to surrender to the whim of fate.

Fear was not something with which Cyril was well acquainted, but he knew it now and knew it intensely. After the meeting with the tsar, he went home and instructed his wife to pack all their valuables away in the secret vault in the basement and be prepared to leave at a moment's notice. He wanted to flee now, but his natural greed was still a bit stronger than his growing fear. He couldn't bear to lose all he had gained if there was still the slightest possibility of beating the current political upheavals.

As he left, he glanced wistfully around the grand Fedorcenko palace. Although he had not had a chance to bring the place back to its former glory, it was still richly opulent—a symbol, in Cyril's mind, of what Russia was all about. The glory of tsarism, the wealth of aristocracy, the pomp and circumstance of Holy Orthodoxy. These were things worth fighting to save.

Worth dying for, too?

No . . . Cyril supposed not. Saving his own neck was all that truly mattered.

When he returned to his office, he had a call from Rodzianko, the president of the Duma. Apparently the tsar had agreed to speak to the Duma the next day and announce his intention of forming a ministry of confidence. Cyril nearly dropped the telephone receiver in shock. Where had *that* reversal come from? Two hours before, the man was firmly set on the status quo. Now Cyril was truly afraid.

He immediately caught the next train back to Tsarskoe Selo.

"I was about to telephone you," the tsar said as Cyril entered his study, "to let you know I will be leaving for Stavka tonight."

"Your Majesty, I am confused. I heard you would be addressing the Duma in the morning?" Cyril only barely kept his tone controlled.

"Oh, that . . . I've changed my mind."

"What about the ministry of confidence?"

"No, it was a mistake. I will try to return in a week or so. Then we can deal with these problems. I think they can wait. Things will settle down a bit."

"Yes, Your Majesty." Cyril should have been relieved. But the dull ache in the pit of his stomach flamed to life with a vengeance.

Nicholas wrote to Alix from Stavka, "Am finally able to relax a bit. No troublesome ministers to contend with. I've been reading a French translation of Caesar's *Gallic Wars*. I look forward to whiling away my evenings with a few games of Dominos. Kiss the kiddies for me."

Alix sat at her writing desk, dipped a pen in ink, and began a reply to her husband. She wrote, as she had so many times before, encouraging him to be firm, to be the autocrat he was born to be.

But for the most part, her letter was dominated with troubles at home, that is, with the children. Olga and Alexis had come down with measles. They both had high fevers and were confined to their beds. It was Alexis's first crisis since the death of Grigori, and Alix felt her Friend's loss more acutely than ever. Within two days, Tatiana and Anna Vyrubova had both gone to their beds with the infection. Alix spent all her waking moments going between the sickrooms, tending and fretting and praying.

Disturbing reports began to filter into the Alexander Palace about disorders in Petrograd. Vlasenko frequently assured her that matters were under control. But with three sick children to tend, Petrograd was the least of her worries.

Besides, she simply did not believe in the possibility of revolution.

When it happened, it was like a match set to dry brush. A moment of smoke, then—puff!—a conflagration. It took even those who had seen it coming by surprise.

Paul could barely make his way through the crowds to get to his office in the Tauride Palace. The huge lines of people waiting for bread and meat and tea were more rowdy than usual. Several shops had been broken into and sacked. Nearly all Petrograd workers were now on strike, surging idly through the streets, discontented and angry. They seemed not at all affected by temperatures of forty below zero.

And now a new sight could be seen in the streets. Red banners, red flags, red sashes, and armbands.

The color of revolution.

It had come!

He didn't know whether to weep or laugh. For over forty years he had been working for this moment. But now he suddenly was gripped with a fear that it would be a bloody, violent event. He had always known that in theory, of course, but now he *knew* in the very depths of his soul. He only prayed that out of the ashes and blood a new and better Russia would rise.

Impulsively, Paul took a red armband handed to him by one of the workers and slipped it over his jacket sleeve. It helped get him through the mob gathered in front of the Tauride Palace. Among other demands, they were shouting for the dismissal of Vlasenko. Paul smiled.

Some Petrograd residents were doing more than shouting. A mob of about fifty had attacked the Vlasenko residence. Luckily, Cyril and his wife, having been warned of trouble by one of their few loyal servants, had vacated the palace early that morning. Poznia was staying with a cousin in another part of the city. Cyril had managed to get to his office, where he was frantically burning incriminating papers. He had ordered the arrest of the insurgent leaders, but there were no real leaders, and the few that he could get his hands on were replaced quickly by others. Hope of quelling the uprising was quickly fading.

While he was at the office, the report came of the attack on the Fedorcenko estate. The house had been set on fire, and over a quarter burned before the harried firefighters, who were busy quelling fires in many parts of the city, arrived and contained the blaze. The malcontent workers had robbed the place as well. Cyril only hoped the vaults had not been discovered.

Anna and the other women and the children stayed inside as much as possible. Little Katrina sat by the window gazing out on the street below at the roaming insurgents.

"Grandmama, why are they wearing red and carrying red flags?"

"You know, in Russian *red* is the name for 'beautiful.' "

"It doesn't look very beautiful."

"No . . . but many think a revolution would be a beautiful thing."

"Do you?"

"I think it might be a necessary thing. I'm not sure it will be so beautiful."

"Are you frightened?"

"A little, sweetheart. But God will protect us."

"I still wish my papa was here."

"So do I, but we'll be all right." Anna put her arm around the child. "We have each other, we have our faith, and especially, we have our love. It is so much more than many of those people out there have."

"Maybe they wouldn't be angry and yelling if they had love, Grandmama."

"If they ever had it, they have forgotten about it just now. But we will be strong if we don't forget. Your uncle Yuri is fond of the saying, 'A threefold cord is not easily broken.' That's what our family is, Katrina. *Together* we are a strong cord."

"Is Papa weaker because he is not here?"

"No, because he is still part of us, as are Misha and Uncle Andrei. The strength of the cord is in our hearts, and that we can always take with us. We should pray for them, though, that they don't forget and lose heart."

"I'll pray for the angry people outside, too."
"That's a wonderful idea, sweetheart."

Yuri had to walk to the hospital. There were no trams running, no public transportation of any sort, and he dared not take the motorcar or a carriage, for there was no telling what the mobs would do to such symbols of the nobility. Perhaps he should have heeded Katya's pleas and remained home. But he had to work.

Those first weeks after Rasputin's death, Yuri had stayed away from the hospital. He felt a murderer had no right to practice medicine. Then the idleness nearly drove him mad. His mama had encouraged him to go to church, to make confession. But he simply wasn't ready to face God.

It had been Uncle Paul who had helped him the most. Paul, of all those close to him, knew what Yuri was suffering. Paul had once been a terrorist. He'd had a hand in planting bombs and had come close to killing a tsar, only a faulty wire preventing his deed.

"How did you live with yourself, Uncle Paul?"

"Each man must find his own way, I suppose. For your papa, that way was the path of God."

"Yes . . ." mused Yuri. "I had almost forgotten the reason he had been sent to Siberia. He killed a man, too . . ." Yuri shook his head miserably. "How it must grieve him to see that I didn't learn by his mistakes."

"It's not too late to learn."

"I can't undo what I have done."

"No, but you can—you must—go on, somehow. Your papa did so with God's help."

"I can't face God, Uncle Paul, I just can't. Every time I try I can't get past the fact that I did wrong fully realizing it was wrong—even if I believed it was for the right reasons. It's not right to blatantly sin and then expect God to forgive you."

"I wouldn't know about that, Yuri."

"That's why I've come to you, Uncle. I can't accept the answers my mama has right now. I need *something*, though, to help me survive."

"What I did," offered Paul, "was to throw myself into my cause."

"I have no cause."

"What about your work?"

"I am no longer worthy—"

"Stop it, Yuri! Now you are whining. If you have no work, no cause, and no God, then you may as well just end it all. Why go on indeed?"

Yuri looked at his uncle with surprise, then a shadow of a smile flickered across his lips. He wanted to live, and something deep within, an irrepressible seed of hope, gave him the sense that he would someday get beyond his present misery. Thus, he decided to take Paul's suggestion. He would go back to work. He might not be worthy, but his hands and his mind were still perfectly capable. He wasn't going to purposefully kill another human—he was sure of that, if nothing else.

He had been back at his post for a week now, and with each minute he felt himself coming more and more to terms with what he had done. But it was not good for his morale to see the mobs in the streets, shouting hateful epithets against the tsar. Yuri had risked everything to save the tsar, and now it appeared as if all his suffering would be for naught.

65

Day by day the crisis mounted rather than diminished. Several government buildings had been taken by the rebels. The Okhrana building had been gleefully sacked and its hated occupants chased out or arrested. Many police stations around the city had also been captured, and the police who did not don civilian clothes and join the rebellion were pursued and arrested.

On Sunday morning, Paul was awakened by the telephone to hear Kerensky's excited voice. "The Pavlosky Guards mutinied last night! The Volhynsky and Preobrajensky regiments quickly followed suit. They refused to lift a hand against their own people. The Cossack Guards rebelled a few hours ago, killing several officers, arresting others."

"Sasha, if the tsar can't count on his guards, then he is truly lost."

"I'm trying to get a message now to these units to come over to the defense of the Duma. Pavushka, you must get here quickly."

"I'll get there as soon as I can, Sasha. But—" He glanced at his wife. "I'll see you soon."

Paul wished now he had spent the night at the Tauride Palace. It was a good half-hour trip from his flat on Vassily Island to the Duma headquarters, especially when no trams or buses were running. But he had been worried about Mathilde. She hadn't been well lately. He looked over at her now, sitting at the kitchen table studying him as he spoke on the phone. She looked pale and had lost weight. Yuri had examined her and feared she might have cancer, but he had wanted to perform some tests before making a conclusive diagnosis. There would be no tests now with all that was going on in the city.

She smiled at him, perhaps perceiving his concern and his inner turmoil.

He told her what Kerensky had reported.

"You must go," she said simply. "We have both worked too hard to miss this. You must go for my sake, too."

"I'm going to take you to Anna's place on my way. You shouldn't be alone today."

She shrugged. "I'd like to spend some time with Anna."

By the time Paul arrived at the Duma, the soldiers had not yet come. Some of the Duma deputies ridiculed Kerensky about his tardy troops. Then about thirty of the socialist leaders met in a private session to discuss their response to recent events. The previous evening the Duma leaders, of whom a large contingent were Kadets—moderate bourgeois who supported a constitutional monarchy along British lines—had taken the small step of forming the Provisional Committee of the Duma with Rodzianko as chairman. They were dragging their feet, though. Rodzianko still hoped for a decisive move from the tsar. The Duma president continued to believe that forming a ministry of confidence would appease the masses.

Thus the left-wing faction of the Duma, including for the most part, Social Democratic Mensheviks, some Jewish Bundists, and the Social Revolutionaries, of which Paul and Kerensky were part, met in a private session. Their immediate intent was not to usurp power, but rather to act as a protector of the revolutionaries in the streets and to ensure that the gains made by them were not lost. They formed the Petrograd Soviet, led by Kerensky and the Menshevik, Chkheidze.

In the meantime, the Provisional Committee called for Vlasenko to resign. But the fat old count said he'd commit suicide instead. Paul was a little disappointed that someone talked him out of it. Finally, the Grand Duke Michael said he would take over leadership of the government if the tsar approved.

The tsar, still at the Front, did not approve. His country was falling down around him and still he refused to compromise.

Nicholas's only action was to send his adjutant general to Petrograd with a battalion of his most loyal troops, men who had all received the St. George cross for valor. They were to make only one stop, at Tsarskoe Selo, to make sure the royal family was safe.

The tsar prepared to depart Stavka shortly after the departure of the troops. He had his train routed the long way back so as not to impede the speed of his general.

He was still not seriously worried. He had made it through 1905, with many crises in between. He would survive this. When he received a telegram from Rodzianko, he did not take it seriously.

"Your Highness, situation in Petrograd serious," the wire warned, "Anarchy reigns in the Capital. The government is paralyzed. There are mobs creating violence in the streets. A ministry must be formed that is trusted by the people. I pray the wearer of the Crown is not blamed for the fall of Russia."

Nicholas looked at his aide and shook his head. "I'm not even going to reply to this nonsense. Rodzianko 'cries wolf' too often."

He did send a telegram to Alix informing her of his departure. "Hope to see you soon. I pray the children are well. Perhaps you ought to expose Maria and Anastasia to the infection so they can get it over with."

Most of the ministers had fled. Those few that remained, including Cyril, were holed up in the Admiralty Building with the Grand Duke Michael. They had had to flee their first stronghold, the Winter Palace, when disloyal troops overran it. The Admiralty was now besieged by rebels, and the defenders had only fifteen hundred loyal troops to protect them. Several other government buildings were also under siege. The District Court Building had been burned down. At least one of the main arsenals in the city had been seized by the rebels and mutineers.

Twenty-five thousand troops in the city had revolted. That amounted to only five percent of the city's force, but, with their military training and access to weapons, they were enough to turn a disorderly street revolt into a viable threat.

Soon Cyril learned that the revolt had spread beyond the bounds of Petrograd. Rebels had taken control of the Kronstadt Naval Base, and a general strike had begun in Moscow.

But Cyril's most immediate concern was the troops outside the Admiralty. They were pressing in closer, and the defense of loyal troops was breaking. The grand duke decided to escape to a new haven. Cyril made the same decision. But where could he go? Everyone hated him. If the soldiers or workers captured him he was doomed. Other ministers had already been arrested, but none was hated more than Cyril Vlasenko. It would take very little for them to shoot him.

Cyril suspected even Michael despised him, but, as a member of the royal family, the grand duke felt duty bound to extend protection to Vlasenko. This time, however, Cyril couldn't follow Michael. The grand duke intended to take refuge in a private home.

There seemed only one recourse for Cyril. Donning a haphazard disguise and sneaking through back alleys, he made it to the Tauride Palace, and there placed himself under the protection of the Provisional Committee. Locked up in a meeting room with several other hapless Imperial lackeys, he gave up all illusions that he was still Minister of the Interior. Why had he ever coveted that position in the first place? From the first it had brought him nothing but misery. Now it was likely to get him killed.

66

Anna's working-class neighborhood escaped major violence. She had heard an occasional shot being fired, and of course there were the endless crowds surging through the streets. But since most of the anger of the mobs was directed against symbols of government and the aristocracy, she did worry about Yuri and Katya. Many residences of the nobility had been attacked. While there was phone service, she kept in contact with her son's family. She tried to encourage them to come to her place, but Yuri declined. He knew her flat was already overcrowded, and his family would add not only Katya and Irina but Countess Zhenechka and Teddie as well, not to mention several loyal servants who could not be left to fend for themselves. Besides, so far the Zhenechka home had been left unmolested.

That morning, however, Anna called Katya and sensed her daughter-in-law's growing anxiety. Her home was not far from Litovsky Prison, and at that moment the insurgents were attacking the prison in hopes of "liberating" the prisoners. These were not political prisoners but, for the most part, real criminals.

"I don't know, Mama," Katya told Anna when she suggested again that they come to Vassily Island. "Yuri's at the hospital, and I don't want to leave without him. Besides, the thought of crossing town is just as frightening."

"Call him and talk to him about it, then call me back," Anna suggested.

"I haven't been able to get through to the hospital," Katya said. "But I'll keep trying."

That was the last call Anna received. When Anna didn't hear from Katya in an hour, she tried to call again, but the line was dead.

Anna was fretting over this when she heard a discordantly cheerful voice in the foyer.

"Papa!" exclaimed little Zenia.

And that was followed by a peal of familiar laughter, then Mariana's voice, "Daniel!"

"And look who I've brought with me!" came Daniel's voice.

By then Anna had reached the foyer, and she could not believe her eyes.

"Andrei!" she cried as she took her son's husky form in her arms.

"Mama. I am so sorry—"

"None of that, now," Anna scolded gently. "There's nothing to be sorry about." She kept her arm tightly around him as they moved into the parlor and were joined by the rest of the family.

Andrei and Daniel chatted excitedly about their journey to Russia and some hair-raising moments as they passed through war-torn Eastern Europe. But the conversation quickly turned to the Petrograd revolt.

"My timing couldn't have been more perfect if I had planned it," laughed Daniel.

"We always did say you had a nose for news," said Andrei, "but who would have thought that nose could smell out a revolution from hundreds of miles away."

It didn't take long for the women to impart the scanty information they had about events in the city.

"Where are Yuri and Talia?" Andrei asked.

"Talia is at her flat near the theater," said Raisa. "She has been afraid to venture out or else she would be here. A young man she knows in the ballet company was going to try to get her here tonight. But her telephone is out, so we have no idea if that is possible."

"It might be safest for her just to stay put," said Andrei. "Or perhaps I can go get her."

"There haven't been any major disorders where she lives, so I think she'll be all right."

"Andrei," said Anna, "if you would like to help, we are much more concerned about Yuri and Katya. They live near the prison, and this morning there were riots over there and a rumor that the prisoners might be freed. The phone is dead and I can't get through."

"I'll go right away," said Andrei.

"I can give you a hand," said Daniel.

"I think you ought to stay here, Dan," said Andrei. "That crowd outside looked as if anything could set it off. Have you women been here alone since this thing began?"

"Not alone, Andrei," said Anna. "God has kept us safe."

With an affectionate smile, Andrei said, "That is just what you would say, Mama. How I've missed all that!"

As he pulled his coat back on, she kissed his cheek. "Welcome home, son! I wish I didn't have to send you out again so soon."

"I'll be back in an hour," he said. "Then we can talk the whole night through."

As Anna walked him to the door and watched him leave, a terrible thought came over her. She had not thought of Bloody Sunday all day. But now she remembered how Sergei had left her in the morning, neither of them having the slightest premonition of the tragedy that would come.

"Andrei!" she said, stepping into the hall and grasping his arm. "Maybe you don't have to—"

"Oh, Mama . . ." Did he see the old fear gripping her? "You mustn't worry."

"I can't help it."

"I'll be back. I promise."

She let him go. What choice did she have? But she stood there watching until he disappeared down the stairs and out of her sight.

Andrei had been shocked when he and Daniel had arrived in Petrograd and found the place blown apart with revolution. On the way to his mother's, they had stopped at the newspaper office and there learned a few more details. The disorders had begun several days ago, but no one had any reason to believe this would be any different from the 1905 revolution, eventually crushed by the government. Then the army regiments revolted, the Imperial ministers fled, and Vlasenko had surrendered to the protection of the Duma. And the Duma was shaping up more and more as a provisional government, though no one was using that particular wording yet.

Andrei wondered what Lenin would think if he realized what was happening. What would he do? What *could* he do? It would not be as easy for him to reach Russia as it had been for Andrei. Daniel had arranged for Andrei to travel as an employee of the American Diplomatic Corps as an interpreter. His special passport had been readily accepted at most borders, although they had been detained in Germany for two days before they were granted passage.

All the while, Andrei had only been thinking of seeing Talia. He had not dreamed that anything could possibly supersede that goal—and nothing short of a revolution would have. Now he had to put it off once again. It couldn't be helped, of course. His brother's family's need was far greater than that of Talia. Besides, Talia had a "young man" to watch out for her.

The words pricked painfully at him. Who was this young man? What was he to Talia? Andrei's imagination soared wildly. It must be someone who cared for Talia, if he was willing to take risks for her. Someone special.

All Andrei could think was that he was too late. He was certain he had lost Talia—again.

His mind spun in turmoil as he crossed Nicholas Bridge, knowing he would pass within a few blocks from where Talia lived. It would be so easy to make a detour. But this was not the time to indulge his personal whims. He had stopped a few people on the street to inquire what they might know of the neighborhood where the Zhenechka mansion was located. Those who had any information at all only confirmed what was feared. Rioting had broken out, and several fires were reported. Andrei could not afford to stray from his destination. Perhaps on the way home, if Yuri was with them to escort his family, Andrei could leave and go on to Talia's. If he dared. He still wasn't certain if he could risk another rejection.

Near the Admiralty, he was stopped at a barricade. The insurgents wouldn't let him through, but to go around would mean costly time. He had a difficult time convincing them he was one of them. Finally an old acquaintance recognized him.

"Andrei! I thought you were out of the country."

"I was, but I returned to see my family."

"Weren't you with Lenin? Will he return to Russia? The Bolshevik cause won't stand a chance without him."

"He will move heaven and earth to get here once he learns about all this." Andrei paused and looked around at the men manning the barricade. "What's happening here?"

"We're holding the Admiralty. Can you imagine? Stick around and join us."

"I must take care of something first. Can you get them to let me pass?"

"Yes, of course." The man fished in his pocket for a moment, withdrawing a torn strip of red cloth. "Wear this; it'll help you through the streets."

Andrei took the cloth and tied it around his arm, then followed his friend to the other side of the barricade. He wondered what the man would think if he knew Andrei was on his way to give aid to a family of aristocrats. Or, if the fellow knew that Andrei himself was an aristocrat, a Russian prince? Andrei hadn't given that much thought until now, but he suddenly realized the line between nobles and commoners was becoming more and more pronounced. Would that line also come between him and his brother? Yuri had killed Rasputin, but he had done it to save the monarchy. It was clear where his loyalties lay.

But Andrei did not veer from his path. Yuri was still his brother.

67

Dark clouds began rolling across the sky as Andrei strode along the quay to the Trinity Bridge. A biting wind accompanied the clouds. Foul weather was coming, and Andrei only hoped the gains of the rebels were advanced enough so that a blizzard would not force them to give up ground.

Crowds of people and soldiers were milling around everywhere. He had seen a group break into a police station near Nevsky Prospekt. He wondered if soon he would join the rebellion. It was what he had wanted all his life. For the last two years with Lenin, they had talked of little else. And he had all but given up his art in order to immerse himself in the cause.

Andrei had no stomach for pillaging and burning and torturing his foes. Yet he had always known there would be no other way to freedom for Russia but by violence. How else would the Romanovs loose their three-hundred-year grip on Russian society? He simply had not considered the actual *acts* of violence. And he had never pictured himself committing them.

He knew he was approaching a time in his life when serious choices must be made. And he felt the need, more strongly than ever, to see Talia, talk to her, to voice his dilemma and hear her gentle, sweet, wise response. Wistfully, he glanced over his shoulder.

Talia, I might live without your love, but how will I ever make it without your friendship?

He wanted to weep for the deep sense of loss he was feeling. But he didn't. He just kept walking. For the first time since he left his mother's flat, he was grateful he had a task to perform.

At the bridge, Andrei crossed to Petersburg Side, the island where the Zhenechka mansion was located. The moment Andrei crossed, he began to realize just how urgent that task was. Plumes of smoke rose all around. To his left, where the island of the Peter and Paul Fortress fronted Petersburg Side, he could see that the Fortress was in the hands of insurgents. A red flag flew from one of the rooftops, and dozens of men wearing red roamed inside the yard.

Andrei reached Petersburg Side unmolested. Mobs were everywhere, some dressed in shabby prison clothes and looking decidedly dangerous. Andrei passed among the rebels without much difficulty. He looked every bit the rebel himself—as indeed he was. And he was rather an intimidating rebel, to boot.

He neared Grebetsk Street. The police station not far from the Zhenechka home was ablaze. An angry group of rebels was pushing its way down the street, evidently stopping at all the residences, but steadily getting nearer and nearer to Andrei's destination. He broke into a jog. Since he was coming from the opposite direction of the approaching mob, he made it to the mansion well before them. The gates were unattended—maybe the gatekeeper had gone off to join the rebellion. Andrei lifted the latch and found the gate unlocked.

He rang the bell at the front door several times, the sounds of the mob getting closer with each passing moment. The family inside probably afraid to answer their door, but, in the event one of them had a firearm, he didn't like the idea of entering uninvited. He rang the bell again. Finally, desperate, he tried the door. It was locked, but as he gave it a push it opened. Apparently someone in their haste had not shut it firmly.

"Is anyone home?" he called. "I've come to help you." Suddenly he realized that no one here knew him and had no reason to believe he was Yuri's brother. Louder, he yelled, "Hello!"

Then he heard a sound. Had the rebels already been here? Was he walking into an ambush?

"I'm coming in," he warned, "I mean no harm."

"Stop right there!" came a woman's voice.

She entered from a doorway off the foyer. She was young and very beautiful with amber hair and pale, fragile features. In both her slim hands she held aloft a great medieval sword. She was obviously no servant, and Andrei instinctively knew this must be Yuri's wife.

"Are you Princess Fedorcenko?"

"Get out of my house!" she demanded. "You've no right—"

"Please! We haven't time for this," he said. "There's a dangerous mob heading this way. You must leave at once. I've come to help—Anna Fedorcenko sent me."

"Anna—?"

"My mother."

"Your—" Her gaze became more incisive as she studied him closely.

"I'm Andrei Sergeiovich, Yuri's brother. You must believe me. I know we don't look much alike, but—"

"No . . . I see it . . . and I hear it in your voice." A smile twitched at her lips, and Andrei saw that her hands were shaking as they held the sword. She had been scared to death, yet she had bravely come to meet the danger. Andrei fleetingly thought that Yuri had made a good choice of a wife, even if he had broken Talia's heart in the process.

"Are you ready to go?" Andrei asked, urgency preventing him from dwelling on further introductory comments. "Katya, isn't it?"

"Yes," she said as she lowered the sword. "I packed a few things for each of us this morning. There are only six of us. All the servants but three have gone."

"All right. Get everyone together, and we can leave through a back way—I assume there is a back way?"

"Yes, I'll show you."

The princess turned back into the room she had come from, and now Andrei could hear voices as she explained to all what was happening. Suddenly louder voices rose from outside, and only then did Andrei realize he had not shut the front door. As he rushed to remedy that mistake, he saw a dozen men running toward the house, shouting and carrying torches. Andrei slammed the door shut. But the mob clamored up the porch steps and pounded on the door. Katya and her companions chose that moment to enter the foyer, but Andrei signaled them to get out of sight and stay quiet. Maybe he could convince the mob the house was empty, that the aristocratic residents had vacated long ago. It was worth a try.

He opened the door.

"Let's clean out this nest of aristocratic scum!" cried the man at the front of the gang.

"No use," said Andrei. "They're all gone."

"Gone!"

The mob shoved past Andrei and began fanning out through the foyer. If they began a thorough search, Yuri's family was finished.

"I tell you, I've looked everywhere. They've fled," Andrei said, scowling convincingly.

"Who are you? A pandering servant of nobility?" sneered the leader.

"I am not," Andrei retorted. "I am Citizen *Malenkiy Soldat*."

"*Malenkiy Soldat*. . . ? I've heard that name—"

"Of course you have. I am a Bolshevik. I've only just come from Lenin himself."

"He's here?"

"No, but he will be soon. Now quit wasting your time here. Find some real aristocrats—"

Andrei stopped, distracted by the sound of beating footsteps, followed immediately by a door being flung open and the sudden appearance of a panting, disheveled figure. Yuri!

"What have you done with my family?" Yuri cried. He pushed aside one of the rebels as he strode into the foyer, looking frantically all around.

Another man jumped on Yuri and held him firm. "I got me one!" the man shouted as Yuri struggled to get free.

"You didn't look so good, after all," the leader said to Andrei. "Search the rest of the house. There must be more."

Half the mob started tramping through the house, some running up the stairs, others opening doors on the lower level. From one of the rooms someone yelled, "I'll burn 'em out of their hiding places!"

"Wait!" said Andrei to the leader. "You can't do this."

"Why not?"

Andrei didn't hesitate with his reply, for it was the only thing he could think of that might save the situation. "This is the man who killed Rasputin. He's a hero."

"What's this?" The leader frowned skeptically.

"I've been sent here by the Petrograd Soviet to bring him in for questioning—and possibly a commendation."

"What proof have you?"

"He's Prince Fedorcenko," said Andrei.

Another man in the crowd piped up, "That's one of 'em! I heard the name, but they never could prove it, so he didn't get arrested. Everyone knew, though, all the same."

The leader now looked at Yuri. "Are you Fedorcenko?"

Yuri licked his lips, seeming hesitant to answer. He looked at Andrei, only his eyes showing recognition of his brother.

"Yes," Yuri finally replied.

"You don't seem so sure."

"I'm not proud of being a murderer."

"Prove you're Fedorcenko, and I'll let you go."

Yuri took his wallet from his pocket and handed it over. It contained his hospital identification and his military pass.

"All right. We'll clear out," said the leader. "But you better clear out, too. I can't promise what anyone else will do. The jail has been liberated, and there's some rough types roaming the streets."

He called an order to his companions and they left the house, some less willingly than others. Only after the last man left did Andrei smell smoke from upstairs.

"We better keep moving," Andrei said. "Your wife—"

"Where is she? Katya!"

"She's fine. I got here before those fellows. But there'll be more, others who may not be as impressed at meeting Rasputin's killer."

"Andrei, I meant what I said back there. I am ashamed of what I did."

"I'm not surprised. We'll talk about it later. Now, let's move."

Andrei turned toward the room where Katya was hiding, but Yuri grasped his arm. "At least I can say thank you. You saved my skin—and my family's, too."

"We're brothers, Yuri," Andrei said impatiently. "Now, come *on*!"

By the time they gathered everyone together, flames were visible on the upstairs landing.

"My house!" the elderly countess murmured, then said no more as silent tears spilled down her cheeks. Not only her house, but the only world she had ever known was going up in flames.

Andrei was more worried about the appearance of his charges. They all had on heavy winter coats and fur hats and muffs—all of the highest quality and fashion. Even Yuri was dressed in a suit and overcoat of fine, aristocratic tailoring. They would be warm enough, but their dress shouted "aristocrat." There was nothing to be done about it now.

Katya suggested bringing along the sword for protection, but it was heavy and cumbersome and the blade was dull. There were no other weapons, but that was just as well. Andrei would kill to protect Yuri and his family, but if they were unarmed, they might not be placed in such a position in the first place. Andrei did not *want* to kill anyone, especially his own political comrades.

Yuri led them along to a passage that, by way of the cellar, would lead them to the street. He said he had seen the mob on his way home from the hospital and had entered the house by this way. The passage led to an alley behind the mansion. They kept as much as possible to back streets, and the gathering night offered some additional protection.

And for the first time in ages, as he herded the group through the waning dusk, Andrei prayed.

68

When they crossed the Trinity Bridge, a group of soldiers challenged them, but let them go when Andrei told them the aristocrats were his prisoners and he was taking them to Tauride Palace.

Yuri looked with amazement at his brother as they set off again. "I didn't know you could think so well on your feet, Andrei. You've quite a talent for it."

Andrei shrugged. "I suppose my impetuous tongue is good for something."

On the south side of the river, they paused for a brief rest in a deserted alley. The older women were winded, and Irina had started to cry. Andrei considered taking them to the Duma building—it was not far, and Uncle Paul might be there and thus could vouch for them. But he had glimpsed the mobs demonstrating in front of the palace. It would be too risky passing among the demonstrators, especially with the way his companions were dressed. Besides, he had heard the situation inside the palace bordered on chaos itself. Rebel groups were coming and going, attempting to plead their cause before the quasi-government. And the government was in no less disarray with the Provisional Committee, consisting mostly of liberals and monarchists, in constant dispute with the socialistic Petrograd Soviet.

Andrei discussed these things with the group, and they unanimously decided that they wanted to get to Vassily Island and Anna's. To all, Anna's home stood out as a haven, perhaps the only true haven in the revolution-torn city. It was a long way to go on foot, but it was almost dark, and perhaps the roaming mobs would seek shelter from the freezing cold of night and the coming storm.

They continued on as snow began to fall. When they reached the Admiralty, the barricades were still in place and there were no friends this time to get them through. They went the long way around. Countess Zhenechka was limping and having trouble breathing. Despite her fancy, fur-lined boots, her feet were frozen and sore. She had never walked so much in her entire life. The other women were doing little better. Though Yuri was carrying the child, each woman had a heavy carpetbag in hand. They stopped again for rest in another alley.

They had rested no more than a minute when three men, one carrying a torch, appeared at the entrance of the alley. It took them several moments to get close, for it was a long alley, and Andrei and his companions were near the far end. Still, there was not enough time for Andrei to get his companions moving. Perhaps the newcomers were not dangerous.

"What have we got here?" asked one of the men when he was close. His voice was deep and grating and definitely not friendly.

"Just some women and a child," Andrei said.

"What about you, then?"

"Leave us alone." Yuri had given Irina to her mother and come up next to Andrei.

The men drew close, the torch illuminating the refugees clearly.

"Come on," said Andrei to his companions. Maybe if they just started moving, the men would let them go. But when the countess moved away from the wall, her legs seemed to fail her, and she crumpled to her knees. Teddie and one of the servants helped her stand, but she was far too unsteady to move. She needed more rest.

"A bunch of bourgeois rats fleeing a sinking ship," laughed one of the men.

"These are helpless women," said Andrei. "Let them alone."

"I don't care what they are! They're the enemy!" The man started toward the women.

Yuri blocked his way. "Take another step and it'll be your last!"

"Well, I'll be," said the man. "You're Dr. Fedorcenko—one of *them*, too." He turned to his companions. "This is the butcher that took my arm."

Andrei now noticed that the man's right sleeve was pinned up. At first, when the fellow indicated he knew Yuri, Andrei had hoped that would be their salvation. Now, of course, it was obvious the man was filled with malice.

"I remember you," said Yuri. "You had gangrene up to your elbow. You would have died if I hadn't amputated that arm."

"I don't believe a word of it! I was just another serf—one of the masses to sacrifice for the rich promieshik and for the traitor emperor. The tables are turned now, though, ain't they?"

"Let's shoot the lot of them and be heros," one of the men said. He pulled out a pistol he had hidden in his belt beneath his coat.

"Come on," said Andrei, "you don't need that."

The one-armed man laughed. "I like that idea."

Andrei could hardly believe it when the man raised the weapon and started to squeeze the trigger. Without giving it a second thought, Andrei threw himself at the gunman, grabbing his arm and deflecting the pistol as they both crashed to the icy ground. The pistol fired, and the bullet struck another of the comrades. The amputee, filled with rage, lunged for Yuri. But Andrei saw no more—he had to concentrate fully on his own struggle and the pistol that was still dangerously gripped in his adversary's hand.

The man wasn't as big as Andrei, but he was strong, and he kept his finger on the trigger. Andrei had to exercise some care as he attempted to disarm the man. He had no luck beating the hand against the cobbles. He was able to get a couple good blows into the man's face, but as he did, he loosened his hold on the man's gun hand. In a split second, the man gave a hard push, raised the pistol, and fired.

The impact of the explosion was like a fist in his gut. It took a couple of heartbeats before Andrei felt anything besides the shock that he was hit. But when the pain became a reality, he swallowed it down. He couldn't let the man get loose, he had to hang on and try to get that gun. He had to . . .

His vision started to go black. But he fought it. He couldn't faint.

He had to get that gun. Sheer desperation forced Andrei to shake off his shock before his opponent could react. He went for the pistol, while the man's grip slackened from his own surprise at wounding Andrei. In a moment Andrei was able to knock the gun to the ground, and in another lurch, with pain piercing through his body, he managed to wrap his own hand around the weapon.

Andrei's foe regained his wits and lunged toward Andrei and the gun, but it was too late. Andrei fired over the man's head.

"That's the only warning I'll give," Andrei panted. But his hand shook as he aimed the gun. The pain now hit him in full force. Beads of perspiration formed on his forehead. His vision was blurring. "Get . . . out of here or . . ." His mind went blank for an instant before he remembered what he was going to say. "Or I'll shoot you both."

The two assailants gathered up their wounded comrade and retreated from the alley without another word.

The gun slipped from Andrei's hand, and he fell back on the cobbles.

"Andrei!" Yuri cried and ran to his brother.

Andrei's heavy coat was already soaked with blood. Yuri opened it enough to see the wound. The bullet had penetrated his side, no more than two inches below his heart.

69

"Dear God!" Yuri breathed. It was the only prayer his tortured mind could utter. But his medical instincts bolstered him. He tore off his wool neck scarf and packed it into the wound. If he could keep pressure on it for a few minutes, he might staunch the flow of blood.

But he didn't have even a few minutes. A dozen men appeared at the far end of the alley. And the amputee whose life Yuri had saved was at the head of the gang, leading them to the horde of dangerous aristocrats.

"Katya," Yuri said, "take everyone and run."

"What about you?"

"I'll help Andrei. Hurry!"

She hesitated only a moment before she obeyed and herded the family toward the end of the alley.

Andrei clutched at Yuri's sleeve. "No . . . they won't make it alone . . . you have to go—"

"I'm not leaving you." Yuri put an arm around Andrei and tried to lift him.

Andrei struggled to gain his feet, but he simply did not have the strength. Yuri tried to lift his brother in his arms, but it was impossible. Andrei was too heavy for him. Giving one desperate, final tug, Yuri slipped on the ice and they both crashed back to the ground with Andrei crying out in pain.

"You have to try to stand," Yuri pleaded.

"Even if I could stand, I'd slow you down."

"Then we'll die together!"

"Don't be . . . foolish, Yuri. Get your family out of here . . ."

"I can't leave you."

"I . . . I'm not going to . . . make it—"

"You will!"

The mob had spotted them now and was shouting and cursing at them. But they were approaching cautiously. Perhaps the amputee had warned them about the pistol. If they had been seriously armed they would have come with weapons drawn. Still, a dozen men, even if armed only with knives and clubs, could easily overtake two men and a single pistol.

"Get me . . . the gun . . ." Andrei said. "Then run, Yuri. Protect the women . . . you must!"

There wasn't time to argue, and Yuri couldn't drag his brother away—he had already proved that with his puny efforts before. Even though Yuri felt completely inadequate to help them, the women couldn't make it through the city alone. And certainly Katya would not leave without him. He saw out of the corner of his eye that, having herded the others to the opposite end of the alley, she was indeed returning for him.

Yuri gave Andrei the gun, then helped him to lean against a wall.

"Yuri, there was no choice . . ." Andrei said. He fired once into the mob. "I love you, Yuri. Now go!"

Yuri hesitated another moment. *Sacrifice the one to save the many*. It didn't seem so logical now. He glanced at the women. They were not in sight—except for Katya, who was moving toward him. Yuri looked at his brother. How could he make such a decision?

The mob started moving again. Andrei fired, and one of the attackers screamed.

"Run, Yuri!" Andrei cried.

He pulled the trigger again, but the pistol produced only an empty click. Realizing he was leaving his brother with an empty gun, Yuri turned back. Then Andrei slumped over. At the same moment the mob, seeing that the pistol was no longer a threat, broke into a run, heading straight toward Yuri and Katya. The rebels had no interest in a fallen enemy with a useless gun. There was no other choice now for Yuri but to shepherd his family to safety. And perhaps Yuri could do some good for his brother by drawing the mob away from him. He took Katya's hand and ran, pausing once to look over his shoulder, but Andrei had not moved.

The others were halfway down the street, but Yuri and Katya soon caught up to them. Yuri quickly took Irina from Teddie, and, still holding Katya's hand, urged them all to keep moving. He had no idea how they would outrun the mob. Countess Zhenechka was nearly spent. And now the snow was coming down harder, driven by an icy wind. Their only hope was that the storm would slow down the mob as well.

He turned down the first street they came to, hoping to lose their pursuers. But Yuri and his family were too slow. The mob spotted them. He must find another means of escape, for they could not keep up this race for much longer. Perhaps a place to hide—

Then he saw it.

An empty delivery wagon was parked outside a shop. The horse hitched in front looked as old and worn as Yevno's old workhorse, but Yuri figured it would do the job.

Yuri herded everyone into the back, then jumped into the driver's seat, giving the old nag a flick on the rear with the crop. The animal lurched forward at a leisurely pace, obviously not accustomed to hurry of any kind. Yuri snapped her rear again, this time harder. The pursuers were close now. Glancing over his shoulder, Yuri saw one try to jump into the back of the wagon. Katya and Teddie pushed him out. Another man took his place, and from somewhere in the wagon, Katya produced a stick and began beating at their attacker. Holding up his hands to protect himself from the flailing stick, the man fell off.

Finally, the horse started moving. But the noise of the mob, along with Yuri's frantic yells at the horse, brought out the delivery men, who also gave chase to the wagon. Finally the old mare caught her stride and showed more stamina than outward appearances might have indicated. In a couple of minutes the mob was left behind, with no hope of catching up.

The shouts of the mob faded into the distance. The alley, which a moment before had been a riot of activity, suddenly fell into complete silence. Andrei could hear only his own shallow, labored breathing. At least he was still breathing. Andrei had slumped over when the gun ran out of ammunition, hoping Yuri would think him dead and thus give his attention to the living. But he had the feeling his ruse had only worked because, with the mob bearing down on Yuri, he'd had no other choice but to flee.

Their chances of outrunning the mob were slim, but he hoped Yuri and his family would make it to safety. Maybe his mama was praying for them; maybe her God would somehow rescue Yuri and his family. Andrei had no hope for a similar rescue for himself. He didn't think he'd last much longer. He'd never known such pain before, not even when he had been shot in the shoulder on Bloody Sunday. He could feel that he was still bleeding, although he couldn't look at his wound. The sight of the blood made him as sick as the pain itself, and he didn't want to take the chance of passing out.

Was he to die alone, then, in a dark, deserted alley? He never thought that's how life would end for him—not that he ever thought much about his end at all. Yuri was the one to ponder such things. Andrei just assumed he'd live forever.

Suddenly another sound joined that of his breathing—a small scuttling sound. When he glanced to his side, he saw a rat creep toward him.

"Well, I'm not alone, after all . . ." he murmured to the creature.

The rat scurried under a pile of garbage, and silence reigned again. The pain throbbed incessantly now, and he tried to lie flat, hoping that would help. But the movement only made the agony worse. For a moment he blacked out, then he willed himself awake again. As long as he was conscious, he might be able to stay alive.

"I don't want to die here," he thought.

He wanted to be with his family, with the people he loved. He wanted to see Talia one more time, to tell her how much he loved her. . . . But it was too late for that . . . he'd never see her again . . . her wide, doe eyes, her tender smile . . .

Consciousness began to slip from him again. He couldn't fight it any longer. At least then maybe the pain would go away. . . .

"Kitty, kitty!" came a sweet voice into Andrei's clouded mind.

"Talia. . . ?" Andrei murmured. "I knew you hadn't given up on me . . ." But even as the dreamlike thought arose from his delirium, he sensibly told himself that Talia had no cat.

But she might have one now . . . how do I know. . . ? I'm sorry I stayed away so long . . . maybe her young man . . .

What a fool I was. . . .

"Here, kitty!"

The voice was sweet like Talia's, but there was no way she could have found him here. He was only imagining it. . . .

It was fitting, though, that his last thoughts were not of the revolution that had so dominated his life, but rather of Talia and Yuri and his mama . . .

Ah, Mama . . .

He was sorry that he had to be the cause of more loss in her life. Mama's dear face, twisted with pain and grief, was the final image in his mind before everything went completely black.

Yuri paused outside his mama's apartment. He dreaded having to go in there and report the death of her son. In fact, he was tempted to leave Katya and the others at the doorstep and turn around and head back to the place where he had left Andrei. Maybe he was still alive. And even if he was dead, Yuri could not leave his brother's body out there to the whims of the marauding rebels.

He *would* go back after him, but first he had to tell his mama. Another minute or two would probably not make much difference to a . . . dead man—but it would to his mama. He feared what this loss would do to her. Andrei was her baby, and though she loved all her children equally, Yuri knew Andrei held a special place in her heart. He was the youngest, the rebel, the one she always had to work so hard to maintain a relationship with.

And Yuri also wished—desperately—that Andrei had not died

saving *him*. Yuri had enough blood on his hands. How could he bear this?

Katya patted Yuri's arm. "Are you going to knock?"

He nodded and, with a ragged sigh, pounded on the door of the flat.

Anna opened the door. "Oh, thank God, you are finally here!" She gave Yuri and Katya and Irina a hug. "Come in! Did Andrei get through? I hope you didn't have trouble getting here."

"Mama . . ." Yuri began, but words caught in his throat, and he could say no more.

"You missed Andrei, didn't you? Well, he'll find his way back. You must be freezing, and I have little heat to offer you except warm bodies. It's a good thing there are so many of us."

"Mama," Yuri tried again, "there was trouble. Andrei—"

"What about Andrei? You did see him?"

"We were attacked by some ruffians. Andrei was—"

"Hurt?" She spoke the word so hopefully, as if unable to consider any other possibility.

"He was shot. I had to leave him in order to get the others to safety. There was no other choice, you must understand. I would have never left him, but I had to think of Katya and Irina and the other women. I'm going to go back now to get him. I'm—"

"He was only wounded?"

Yuri's hesitation was not the answer she sought.

"No!" Her knees seemed to go weak and she staggered back. Daniel, who had joined the group, caught her.

Yuri looked at his brother-in-law. "I wouldn't have left him, Daniel. I had no choice."

"I know that, Yuri. Your mother knows that."

"I'm going back for him right now. I just wanted to get my family to safety."

"Then he's not. . . ?" Daniel's voice held the same note of hope.

Yuri looked away. He had seen men die on the battlefield from far less serious wounds. But it wasn't just the wound itself that was dangerous. The bleeding had been profuse, and he had been left to bleed now for half an hour. But the weather was as likely to kill Andrei as the wound. It had been thirty below in the daylight, and even if the storm raised the temperature a few degrees, it was still too cold for a man to survive long, exposed and unprotected in an alley.

Yuri did not relate all these things to his family. For now it might be best to keep a little grain of hope alive—it would lessen the blow of the final realization that Andrei was indeed gone.

Nevertheless, Yuri was hardly convincing when he said, "He may be alive. I've got to find out."

"I'll go with you," Daniel said. "You'll need help to bring him back." Was he thinking of that awful day on Bloody Sunday when he had carried a wounded Andrei back to his mama? The day their papa had died?

Yuri did not argue. He was glad for the company on this grim errand.

Outside, they were greeted with a full-fledged snowstorm. Wind howled and snow swirled everywhere. It was crazy to venture out in such elements. But Yuri felt crazy—insane with grief and guilt and pain.

They drove the delivery wagon to where Yuri had commandeered it—that is, to where he *thought* he had taken it. In his haste to get away, he hadn't paid much attention. And the storm made it even more difficult to pinpoint the location. From there, they went on foot because the wagon was useless, negotiating the many narrow alleys, trying to find the alley where Andrei had been left. But everywhere they looked they found nothing. All were deserted.

Yuri was now completely confused. They had gone down so many alleys and back streets in their flight. He grew frantic, running down the streets like a wild man, slipping in the ice, pulling himself back up, racing down another alley.

But nothing!

Even the rebels had taken shelter from the storm. The streets were deserted.

Stumbling, his feet frozen, his eyes nearly blinded by the storm, he turned into another alley. Daniel, who had barely been able to keep pace with Yuri's frenzy, raced up behind Yuri.

But this alley, too, was empty.

Yuri spun around, ready to tear off in another direction. But Daniel caught him.

"Yuri, it's no use—" Daniel yelled above the wind.

"No! He's got to be here. I have to find him!"

"You've done your best."

"How could I be stupid enough not to remember where he was?"

"Anyone would have had trouble in this storm."

"Daniel!" Yuri cried, his tears freezing on his cheeks. "I can't go back without him."

They searched for another hour, until they were both so frozen they could barely move. They tried to find the wagon again, but either some kind soul had taken the horse to shelter or they were hopelessly lost. It was another half hour before they came to the familiar area of the Admiralty. Everyone here had taken cover from the storm; only a few guards braved the elements. The streets of Petrograd were quieter than they had been in days. It had taken nature to quell the force of the revolution, to do what the tsar of all the Russias had been impotent to do.

In complete despair, Yuri turned his face toward home. He had failed. Even if Andrei had survived his wound, he would never survive exposed to this storm.

70

The Imperial train had made it to Pskov. It had been forced to detour here because rebel troops had blockaded the southern route. In Pskov, Tsar Nicholas received another telegram from Rodzianko. The Duma president made it clear that the time had passed when the tsar could appease the people with a mere "ministry of confidence." Now there was only one possible way the tsar could hold back the revolution and save the monarchy.

He must abdicate.

Nicholas read the latest telegram and glanced around at his advisors, all seated with him in his private railway car, all deathly silent. He rose from his seat and wandered aimlessly to one of the car windows and lifted the shade. It was dark outside, there was nothing to see. But he simply could not focus on the overwhelming decision set before him. Why now, of all times, was he separated from his dear Alix? He needed her strength more than ever.

Through the night he struggled over his decision. Were there any alternatives left to him? With the defection of the Guards, how could he hope to wrest back his Capital? But even if he could find enough loyal troops, the result would be civil war. Nicholas simply did not have the heart to set Russians against Russians, especially when the hated Germans were still undefeated. In the end, it was patriotism, and love for Russia, that prompted him to make the most difficult, soul-wrenching decision of his life.

The next morning he met again with his generals and advisors in the same place as the night before. Only the silence changed; now it was charged with expectation.

The tsar was pale as he spoke, and his voice, though resolved, lacked force and confidence. "I will abdicate the throne in favor of my son."

A collective sigh of relief rose from the group, and each man crossed himself.

Crossing himself also, the tsar thanked the men in the room for their faithful service. He did not say that he was more relieved than any of them over his decision. The shackles of rule were finally loosed. He was a free man. And still he had saved the Crown and passed it on to his son. Yet later, after more thought on the matter, he spoke to Dr. Fedorov and realized that, too, was a fantasy.

"Doctor, is my son physically able to bear the responsibility of rule?" asked the tsar. "Please be frank."

"Your Highness, it is a fickle disease that afflicts your son. He could live to be an old man or a mere bump could kill him. He will always be at the mercy of his disease. And, of course, you know, Your Highness, that you and the tsaritsa will most certainly be exiled from Russia and forbidden contact with your son."

Nicholas had, of course, known that. But in a last desperate attempt to save the throne for his son, he had blinded himself to those facts. Now, facing them squarely, he realized he could not bear to be separated from Alexis. And the empress would be devastated by it.

Still, clinging to a tiny shred of hope, Nicholas reconvened his advisors and informed them he would turn the throne over to his brother, Michael, instead of Alexis.

"Ilyich! Ilyich!" Stephan Kaminsky raced down the street to catch up with Lenin, who was returning home from a day at the library.

Lenin turned. "What is it, Stephan? You are making a scene."

"You'll make a scene, too, when you hear the news. The tsar has abdicated!"

"What?"

"It's true, Ilyich. The revolution has succeeded at last."

"I can't believe it." Kaminsky handed him several newspapers and he read the headlines in utter astonishment. But it didn't take long for his stunned mind to click into gear. "Stephan, we must have a meeting of the Central Committee immediately. Spread the word, get as many as you can to meet at my place as soon as possible."

The next day half a dozen Bolsheviks gathered in Lenin's Zurich flat. Lenin had hardly slept the night before as he deliberated over all the ramifications of events in Russia. He sent several letters to comrades in other parts of Europe, and one to the leader of the ragtag group of Bolsheviks in Russia. Who knew if the letters would get through? But he had to make the attempt, for it was important that his tactics be clearly spelled out.

We must neither trust nor support the new government. Be especially suspect of Kerensky. Our only hope of victory is to arm the proletariat.

His main concern for the moment, however, was getting back to Russia. And toward this end, the group in his flat began brainstorming ideas.

Because there were no legal ways to travel, they must avail themselves of illegal methods. A dozen improbable ideas were mentioned, including stealing an airplane, flying to Russia, and landing in a field somewhere.

Lenin suggested that he travel on a forged Swedish passport.

Krupskaya chuckled. "That would never work, Ilyich. You would fall asleep on the train, dream of Mensheviks, and start cursing aloud in Russian, giving yourself away completely."

"There must be a way!" exclaimed Lenin, frustrated. "I must get to Russia soon, while the Provisional Government is confused and weak. Once they gain a foothold, once they establish a power base, we might never be able to usurp control."

They discussed a route through France and England and thus by sea to Russia—after all, these countries were allies of Russia. But aside from the difficulty of traveling via the North Sea at that time of year, there was the even more difficult prospect of France and especially England lending support to a bunch of Marxist socialists whose express purpose would be to disrupt the newly formed government of Russia. Lloyd-George of England well knew that Lenin opposed the war, and thus would be very ill-disposed toward supporting anyone who was avowed to pulling Russia out of the conflict.

"What about traveling through Germany?" offered Stephan.

The Germans had made overtures in the past through Parvus, and there was no reason to believe that they would not still be favorable to the concept of introducing a rival faction into Russia. The new government was apparently committed to continuing the war, while the Bolsheviks were not. More chaos in Russia would only help the German cause. For Lenin, however, it was a sticky situation. To seek aid from Germany might brand him with the stigma of colluding with the enemy. But Lenin was desperate enough to try any reasonable idea.

"Let's pursue the possibility," he said. "But I don't want any Russian to deal directly with the Germans. Stephan, contact Fritz Platten, the leader of the Swiss Socialist party, and have him open negotiations with the Germans. I'm sure Parvus would act as a go-between."

71

Paul had braved the blizzard to bring the news of the tsar's abdication to his wife and family. Anna felt a little bad for him that it wasn't received with the ovations he had expected, but he understood when Mathilde drew him aside and explained the situation.

Anna, however, didn't understand—she couldn't understand. She had sacrificed Sergei and Andrei to this cause, to freedom for Russia. It just did not seem worth it. What would it matter if Russia did change, suddenly became a democracy, or constitutional monarchy, or a socialist state? The many women who had given their husbands and sons would never be free, not from the bondage of their grief.

Maybe that was selfish of her. Neither Sergei nor Andrei would have done anything less than die for what they believed in. But the heroes who died did not have to live with the ache of emptiness in their hearts.

Oh, Andrei! My baby! Have I truly lost you? Will I never again look into your dear eyes, filled with such zest and vitality? So sure of yourself, so ready to jump into a fray. Impulsive, gentle, and exuberant, with the look of a fine peasant, and the soul of a sensitive artist. How can you be lost to me and to those you touched with your wonderful spirit?

Anna wandered over to a window and pulled back a corner of the drape. She was hardly aware of the conversation from the fifteen people gathered in her parlor. Watching the swirling snowstorm, she became entranced by it. She felt as if she were out in its midst, cold and so very confused. It was fitting that such a storm should rage this day.

And despite her grief, she could not help thinking of Russia. What would become of it now? Was it cold and dead, as she feared her son was? Or was there yet hope that it, too, might rise above chaos and death? Then old Papa Yevno's words crept into her consciousness: "Anna, always remember, where there's life, there's hope."

In Paul's mind, Russia was being reborn. Perhaps he would even insist that Andrei was still out there alive . . . somewhere.

Anna tried hard to have such hope. She prayed that God would reach into her grieving heart and bolster the places where her hope failed. She prayed that somehow God would help her to see beyond her pain.

Then a little squeal of laughter caught Anna's attention. She turned her gaze away from the window to a corner of the room where Zenia and Irina were playing together. Something had amused Zenia, and she was giggling loudly. Mariana glanced at her mother, then leaned down and gently hushed her uninhibited daughter.

"Let her be," Anna said. "Perhaps she can teach us something, eh?" Sighing, she turned back to the window. "But I don't know what. . . ."

Yuri came to her and put his arm around her. He was, undoubtedly, the most miserable person in the room—perhaps even more so than she. He felt responsible for what had happened to his brother, maybe even responsible for what was happening in Russia.

Because of his part in killing Rasputin, the revolution had been set off. Since he had returned home late last night from his unsuccessful search for his brother, Anna had not been much comfort to him. He had been nearly frozen to death himself and as discouraged and dejected as a man could be. But she had been too wrapped up in her own pain and grief.

Now she attempted to make up for it. She put her arm around her son and held him tightly. "Look to the children, Yuri," she said. "They are our reason for going on; they are our reason to hope. And, yes, they can even be an example to us."

"Do you expect me to laugh like little Zenia, Mama?"

"No, Yuri, not yet. But we musn't forget how to laugh, nor that laughter exists and is a good thing."

"I'll never—"

"Hush, son. Don't say 'never.' Mourning only lasts for a season. I have mourned, Yuri, I know. Then joy returns. *It will return*, do you hear?"

"I'm afraid it won't. I fear I will always feel this way—like I'm walking through quicksand, reaching out and struggling to find some solid ground, but there is none in sight. I'm sinking, Mama."

"Hold on to me, Yuri."

"How can you bear it?"

"God will find a way."